WINNER "STORY TELLER OF THE YEAR"
"TOP TEN BOOKS OF THE YEAR"
Independent Publisher Magazine

"Jack Fritscher's gift for language makes me think of the poet Dennis Cooper."
—Ian Young, *The Body Politic*, Toronto

"All of this is expressed in subtle, fine writing. Fritscher is a polished writer, editing his work to the bone so that the entire mood points only to the feeling he wishes to impress on the reader. One thing for sure. This fellow is a super writer."
—Virginia Sink, *The Tribune*, Oklahoma City

"Powerful...outcast, and at times cruel...young men forced to shun sexuality. A distinct insight into seminary life for both Catholic and non-Catholic."
—John R. Selig, *ForeWord* magazine

Fiction. Fritscher. Frisson.

"Genres collide. Postmodern and deconstructed, *What They Did to the Kid* straddles genres, magically shifting shape in the reader's hands. Jack Fritscher is novelist and memoirist—my favorite kind of both."
—Mark Hemry, editor,
Chasing Danny Boy: Powerful Stories of Celtic Eros

"This novel of the secret culture of priests and boys locked away in a seminary boarding school joins excellent company with Robert Musil's *Young Törless*, James Joyce's *A Portrait of the Artist as a Young Man*, and Calder Willingham's *End As a Man*."
—Harold Cox, editor, *Checkmate* magazine

Jack Fritscher, seminarian attending the
Pontifical College Josephinum, visiting home, 1959

What They Did to the Kid
Confessions of an Altar Boy

Jack Fritscher

Palm Drive Publishing®
San Francisco California

For Leonard J. Fick,
Ruth Haungs,
Thomas R. Gorman,
and Mark Hemry

Acknowledgements

The author gratefully expresses his appreciation for grants from the Michigan Council for the Arts and the National Endowment for Humanities.

Here's for the plain old Adam, the simple genuine
self against the whole world.
—Ralph Waldo Emerson, *Journals*

Jack Fritscher is a graduate in philosophy from the Vatican's prestigious seminary, the Pontifical College Josephinum (1953-1963). He is the author of seventeen books of nonfiction and fiction, including the comic novels *What They Did to the Kid, Some Dance to Remember,* and *The Geography of Women* as well as his six short-story collections such as *Sweet Embraceable You: Coffee-House Stories* and *Stonewall Stories.* He has also written two screenplays and two produced plays, one of which, a musical comedy, was staged by the Josephinum Glee Club in 1959. From 1957 to 1963, he was assistant editor for the national magazine *The Josephinum Review,* was founding editor of the Josephinum college magazine *Pulse,* and was published frequently in the Catholic press before moving into GLBT publishing.

With his 1967 dissertation, *Love and Death in Tennessee Williams,* he received his doctorate in American literature from Loyola University of Chicago where he taught. A prolific contributor to GLBT magazines, he is noted as the founding San Francisco editor in chief of *Drummer* magazine (1977); and as its most frequent contributor for twenty-four years, he has become the keeper of its institutional memory in his series of history books, *Gay San Francisco: Eyewitness Drummer.*

With more than fifty years as a published author, he remains a working scholar of American popular culture cited particularly for his books *Popular Witchcraft* (1971) and his controversial memoir of art and Catholicism, *Mapplethorpe: Assault with a Deadly Camera.* (1994).

Having penned *What They Did to the Kid* in 1965 as a stand-alone novel, he subsequently continued the story of Ryan O'Hara in his award-winning signature book, *Some Dance to Remember: A Memoir-Novel of San Francisco 1970-1982.*

He lives near the Golden Gate Bridge with his spouse of more than thirty-two years, Mark Hemry, and their Border Collie, Guenevere.

Information at www.JackFritscher.com

Author's Note

Yes!

I confess!

I was for six years, at the Pontifical College Josephinum, a school-mate of Bernard Cardinal Law who became scandalous in the priest sex-abuse cover-up. But I ripped nothing from the headlines. I wrote *What They Did to the Kid* from journals I kept when I lived inside the seminary culture of the 1950s and 1960s that produced Vatican II period's crop of accused priests. I wrote this memoir as a positive "novel of the closet," not as an exposé, well before media focus on the sexual judgment of priests. *Kid* is a cautionary tale of how a boy's emotional growth becomes stunted at 14, which may explain why some priests later in life seek out the familiar company of 14-year-olds.

What happens to a boy when he is 14 marks him for life. At 14, I was recruited by the Catholic Church into the custody of priests. It took me ten years to escape and then grow up. For all that, *Kid* is a comedy of coming of age, coming out, and coming unglued.

—Jack Fritscher
www.JackFritscher.com

1

June 1939

Falling into the liquid of time, born, he worked his way into reason. All about him he remembered leaving the darkness, finding first his fingers, his hands, his feet, the faces of his parents, and a great dangling bird twirling above his crib. The bird caught every draft that swept his room and circled the timeless days when twilight became light only to fade to twilight again. Screaming in the darkness, he could not make them understand the sounds he formed on his uncontrollable mouth which could not speak words. In limitless wrath he screamed, crying and relieving himself in frustration.

The faces smiled down at his squalling formless words, washing and patting him with oil and powder, pointing and pulling at him, taking him one day, after he first could walk, to a white room with a doctor who pulled back the skin that was so tight he had to hold himself. He cried, hurting every day since he could walk. The doctors rolled him down a tiled hall, through doors that thumped when hit by his gurney, swinging open to a nightmare room echoing with his wordless screams. Down and back they pushed him, with gas and masks back into the unmade darkness from where he had crawled and scratched his way to a demi-consciousness. Down and back they pushed him, weak and unformed, no chance against them, frustrated, without even having found the words for anything, overcome finally, crying for being pushed untimely back into the darkness before the time that time had begun.

To be lost too soon with everything gone, taken and pushed back, to fall down the wordless black void and hang there endlessly swirling no place, out of time, like the huge red and green and yellow bird floating obscurely, at the edge of vision, once over his bed. In all the summers forever after, sitting in the darkness on his porch, he could not believe he had survived to find the words, though in the finding he exorcized nothing of the formless sensible time of terror and fear that seemed his alone even during the years of the shortages and rationing and blackouts of the great war when he first came to consciousness, and all the adults were brave but afraid.

Christmas 1942

Christmas Eve taught me time. Clock. Calendar. Anticipation. Three nights before Christmas, Charley-Pop carried me out to the dark street where my mother sat with the neighbors in a one-horse open sleigh. He bundled me into her lap and two little girls looked at me and sang, "What Child Is This?" and laughed and sang the words again.

My father climbed up next to Mr. Higgins and the horse clopped off with everyone singing and laughing. We glided down the street, dark with night, dark with war, dark with ice.

A boy skated by us, waving, then waiting, grabbing hold of the side of our sleigh, with his smiling face close to mine, laughing, then swinging off on his own speed, falling into a drift, scattering snow like an angel, like that dead boy who had lived next door, who liked to throw me into the air, and died in the war.

Our sleigh passed dark houses. The two little girls shouted "Yoohoo, Santa!" to make me look, because I was three, and for the first time in my life waiting for something the way my mother was waiting for my brother to be born. I could feel him next to my face inside her stomach, and I wondered "What Child Is This?"

I fell asleep looking up at the clear cold sky lit with stars behind the tree branches whirling by.

Two nights before Christmas, Charley-Pop set up a little tree and me beside it and took a long black electrical cord and a pliers and taped twelve light sockets to the wire, and pulled out twelve big light bulbs, red and green and blue. He took my hand in his and turned the bulbs from dark to bright, and held me in one arm while he draped the lights in the tree.

He was twenty-four and crying and my mother was twenty-one and crying, and I was three and afraid to know why, and the next morning, under a huge clock, I stood shivering next to his legs in the snow while he kissed my mother at the train station, where all the men were kissing all the women good-bye, and the troop train steamed and roared, and he was gone off to the Induction Center upstate in Chicago.

In the crowd of ladies and children, we all began to cry, because we all knew more than one dead boy who had gone to war and never come back, and the women said, "Maybe they'll be 4-F, maybe have flat feet, maybe not able to see without their glasses, maybe maybe maybe."

At home, I sat looking out the window, through the glass pane reflecting my father's Christmas lights that he made because of the shortages of everything, watching the snow fall, and measuring the dark, the way night fell on snow, waiting all evening, waiting for Santa Claus, waiting to go to Christmas morning Mass to see the Baby Jesus, waiting for my daddy to come home.

Carolers walked down the street singing "Silent night, holy night!" It was the night before Christmas. Christmas Eve. The clock ticked off minutes. My mother pretended for me that there was no war, no fear, no panic. We put out Christmas cookies and a bottle of Coca-Cola for Santa, and late, sitting up together, my mother said, "Look at the time! How time flies! You better go to bed quick! No 'Yoohoo, Santa!' tonight. Santa won't leave any toys if he sees you see him."

I believed her. I believed all of them. I knew I had no proof other than their word, so I believed everything. She tucked me in bed, and I thought of how we had stood together in the department store line to see Santa sitting in Toyland, and I asked Santa to bring my daddy home to me. He could whistle "White Christmas" and knew how to cut figure eights wearing hockey skates on the frozen lagoon in Glen Oak Park and could make Christmas lights out of an old extension cord and was good at driving his truck at the defense plant and I fell asleep praying to Santa Claus, and the Christmas Angels, and Mary and Joseph, and the Baby Jesus to bring my daddy back home to me. In the morning, in the magic of Christmas morning, I woke up to the voice, to the smell of the sweet breath, to the face of my father—with the 4-F eyes and the war job in the defense plant—who picked me up and hugged me and kissed me, and I said, "Daddy Daddy Daddy."

VJ Day, August 14, 1945

After the circumcision and the air-raid blackouts and the tonsillectomy and the supper-table stories of children starving in Europe, fear kept me quiet until the summer the war ended. Meredith and Beverly sat for hours on our front porch that rambled all around the first floor of the big gray duplex at the corner of Ayres and Cooper. They rented the downstairs and we rented the upstairs from a ninety-eight-year-old woman whose name was Peoria Miller. Meredith said she was the first girl born in the town of Peoria when it was no more than a settlement on the Illinois River.

Meredith, who was Beverly's husband, liked to rock on the porch, smoking hand-rolled cigarettes, on guard to chase me from our mutually-owned porch swing. I wore short pants cut from the same material as his best suit and this coincidence, I thought, gave us a fighting equality. He may have been an air-raid warden, but he was small and scrawny and seemed only a bigger kid than me, always bullying and tattling and pointing his finger at me, saying, "Lickety-lickety."

"Sonny boy, quit tangling those chains and get the hell out of our swing."

I defied his thin line of moustache and twisted the swing around one more full circle.

He shook his raised fist at me.

"Lickety-lickety," I said.

"Don't you mock me," he said.

"Let him alone, Meredith. He's only a kid."

"Aw, Bev," he said.

"Aw, Bev," I mocked.

"Ryan O'Hara," she said to me, "you go upstairs, young man, right now." She turned to Meredith and hissed, "I said, *sit down*. I mean it. You're making yourself nervous." Beverly was bigger than her husband. She told everyone Meredith had been sent home from the Army training camp, because he was "nervous from the service." She measured out her words, *sit down*, like venom from an eyedropper. He sat down. His obedience shocked me. Sometimes they fought so loud we could hear it upstairs and my mom and dad shook their heads. We had lived in Peoria Miller's house a long time, from even before I could remember, when they moved in. I felt that gave me first dibs on the porch swing to do whatever I wanted which was anything he hated, especially winding the big swing up, twisting it around and around until the two chains tangled into one thick knot that lifted the double seat high above the floor. Then anyone could jump up into it and ride it down while it jerked and lurched faster and faster to the floor.

Once when I banged the swing into the house wall, hard, Meredith came running out from their apartment. He had jumped up from the dinner table with one of Beverly's dish-towels tucked around his middle, screaming he'd kick my fanny, *lickety-lickety*, over the rail into the bridal wreath bushes if I ever did that again because the sudden bang made the war sound like it had come to our corner of Ayres and Cooper streets.

I did it again. After Beverly made peace between Meredith and my parents, and everyone agreed not to quarrel over the children, we sat long and late on the front porch. But this summer hadn't near the dash of the few summers before, the first I could remember, when the lights had to be turned off and the air-raid wardens patrolled the sidewalks.

Across our river, the factory where my father worked had turned into a war plant and steamed day and night because even as far inland as the

Midwest everyone feared the bombs could come. At first to me the black-outs were all as much a game as teasing Meredith who a Christmas or two later, panicking nervous, dropped dead at the produce counter in Kroger's Grocery where he worked. I never felt I caused him to keel over and fall in an avalanche of cabbages and potatoes any more than I felt I caused the war. But somehow I understood his fear.

They're coming, Mommy. Big and ugly. Germans. Mommy-Annie Laurie, help me run. Help me, Daddy. Tojo will get me. Help me, oh help me. Crying. Screaming. Falling out of bed. Hiding from dreams under the covers at night, *nobody loves me,* grew out of the cold hungry days when food was rationed and hand-me-down clothes were sewed and resewed. Walking everywhere, because there were no cars and no gas for cars and no rubber for tires, the grown-ups could only half-hide their fears. A silent anxiety ferreted my family out, tracked us like all the other mothers and fathers and children watching in horror in the blaring movie newsreels, *armies, tanks, captured soldiers,* and out through our darkened streets, *bombed cities,* and into our home, *refugees in rags,* where our radio, *it's not over till it's over over there,* and the newspaper, *dead bodies, our boys,* and the can of bacon-fat drippings in the icebox, *children starving in the snow,* told us the enemy was stronger than mortal danger itself.

"Bombs over Tokyo! Bombs over Tokyo!" Thommy shouted. He was four years old.

"Look out, Beevo," I said. "Thommy's dropping rocks out of the tree."

"Bombs over Tokyo!"

"Cut it out, Thommy." Beevo whooped a war cry. He was eight and he was Meredith's nephew.

"Bombs over Tokyo!"

Beevo waved a shiny hatchet in the air like a tomahawk.

My brother, Thomas a'Becket O'Hara, missed Beevo with another rock. I didn't know it then, but Thommy didn't even remember what Tokyo was. He was only three when the war ended and learned things like *Tojo* and *Tokyo* from us older kids. We might have told him some of the things that happened, but he could never remember stamping tin cans flat in the kitchen for scrap drives or going to Jake Meyer's store with ration stamps or having no car or no tires for the cars some people had. My uncles, framed and smiling in photographs on my father's piano, were fighting in the war and, my father, whose war job was working in a special factory, said we had to eat things we didn't like because children were starving in Europe. Everything seemed somehow significant, because every day gave me new words for new things.

"Get out of that tree, Thommy," Beevo said.

"Bombs away!" Thommy dropped small rocks down on us.

"Get out of that tree or I'll chop it down," Beevo said. "It's my tree."

"Go on, Beevo," I yelled. "Chop it down."

Our dog, Brownie, barked up at Thommy.

"This is Beevo to Thommy. Beevo to Thommy. I'll count to three, then I start chopping."

"Bombs away!" Thommy screamed.

"One...two..." Beevo strung out the count.

"Go ahead, Beevo," I said. "It's your tree. Chop it down on him."

"One more chance. One...two...three!"

I stood back, delirious in the fight, wanting to be the first to yell, "Timber!" I shouted the word a few times to test it out, like the movies, running in circles around the smooth trunk. "Timber! Timber! Timber!"

The frenzy on the ground agitated the little boy in the tree. Frightened, he lowered himself three branches. "Don't timber me," he pleaded.

"Don't come any farther," Beevo said, "or I'll chop your foot."

"Come on, Thommy. Don't let him scare you."

"Don't come any farther."

Thommy moved down two more limbs, looking at me, above Beevo's head.

"I'll chop your foot," Beevo warned.

My little brother looked like a baby bird sitting up in the deep green of the tree. Unlike me, he was blond and fair and he sat perched on the branch beginning to cry because his rocks were all gone and he could not comprehend us dancing around the trunk in a shower of wood chips and our own dog barking at him.

"Don't let it fall toward the mailbox," I said. "Johnny the Mailman will get mad and call the police." I turned to look across the quiet street at our big gray house. No mother in our window. Annie Laurie was away in the other rooms cleaning and fussing with the furniture that had been her own mother's. Even the elm trees, monstrous around the big corner house, were still. Only the trebling of the pigeons in our old carriage barn came from across the street.

"You won't chop my foot," Thommy cried.

"Wouldn't he, smarty. Come down and see."

"I'm coming down."

That was the last thing Thommy said before Beevo smashed his ankle with the hatchet. Blood spurted up all over his sunsuit and he fell from the tree. Brownie barked and yelped and ran for the bushes. The noise I made as I ran across the street tore down the afternoon, caused the pigeons to start up and circle the barn, brought mother from upstairs, and Meredith from down.

"Oh my God, my baby!" There was blood all over. On me. On Beevo.

"I didn't mean to," Beevo cried. "We were only playing. He put his foot right in front of the hatchet. I didn't mean to. My hand slipped." The weapon hung limp in his hand, a bright sacrificial silver, dripping blood, exactly like the movies.

"We told him not to come down," I said. "Thommy's foot slipped. Beevo's hand slipped."

Meredith pushed Beevo towards the house and carried Thommy to his car and set him in my mother's lap. Brownie jumped up into my lap in the back seat. We raced through the streets with so much blood all over us I thought he'd never stop. I sat hiding behind the dog, alone in the back seat, unnoticed. His blood was on me and no one noticed. No one mentioned what I had caused. Saying nothing, they said everything, *ringleader, cheerleader,* and I willed myself, full of guilt, isolated and alone with the dog in the back seat, not to cry, but Meredith, unable to contain himself, turned and looked a full *lickety-lickety* at me, and sorrow welled up inside my heart and sucked air into my throat that turned to gasping sobs.

Two nights later, Thommy was running with Brownie and playing hide-and-go-seek with us around the tables at Michael and Nellie Higgins' lawn party. He was only four that summer when I was seven and he really wasn't too good at playing yet. But we let him because the summer before he'd been too little to do anything. He wasn't the only thing that had changed.

Last summer, when the neighbors gathered next door at the Higgins' house, the parties had been every bit as fun as tonight. The air felt as warm and soft. The lanterns strung up between the grape arbors hung with the same sweet glow. Even the grass felt the same as last year. But the music now that crooned so softly way up on the porch where the boys were with the girls had been louder and different. Last summer everybody knew somebody who was coming home from the war, the war that had been over for two whole wild honking crying happy days. I learned all the words to the song, "Oh, Would You Rather Be a Colonel with an Eagle on Your Shoulder?" And we all sang back, "Or a Private with a Chicken on Your Knee?"

I took that song so literally that Victory over Japan almost disappointed me on VJ Day. The frenzy struck with the news that came over the radio on WMBD Peoria. Cars and trucks and buses spewed crowds into our small downtown. Girls shredded paper out of office windows, instantly releasing all thoughts of rationing and hoarding and saving for the scrap drive. An impromptu parade picked up in the streets. People danced on the sidewalks. Conga lines snaked one-two-three-four-conga! Thommy didn't know why the celebration was happening, but he yelled as loud as me on top of our Hudson parked in front of the Palace Theater where the marquee showed one big word: *Victory!* I didn't see any eagles or chickens in the swirl of noise and music and toilet paper rolling out of the windows. The few soldiers who happened to be in town were getting kissed by every girl there was. A crowd of farmers hoisted some sailors to their shoulders and started to carry them down the street and everybody cheered and I cheered and screamed and cried and went wild on the colors and the noises and the people pushing into each other, laughing and hugging and crying. My father kissed my mother and they both kissed us.

I had heard stories and seen the newsreels of the horrible things that happened to children, hung from their thumbs in the village square in some faraway lands. I cried uncontrollably because I was so glad it was over so it wouldn't happen here, in our downtown square, to me. The anxiety left like escaping steam. The void filled with a supercharged emotion that made my brain useless. All I needed was my body that tingled from top to bottom with the excitement of the wild streets. Ever since I could remember, from the dark timeless time to the beginning of my consciousness, the world was at war and now it was over. We were safe. But unseen by anyone, inside my chest, lay the angry marks made by the escaping fear. The jolt of new wild emotion whipped suddenly across the old anxiety like a long red welt from a willow branch that snaps back at you on a trail in the woods. Understanding much too little, I was exposed to feeling a little too much. I took the A5 Army patch a soldier in khaki gave me and put it away in my secret shoe box with my First Communion prayer book, and my first rosary, and a black-and-white snapshot I'd taken of Brownie and wrapped in wax paper with a lock of her fur.

The lights hung low and the ice cream lay melted in a hundred abandoned dishes when I crawled into daddy's lap on the Higgins' porch. The evening was late and a small breeze played with the napkins out on the green lawn. The music died away to the murmur of crickets. A girl laughed down the sidewalk, *pretty girl,* and disappeared into the dark shadows of the big elms. Another shadow, larger than hers, *handsome soldier,* darted, followed, and was gone. On the railing, my jar with sugar blinked on and off, full of lightning bugs.

My daddy felt warm and smelled of cigarette smoke. With my ear on his chest I could feel his heart thumping in quiet time with the rocker and his voice came low from deep inside. He was humming some old Irish song, *Mary of Dungloe*, half to himself, a bit to me and Mr. Higgins smoking in another chair. I felt like running in and telling my mother. We could hear her in the kitchen rattling the dishes with Mrs. Higgins. Their voices sparkled clear, out into the night. Half-awake, I listened to them. Once when my mother laughed inside the house, I laughed because she did and daddy laughed because of me.

I was nearly asleep when the women joined their husbands on the porch. Mrs. Higgins helped mother lift Thommy from the glider into her lap. I stayed in the rocker without moving, listening to their swing creak as heel and toe they pushed. My jar of little firefly lights on the railing seemed to go up and down, if I had known it then, like harbor lights seen from a rolling ship.

"Your brother, Father Les, is he in a parish yet, Charley?" Mr. Higgins spoke to my father. His voice was as old as my grandfather's, but a painting business and many cigars made it thick and deep. Mike Higgins had always been a success. He wanted everyone else to be.

"Yes, Charley," Mrs. Higgins said. "Michael and I were wondering at supper this evening about Father Les. He's such a fine-looking young priest." She sat perched in the swing like a tiny nervous oriole. Her eyes softly caught the lights from the elm-shrouded street lamp. The fullness of her hair made shadows on her face and her face dropped shadows down her thin breasts. I knew she smelled of strong verbena, but she looked fragile, as if she would be cool and hard to lean against. Her white hands neatly smoothed her dress. My mother had told Beverly that Mrs. Higgins could teach the world a thing or two about how to smooth and fashion a husband from a man. Beverly had told my mother, "Annie Laurie, you know who wears the pants."

"Father Les is stationed at Collinsville now," my mother told the Higgins. "The bishop sent him downstate as soon as he came back from overseas. It's a small country parish, that's true, but it gives him a chance to rest."

They said he had to rest from the Battle of the Bulge in Belgium. He'd been a chaplain in the Fifth Army and had buried dead bodies, and parts of them, that everybody said was terrible. But I wasn't sure what death was, so I believed them as I believed them about everything, because I didn't yet know where Europe was, or Belgium or France, or, worse, Germany, or exactly if they were far enough away so the bad things that happened there might stay there and not come get us here.

"Father Les should be made a pastor soon, I should think," Mr. Higgins said. "He did the Church no end of good being in those photographs."

"Yes, dear," Mrs. Higgins said to my mother, "that was so terribly thoughtful of you to write into the *Journal*. I know that anybody who might have missed the pictures in the magazine was glad to know Father Les is your brother-in-law."

My uncle, the Reverend Ryan Leslie O'Hara, 33, *Major O'Hara, Chaplain O'Hara,* burying the dead in the largest military cemetery on the Western Front, at Henri Chapelle, had been in *Life* magazine, April 2, 1945, page twenty-seven, in a famous Wirephoto also published in *Time* magazine and a hundred newspapers. My picture, age five, was in the Peoria newspaper, page three, sitting on Charley-Pop's lap, and the lady reporter, *camera, red lipstick, nylons, Annie Laurie said,* wrote we were namesake and brother of the famous, brave priest who stood over a hole in a barren field of a thousand open graves, burying the young dead boys, his white surplice billowing in the Ardennes winds, his handsome face beautiful as a manly young Irish saint.

"That's what wrong with war," my uncle said in the newspapers, "all those crosses." He waved at the white markers on 25,000 graves, *dead boys, 18, 19,* stretching as far as the eye could see, *dead men, 24, 32,* across the green and muddy Belgian hills, silent, but for the *flap flap flap* American flag flying permanently at half-staff and the sounds of cannons not far off. Every day from the Western Front, Uncle Les rode forty miles back from the German battlefields with the dead young soldiers, *Nazi massacre at Malmedy,* escorting their torn bodies from Germany to Belgium, to bury the dead American boys no American wanted buried in German soil.

All the dead soldiers carried the same things: *a photograph of someone they loved, a pocket knife, a saint's medallion, for Catholic boys, or a rosary, a pen and pencil, and a one dollar bill to remind them of home.* All night long he heard Confessions, and in the mornings, riding back to the front, he said Mass four or five times from the hood of his Jeep, and gave Communion under fire in trenches, knee-deep in mud and blood, and took letters to be mailed. The picture of the "Combat Chaplain Saddened by War, Shot by William C. Allen for the Wartime Still Picture Pool" was framed and hung in our front hall and we always said, "Oh yes," when callers noticed it. "Oh yes, and Ryan is named after him."

His favorite song was "Stardust" and I loved him saying the songwriter's magic name, "Hoagy Carmichael," singing the song for us, folding us singing along into his singing. Once he sent from France a seven-inch white vinyl record printed with a Red Cross label that said, "A Personal Message from a Service Man through the Facilities Provided by the American Red Cross." On one side, Uncle Les sang "Stardust," *wondering why he spent the lonely nights*, and on the other, "That's All That It Was (But, Oh, What It Seemed to Be)." I imagined him, the way we saw the world in movies, in black-and-white, in liberated Paris singing into a silver microphone, seining smoke from his cigarette, smoke forming words, *stardust*, coming from his mouth, smoke curling around his smile, smoke inhaled again up his nose in a quick uptake of breath, smoke around his head in a halo.

"Being a pastor has obvious advantages over being a second assistant priest, or even a first assistant priest," Mr. Higgins informed us. "Why, the other day I visited Father Fitzgerald..."

"Michael!" Mrs. Higgins sat up, stopping the swing of the glider.

"Mrs. Higgins," he said, "I certainly am not going to mention any check."

She threw herself back into the seat, her command ruined, her eyes raised. I heard my father laugh a little. My mother smiled.

"But surely, to speak of it, a pastor is a man of experience and Father Fitzgerald will certainly know what to do with the donation. If there's anything Father Fitz knows about, it's how much business sense it takes to run a parish. That's one thing Father Les will have to learn, Annie-Laurie, money. Even in the cloth and collar, it's money." He leaned forward assuringly. "But don't worry, my girl. He'll learn. Church and charity. He's a great fine lump of a lad, that brother-in-law of yours. He's as smart as his brother," he smiled at my father, "whom you were smart enough to marry. With the war and all he'll be a pastor before you know it."

Michael Higgins went on and on, building my uncle's career out of church and congregation, telling a story of Uncle Les becoming a pastor, then a monsignor, maybe even a bishop with purple robes and a purple hat and a great big black car, adding it up, ruling over a diocese of a hundred parish churches and a hundred schools, and a thousand priests, and ten thousand nuns, and fifty thousand Catholic families, and a million school children. Half-asleep there on the porch I heard all the things I had ever heard anyone say about my uncle. My father shifted in his chair, a little uneasy. He lit a cigarette and the match sputtered in the dark, its sudden sulphur brightness painful to my eyes. I slid from his lap and went to my mother on the glider. Nell Higgins reached over and touched my head.

"Poor Ry," she said, "so tired. I think when you're big, you'll be a priest like your Uncle Les, won't you."

"Yes, ma'am," I said.

"Imagine. You, Father Ryan O'Hara."

"What's more than Les?" My father loved his brother.

In my mind, I could hear Uncle Les singing a song he'd learned in Belgium when he was lost in the Battle of the Bulge. French children sang it, or maybe Belgian children, and he taught me all the sounds, but I had no idea what it meant when he and I sang together, with him teaching me to be his little echo on the *ollie oom, ollie oom.*

"Ryan," Nell Higgins asked, "can you sing that little song your Uncle Les brought back from France?"

I sang, not understanding a word, "Dess lardenn melodien econterr melodien. Ollie oom, ollie oom, ollie oom, ollie oom, ollie ollie ollie oom lay ollie oom."

Falling asleep cradled so soft in the swing, I heard my mother say, "A priest like his Uncle Les. He always has said that's all he wants to be."

May 1, 1953

"That's all I want to be, Father. That's all I ever thought about being." I sat across from Father Gerber in the little room outside the principal's office. It was May Day in the month dedicated to the Virgin Mother of God. Father Joseph Gerber was the pastor of St. Philomena's Parish and Sister Mary Agnes was my eighth-grade teacher and the principal of our school. I felt flushed rose that I could talk to him. The last month of eighth grade was time to be adult. Sister Mary Agnes herself, playing a record of Frank Sinatra singing "Young at Heart," led off a classroom practice dance right in the rows of desks to instruct the proper distance between boys and girls. Our Mothers Club arranged graduation robes and diplomas and breakfast. A full-grown priest who could actually make dreams come true took a real interest in me. I was almost fourteen and flattered. His attention proved I was right and my classmates were wrong, because they were all so smart, and I couldn't be like any of them. I had made up my mind.

My conviction jelled earlier in the spring when Billy O'Connor ran into Barbara Martin in the cloakroom during lunch hour. Only he had been pushed, and Danny Boyle had done it. He pushed himself into Billy and knocked Billy into Barb so he could bump her sweater.

"Quit your bawlin'," Danny said. "You ain't the first girl's been bumped."

"And you bumped them all," Barbara wailed. "I'm going to tell Sister."

"She's solid." Danny, unruffled, preened.

The boys standing around laughed. I edged away, pretending I never heard it ever happened because I wasn't sure what really had happened. I only guessed the edges, especially when a few minutes later, after the bell, the girls were excused and the boys held after.

"Daniel Boyle," Sister Mary Agnes looked stern, ruler in hand, "what did you do in the cloakroom?"

"I watched queerbeer Billy trip over Barbara."

"You needn't call William names," she cried, "and add uncharity to your impurity."

"I watched Billy bump into Barbara," he said.

"You mean you pushed William into Barbara as an excuse."

As an excuse for what?

"Daniel Boyle, tell me. You shave already."

"Yes."

"Yes, what?" She slapped his hand with the ruler.

"Yes, *Sissster.*" He hissed out the word.

"Do you know what a beard is, Daniel?"

"A big hairy deal."

Laughter rolled through the room.

"It's the mark of Cain, young man. Because of the first male's sin of impurity, man's face has grown covered for shame." She waved the ruler. "Did you realize that?"

"No, *Sis*ter."

"Do you know, Daniel Boyle, that to jostle a young lady is a serious sin of impurity? Do you know it will make your face grow dark with hair? Do you know it will make your soul grow blacker still?"

I felt my smooth chin and my stomach in the area of my soul.

"You young men of tomorrow must be like the young men of yesterday. Oh, I fear for you. I fear for you," she said with menace. "You must be pure and keep all black spots off your souls like all those young saints who died when they were your age." She brandished the ruler. "Nothing is worse than impurity. You must never look at bad pictures or say impure words that make your mouth dirtier than the bottom of a sewer. You must die before listening to impure conversation because you could commit mortal sins that would make your souls black and filthy and keep you from going to Communion and receiving Our Lord's body and blood, soul and divinity into your hearts."

She paced before the chalkboards, her face flushed inside her white and black oval. Outside the windows, the other classes were leaving school amid shouts and the rattle of cars and the roaring smell of the worn yellow buses. Danny Boyle had sat down unnoticed in his scarred desk.

"It's wrong, as you've been told before, to look longingly at the parts of your bodies nobody ever sees. If you do, you will commit a black, black sin. If you go to Communion so disposed, you will only make Jesus suffer more. You will drive one more nail into His body, or beat Him once more, or spit on His sweet face, or push one more thorn into His precious head. Not this, oh please not this, young men, to the Sweet Babe of Bethlehem."

Danny Boyle was carving his desktop with an Eversharp pen. Sister didn't notice. She was telling that story again about Ted who had committed a mortal sin with a girl and how driving home he was killed and plunged into the deepest, hottest pit of hell where it was so terrible Lucy and the Children of Fatima fainted when they were gloriously gifted with a vision of it.

"Impurity is the worst sin of all," she concluded. "Boys can always be impure at the movies and women in the movies are the worst temptation of all."

I felt hot with shame. I went to the movies, but I always sank down to try to keep the back of the seat in front of me, especially at 3-D movies, between me and the actresses' chests.

"Athletes of Christ are pure and good and clean. As you live, so you'll die."

I knew this was true. Boys had to be really careful around girls.

"Go," she said. "Sin no more. Do not make Jesus weep."

I moved with the class shuffling in a rush toward the door, my resolves renewed. I didn't mind missing my bus. I could think on the long hike home and I would say a prayer for my father who would be angry I was late and who would curse and say, damn, what's the bus fee for anyway? And I would say a grateful prayer for the nuns that God had given to preserve me, and for my dad who was always watching out for me.

"Look out, Ry," Danny's gang of three boys shouted. They pushed by me down the steps.

Their hero appeared at the top of the divided stairs.

"Oh, Danny Boy!" I sing songed the nickname he hated most, in a high voice imitating Barbara Martin. "Oh, Danny Boy!"

He slung one long leg over the median banister and slid down the flight, screaming past me as loud as he could: "The nuns are *coming!*"

May 14, 1953

I thought we would all be on our guard at the real spring dance, but the party was our first one that wasn't a kid's birthday party run by adults, so we were on our own, and hesitant. Mostly the guys watched and the girls danced and stood together around the plaster statue of the Virgin brought to Barbara Martin's knotty-pine basement from the classroom. After about an hour, three of us went outside to see where some of the wild ones had gone to sneak a cigarette, blow smoke rings, and spit.

"What you doin' out here?" Danny yelled. Smoke came out of his face.

"Mind your own business," Billy O'Connor said.

"Is that clumsy Billy who bumps into girls?" Danny asked.

"Mind your own business," I said.

Danny walked toward us, his voice singsonging back at me, "Mind your own business." He danced a little dance like a boxer. "Mind your own business. Chick, chick, chicken!" Danny advanced on Billy. "Come here, lover boy!"

Danny Boyle's gang of three stepped in behind him. They started after Billy. I pushed him to the door, but they grabbed him back. Danny Boyle flipped out an open pocketknife. He shoved Billy against the house wall, grabbed his belt, and held the knife in his face. "Hey, clumsy Billy, you been fixed? Maybe I should ask old sweet tits Barb."

"Don't talk dirty," I said.

"Shut up, or I'll fix you."

"You and what army?" I said. "Let him go." I made a fist.

"You telling me what to do, you ass-kisser?" He let go of Billy's belt and came toward me. "Go kiss your sweet nun's ass, Ry. Go brown-nose till it falls off." He closed the knife in his hand and shoved it into his pocket. "I don't need this to fix you!" He made two fists and jumped at me.

We pushed at each other. Danny threw a punch and missed. Billy and I laughed and bolted inside, hooking the screen door. Danny led his gang circling the stoop making finger signs. "Chick, chick, chicken!"

I shouted, "Oh, Danny Boy!" The three of us started singing high in the back of our noses, making fun of big fat opera singers to make fun of Danny Boyle: "The pipes, the pipes are calling! Oh, Danny Boyle! The cops will come and haul you off to jail."

Billy flicked the porch light fast, on and off, and the gang charging toward our door scattered back into the shadows of the yard.

"Chick, chick," Danny Boyle yelled back from the dark. "I rule the roost around here!"

I crowed back, "Cock-a-doo-doodle-doo!"

The challenge thrown down between us charged us up like some contest between the bad boys and the good boys. If Danny Boyle could show himself the best of the worst, some other boy could be the best of the best. My Uncle Les had bought me a two-year subscription to *Catholic Comic Books* starring Chuck White, All-American Catholic Boy, who in page after page of cartoon strips was the best of the best.

The Sisters had insisted something bad could happen between boys and girls. I didn't know what it was, but I was very careful because they said you never know when you'll die and go to the deepest part of hell for all eternity with not even a drop of water. But I could always sense when someone was sniffing around the edge. The recess before, Danny Boyle had been impure on the playground with all the girls. He swung a pale old rubber balloon around on a stick, waving it in their faces. They laughed and ran and came back laughing more. I knew they were not being good and I thought we'd all better pray for them that they didn't get amnesia while they had a mortal sin on their souls because they said if you forgot to be sorry for a big sin you'd go straight to hell.

Later I was glad when Father Gerber came into the classroom because he could forgive sins and make your soul as white as snow. I felt better than Danny because I was careful and always confessed impure thoughts about going to the bathroom and was careful not to watch the whole screen at the movies. At least I didn't run around being impure out in the open. It was hard enough trying not to think of girls going to the bathroom.

"You boys and girls," Father Gerber said, "are going to be graduating in three weeks and next fall you will start high school. As you become young men and young women you will discover that you want to do much good for the greater honor and glory of God. Some of you will become mothers and fathers. But to some others of you the Holy Ghost, the dove of peace, will whisper in your ear that you should become sisters and priests of almighty God."

I knew what was coming. Every year Father Gerber came to the graduating class and asked the same question. My answer was prepared. I was different from all my classmates. My best response to their sex and stupidity was the safety of a vocation. I recognized what I needed. I saw the way out. I sat on the edge of my seat waiting to raise my hand to volunteer to become a priest.

"No greater vocation on earth can come to a man or a woman," Father Gerber said. "Only the finest children of Christ are asked to carry on God's work. You girls have seen all the good that the Sisters do. Teaching and nursing and praying for long hours before the most holy Blessed Sacrament. What greater life could be yours than as daughters of Holy Mother Church? You boys know that the priest calls God down from heaven, body and blood, soul and divinity at the consecration; that the priest helps the sick and must go to help the dying even risking his own life in burning buildings and caved-in mines."

"Would you risk your life for me, Ryan?" Barbara whispered.

"Barbara!" Sister Mary Agnes snapped.

"The time is short," Father Gerber continued, "and the day of your graduation is at hand. This is the biggest chance in your lives." He looked about the room at Monica and Audrey and Ara Ann shining over girls like Barbara. "How many girls in here would like to seek the challenge of the Sisterhood?"

We all sat quietly, straining to see whose hand went up. The girls sat stock still, poised like stones in a Virgin grotto of varnish and chalk. No one moved. No hand was raised.

"Is there no one," Father Gerber repeated, "who seeks the challenge of the Sisterhood?"

Danny Boyle whispered, "I would."

Sister Mary Agnes spoke, over the snickers, too loud, from the back of the room. "Some of the girls are indeed interested, Father. I have talked to them, but they seem to think it better to wait until after high school."

"I'd rather be the mother of a priest," Barbara said.

"And I'll be the daddy," Danny whispered.

"Maybe it's the times," Sister Mary Agnes said. "Girls today."

"That's prudent thinking, girls, that you want to wait to be sure." The priest looked at the nun in a way that made her look like she hadn't done her job. "But it's best not to keep almighty God waiting. It's a far more blessed thing to save your vocation from the temptation of high school and go to the good Sisters' convent as soon as you take off your graduation gown."

A few boys snorted at that, but there were no volunteers. Father Gerber reddened, then recouped. "How about all these fine young men, Sister? Who here now is thinking about being a priest?"

I sat a minute savoring the delicious moment of my perfect ascension into heaven. I had settled on the seminary by myself and the fact I could declare it in the very faces of the impure was incidental glory. The heads turned toward me, mouth-breathers marveling a little as I was ushered up from the long rows of desks and pencils and books. This moment of affirmation, of stated resolution, of perfect nya-nya-nya, was enough to separate me from all their stubborn childishness massed together in one room. For the first time I knew I was more than a name in their alphabetical order. I was apart, independent. I liked the taste. My exit toward the door was all topping, because behind all the payoff I knew this was only God's will.

"So long, chick, chick, chicken," Danny whispered.

I marched toward the door like a slapped soldier of Christ. Truth and justice and purity walked with me and I resolved ever to be so good. For I had never been so perfect. The priest held out his hand and made me his equal. I would be cut fabric and soul in his image. I would be a priest like Annie Laurie's favorite actor–she called him "Monty Clift" like she knew him–who refused to tell the police a killer's Confession in *I Confess*. I'd be a priest like Bing Crosby wearing the collar and singing and taking care of women and children in *Going My Way* and *The Bells of St. Mary's* where he tried not to be in love with Ingrid Bergman who was a nun. I walked past Danny Boyle. I whispered, "We'll see who rules what roost." I imagined him years in the future as the father of six sets of twins coming to ask me in Confession if he for God's sake could use some birth control, and I'd say *lickety-lickety, no* and make him for penance say twelve rosaries and the fourteen Stations of the Cross twenty times.

In his office, Father Gerber asked me to sit down. "You've thought long of being a priest, Ryan?"

"All my life, Father. That's all I've ever wanted to be." My words were inspired.

"Knowing the O'Hara family so many years, I can certainly believe you. Surely you've talked to your uncle, Father Les, about your vocation."

"Last Christmas I told him I was thinking about going away to the seminary, but he thought I better wait until after high school and maybe some college."

"He risked waiting?"

"Yes, Father."

"You see, Ryan, your uncle was very, very lucky. Many boys who wait until after high school don't wait at all. They turn their backs on God and lose their vocations dancing and dating. Many, I dare say thousands, lose their vocations this way. And perhaps their souls. Even our good Holy Father desires that vocations to the holy priesthood be nurtured from a tender age. Which is certainly the eighth grade. Holy Mother Church has counseled this for centuries."

"Yes, Father."

"I myself skipped my last year of grade school. I went directly from the seventh grade right into the seminary."

"That's wonderful, Father."

"I've never regretted it. Thanks be to almighty God."

"Yes, Father."

He picked my mind and moved words and arranged thoughts so I became kin with him. My will and my true heart rose up to meet him. Danny Boyle and Barbara Martin really didn't matter, because I had a divine vocation. I listened to his sound advice. I might lose my sacred calling. Jesus would whisper only once, and only into undefiled ears. "Now," Father Gerber said, "now is the time. Souls are waiting. The night is passed and the day is at hand. Jesus has no hands now but yours. Come to Me, He cries in the night. Be Mine. Be Mine. If you say *no* to your vocation, thousands may burn forever in hell because you gave no hands to help them, to baptize and bless them, to anoint and absolve them. If in your pure heart, He calls you away from the world, if He asks you to do more, to give more, to bleed with Him on the Cross of the world, then you should, nay, you must, go to Him now. Give Him all, now. Now is the time. Before the world and the flesh and the devil rip you away from your holy Saviour. Now, Ryan, now. Remember, Jesus needs you to work in the vineyard of Holy Mother Church. Christ needs you as his priest. You can be an *alter Christus, another Christ*. Now, Ryan Stephen O'Hara. Now."

May 31, 1953

"I, the soothsayer, the prophet of the Class of 1953, beheld or dreamed in a dream how that we of '53, or most of us (I added that to leave out Danny Boyle), were united in a great orchestra." I did believe this, these words I memorized for the graduation breakfast. I looked down into their faces and the eggs and pancakes and the bouquets of peonies on the cafeteria tables. Already I was forgetting them marching off into the anonymity of their high school. I stood confident, without stage fright, facing my classmates and their parents, knowing I was singled out.

Something so great and big had touched me that something rose out of me and separated from me in the same way I was separated from them.

God's grace came down upon me and some ideal me took my place.

I would be the spiritual leader of the orchestra. I would forgive the impure. I would forgive the boys who bumped into girls and would make sure they all got saved even if they didn't deserve it. I stood before them with the promise to save them from their own sinful natures. I pledged myself to them. I was, after all, only three weeks and one day shy of my fourteenth birthday, and, I felt, late already, older by two years than the accomplished boy Jesus in the Temple.

"Har," Danny Boyle said, "Har dee har har."

September 7, 1953
Labor Day Weekend

The last Sunday of the summer, the September Sunday before I left for the seminary, I wanted to be left alone. In four days I would abandon everything for the honor and glory of God. From here on out I would be pure and holy and kind to all, never raising my voice or quarreling with Thommy or being envious or gluttonous, fighting even harder the snares and wickedness of the world and the devil and the flesh. I had saved a dollar to rent a horse for an hour to ride fast as I could out the trail and into the woods. I wanted to feel the big horse heave and jounce and fly beneath me. I planned to give my good old dog, Brownie, a bath and a currying, and I'd pack up all my most precious secret stuff into my shoe box and put away childish things forever.

After Mass, Dad suggested a driving lesson I didn't really want as much as I wanted him to drive me out to the stable to rent a horse. But I was obedient. I drove our big blue four-door 1948 Plymouth down an old dirt road, shifting on the steering column, grinding gears, *"first" and "second" and "third,"* working my feet on the clutch and brake pedals, popping the clutch, riding the clutch, herking and jerking, because I hated driving. A mile down the lane through the woods, I coasted to a stop inside a glade of maples and oaks. I announced I'd had enough. "You'll have to back us out," I said. "You know I can't find 'reverse.'" I gave my dad the wheel. Something was on his mind.

"Ryan."

"Yes, Dad."

"Because you're going away to school and all, there's some things I, well, I think I ought to tell you. Since you're growing up and all."

He was skirting the edges. I knew the area and I remembered Sister's words not to listen to impure conversations. My mind puckered and turned in on itself.

"I know when I was growing up and it happened I thought maybe something was wrong with me. I worried maybe I'd been hurt. But it's natural and nothing to worry about."

"I know," I said, trying to end it, trying to shut it out. I wanted out of the car. *Suffocation.* He was always so good to me. I wanted to run out into the hot September sun, off through the dusty goldenrod. I willed not to panic and my hands were folded hot between my knees and a bead of sweat rolled down my cheek to my chin and down my throat.

"A boy grows up to become a father."

But I'm not going to be a father, I wanted to shout. I ached all over wanting to find the words to exorcise this devil in this man I loved who was subjecting me to hearing this. He had wanted to be a father. That was his vocation. I had to stop him. Because if I didn't know about impure things I couldn't be tempted and then I couldn't lose my soul in fires hotter than the chrome on the dashboard.

"Do you know what I mean?" he asked.

"Yes. I do. Sister at school explained it all to us," I lied. "I understand." But I didn't. *Liar.* I had no inkling. *Liar, liar.* I didn't need to know what he was saying. *Pants on fire.* There would be no girls at the seminary. No temptations.

"Am I relieved!" he said. "I certainly wouldn't want you to worry about those nights the way I did." He looked at his watch. "Shall us men stop and get a milk shake?" He smiled.

Thank God, he dropped the subject. My soul was completely safe, because I hadn't the slightest idea of what he was saying.

"I'd rather just go home."

He looked a bit disappointed.

"Or maybe to the stables. I saved up a dollar so I can rent a horse and go riding one last time."

"It's God's will for you, I guess." He rubbed his chin.

I felt for him, sitting sweating with him in the hot car parked in a lane of goldenrod, that he would have to get used to my being gone.

"I know it's God's will," I said.

"Okay. Because you say so." He turned the key in the ignition. "... Ryan."

"Yes, Dad."

"Son. You really do want to go away to school? I mean, leave town, and your mother, and Thommy, and Brownie?"

I looked at him and loved his kindness, his generosity to me. "Yes. More than anything."

"You're not going away just for us? We don't want you to become a priest for us."

"No, Dad. Gee!"

"I want to make sure you go because it's what you think is right."

"It's right. I want it more than anything. More than anything in the whole world."

I did, sitting with him in the car with the sun beating down. I did want the priesthood more than anything. I knew it then, eight years after the World War. I had known it all along from the first moment the shadow of the War's wild violence had crossed my three-year-old life in 1942. I had known it, sitting in dark movie theatres, from the cruel atrocities in the blaring black-and-white newsreels of marching soldiers and orphaned children and bombed cities. I knew it covered with my brother's blood. I had heard Michael and Nellie Higgins, man and wife, suggest my whole enduring life on a summer night. But even before these things I had known it, perhaps from before time. I could save people.

No matter how silly I was or scared or immature or full of myself, my vocation had been whispered to me out of some cosmic Pentecost when a Holy Ghost bird of red and yellow and green circled above my crib, in the wordless time before I recognized words, making me later imagine what primitive people felt like when huge birds with claws and beaks and teeth hungry for human flesh flew overhead. Some virgin, I knew from Hawaiian movies like *Bird of Paradise*, had to be willingly sacrificed to keep the cannibal bird away from the cave door.

The threat of that flapping violence mixed all my war-torn sympathy for a fallen world into a small green-apple ache, straight from the Garden of Eden, cramping my soul and my heart. An ache of appeasement inside me burst in my chest like the hot red bloodspray of a spear piercing my side, *Jesus' side*, spreading through my body, reaching up to my face, burning my eyes, and I knew I wanted to offer myself up like Christ on the Cross. I could taste the holy life of my heroic uncle anointing dying soldiers on the battlefield.

Cosmic desire had lodged in me, moved me to find how the Word was made Flesh, how missionaries became martyrs, how virgins became saints. My vocation was right and good and I would embrace it willingly like a whole holiness I remembered from before I was born, and being born, was in danger of losing. Through Ordination to the priesthood, I would humbly renounce the whole proud and wicked world and save it by going my way.

2

Fall 1953

North America. Ohio. Misericordia Seminary. September. October. November. Maps and clocks. *Tick. Tick. Tick.* After the hot waxen weeks of the long fall, I awoke one morning in the cold rain. I could read the drizzling pre-dawn sky outside the tall row of dormitory windows. Another overcast day. All around me, in nearly one hundred beds, classmates lay snoring in lumpen disarray, asleep in tangles of blankets, their unconscious faces more innocent than when awake. At the far end of the sleeping hall a student-prefect padded to the washroom to begin his day. The door thunked closed after him. My watch ticked close to my ear, loud as a sound effect in a movie. The prefect's toilet flushed in the muffled distance. For the first instant in my life I was rationally conscious of time. I had twelve years to go to be a priest. I was fourteen years old.

Sixty-three days had passed since September when I had left my family and the world behind. Then, in that gentle late Indian summer, before the drizzle of this morning, the Ohio autumn had sifted down, dry and golden, on the river valley below the seminary. Across that valley, four hundred miles away to the west, was home. The wind sweeping up the long hill from the river, from the patchwork orchards on the far rim of the valley, had blown only the day before across my home on the flat Illinois prairie. Letters from home took three days. The weather my mother invariably mentioned traveled with the post and was hanging in Ohio over Misericordia Seminary at my reading.

By November the summer sun had gone thin for the winter. Gray sky was Ohio sky. The seasons became another kind of clock in my isolated new life. Already I was forgetting what autumn in the world had been. Even that first day, after the first meeting with the priests of the Misericordia faculty in the reception garden, after I had kissed my parents good-bye, and they had driven out the long drive leaving me alone for the first time in my life, things had needed adjusting. I was an Irish-American boy in a German-American seminary.

September 7, 1953

Welcome to Misericordia Seminary!

"Misery loves company!"

"You're from Peoria, Illinois?"

"My God! Can anything good come out of Peoria?"

"Peoria's strictly a vaudeville joke! You know what they say..."

"...If it plays in Peoria,..."

"...it will play anywhere."

"We're the Rimshot Brothers."

"Ka-boom!"

They actually were brothers, each playing the other's straight man.

"I'm Peter. He's Heinrich. We're the Rimski's."

"You can call me 'Henry,'" Heinrich said.

"Or you can call him 'Hank,'" Peter said. "'Heinrich, Henry, Hank.' Get it?"

"What do you do?" Heinrich Henry Hank Rimski said. "I mean besides being from Peoria? Do you play any instrument or sing? Peter was in a show at a mountain lodge last summer." Hank motioned toward his older brother, who grinned. Neither wanted a plain answer.

"You were?" I asked.

"Really, Peoria," Peter Rimski said. "Hank, this must be the kid's first day away from home."

"As a matter of fact, we drove in this morning," I said.

"Can it, Peoria."

"My name isn't Peoria. It's Ryan O'Hara."

"We're from Howl and Bellow. Or is it Bell and Howell? I never can keep us straight," Hank said. They leaned together, laughing.

"I think I got to be going," I said. "So long."

"Wait a minute," Peter said, breaking away from Hank. "We'll show you around."

"I can manage okay."

"Come on. Let us show you," Hank said.

"Why?" I asked.

"Because you're a live one," Peter said. They both laughed. "We can tell you've got personality."

"How long've you two gone here?"

"This is my first year," Hank said.

"Then we're in the same class," I said.

"Yes," Hank said, "but I doubt it."

"You should know," Peter said, "that our father studied here at Misery for six years and we know everybody."

"Your father was a seminarian?"

"In this seminary, yeah. He was in Father Gunn's class. But he quit."

"I never thought of that happening. An ex-seminarian being somebody's father, I mean. That's funny."

"What do they teach you in Peoria, kid?" Hank pretended disgust.

"Ever been there?" I asked. "Where you from?"

"P. A.," Hank said.

"The great state of Pennsy." Peter mimed a cheer that reminded me of a girl.

"Are you both in my class?" I asked.

"Never," Peter said. "I'm fourth-year high school, a senior, and you're a freshman like Hank."

"See those guys playing touch football over there, Peoria?" Hank asked. "You ever play?"

"Around the neighborhood. Never on a team."

"Here everybody plays. Except my brother," Hank motioned, "who's got a medical excuse. You'll play and learn to take it."

"Take it? He doesn't even get it," Peter said. They both roared.

"Who said I couldn't take it?" I asked.

"I'll bet he doesn't even own a jock," Hank said.

"God. I'll bet he doesn't need one."

"You got one, Peoria?" Hank asked. He was bigger than Peter, who was bigger than me. "I asked you do you got one?"

"One what?"

"You got a jock?"

"You know," Peter motioned, "a jockstrap. A bag for your bowling balls."

"Sure," I lied. "Sure I got one." I didn't know what they were talking about.

"Good," Hank said. "You better. Because if you don't, when you die all maimed up, Saint Finger will wave his Peter at you. Or is it...hell, I never can keep it straight."

I wanted to change the subject because this was impure. I had only been at the seminary three hours, had watched my family drive off in our big blue Hudson, and people who were going to be priests were talking impure. "Where'd you say you were from in Pennsylvania?"

"What's it to you, Pee-oh-ree-ahh?" Hank said. "Up yours, I guess." He ran off, leaving Peter staring at me.

"Pittsburgh," he said. "Ever been there?"

"This is as far East as I've ever been."

"Hank always did like a good pimping," Peter said. "Why not let's go inside and see who's here?"

We walked from the garden out across the playing fields. Intense blue sky outlined the huge red brick buildings. I was seeing Misericordia Seminary for the first time. The green bronze cap of the bell tower pointed twenty stories high, up and over the hive of buildings at its foot. From miles away, people could see the gold cross on top rise above the surrounding Ohio woods and farmland, a tower of German Catholicism on the American prairie.

Below the imposing tower, gray slate roofs covered all the buildings, including the high-vaulted chapel roof from which, Peter said, a mason had fallen and been killed during construction in 1907. Lower, but tall at four stories were the buildings with classrooms on the first and second floors, and dormitories above. The doorways and windows were framed in limestone set into the red brick. The refectory where we ate was a huge Gothic building with leaded glass windows. Miles of long corridors and tunnels connected all the buildings exactly like my father's best friend, a Mason, had predicted.

The Gibraltar-like front-entrance building where the priests lived, each in a small apartment, continued, Peter said, "the formal Flemish Renaissance tone. The suite for the Apostolic Delegate, Archbishop Amleto Giovanni Cicognani, is always kept available for his frequent visits from Rome. Apostolic Delegates to the United States eventually always become cardinals, and, sometime, someday, Pope."

In that main residence lived the forty or so priests who were to teach the hundreds of us boys how to be priests. In the building nearest to the priests lived a small group of students, ages twenty-one to twenty-five, closest to Ordination to the priesthood. The forty or fifty of them studied theology in Latin textbooks and learned to administer sacraments like Confession and Extreme Unction and practiced saying Holy Mass. Between their theology department and our high-school building lived the collegians, two hundred of them, who studied the humanities and majored in philosophy, and who never spoke to the three hundred of us high-school boys.

Like Gaul, the seminary was divided into three parts, but all three parts were united like the Trinity. All these buildings connected with one another through off-limits tunnels and forbidden corridors that passed under and through the chapel, the one place priests, theology students, collegians, and high-school boys congregated. All told, five hundred boys and young men made their way through the twelve years of study for the priesthood.

"Misericordia is a community built around the tabernacle," I said.

"But you better never find any communication between departments," Peter warned. "We can't speak to theologians or collegians, or them to us or to each other. There's three departments. Four years each. High school, college, and theology. If you fraternize across the boundaries, you'll get shipped."

"Why?" I asked. "The collegians and the theology students are closer to the priesthood. I'd think they could help us some."

"It's part of the plan, part of the game. Rules. Penalties. Go directly to jail. Collect two-hundred dollars. You'll get a rule book," was all he said, dropping the subject.

For the first time I sensed the boundaries and secrets signified, but not revealed, in that calibrated tangle of sacred buildings. I determined then and there to learn the mystique, for that mystery could make me holy, make me a priest, and set me apart forever. I knew it would have to be learned slowly, the word for the mystery. I knew it had to be learned inside. Inside Misericordia and inside me.

No driver speeding down the highway and catching the first glimpse of the red-brick sprawl on the hill could ever guess at Misericordia's maze of secrets, could ever really comprehend the inner strength and recesses of the cluster. Isolated in a clearing of Ohio woods, a mile from the nearest roadhouse, Misericordia stood, cloistered and alone, enigmatic on the valley rim, no more than a landmark telling tired salesmen only sixteen miles more to Columbus, a drink, and bed. But to the thousands of teenaged boys who entered and stayed, marking the years from one to twelve, the seminary stood as a house of search and journey, winter and summer, in season and out.

That first day I did not know the seminary. It was, if one of those passing travelers had asked, a place where boys can study to be priests. That was it. That was all. If a boy believes he has a vocation, if he feels God has called him to the holy Catholic priesthood, all he has to do, *God told me*, is announce his belief and his feeling.

That surety of vocation I had with all my heart and soul. Everything was settled. I questioned nothing, because God would take care of me. I knew His general plan, but His details were a holy mystery to be revealed through prayer, studies, and sports.

But I had hoped that something of what I had seen of boarding schools in the movies was true. I hoped that in the dormitory where Peter guided me, kids would be sitting around, laughing, bursting into some song.

"I do play the ukulele," I told Peter on the way to the building.

"Key of 'C'?"

He sounded so snotty.

"I can play 'Ain't She Sweet?' and 'Danny Boy.'"

"Of course, you can," Peter said. "Because you are ha ha ha a real 'Danny Boy.' He stuck out his lower jaw and repeated himself, "Of courssse, you kahn. Becawze you awh." He was his own favorite fan. "I play the accordion and the piano. Hank plays the drums and we both sing. We could play vaudeville in Peoria."

"If it plays in Peoria," I said. "That's what they say: it will play anywhere."

"So Peoria is the ultimate audience," he said, studying my eyes, considering my challenge.

"Go figure," I said, "what that makes me...to you." *Ka-boom*. I was learning fast that the freshness of freshmen was survival.

"What did you say your name was, Peoria?"

"Ry." I bit my lip. "Ryan," I said. I had decided "Ry" and all the things he'd done before were going to be put away like the things of a child. Exactly as Saint Paul said. Now that I was older in a new life, away at school, I wasn't any longer little "Ry" O'Hara.

But lying half awake in the cold November morning, remembering, knowing the electric matins bell was about to wrangle the sleeping dorm, knowing another day out of days was to begin because time had me cloistered where priests wanted me, because the timeless Priest Jesus seemed never so far away, I never felt more like poor little lost "Ry."

My classmates' November talk of the coming Christmas vacation—everyone counting the days backwards in white chalk on the blackboard—stirred in me the old worldly troubles of the early autumn, of my first night sleeping in a room of ninety freshman boys.

"Only ten percent of new boys make it through the twelve years to Ordination to the priesthood," Father Gunn had told us our first night after lights-out.

Blankets rustled. Someone farted. Boys laughed into pillows. I pulled the blanket and sheet up close to my chin. The dormitory had been dark except for the exit lights burning over the door. The settling sounds began to quiet and from under them, up and over, rose the whooshing sound a black voile cassock makes around walking ankles. Father Gunn, the disciplinarian, a Marine Corps chaplain during the War, was pacing the long center aisle. He paused under the bright pool of exit light, his solider's face prologue to his speech.

Early that first day my family had met him, Father Gunn, who introduced himself as the priest who always introduced himself, told us all manner of things—of how he was hard to trip up on names because if he forgot a boy's name, he always asked, "What's your name?"

When the boy said, like my name, "Ryan O'Hara," he'd say, "Oh, I knew your *last* name. It's your *first* name that slipped my mind, Ryan, old boy."

"Old boy," he called me that on our first meeting and I was thinking how easy the welcome, because I had feared he'd call me what I was, a new boy.

"Old boy," he said, "you'll be surprised how quick a good boy can become a priest." He smiled. He cracked and wrinkled up his great athletic face and smiled a slow handsome smile, displaying all his teeth, perfect and white. "We'll whip you into good shape here," he said.

Late in the dark, that first night, my parents gone, alone with all the other new boys, I lay on the hard cotton mattress in my brown metal bed, watching Father Gunn establish his command presence among us, him patrolling like a sentinel in the dim dormitory light, his rosary swinging from his right hand.

"All right, you men, listen good to what I have to say." He paused.

Around me some freshmen sat up in bed or rose to a halfway rest on their elbows. I lay quiet and listened. Four beds away I could see Hank, huge as the grade-school football player he'd been, outlined in the darkness against the dormitory windows. I wondered where in the building his brother was sleeping with the seniors.

The end of the first day of my new life had left me very tired. Strange sights and sounds and smells had greeted me all day long. In the cool, unwrinkled sheets that smelled of disinfectant, with my new black khakis hung over the head of my bed, I felt that on this day the end had ended and the beginning had finally begun.

Father Gunn called us men and I lay back to listen to him, waiting for him to tell me what to do to be a priest on my first night in the seminary.

"A lot of you are away from home for the first time and you're going to feel lonesome and maybe want to cry when you think about your families and friends and the good times. Many a night for the first nights it's nothing to have homesickness. But if you're men, you outlive it.

"When I was a chaplain in the Second World War, a lot of the young Marines, they were out for the first time. Up at the front and plenty scared.

They came up to me and couldn't say anything. Maybe looked at me kind of funny and started to cry.

"Men, everybody gets lonesome for the good things. Anybody here thinks he's not going to miss his ma's cooking, and his own room, and all his friends is wrong. If not tonight, you wait a few days. I guarantee it. Because you miss your folks is no sign you haven't got a vocation. It's only God testing your vocation to see how much of a man you are and if you can take it. One way or another you've got to pay for your vocation.

"Go ahead and cry. Get it over with and make a prayer out of it. Don't any of you think of leaving because you're homesick. You come down and talk to me and we'll straighten it all out. I make appointments with anybody. There isn't anyone going to go home the first two weeks because he's a weak sister. Nossir. You've got to take it.

"Hear me good one more time. I don't say these things for money or to fill up the time while I wait for some civilian boat. You've got to be men, manly men, especially nights here in the dormitory. There's rules of the Grand Silence to keep for the Christ you're to receive in Holy Communion the next morning. Don't be afraid to say extra prayers at night.

"Many's the night I've walked through the seniors' dormitory and seen hands, precisely where hands should be, out on top of the blankets, the rosary wrapped tight around the fingers, and the man there asleep on his rack.

"A priest should have a tender love for God's mother because she is the mother of priests and therefore your mother because you are future priests."

I thought of Annie Laurie halfway home in a motel, with Dad and Thommy, and lost all track of what Father Gunn was saying. I thought of our car and our house on a street of Chinese elms and my old school, and Sister Mary Agnes, and my dog, Brownie, who was almost ten years old, because my dad had given her to me before I went to kindergarten.

I knew my family was gone. Tomorrow they'd be even farther from me than tonight. Homesickness sat on my chest like some panicky choking thing and pressed a single syllable, *uh*, from up behind my mouth, and my eyes crinkled. I wanted to cry but would not.

The whooshing of Father Gunn's cassock stopped. He blessed us with his night blessing and was gone. Inside our dim, vaulted dormitory high up on the fourth floor, I was left to hear in the Grand Silence the world's music from way across the grounds, a miracle from the roadhouse a mile away. From across the highway, up and over Misericordia's stone fence, came sounds of golfers' laughter from the night-lighted driving range. The hollow hit of driver and ball pucked solid through the warm September night, and echoed through our settling dorm where summer was for us officially over.

Everything was gone from me. Alone. For God's sake, I prayed, for His sake.

Then came the long march of mornings at Mass. The autumn grew colder, and the Ohio dawn came later. When the Grand Silence of the night ended after breakfast, the dorm, where we returned to make our beds before classes, erupted with the suppressed wildness of our small lives. For days the only adults we saw were professors in the classroom. Few of the priests associated with us. The younger priests were not allowed to mingle with us. The older priests did not want to. Our parents knew nothing, trusted everything, and relied on the will of God.

Hank stood at the foot of Dick Dempsey's rumpled bed. He was looking for trouble. "Dempsey better get that mattress out of here. He wet the bed again. It's enough to gag a maggot. He's too lazy to get up and go to the jakes. Every night he lays there and pees all over himself."

A curious crowd of hungry, excited vultures of prey began to gather. They were the terrible birds of my childhood circling over my crib.

"Hank, we should do something," Porky Puhl said. "Can't we tell the dorm prefects or Father Gunn?"

"Porky, Porky, you are too stupid to keep breathing." On cue everyone laughed at Porky. "God knows who can stand breathing here." Everyone always laughed at Hank's menacing jokes. "Gunn already tried to burn three of Dickie Dempsey's mattresses. They were too wet. They went up in steam." *Ka-boom.*

"We gotta do something," Porky Puhl insisted.

"What do you suggest?" Hank asked. "We should tie Dickie's dickie in a knot maybe?"

I pounded my pillow, pulled up the spread, tucked it, and walked past the group.

"Hey, Ryan, Ry-Anus."

"What?" I said very flatly. Hank had a mouth on him.

"I'm declining your name in Latin," he said. "*Ryanus, Ryani, Ryano, Ryanum, Ryanibus.*"

I hated his vicious sense of humor. I was beginning, more than ever, to hate Hank. His wildness was spreading, attracting, and creating boys in his image. Every day the ninety boys in our class clicked a bit this way and a bit that, forging new alliances. Our freshman class was working out a group identity, pushing boys up and down the pecking order.

"Hey, Ryanus, fella. Ryanus." Hank put his arm around my shoulder. "Dickie Dempsey's your friend, right? What do you suggest we do to make him stop peeing in his bed?"

"Let him alone."

"But, Ryanus, he stinks up the whole dorm. Maybe you don't mind the smell."

"I smell it."

"But you don't mind it."

"I mind it. So what? He and Father Gunn come up here every morning at recess to change the sheets. He can't help himself. He's embarrassed. He's nervous...from the service."

"Nobody's that nervous,'" Hank said. "He goes all day without ever standing at the jakes."

"Maybe he squats," Porky Puhl said.

"Maybe he drinks it," Hank went on.

"Maybe he's modest," I said.

"Hank!" Porky sounded the attack. "Look who's coming in the door. The Great Pisser himself."

"Shut up, you guys," I said.

"Shut up yourself." Hank moved towards Dempsey.

Everyone stood, perched in shifting pecking order, waiting to go with the winner. Three mornings before, Hank and his clique had wrestled Dempsey to the floor, ripped open his shirt, held him down spread-eagle, and given him a "pink belly," twenty hands slapping his belly fast and hard.

Misericordia was a school where the wrestling never stopped.

Our bodies cast us all in inescapable roles. Dick Dempsey was a walking target, tall and thin. My grandfather O'Hara said "Dempsey" was a name as Dublin as could be. A shock of red Irish hair fell over his milk-white forehead. His nose was arched and his face was much too bony. His neck was long and when he swallowed, the big lump in his throat went crazy. He was a good kid.

"Hey, Dickie Lickie, Dummy Dempsey," Hank said.

The group shifted expectantly.

"You peed your bed again last night, didn't ya, ya old wetback."

Dick ignored them all, reached for his pillow, placed it at the dry end of the bed.

"You tried to cover up the pee spot with the blanket, but we could smell it. All over the place. Like some stupid puppy."

Dempsey pulled the faded blue spread over the bed. He ignored Hank completely. Standing in the group, I could feel their frenzy rise, electric.

"Like some stupid puppy that pees on the rug. Listen, you stupid shit. Quit making that bed and listen. What are you going to do about it?"

Dempsey, tight lipped, clapped his slippers together, twice, and placed them deliberately at the foot of his bed.

"Dick, come on. Let's go," I said. "We've got class."

"Shut up, you priss. Ryanus, you big *priss*." Hank turned to Dempsey. "Listen, you puppy. You know what we do to stupid-shit puppies that piss on the rug at home?" He reached for the covers and in one thrust stripped the bed right down to the acrid yellow damp. "We rub their noses in it."

He jumped on Dempsey, grabbed him in a full-nelson wrestling hold, bent him over the bed, the palms of his hands finger-locked flat behind Dempsey's red head, pushing his rosy face ha ha ha down, inching his mouth closer and closer to the cold sodden sheet.

"Cut it out," I said. "Stop it." I gave Hank, who was as big as a twenty-year-old, a push that hardly moved him.

The mob, uneasy, broke up into sheep.

"Hey, come on," someone said. "A joke's a joke."

I pushed Hank again, hard as I could, with the first bell ringing for class, as he shoved Dempsey's face into his own cold urine. Hank released him, threw him face down across the bed, and turned on me.

"Just you wait, Ryanus. Nobody pushes Heinrich Henry Hank Rimski. Just you wait."

He was Danny Boyle all over again. Boys like Danny were everywhere.

October 31, 1953
Halloween

The clocks at Misericordia ran on their own sweet time. At the end of every finite minute they hummed and the big hands all jumped together in one big nervous *tick* to the next tiny black etching. Time defines a boy's life. The watched clocks moved so slow, we Misericordia boys existed outside of time, bound on the east by the busy highway and on the west by the slow-rolling river, forbidden to leave the property. We could be an hour or two hours behind the people walking down the streets of Columbus, Ohio, and into the Colonial Drugstore.

Those ordinary laypeople in town had always to know in the back of their minds that five hundred boys lived outside the town like little ghosts, white as sheets, living lives of starched linen conscience under the bell tower that chimed every fifteen minutes. They could drive past the Gothic red-brick buildings of Misericordia, imagining the fearful quiet and the holiness of boys forbidden to have radio or newspapers or magazines.

We did not know what happened in their town or what they heard of the world on their radios driving past. In their profane time they must hardly have thought of us boys and men, isolated and rural and alien, living outside time where the jumping hands on our clocks taught us every minute how long eternity actually was.

To be out of the world's time, I searched myself for the word that would lock me into the eternal, away from the awful possibilities of changing time where any moment could bring temptation, or an occasion of sin, that could undo a whole lifetime of doing good. This was how I would save Danny Boyle and Barbara Martin and myself. At moments, in the classroom or in the chapel, I would believe that the *tick-tock click-clock* of time was beginning to turn into eternity. But the other seminarians didn't. They refused to leave time behind. They indulged in finite measurements of time and brains and sports and looks and piety. I had thought to enter a community that understood what I understood. But these boys studying to be priests proved as foreign to me as everyone else I'd ever met. The twenty-four-year-old priests in the Ordination class of 1953 were so old-fashioned they'd been born in 1928.

Misericordia was no quiet pocket out of eternity. It was about the same as any other adolescent boarding school that drilled boys through foreign language and literature classes in novels—German ones, *Die Verwirrungen des Zöglings Törless, Young Törless,* and Irish ones, *A Portrait of the Artist as a Young Man,* and Southern ones, like *End as a Man,* about military academies with secret initiations and uniforms and cliques run by blond bullies with flattops where Hank could have played kingpin.

The inspirational pictures of seminaries sketched on the back pages of the *Sign Magazine,* and all those other Catholic magazines with athletic, smart-looking seminarians recruiting vocations, stretched the distance from appearance to reality the way faces in *Life* and *Look* and *Sports Illustrated* photo ads promised a boy could become an ideal boy by using the product. Priests needed squared- off wrists like the full-page Speidel Wristwatch ads, and teeth like the Colgate Tooth Powder ads, and chins like the Lucky Strike ads. I had felt, like the young men in the Misericordia Seminary recruiting advertisements, each and everyone handsome and athletic as a blond German Jesus, an apostolate to the whole world. By entering the seminary, the priesthood, I could become perfect like my Uncle Les.

Finally, I knew I must somehow bring the word to even these chosen ones, these profane seminarians, as John the Baptist had brought the word to the Chosen People of Christ who was Himself the Word. If I could hold my breath for twelve years, I could be ordained a priest.

November 19, 1953

Porky Puhl swiped down the chalk rail one last time and gave the wet rag a two-handed jump shot into the wastepaper basket. He looked content with himself, even from the distance of my fifth-row desk. We were alone in the classroom, recess time, except for Lock Roehm studying Latin second conjugation *moneo, I admonish,* in the back corner.

"Lock, lock, who's got the lock, Lock?" Porky said.

Lock and I ignored him. We were studying conjugations of verbs for Father Polistina's daily Latin quiz next period.

Porky turned to his newly cleaned blackboard and began drawing an arty frame, something that was occasionally acceptable, to surround the Latin teacher's chalk talk. On the far left panel he sketched a turkey, this Wednesday class before Thanksgiving, and in a cartoon balloon coming out of the turkey's mouth, he printed: "For Daily Latin Saying–Write Right Here!" In the upper corner on the far right panel, where the day before he had written "24," he wrote in huge blocks, "23."

Porky stood back. His fat face grinned like a full moon in a German almanac. He lobbed the chalk accurately onto the rail and said, "That's the time."

"What?" Lock Roehm asked, not looking up, his finger tracing the page of *Englman's Latin Grammar.*

"That's the countdown. Only twenty-three days left till we go home for Christmas."

"Amazing," Lock said. He looked up. "You can count backwards."

"That excites you, eh, Lochinvar?" Porky clapped his hands together.

"Yes." Lock pulled off his glasses. "As a matter of fact, it does excite me."

Back in September, our first day, Hank had swiped at Lock. "Lochinvar's not a saint's name. You have to be baptized with a saint's name. You can't make up names. What kind of name is Lochinvar anyway?"

Lock had said, "It's a hero's name." I had liked him standing up immediately to Hank's bullying. "My middle name is Thomas for Saint Thomas Aquinas, the most brilliant theologian the Church has ever seen."

"Are you taking the train?" Porky asked.

"Plane." Lock said it flat. "After all, it is 1953."

"Bet you won't get reservations what with Ohio State going to play Southern Cal." Porky challenged everything.

"They're already confirmed by mail," Lock said.

"You planned way ahead. Big, big man."

"I always know how I'm going where I'm going."

"Doesn't everybody." Porky pushed the prof's chair in under the desk. "The train's good enough for me." Then silently, dramatizing his nonchalance, he walked down the aisle toward Lock's rear seat.

"You know," Porky said, "there's only seventy-four boys in our class now. Counting the three that left the first week, the one that didn't show at all the first day, and the six dummies who got shipped first quarter for grades—that's ten already left from our class. Seventy-four out of eighty-four. After only one quarter. I figure after the first quarter of our junior year, we'll be in the hole."

"Gee." Lock crossed his perfect blue eyes. "Only forty-seven more quarters till our Ordination."

I looked at him. I had never thought of counting the time that way. I'd never thought about dividing it up in sections or anything. It was always: "Well, Ry, you're going away to study for the priesthood. How long will it take?" I always said, "Twelve years after grade school, sir." But in my mind it was all one vast blank time when I would study Latin and pray fervently and be sportsmanlike on the ball field. Lock Roehm had said forty-seven quarters and suddenly the twelve years unraveled into terrible, tangled possibilities.

He could do that, unravel things, Lock could. Even in class he always stood head and shoulders above the rest. He had the best answers and wrote the best papers and all the priests showed him a kind of open, grown-up respect.

Misericordia was a very German school and Lock Roehm looked very German. He had blond hair and white sharp teeth and fair white skin with a lot of moles and the kind of mythologically perfect Greek body Germans idealized. He was incisive the way he looked and the way he acted. He had "Cardinal Roehm" written all over him, even standing in class, called out by Father Polistina to recite Sir Walter Scott: "Young Lochinvar is come out of the West. So faithful in love, and so dauntless in war, there never was knight like the young Lochinvar."

No one laughed.

Incisive. Lock had told me he had read nearly the whole dictionary in English, Latin, and German, and learned a word a day. Somehow I thought Ryan Steven O'Hara is not blond and fair and German like

Lochinvar Thomas Roehm, but I can learn a word a day and I started reading the dictionary. If the Holy Rule of Misericordia had not forbidden special friendships, I would have picked Lock Roehm as my best friend.

"The first thing I'm going to do on vacation," I broke in, "is drink about six Cokes and see any double feature at the Palace Theater."

"Crap," Porky said. "I'm gonna see me some basketball. The Celtics maybe. My buddy wrote he can get us some tickets. I'll see my cousin play for Monessen High at least twice."

"Does your cousin dribble better than you?" I asked.

"How would you know anyway?" Porky said.

"I'd know," I answered. I walked up to the blackboard and added an extra fold to his turkey's craw.

He came running to the front of the classroom. "Hands off!"

"I'd know," I repeated. "On a basketball floor I can look down on the top of your head and see the dandruff flaking off."

"Fuck you," he said. "Fuck you."

His forbidden language spun me around into a kind of fit. I dropped the chalk and lurched toward the window. "Stop it," I yelled, my arms going rigid.

"Fuck you, Ryanus."

I clung to the window, my forehead against the freezing glass. "Stop it, Charles Puhl. Stop it!"

He picked up the fallen piece of chalk and struck the four letters across the clear blackboard. "F-u-c-k, Ryanus, f-u-c-k," he spelled.

"Stop it. You're dirty. Dirty!"

"Get thee to a nunnery, Virgin Mary." He turned and stalked from the classroom.

Lock Roehm came toward me.

"Erase it," I begged. "Please, erase it before I have to turn around."

"Look at it," Lock said.

"No. It's a sin. A mortal sin."

"Look at it," Lock repeated.

"No. I can't. In conscience, I can't. Please erase it."

"Do you know what it means, Ry?"

"No. I don't want to. It's bad—that's enough to know."

Lock made a clucking sound. "You are very much a simp, Ry. You're always talking about words and how important they are to you. Yet you stand nearly falling out of the window because of a word."

"Words are powerful. I've told you I think there's a word somewhere that can save us all. Jesus was the Word made flesh. To find His secret we have to find the new word for our time."

"Ry, get real. This is a word on the blackboard."

"I've never said it."

"It's four letters."

"I don't need to spell it. I'm not going to write it."

"Crimanetly, Ry, turn around."

I turned halfway, facing him and all his blond Germanic confidence. "I can see you, but I won't turn any further till you erase the board."

"Ry, crimanetly. Understand things, will you? The four letters in that word are based on old English law. So many people were charged with this particular crime that the bored police scribe abbreviated it: F period, U period..."

"I know how it's spelled!" I said.

"The four letters simply abbreviate 'For Unlawful Carnal Knowledge.'"

"Don't tell me what that means."

"Read the Bible, for cripesakes."

"Yes. Yes, Your Grammarship."

"Act your age," Lock said.

"You're disgusted. With me you're disgusted," I said amazed. "You're disgusted with me and not with Porky Puhl."

Lock picked up the wet cloth and began wiping off the four wide scrawls of chalk. "I'm not disgusted," he said.

"You are. You are too," I said. "You're so smug. You think you're so mature and you understand things just because your father died and you can be the head of your family."

Lock was totally silent. He finished his last swipe and his silence was awful. Finally he turned to me and said simply, "Ry?"

"What?"

"*Fuck* is a word." He threw the wet cloth back into the wastepaper basket. "*Fuck* is the word for you. Fuck you!" He went out to the drinking fountain in the hall.

I looked up at the crucifix hanging over the blackboard, begging Jesus would not convict me of taking part in Charles Puhl's impurity. Then I left the classroom, walked past Lock Roehm, who until that moment had been one of my crowd, and went into the washroom to scrub my face and eyes with freezing water.

December 3, 1953

The first week in December I spent reading an underground copy of

Oliver Twist. The priests warned not to read anything except assigned books; but forced day and evening into six hours of study hall, even after a day of classes in Greek, geometry, civics, and ancient history, I couldn't find enough to do. Every day a Latin assignment. *Gallia est divisa in tres partes.* Translation line by line was as tiresome as decoding. And always some English. That was best. And algebra which was terrible and religion lessons that Rector Ralph Thompson Karg came to teach us, regular as orthodoxy, three times a week. He warned us that every minute of wasted study time was stolen from God and endangered our vocation.

The Father-Treasurer, Gilbert Durst, often climbed up the five steps to the reader's lectern in the refectory to berate us about how expensive was our food and study. He told us that we were wasting the money of poor people who sent in dimes and quarters to support the seminary up on the hill to help boys become priests because God called them. Gibby Durst carried inside his cassock a worn envelope which he produced periodically and read aloud at our silent meals while the food grew cold. It was from an old and blind German lady in Mankato, Minnesota, who sent fifty cents *"für die armen Studenten, for the poor students,"* he said. "You boys have," he emphasized, "more than she."

Lock Roehm always said the Father-Treasurer was no better than a butcher doing a thumb job on a scale. All five hundred boys were on full scholarships for tuition, room, and board. A boy had to keep very good grades, play sports, and work on the cleaning crews to keep from being shipped out by the Father-Treasurer, or the Father Disciplinarian, or the Rector himself, all of whom ultimately had more power than the Pope over a boy's vocation. If God called a boy, how could humans, even if they were priests, tell a boy he had no vocation, unless the priests spoke directly for God.

Even though reading *Oliver Twist* didn't seem like stealing, especially from the blind German lady, I wrapped the jacket in plain brown paper, elaborately penned *Misericordia* across it, and read it, pretending I was studying an old Latin book for translation, not bothering anybody.

In three days of pretended work during half my study periods, dodging glances of the watchful priests, I had gotten to the part where Fagin sends Nancy to look for Oliver. That was when Father Gunn came into the hall for one of his Son-of-a-Gunn pep talks. When I think of the good times, he was interesting, at least better than the study halls, but not so good as Dickens. I closed the volume of forbidden fiction and hid it in plain sight on the edge of my desk. A kind of cheap thrill rushed through me.

"Men," Father Gunn said, slightly out of breath. His cheeks were fiery, his black hair damp from the shower. I had spied him earlier out the study-hall window running his daily twenty laps around the frozen cinder track.

"I promised to talk to you about studying soon after first-quarter exams in October. Time's been slipping by like time always does. While I don't want to keep you long from your studies, I do want you to be good priests. So understand it's God's will that now, today and every day, you study your lessons seriously. Maybe some poor soul will be saved from the fires of hell because you studied your Latin well. Studying is now your vocation in life.

"The seminary's not supposed to be a bed of roses. Vocations are hard to come by and have to be paid for. Either in the seminary or after Ordination. I swear to you, it's far better to pay for your vocation before Ordination. Not after. God help you. Your endurance in study and prayer is one way to pay off the debt we owe God and His Blessed Virgin Mother for giving us the highest vocation in the world."

He marched, talking, up and down the main aisle of the study hall, between the rows of varnished desks and craning freshmen. He punctuated his words with his powerful hands, the same hands that called God down to earth every morning, the very hands that he'd told us had given the sacraments to dying soldiers.

I thought of my priest-uncle, his chaplain hands, and his mother, my grandmother, Mary Pearl O'Hara, who had on the lilac wall of her room a framed poem about the wonderful hands of a priest. She herself wrote out a copy of it especially for me. "You have beautiful hands," she said. "You have beautiful fingers. I have arthritis." She held her sweet fingers up for me to see. I kept her poem, so hopeful, so sentimental, in my shoe box.

"The Beautiful Hands of a Priest"

We need them in life's early morning.
We need them again at its close.
We feel their warm clasp of true friendship.
We seek them when tasting life's woes.
At the altar each day we behold them,
and the hands of a king on his throne
are not equal to them in their greatness.
Their dignity stands all alone.
And when we are tempted and wander
to pathways of shame and of sin,
it's the hands of a priest will absolve us

–not once, but again and again.
And when we are taking life's partner,
other hands may prepare us a feast,
but the hands that will bless and unite us
are the beautiful hands of a priest.
God bless them and keep them all holy
for the Host which their fingers caress.
When can a poor sinner do better
than to ask Him to guide thee and bless?
When the hour of death comes upon us,
may our courage and strength be increased
by seeing raised over us in blessing
the beautiful hands of a priest!

My father had said, "Ryan, never touch my tools. Be careful of your hands. You can't work on the car with me. You can't lose your hands and lose your vocation." My father looked forward to my Ordination Day. My Uncle Les and Father Gerber both had instructed him that Canon Law decreed that a boy with damaged hands could never have those hands anointed for the priesthood. I couldn't touch pliers or saws or car parts.

The very first days at Misericordia I had wanted to obey everything the priests told me, so I could learn the priestly mystery and feel the chill go down my back every morning when as a priest I would say the words of consecration, "*Hoc est Corpus Meum, This is My Body*," and hold Jesus in my hands.

"The sophomores," Father Gunn said, motioning to the sixty-three second-year boys drawn up in shorter aisles at the rear of our large study hall, "have stepped one year closer to the priesthood by one-hundred-percent keeping their part of their deal with God."

He wanted all of us to be fine-looking, broad-shouldered young priests marching out to all the people in the world who were sinning and dying and who would fall like starlings to the oil fires of hell if we didn't learn to save them.

Danny Boyle and the German lady who was blind, and Porky and Hank and even Father Gunn needed my dedication to duty. My obedience could eventually cure all kinds of blindness. It could lead me to the words and introduce me into the mystery. I renewed my summer determination and let poor lost Oliver Twist go his hapless way. "*Ich habe Dienst*," Father Gunn kept repeating. "*I have a duty.*" Despite everything, worldly temptations and desires especially, to God, "*Wir haben Dienst, We have a duty.*"

I was an Irish-Catholic boy in a German-Catholic school where German was taught one hour a day four days a week for six years to instill the discipline that comes with language.

December 5, 1953

Two nights later, on the eve of the Feast of Saint Nicholas, our sober *Dienst, duty,* of the study hall was suddenly interrupted by an old German custom. The older boys had kept this one secret well. All its pleasurable violence depended on surprise.

Exactly fifteen minutes into the evening study period, when the ink bottles and blue-lined paper and Ticonderoga pencils were finally settling into concentration, Saint Nicholas himself, in full ancient bishop's robes and mitre stepped, an old fantastic, very quietly into the front of the study hall.

Only those very close to that door noticed his silent entrance. His beard, white and long, covered his golden chasuble. In his left hand he carried a wooden shepherd's crook painted gold. I thought he might be a vision.

Like a rock dropped into Misericordia's pond, little Lake Gunn, the old man's entrance sent concentric ripples out from the doorway as more and more new boys looked up to see him standing before us, a silent apparition. Slackjawed, no one said a word. We all saw the same apparition.

Saint Nicholas stood, stock-still, serious, silent, watching us. Suddenly all the lights went out and from behind us a wild scream ran toward us through the darkness. Every freshman whirled in his seat, sat frozen in his desk. The lights came on. We fell back.

A short creature, filthy in dark rags and black-caped hood, raced screeching up and down our aisles beating at us, hitting mostly the desk tops, whipping at us with his leather flail. He stopped, threatening individual boys around the room. Two rows away he smelled of onions and garlic and things he caught at night like the dead rats hanging on his belt.

He wore a shoulder harness of sleigh bells that never stopped jangling. He was a conjure man, running like some campfire horror from a Boy Scout story through our startled study hall. His cape, billowing black, caught books from desk tops, dragging them to the floor. *Oliver Twist* crashed down, flopped open to the title page.

He ran in dark circles around the white-robed Saint Nicholas. He shrieked that his name was "Ruprecht!" His menace swooped through the study hall. He pulled out a long list, with names, he cackled, and the names were connected to all the things we freshmen had done wrong, misdeeds, real and false, that he was going to call us out for, to make us eat rats, for all the boys to see.

Suddenly a scream louder than this demon's own brought him to a standstill.

Curdled, but beginning to suspect a joke, we new boys turned.

Russell Rainforth, the most worshipful of all the upperclassmen, the president of the sophomore class, had stopped the accusing specter dead in his tracks. Russell half-stood in his desk, his lips pulled back baring his white teeth.

The older boys stared bewildered at Russell's upstaging.

He screamed again, paused almost as if testing, then repeated the scream. *Crazy.* The blood drained from his face. All his books fell to the floor. His eyes went wide and wild and he charged up the aisle toward the creature humped up in black.

Russell lurched and howled, his the only movement in the frozen room of more than a hundred boys.

He had gone ten steps before Father Gunn burst in and hit him square on the jaw.

He careened and fell to the floor and lay whimpering and twitching with the blood running out of his ear and his mouth and all over his shirt.

The priests tied him quickly to a chair with their belts and carried him out half-conscious to the infirmary, and later, that very night, from there to a hospital and we were never to see him again.

In that first moment, in the tense vacuum their sweeping him out had left, I felt the dead silent air that a tornado sucks out of a room.

The priests had everything under complete control.

Boys' whispers began, fell, murmured.

Father Gunn, returning instantly back into the middle of the wrecked study hall, amid books strewn all over, said, "Pray for Russell Rainforth."

I did on the spot. For him and for myself that God would not let my vocation be taken away by such a powerful sign.

"Carry on," Father Gunn said. "Proceed and carry on."

The creature in black, Ruprecht, Saint Nicholas' assistant, moved slowly toward his dramatics-room bishop. He tried to recover his spell, but the fun was gone. His warts and Max Factor scar no longer looked real. Ruprecht was only Hank's brother Peter with ropes of plastic spit hanging from between his blackened teeth.

As Ruprecht-Peter, recovering his role, read from the Bishop's big book the names of various new boys and their humorous offenses, some laughter returned. The second-year boys tried to cover crazy Russell's disgrace by laughing too loud.

When finally Ruprecht-Peter hunted out Dick Dempsey and whipped him into the center of the room, the laughter slathered with anticipation. When old Ruprecht-Peter handed Dempsey an empty milk bottle, a roar went up that turned the Saint Nicholas charade back into comedy as freshman after freshman was humorously shamed.

I was disappointed Ruprecht didn't pick on me. I had done nothing awkward or disobedient enough to be included, but I felt the scorn quietly implicit in being ignored. Peter Rimski hadn't even bothered to make up something silly against me. I wasn't part of a clique.

Afterwards, the priests handed out hard candy and allowed us to go to the recreation room for ping-pong and shuffleboard and singing carols around the piano.

"You know why Russell cracked up, don't you?" Hank was in the center of his group of six boys surrounded by eight more boys who wanted to be in the first six. They stood around him like spokes around a hub. His shoulders were thick and he was almost overweight. His voice was deeper than most of the new boys and at the neck of his shirt tufts of hair curled out. He spoke with authority, like an actor playing a seminarian impersonating a priest trying to be a bishop.

"My brother Peter found out what's going on. Russell will be put in an insane asylum, because he made up his mind when he came back to Misery this year he was going to ace his studies. When he got elected class president, he knew he had to set a good example, so he stopped everything. Quit playing football and basketball and studied all the time. So he snapped. Like that."

He clicked his fingers and shook his head, staring down the group around him. "Peter and I knew things like this happened here because our father went here and this is a real tough seminary. You gotta know what you're doing. Or else they put you away in an insane asylum."

I heard enough. I walked away. I'd seen crack-ups in the movies. I prayed no crack-up would happen to me, that I wouldn't be carried out of a study hall full of laughing boys, as mocking as Roman soldiers making fun of Christ, with my arms twisted behind my back, my hands tied together, and blood running out of my nose and mouth. I ate candy, considering why Jesus made a distinction between the sparrows He kept His eye on and the seminarians He didn't. I was sure God understood when I went to my desk the next day and picked up *Oliver Twist* where I had left off.

Father Gunn warned us very strictly, almost with the Seal of the Confessional, not to mention Russell's accident when we went home for Christmas. "Rector Karg," he said, "feels your parents might not understand. If Catholics get the wrong impression about seminaries, non-Catholics will never be converted, especially if they see anything but a clean bill of health on our altars. Priests and seminarians are to be like Caesar's wife: above reproach. Actually," he added, "you boys have an obligation in charity not to tell a soul. Not even to ever mention Russell among yourselves again."

On December 19, I took a Greyhound bus across the frozen Midwest flatlands to the snowy river valley of Peoria. I felt very responsible, trusted with our seminary secret, not mentioning Russell Rainforth. I had never before kept a secret from my parents. I felt old. Older than when I had gone away in September. Summer was gone. I had been away at school. That meant something very special that first Christmas, serving midnight Mass, combed hair, perfect teeth, in our parish church decorated with pines and ribbons and candles. The choir soared into *"Gloria in Excelsis Deo, Glory to God on High."*

Leaving my soul, I levitated above the congregation. I was more than an altar boy in black cassock and starched white surplice serving Father Gerber in his white vestments. I was a seminarian swinging the gold censorium of burning incense out three times on its golden chains right into the faces of the congregation.

The church was packed with two thousand people standing behind Barbara Martin standing in the front row closely next to Danny Boyle crossing his eyes at me, cocking his head, and sticking out his tongue.

Returning to Misericordia in January, I could remember nothing significant about that vacation except that the ceiling in our house seemed lower. My family, the Higgins, my dog, Brownie. Nothing had changed with anybody.

But everything was changing with me.

Spring 1954

In February, the "Apostleship of Prayer" leaflet for seminarians featured Saint Valentine, the priest, as Patron of the Month, with the special mission intention of "Social Justice in Africa." I was reading the dictionary and happened on *puberty*. I had read a lot and knew whatever *puberty* was, at fourteen, *pubertas* was supposed to be happening to me, *the puer, the boy*. My father had tried to warn me something would happen. The priests had warned me.

"What happens to a boy when he's fourteen," Gunn had said, "marks you for life."

He scared me, but it sounded wonderful, like a secret club of brotherhood. I knew from my grandfather's *National Geographic* that some tribes initiated their boys and I wondered if that's what it was. Some secret ritual nobody ever talked about where they came in and surprised you and took you out somewhere and maybe painted you all green and purple and showed you a quick glimpse of a naked woman and then said you're a man now.

I really doubted that, because somebody would have leaked something that stunning out. Besides it would be impure to look at a naked woman and even if that was the initiation of the human race, they couldn't allow it to go on in seminaries. I hoped whatever it was wouldn't hurt, and that Hank wouldn't be involved, but I was very worried about the naked pictures, because I had never seen one, and I worried what my real reaction might be compared to how I was supposed to react.

Right below *puberty* I saw *pubes* which I knew was Latin and I was glad because I could chance the impurity to increase the vocabulary. There was an *L.* that was followed by *pubic hair, groin*, and *adult*. I turned more pages and found *genital* and *genitalia* next to *genitive case. Sex* in Latin meant *six.* So I looked up *sex* and *sexpartite* and *sextillion* and *sexton*, which has to do with the Church, and *sexual* and *sexy.*

Noah Webster stated humanity's case so politely I bit off my frustration. He said everything without revealing anything. Males fertilize the ovum. Females have a pistil and no stamens. I remembered a girl with a big band singing "Pistol Packin' Mama" during the War and thought the pun was great, though I couldn't tell anybody, because I wasn't so sure what the pun was. In March, Father Polistina started Latin verbs, copulative verbs, and half the boys laughed as hard as we all had when he had introduced the Latin verb *scio, I know, scis, you know, scit, he knows.* Ha. "Keep saying it," Polly Polistina said, ha ha, and we kept repeating the Church's soft liturgical pronunciation, "*Shee-o, shis, shit.*" Ha ha ha.

My grades were good when spring broke and I was reading *My Friend Flicka* and *Thunderhead* and *Green Grass of Wyoming*, all under brown paper. I imagined myself at night far away from the corral of a hundred beds in the dormitory, out in the cool green West, with a white horse and a life free as an eagle's soaring over the peaks. Flicka had a baby horse, a colt, a stallion that grew up to pursue wild mares across the plains. He'd search them out, fight for them, nuzzle them to marry them.

At the first evening of May devotions to the Virgin Mary, I asked her if nuzzling was for people too. Life's not like the movies, I said to her, and I've no one else to ask. I knew she had a baby, all alone. At least the baby had no earthly father. But I knew everyone else did. I was sure it took two, but how the two got together was beyond me.

My father had tried to tell me something, but I lied and told him I knew everything. I was always lying, white lies, to protect myself.

Absurd of me, I prayed, to get so upset about something completely irrelevant to my celibate choice in life. You can't be tempted to do something you know nothing about. Besides, I had the final exams of my first year in the seminary to occupy me. I wanted to do well with only eleven more years to learn the secrets the priests would surely begin to tell us the next year.

I had one more secret book to finish called *Tales of the South Pacific,* and on one of those first May nights, a character from the book, a girl, came and sat on the foot of my bed. Her dress was red with white flowers that matched the flower in her long black hair. Her arms moved gently, in soft undulations from some really slow hula. She beckoned me to get up and follow her, up and out the dormitory doors, to places I had never seen. I held back.

This was different from the other dream I had once a week about some boy, some boy unidentified in the dark, standing over my bed with a shoe in his hand, ready to use the heel like a nightstick.

I was happy, and the girl came closer, and her white smile and dark skin and darker hair melted me away, like snow running in the first warmth of spring, and I fainted in my sleep which struck me as probably so unusual I never told anyone.

The next morning at Mass, I knelt back unworthy, blushing, as the other seminarians filed past me to receive Holy Communion. Hank, as he stepped over me on his way to the Communion rail, snickered and winked and kicked my leg on purpose. No boy ever did not go to Holy Communion except for one reason.

I resolved, whatever the girl's reason, I could not follow her. I was a seminarian and resolved seminarians must avoid occasions of sin. I confessed to the priest an accidental sin of impurity, but explained I took no pleasure in it.

"I did not, Father, interfere with myself."

He said, "Night time is the worst time. Sin happens in time and takes us out of eternity. Go to sleep at night time."

I said my penance of three Hail Mary's and resolved myself against the girl, and vowed to stop reading worldly books.

3

January 3, 1957

The simple truth was my schooling ran like clockwork. I was seventeen, a senior in high school, four years into the seminary, and able to speak Latin and German. Year after year, I traveled from Misericordia once at Christmas and once in June for the three-month summer vacation to test my strength wrestling worldliness.

My return to my parents' home always reminded me the world was out of joint with my spiritual life, my emotional growth, and my intellectual awakening. I could translate ancient Greek and Latin and modern German, but I could not break the code of life. Unlike Telemachus, the boy in Homer's *Odyssey* who searched for his father, Ulysses, to learn how to live, I had to leave my family to learn my life.

My little brother, Thommy, was fourteen, full of war movies, eager to join the Marine Corps Reserve as soon as he turned seventeen. Thommy was distant from my parents and cold miles away from me. "You're a fake," was all he said.

I punched him on the shoulder. "How fake was that?"

I was seventeen going on eighteen going on twelve. We were Cain and Abel, like all the pairs of brothers in the movies where one wears Blue and the other wears Gray or one is a gangster and the other is a priest. We kept our distance.

"Ryan," Dad said. He opened my bedroom door, tentatively, the way he always did at the end of my vacations. Brownie looked up at him with her big spaniel eyes, sighed, and put her old head down on my slippers. Dad moved some torn Christmas wrapping paper. "Mind if I sit here for a smoke while you pack?"

I pulled a stack of new teeshirts off my desk chair. My mother had sewed my laundry number in all my clothes. My number was 66 and the first day of every school year I had to introduce myself to the boy who was the new 99, because the freshmen boys who sorted our laundry, walking around and around wooden racks hung with five hundred laundry bags, rarely bothered to look at the red period dot sewed in after 66. Once a week, I had to meet with 99 to exchange clothes. There seemed to be a curse on 99, because 99 always seemed to quit or get shipped, and my underwear would disappear with the disappeared boy, and I'd be left with his jockstrap and stray socks.

My dad sat down. "I brought an ashtray," he said.

"Would you hand me those four books?"

He handed over the Modern Library editions of Hemingway, Wolfe, Dos Passos, and Fitzgerald. "You read too much, but I bet you'll be glad to get back to the good old routine," he said. "There's a lot you can say for regular hours and plenty of sleep."

I didn't say it. I loved my father, but he had grown up on a farm before he married my mother, who insisted they live in a town. One set of my grandparents lived in an apartment. The other owned a barn.

He made business with his cigarette, casting silently about for conversation. "Really think I should go back with you. Yessir, that would be the life. Quiet. Regular. Like the farm."

This joke he always made I always played along with, because I loved him so much. What we had in common was growing less each year I was gone from the world. Sundays I wrote long letters. Wednesday mornings Annie Laurie ran down the stairs to the green mail box on the big porch, read my typed pages once, then immediately again to my father over the telephone at his work. They bragged to their friends and to my aunts and uncles that my letters were talky and full, but they could not begin to fathom what it was to be away, as they always said, studying to be a priest.

"Here's the last of your underwear and socks." Annie Laurie put them on the bed. "I soaked them in practically straight bleach to get them white. What's the matter with those nuns who do your laundry?"

"It's top secret," I said. "We don't tell anyone what goes on there."

Through the back of my mind raced the laundress-nun with her note in German that poor literal Father Gunn had read aloud in the refectory, asking if the boys would please stop blowing their noses in the sheets.

"You make it sound like there's some big mystery," she said.

I took the laundry from the bed. "Guess what?" I said. "There is. Dad's going back with me."

"Me too," she said. "All that rest you'll get."

"Aw, Mom, they'd quick put you to work with the nuns in the laundry."

"A beautiful woman like me?"

"Ever heard of Cinderella?" I said.

"Your mother as a nun? A German one at that? As if there's a shortage of Irish nuns."

Annie Laurie shook her head. "They're DP's, displaced persons." She tucked my last book into the suitcase.

"This book?" my father said. "You're going to be the priest, so you have to read everything, but won't this book get you in trouble?"

"Maybe," I laughed. "But everybody's reading Grace Metalious. She's 'in.'"

"*Peyton Place*?" my mother asked.

"It's no different than *Peoria Place*. The stuff that goes on around here!"

"Hasn't it been condemned by the Church?"

I tried to act sophisticated. "It's not exactly on Rome's *Index of Forbidden Books*."

"Priests have to read everything," my father repeated. "A priest has to do what a priest has to do."

"Some of your friends have read it." I snapped the latches on my Samsonite suitcase. If ever a movie is made about Misericordia, the lawns, the buildings, the trees, the classrooms, the gym, the chapel, the boys and young men, all should look the way *Peyton Place* looked in the movies. Perfect. Clean. Crisp. The idyllic Technicolor Hollywood set.

"Every night this week, since New Year's, we've had a houseful of company," my father said.

"Ryan, everybody wanted to see you," my mother said.

"I think everybody did." I looked at her and she was tired from knocking herself out as a hostess. "This house was a solid procession of guests from Christmas Eve to New Year's."

"The more people you see when you're home, the better," she said.

"You need anything, son?" Dad asked.

"I have enough to open a general store," I said.

In the bottom of my luggage lay all my contraband: three bags of Annie Laurie's cookies, the extra books I could not resist, six 45-rpm records, and my shoe box. I pulled the suitcase to the floor and sat on the bed. I was beginning to work at the loopholes in moral theology. I couldn't explain to them my smuggling wasn't a sin, not even of venial disobedience, because it was no serious matter. This disciplinary, institutional rule was only penal law, not moral law. Lock and I had decided that. If caught, I would have to take the punishment. Simple as that. Despite Rector Karg always saying the better thing was to do the better thing.

Besides, reading about the human experience was learning how to be a better parish priest. I could always easily skip the dirty pages, because somebody was always eager to point them out. Besides, all boys knew if you set a library book like the *Dictionary of Slang* on its spine and held the covers between both hands and let go, the book always fell open to the dirty pages. So a boy could find them or skip them. Something like the dirty magazines in our neighborhood drugstore, *Saga* and *Men's True Adventure*, which I'd never noticed, not once, not until Father Gerber warned us against them.

For a few moments we sat silent in my room, my father smoking at my desk, Annie Laurie and I on the edge of my bed. My spread was brown. I had requested the monastic reserve of that, but it was chenille by her choice. I ran my hands over its tufts, conjuring the cotton covers at Misery, all with the faded sameness repeating itself on eighty beds in row upon dormitory row. An equality was in that and an austerity over all. I ached to leave all the luxury my parents offered me. They could never understand that worldly attachments to chenille of any color might keep me from Christ in His simple seamless linen.

"Well." My mother extenuated the word with a puff of breath, as if the grand show of the holidays were finally over.

Parents, I thought, never like to let go. I must remember that when counseling.

She patted her lap and rose. "We seem to have run out of things to say."

"Mmm," I said.

"Or the right to say them," Dad said, grinding out his cigarette.

"Mmm," I said, wondering what they meant. I knew Rector Karg sometimes sent general letters to parents instructing them how to act as parents of seminarians.

They stood together near my door, waiting for me to speak or to rise, I didn't know which. They so much honored my vocation that they had surrendered themselves to let go of me even before I was fourteen, about the same age as Jesus was at twelve when He got lost at the Temple and Mary and Joseph went crazy searching for their lost Boy. On my desk, the forest-green blotter lay slightly flecked with ash. My father held his smudged ashtray in his hand. It was an awkward scene.

"What movie is this?" I tried to lighten the moment.

Annie Laurie recouped. "Ryan, would you like some banana-cream pie before we go to the train station?"

"Cut me two pieces. One for the road."

"Me too." My father seized upon the offer of pie and coffee together. He put his hand on my arm, lightly, then his full arm around my shoulders, and they walked me down the hall. "Good as school is, Ry, I bet you won't taste cooking like your mother's for the next five months."

"That's sure. Not till after graduation. Just think, mom, I won't have to eat any of your cooking. In fact, I refuse to, until I graduate from high school."

They both laughed. Absurd time jokes were part of our kidding. We saw each other on occasions that were far apart. I was seventeen and winter would turn to summer before I would see them again. My birthday was in June. I had become a stranger to them, maybe even a mystery to them that they had to take on faith.

"Brownie can't sit up and beg anymore," Dad said.

"That dog," Annie Laurie said, "can beg with her eyes."

"Those great big beautiful eyes," I said.

"She's a good old dog," Dad said.

Annie Laurie's eyes glistened. Charlie-Pop sniffed and choked. Tears ran down my face. Poor dog. Poor them. Poor me.

"I always really miss you," I said. I wanted to reassure them their loss of my adolescence, all of us bowing our will to the will of God, would gain them the honor of being the parents of a priest.

Leaving my life with them plunged me on my every return to Misery into aching homesickness. Still, we laughed over the pie and coffee. I felt sorry for them, storing me up, so obviously, for the rest of the winter and the whole of spring. My father ran his hand through my hair and down my neck to my shoulder and his touch was the sweet, strong touch of a father.

During the last four years, I had come home seven times, and still, despite the grandeur of their becoming parents of a young priest, they could hardly understand the days and nights of my new life. Their heads and their hearts had listened to sermons on detachment from worldly associations, but actually letting go of my hand after one last kiss at the train station was a great sacrifice. They believed me without reservation that I knew I had a vocation to the priesthood.

Their reward would be great as mine, each in our own way, having given up, on faith alone, father or mother or son for His sake. Oh, I wanted to reach out, to touch them, to take them away with me. Instead, I ate pie in silence. I loved them. I wanted never to leave them and their warmth, but Jesus was telling me to follow Him, and that it would not be easy. He had left His home to die on a cross. I had only to leave my home to go to a place where the priests promised to make me into an *alter Christus, another Christ*.

No one, outside the seminary and in the world, could understand such joy taken in such pain. I had to return from my visit to the world to climb the fourth of the twelve rungs toward the priesthood. With high school ending in the spring, I would be one-third of the way to Holy Orders.

Thommy came in from the garage. He wiped his hands on a red mechanic's cloth. Charlie-Pop liked Thommy using his tools I couldn't touch. "Take care of yourself," Thommy said.

"You're the one," I said.

"See you in six months," he said.

"Love you," I said.

"Love you too." He scooped up a piece of pie in his fingers and walked out.

At the snowy railroad station, from the train window, I watched my mom and dad, between the white clouds of steam, standing in the freezing wind. The heavy glass between us left nothing but the sad last wavings of good-byes. Annie Laurie moved her arm in the quick jerky fashion of women who are exhilarated by the cold.

I constrained myself, holding my palm up and out, pressing on the cold window glass, in a single immobile gesture. Was the cold suction on my palm worldly vanity, spiritual discipline, or movie-acting? Wearing my new clerical black suit, with other passengers watching, I could not afford any show of scandalous attachment unbecoming a seminarian. Priests and seminarians were supposed to set a good example when out in the world.

But deep inside me the vast homesickness welled to an ache of emptiness. I wanted my mom and my dad and my dog. Even my brother. I wanted to fill the void with something. I wanted God to fill it with Himself and His grace. Outside, Annie Laurie jumped lightly, twice, waving briskly while holding onto my father's arm, as the train finally pulled away, leaving them on the cold platform.

The priests told us no vocation was given free. Anything of value has its cost, even with God. I paid the down payment on the price, my palm slipping down the cold glass, sadly, willingly, suddenly realizing my celibate life would always be pulling out of stations, *steam, whistle, chug, movies*, where I loved too much the world where I did not belong.

January 4, 1957

In deep snow, I returned in a taxi stuffed with six other senior-high boys to the red-brick mansions of Misery.

"Yeah," the taxi driver had said, "the Divinity School." Only a Protestant would call a seminary a divinity school. "Seven of youse boys is all I can take. What's with all the fub duck suitcases?"

"Fub duck!" We all laughed. "Fub duck!" We could not stop laughing. Riding all the way back to Misery and up the formal drive where freezing freshmen with shovels were clearing the snow, we chanted, "Fub duck! Fub duck!"

The taxi drove off and we looked up at the huge front door of Misery. "Fub," a boy said dragging his suitcase up the stairs. The Christmas vacation of our senior year slammed closed. Within two hours, Dick Dempsey and I witnessed a shocking scene between three priests that happened so fast that we ran for cover without losing a single detail.

"I've never seen anybody so mad," Dick Dempsey told Mike Hager. He pointed toward the main entrance to Misericordia Seminary where Father Arnold Roth had made a scene. "Father Arnie went storming down the main hall, red in the face, blown up to twice his size, and stalked right out the front door, straight to his car, dragging two grade-school boys he had brought as visitors to see the seminary."

The halls had echoed with the young priest's shouts.

"Arnie struck a nerve," I said to Mike Hager. "He stood up to that cadre of old priests and their prehistoric rules."

"They think this world is their cloister," Dempsey joked. "They're so fub duck."

Lock ran up the stairs towards us. "I was leaving Rector Karg's office," he said. "Arnie Roth told off Father Gunn right in front of Rector Karg. Arnie said it was too damn bad if the faculty couldn't arrange for the two kids, as special guests, to eat dinner here with us in the refectory to see what seminary life is like."

Father Arnold Roth, ordained from Misery only two years before, was from Mike Hager's Wisconsin diocese. He had driven Mike in from vacation only hours before, along with two eighth-grade boys interested in the priesthood.

"Here I miss the fireworks after traveling with him all day long." Mike said. "Those two kids are okay—one's maybe too pious, you know?"

"Rector Karg and the faculty insisted Arnie eat in their refectory," I said, "but they didn't want those kids in there and Father Gunn refused to let them eat with us."

"We might clue them in too much and scare them off," Dempsey said. "So Arnie says what was he supposed to do with the kids anyway, leave them in the car with the heater running?'

Lock said he thought Arnie was even more rebellious as a priest than he had been as a seminarian. "That's one great thing about Ordination to the priesthood," Lock said, "they can't get at you the way they can when you're a lowly seminarian."

"God," Dave said, "I hope he's angry enough to tell a few alumni something's rotten here in lower Denmark."

"I bet you Rector Karg writes Arnie's bishop," I said, "and fawns all around and says, Oh, your excellency, Father Roth came and acted uncharitably."

"Karg can't," Mike said. "He's got to maintain our sanctified institution's sanctified reputation with all the bishops."

"*Yessss,*" Dempsey's voice hissed to a perfect mime of Rector Karg, his lower jaw thrust out, looking heavier than all the rest of his head. "Misericordia Seminary enjoys a prime reputation for turning out o-*bee*-dient, hard-working priests. In every diocese of the country where we have a Misericordia man stationed, the bishop is happy. Yet we must be *'umble,* for only true *'umility* can keep us that way."

We all laughed at his imitation of the ashen-faced rector, who was a simple man, pious, *Hoch Deutsch, High German,* and very nineteenth century. Two weeks of Christmas vacation out in the world had passed since we'd had a good laugh together at an inside joke. Suddenly I was missing my family. The homesickness always swirled up a tornado sucking my breath away.

My heart melted toward my classmates because we shared the same goal. God had talked to each one of us, even the ones like Hank who made you wonder what God was up to. I loved them and I loved being with them. My heart leapt up. Sometimes I could forget the priests had warned us particular friendships could be somehow sinful, our times together could be so good.

"Be *'umble,*" Dempsey mimicked and we roared again, so loud the echoes rang up and down the stairwell.

Hank and John Kowalski, outside our private joke, pushed past us. They carried a length of heavy pipe. "Out of the way, Ryanus," Hank said.

"What you gonna do with that?" I asked. "Shove it up your own wry anus so you'll have a happy new year?" Then I added, "Asshole." Some words were more uncharitable than impure.

Hank banged the pipe against the railing and turned up the next flight. "Who writes Ryanus's script?" he said to Kowalski. "Ski, baby, I remember, don't you, when sweet baby Ryanus would never have said *ass* much less *hole.*" He dry-hawked spit down on us. "Ain't none of your damn business what we're doing."

"Hey, big, strong, and stupid," I said, "You're a real two-ton Teuton. You're a real tank. You're big Hank the Tank."

"Says you," Hank shouted.

Hank and Ski disappeared around the upper landing.

"Why do you antagonize him, Ryan?" Mike said.

"Ryan gives as good as he gets," Dempsey said.

"Hank, Hank the Tank, he antagonizes me." I held my ground. "My dad says when I was three years old I stood on the sidewalk in front of our house and said to anyone walking by, 'I'm rough and I'm tough, and I'll beat you all up.'"

"Forget it." Demspey pulled me around. "Let me show you what I smuggled in from home."

Mike went on down the stairs to spread the Roth story. I followed Demspey off the stairs through the hall, a little mad he was so obviously changing the subject.

After he had stopped wetting the bed, Dick Dempsey got to be one of the most popular boys in our class, except with Hank, who kept doing things to him like putting a pair of panties he'd bought on vacation into Dick Dempsey's bed. "What's that word *dick* mean?" he'd say. "Is that a name or a description?" Despite Hank the Tank, or maybe because of him, Dempsey's stock rose.

Some boys thought Dempsey was a saint.

Little cliques opened and closed and opened again. Gossip put some people up and gossip knocked some people down. *Down* was always easier.

Every boy had a reputation created by all the other boys. A whisper could cause a scandal or an ostracism. Any weakness in any boy was picked like a scab.

All of Misery watched with only one comment: "A boy needs to have his corners knocked off."

My greatest fear, anxiety, and thrill was to try and find out what the other boys were saying about me behind my back. I didn't want my corners knocked off. Who does? I was no Dick Dempsey, because Dempsey would do anything for any boy, even for Hank, sometimes, even, especially, for Hank who ruled him. His charity was noted by some of the priests.

Once in religion class Rector Karg asked Dick, what if some boy vomited in the study hall and Father Gunn told him to clean it up. We all, except Dempsey, started to laugh. He said, "I'd try to see Christ in the sick person and pretend it was Jesus I was wiping up after."

Saint Dick.

"What'd you bring back?" I asked.

"Some records," he said as we entered the senior locker room. "They're in my trunk."

The stowed luggage lay banked on racks against the wall opposite the door. In between in green rows stood the lockers, thirteen inches wide, seven feet high, with one shelf and a tie rack inside the door, stuffed with sweaters and jackets and black khakis. We used to be glad when somebody left Misery, emptying a locker, though using more than one locker per student was strictly forbidden by the mimeographed rules.

If Father Gunn or Rector Karg had known what happened right before Christmas, they would have wished all the lockers had been filled with clothes: one free afternoon four seniors jumped the best athlete in our class, ripped off his shower robe, and shoved him naked into an empty locker. Everybody thought it a great joke except the seminarian in the locker. He wasn't released till after supper.

"Albums or singles?" I asked.

He pulled the records from his footlocker, shuffling through an *Oklahoma* soundtrack, Mantovani's *Music from the Movies*, and three Presley singles.

"Gunn will never pass the Elvis records," I said.

"I'll play those when he's sure not to barge in. He okayed Mantovani and *Oklahoma*, except for a couple of songs like 'Everything's up to Date in Kansas City,' that he made me promise to skip when I played the score in the recreation room."

The door banged open and he slipped the Presley singles into his trunk. Porky Puhl confronted us.

"*Heil, Hierarch!*" I said.

Porky didn't laugh. Before vacation, in a class meeting, we had sent money to a missionary he didn't approve. South America, not Africa, he had said, was where our first charitable allegiance should be. The Spanish Church was more deserving than the African Church. He called us immature and threatened to resign from the hierarchy of the class. We all stamped our feet and laughed for days. "Hierarchy!"

"A little contraband, I see," Porky said.

"Records." Dempsey closed his trunk. "Gunn approved them."

"So did I," Porky said.

"What? Approve them, or bring some contraband back?" I asked.

He looked hurt, as if he had been slapped trying to equalize something. He shifted his hierarchy across his fat shoulders, intending to "maintain it on our level" was how he'd say it. He never recovered from Father Gunn choosing him our class president the fourth day of our freshman year, and everyone realizing by the fourth month what a mistake that was.

"I came back with some educational reading materials." He opened his suitcase, which hadn't been unpacked. "Remember the clipping Rector Karg posted on the bulletin board last month about the Hungarian Revolt?"

"I read about it over the holidays," I said. We saw no newspapers September to June. Television sets were so new and expensive that no priests at Misery had television, and even if stores had given sets away, television was too worldly for us to watch. The radio in our recreation room could only be turned on, by a priest, with permission, for sports or opera broadcasts.

"Look at these," Porky said, producing a notebook pasted fat with clippings like nothing personal I ever had hidden in my little old shoe box of souvenirs from the world. "The Commies shoved the rebels through meat grinders and washed them out through the sewers. Look at this one, Madam Meatball. She shoved glass rods inside the men prisoners and broke the rod so they felt like they were dying when they urinated."

"That I didn't read," I said. Could printed words about bad women cause impure thoughts like dirty pictures?

"Glass rods like chemistry class?" Dempsey asked.

"That's nothing." Porky retrieved the notebook.

"The sins committed in a country's name," I said.

"You bet your sweet life," Porky agreed. "My brother was in the War and he says the Nazis nailed American soldiers to trees right through the groin."

"Stop," I said.

"Then tied wire around their waists to jeeps and drove away."

"God!" Dempsey breathed.

"Do you guys know any more about this stuff?" Porky was breathing through his mouth.

"It sounds like the sufferings of the saints in *The Roman Martyrology*," I said. Every noon, as we sat looking down at our meal, a priest read aloud how the early Christian martyrs were tortured and killed. Saint Agatha had her breasts torn off one day, and by the next lunch, forty Roman soldiers who had converted to Christianity were left exposed to die naked on a frozen lake. "All of them perished," the *Martyrology* said, "except for one soldier who renounced Christianity and then died anyway in a bath of tepid water."

Suddenly, the room shook.

I jumped, almost knocked from the trunk rack. A loud crashing came from the storage room directly above us: metal, and bits of metal, falling on the concrete floor above and rolling in every direction.

Dempsey and I ran from the locker room.

Porky sat staring at us.

We ran up the stairs. The door was locked. "What do they do in here?" I said. We pounded on the door, then listened.

"Locked *doorssss*," Dempsey said in his hissed Rector Karg imitation, "are not permitted at *Missssericordia*."

"Where's Porky?" I whispered.

"Still downstairs catching his breath," Dempsey said.

I pounded again. No answer.

Another smaller piece of metal fell, rolled, was snatched up into silence. Someone inside giggled and someone else told him to shut up. I recognized Hank and Ski. Ha! Caught! Perfect! I pounded again to make them uneasy. Someone shifted close to the door, then moved away.

Dempsey whispered, "Gunn better not find out they locked one of Rector Karg's blessed doors. You can get shipped for locked doors."

We fled on down the stairs. Porky waited for us outside the locker room.

"Ski and Hank are up in the storage room with the door locked," I said to him.

"Not smart," Porky said. "Nobody gets shipped if nobody tells."

"What's going on?" Dempsey asked him. "What are they doing?"

"Lifting, that's all," Porky said.

"Lifting what?" I wanted to know.

"Weights Hank made, Jerkwater," Porky said. "They've got these muscle-building magazines from Charles Atlas."

"Oh," I said. "What do you know!" If I ever wanted to get even with Hank for anything, I had him right where I wanted, behind what Father Gunn, USMC, disliked most, a locked door. "So what do you know," I said. "Hank the Tank has fub duck."

February 1957

Saturday our classes ran until lunch, and our afternoons were free until our five-o'clock study hall. Gunn programmed Saturday afternoons down to fifteen-minute play-and-work periods. His intramural teams did double-duty for the Father-Treasurer as paint-and-scrub crews, washing out the jakes, or painting window sashes in periods between their games. Ski's team painted while Hank's played basketball until two-thirty when they reversed their positions.

During the autumn of my first year, all ninety of us freshman boys alternated playing football and dismantling an old brick house on Misery's property that had been part of the Underground Railroad during the Civil War. It was kind of fun and kind of spooky, especially around Halloween, going down into that cellar and feeling the souls of scared black folks running away, escaping, free.

We chipped all the white mortar off all the red bricks, and loaded each others' arms up with six to eight bricks, and carried the bricks a hundred feet to a big truck, and then ran back to be loaded up with more bricks. From the twenty-story bell tower, we must have looked like busy worker ants. In the deepest snows, our lines of boys carrying bricks circled around a big bonfire to keep us warm. By the spring of that freshman year, some of us could carry ten or twelve bricks, balancing them, and running toward the truck.

"*Ora et Labora*" was the rule: "*Pray and Work.*" *Ora et Labora* had been the monastic rule in the Middle Ages. The senior boys warned us snidely that the German translation at Misericordia of "*Ora et Labora*" was "*Arbeit Macht Frei, Work makes you free.*"

At work and at play we were platooned like Gunnie Gunn's Son-of-a-Gunn Marines, kept moving and busy as boots. He blew his whistle and signaled us out onto the field, no equipment but the mud and the goal posts and the ball he tossed us. I didn't like getting knocked around to begin with, but Gunn drilled us all to play because, after we got ordained, one of our main jobs, he said, would be coaching grade-school teams, because athletes made the best recruits for vocations. That seemed reason enough, but I liked it even less my junior season when Hank the Tank kicked out my two front teeth during our big annual Thanksgiving game, "The Misery Mud Bowl."

In the fourth quarter, our clothes sucked so wet with mud we could hardly move. Mud caked our faces, twenty of us, our breath heaving out in wet puffs of steam, *point, set, hike.* I looked up at Hank's pink hole of a mouth wide open in his face, his big shoulders, back, butt, legs, behemoth rising from the mud, coming toward me in the slow-motion of muck, deliberate, aiming himself, his big boot, toe-first, into my teeth, and in the melee of the play, our side gaining a yard, less than a yard, but gaining, no one noticed that my beautiful teeth, so protected by my mom and dad, shined white, shot white, rootless, falling from my bruised lips through the mud and blood spitting out of my mouth.

Afterwards, after the shock, after the blood, after the dentist, after my permanent dental bridge, after my parents paid a lot of money, Peter Rimski said, "It sort of makes you feel like a real jock to be able to brag your teeth were kicked out in a football game."

"Yeah," Hank the Tank said, "and you were sitting in the stands." *Ka-boom!*

I hated Hank Rimski so much it would have been a mortal sin except I couldn't help my own true feelings. He had injured my body permanently. My hands were perfect, but my front teeth were not. His kicking out my teeth was our secret. I never reported him, because I didn't want to give him credit, especially when he said he did it on purpose. I was afraid of what he might do next.

The pecking order was pecking.

Father Polistina, our classical Latin teacher, began calling on me every day, five days a week, in a class of thirty-eight boys.

Singled out, I prepared my translation of Cicero's *Pro Milone*. Daily I had to be ready to stand up in my desk, the second desk in a long row of six desks, and line-by-line recite my translation and explain the grammar, sometimes for twenty minutes of the hour.

"Be prepared," Lock warned. "Polly's got it in for you."

During my recitations, oftentimes the four or five boys in the row of desks behind me horsed around, joking, putting their feet on the desks in front of them and, slowly pushing with their four or five sets of legs, shoved the connected row of desks, with me standing in the row, forward inch by inch, foot by foot, until the boy in front of me, the boy in the front desk was only twelve inches away from the face of Father Polistina.

"Polly hates me," I said to Lock. "And I hate him. What did I ever do to him?"

For reasons I could not divine, Polly Polistina found my mere existence fearsome, but to me he was only another kind of bully. I vowed he'd never win whatever contest we were playing. He would never catch me unprepared. I honed my daily Latin class performance always to earn B's and sometimes A's. I grew to love my slow-shuffle advance toward Polly as my classmates pushed the row of desks, causing me to tip-toe baby-steps closer to him every day, inch by inch, two feet up to his face.

Father Polistina, Misery's mystic, was a mystery to me, but I obeyed him, studied for him, and hated him, personally hated him for personally hating me for no reason at all.

I thought about the priestly mystery behind things the priests made us do. Especially in the shower. I could go in a stall and be alone, the only time I really was unseen by someone. I could pull the plastic curtain and listen to the water run down all over me, not minding the flaking paint on the Army Surplus sea-foam-green walls or the voices singing four different songs in the other stalls. It was worth it to play a hard game, or endure the slave labor on the free afternoon, to get to take a shower and be alone.

The luxury was kind of a reward, a treat added to the maximum two showers a week. I dawdled a long time even though Rector Karg counseled us to enter, briskly scrub down, towel off, and exit. He said not to luxuriate.

But I refused to hurry, even when other sems scuffed by in shower shoes impatiently flicking, hard, harder, hardest, at the plastic curtains with their towels, or sloshing buckets of pee over the shower top to drown boys in sport. I wasn't luxuriating or interfering with myself or polluting myself. I was drenching myself in privacy, wondering at what Lock termed the nondirective failures of the priests. I was simply being alone for a while in the wild communal world of boys.

The shower and the Confessional were almost alike, except the priest was there to listen when I went to confess twice a week, late on Wednesday and Saturday afternoons.

"Bless me, Father, for I have sinned." I was kneeling.

The darkness of the Confessional smelled like the wet hair and after-shave of the seminarian who had confessed in the box before me.

"It's three days since my last Confession." Outside the heavy green curtain, I heard the shuffling sounds of the thick-soled, thick-souled lines waiting to confess. Through the Confessional screen, I saw the priest bent over, his ear close to the screen, an inch from my mouth.

"These are my sins," I whispered into his holy ear. "I've especially been watching against sins of uncharitableness and have fallen fifteen times since my last Confession. I was inattentive at morning prayers twice and was careless in saying the rosary three times. For these and all the sins of my past life, especially sins of disobedience, or any unknown sin of impurity, I am heartily sorry."

I looked at him, the side of his head, the white hair crested well back on the crown, hoping this time he would say some secret code word that would unite the natural in me with the supernatural outside me.

"My son," he said from beneath his hand, "you do well to guard against sins of uncharitableness."

I locked my fingers together in front of me.

"For it was uncharity that condemned Christ to die so ignominiously on the cross. His precious blood was spilled to fill that very cup of charity that we must offer one to another."

I reached up to touch the crucifix hanging above the screen which framed the priest's profile. My fingers, my priestly thumb and forefinger, touched the painted body of Christ crucified and I thought, "I hold Him now as I will hold Him later in the Host."

The priest hissed at me horribly, "Young man! What are you doing? Put your hand down!"

"I'm sorry," I said. I was very sorry I had the longing touch.

"Be quiet," he said. "Pay attention! For it is in loving others that we love Jesus. In others, we find Jesus."

"I love Jesus," I prayed. "Directly, I love Jesus."

"Are you deaf, boy? I told you once. You can't love Jesus directly. You can only love Jesus through loving others."

"Forgive me for that then too, Father."

"For your penance say three Our Father's and three Hail Mary's. Now make a good Act of Contrition."

"Oh, my God, I am heartily sorry for having offended thee, and I detest all my sins because I dread the loss of heaven and the pains of hell, but most of all because I have offended Thee, My God, who..." I touched my fingers contritely together on Jesus' feet, hoping the word would come.

"Knock it off," the priest said, and slammed the slide closed across the screen, leaving me in darkness while I finished.

"I firmly resolve," I said to the closed screen, "with the help of Thy grace to sin no more, and to avoid the near occasions of sin."

The screen slid open. "Go in peace," he said. Again the screen slammed shut.

I said, "Thank you, Father" to the dark, stood up off my knees, and with a swimming breast stroke pulled open the heavy green curtain and walked out through the twenty lines of three hundred repentant boys waiting, shuffling, murmuring outside the ten Confessionals.

I knelt in a back pew near a pillar. The medieval dark was musk and damp as March. I shivered watching the far-ahead flicker of the red sanctuary lamp casting shadows through the darkened church across the marble altar. Once again a priest had failed to say any key word. Perhaps no one would ever tell me. Perhaps boys who never heard any word of revelation lacked a true vocation. Jesus could not pass by like that, words unspoken between us. I'd find the words to Jesus directly: with nobody between Him and me.

The Lord would take me.

Oh Lord, do take me. My life. My vocation. Wreck me. Break me anew in You. Bring me close to You and Your Virgin Mother and pronounce me a priest forever. To hold You in my hands, having said the consecrating words, while the world crashes in its own violent sins around us. To move out through the streets, to the sick and to the sinners, carrying You in my heart. Oh God. Jesus God. Let the priests themselves deny me the way to You. I'll only crawl onward on hands and knees to Your altar rail. Crucify me with fewer words than You spoke crucified. Let me will nothing but what You will. Let my will be Your will or Your will be my will—or however it goes. See, Lord, I can make jokes with You and talk to You as my friend and brother. You are all I have. My whole family is You. Your souls must be my children because I am not like other men. Let me suffer the fearful violence of Your life in my life. And, Lord, the one thing, *oh no*, the only thing I ask is You deliver me safe from the awful temporal possibilities of temptations. I'm afraid to be too free. I might change or be changed and lose You. So if anything should ever go wrong, *I don't,* if I should commit a serious sin and be about to die, I beg You to remember, *don't want,* that this once, this actual moment, I loved You intensely, *this pleasure,* with all my heart and soul and never really meant to take my heart and soul away. Save me, Lord, from the fires of hell. Oh, *omigod,* take me, Lord. Take me now into Your changelessness.

In the phosphorescent dark, the sanctuary lamp flickering light without heat, real as anything, breathless, I slipped down onto the pew, half-kneeling, half-sitting, hardly breathing, excited, gasping for air, panting, that the whirlwind of grace had passed, leaving me sated and *triste*-ful, a mystic in the Mystical Body of Christ.

Outside the chapel windows the soft urgent cry of doves soothed me against the ruzzabuzza praying of other seminarians entering and exiting from the ten Confessionals.

When the supper bell rang in the church, I walked down the unheated terrazzo stairs to the refectory vowing to speak no uncharitable words to anyone at the table, under penalty of eating no dessert in reparation.

March 15, 1957
The Ides of March

Eight of us boys sat at each table, three to a side, a single at both ends. Every day a different boy started the big plastic bowls of steaming food. Gunn had regulated the drill after a feud at one of the tables grew to such proportions that for almost a week the south end of the table had only potatoes and dessert cookies while the north, who always marched into the refectory first from chapel, hoarded the meat and bread and vegetables and milk. Gunn heard about the feud when the leader of the south stabbed the leader of the north in the hand with a fork. From then on, Gunn himself ate alone, standing on a raised podium in all his Marine Corps presence, keeping watch that all the food started with a different seminarian each day, traveling clockwise, seconds returned counterclockwise, hardly ever making it a third of the way back.

Of the twenty-nine tables, we high-school seniors sat farthest from Gunn's platform, exemplars to the younger juniors, sophomores, and freshmen of Absolute Silence, while a priest read to us, over the clatter of silverware on china, from the *Lives of the Saints* and from spiritual books like Thomas Merton's *Seven-Story Mountain* and *The Life and Death of Maria Gorretti,* the newly canonized Italian saint who at eleven, *no, it's a sin*, had been killed by her rapist, Allessandro Serenelli.

We ate seven hundred meals September to June listening to the readings in silence, except for Saturday and Sunday nights, and lunch on Wednesdays, Saturdays, and Sundays when we were encouraged to practice the social graces we'd need living in our future parish rectories with other priests.

At silent meals, after saying grace, the last boy to be served that day was allowed to call, in the sign language of food, his tablemates' portions. When we could speak, boys announced, "Fair share is two scoops of the noodles and whatever the meat in it is." A miscall meant his starvation. If he were cunning, he could call a fair-share portion small enough to insure that he received a double share before the counterclockwise return. Noodles were hard to capture in two scoops, but hungry boys created tricks like loading a tablespoon with a balanced stack of eight apricot halves while suctioning an extra bonus half onto the bottom of the spoon. Hank invented that, and Porky perfected it.

Gunn, always knocking the corners off, realized how his carefully planned seating arrangements threw mismatched boys together. Inevitably Hank sat across from me, sometimes with Ski and a few of the joy boys from the farm crew, or worse, the elegant boys from the choir, glee club, and opera society who ran around singing snatches of Gilbert and Sullivan like they were always starring in Misery's all-boy version of *The Mikado.*

"There's a new prof coming next year," Hank the Tank said. "Peter told me."

"We'll have him for history." Ski ate like a Clydesdale horse.

"His Ordination picture's in an old yearbook," Dempsey said. "I saw it."

"Looks full of tricks, doesn't he?" Porky Puhl asked.

"He's a friend of Arnie Roth who's no longer a friend of the faculty," Hank said, "after that shouting scene over those boys."

"Pass the bread." Lock was not interested in the gossip.

"I think he looks tricky," Porky insisted.

"Bull!" Hank said. He skimmed the enameled metal bread plate across the table toward Lock. "Peter says he's a real good guy. He can tell."

"How?" I asked. "White horse? White hat?"

"Funny as a wicker bedpan, Ryan, that's what you are," Hank said.

"Compared to the professors we have now, anybody's better." Dempsey ticked me off sometimes agreeing with his own enemy. I liked him better talking about movies or something innocuous like his family's peanut farm and how one summer during a drought it was so hot they planted hay in Lake Dallas.

"Look! It's alive!" Ski pulled a hunk of meat, gristle organ attached, dripping with gravy hemorraging from the noodles. "What is it?" He threw it down on the plastic tablecloth. It wriggled and shook and I turned away.

Porky muttered something low. Boys nearby laughed.

"What'd he say, Lock?" Dempsey asked.

"I couldn't care less," he said, "about the cheap double entendre's." Lock was senior class president and an A student, who had spent the previous Christmas and New Year's with his pastor, who was his mentor, at a ritzy hotel in Havana, Cuba, where they had seen stage shows that were probably a mortal sin, at least for me, because at the New Year's eve show at the Tropicana Hotel, a nearly undressed showgirl had been dropped into Lock's lap and make-up smeared on his good suit.

Hank, who had spent Christmas in New Jersey, pushed his plate away after two helpings. "They call this food?"

"Look," Lock said flatly, "I went to Gunn officially last week and complained about the food."

"So go again."

"The kitchen nuns need time to reorder."

"It's your duty as class president," Ski said to Lock.

"I've got a lot of duties," Lock said. "Lay off."

"Those Hun-nuns from Deutschland only give us more of the same." Hank was working his way up to one of his stentorian scenes. He took a plastic serving plate and licked the lead of one of the dozen pencils he always carried with his slide rule in the plastic pocket at his chest.

"Tank," Ski said, "what you doing?"

"Writing a note to the kitchen." He licked the pencil again.

"Chills, thrills, and vibrations," I said.

"What's it say?" Ski asked. "Let's see."

"We want food," Hank read, "real food—no more of this crap *Kraut Schweinscheit, German pigshit.*" He held the lettered plate up to view. "Sign it, Ski."

Ski looked at us. This was about choosing sides.

"Go ahead, chicken-dick, sign it." Hank the Tank shoved the plate at him. "I signed it."

Ski took the pencil and signed it. He handed it with the pencil to Porky. They looked at each other, then laughed. The plate passed hand to hand around the whole table, gathering signatures, even Dempsey's. Lock set the plate down, decisively, unsigned. His good example was enough for me.

"Hell, " Hank said, knowing better than to push more than his match. He picked up the plate from where Lock had placed it. "Go on, Ryanus. You chicken-dick to sign?"

"I won't," I said.

"Why not?"

"Because if you all jumped off a bridge, I wouldn't jump."

"Why not?"

"Because someone has to applaud."

"Come on, Ryanus," Ski entered in, "You chicken to do something for a change?"

"Say 'chicky-dick,'" I said. "That's the way Hank the Tank says it. 'Chicky-dick.'"

"Why won't Baby Ryanus sign it, why not?" Hank patted my arm.

I arched my elbow sharply at him, clipping his shoulder.

"Watch it, Ryanus." Hank held out the plate. "You sign this or I'll pound the living shit out of you."

Deep inside my chest, my vagus nerve twitched, the way my dad said his twitched, full with adrenalin. I half rose. "Try it," I said, "and die!"

Everybody laughed.

"Try it," I repeated.

"Sign it."

"No."

"Why not?" Hank the Tank knew full well I would sign nothing he had cooked up, not even a good idea. "You're nothing but an ass-kisser," he said, "Gunn's ass-kisser."

"Kiss mine," I said.

"Bare it."

"So you could sign your name there too? Fool's names, Hanko, and fool's faces are always found in toilet spaces."

"Eat shit," he said.

"Then what would I do with your clothes?" If there was one thing a boy learned in the seminary, it was the snarling way to use his mouth.

Far across the refectory, Gunn rang the bell signaling us to stack the dishes at our tables' ends. The clatter of two hundred of us high-school boys passing china and silverware began. I touched the underside of my fork handle to a blot of mustard and passed it directly to Hank.

He winced like an old maid when the mustard soiled his fingers that were more mechanic's than priest's. He cursed and tried to wipe his hand on my black sweater. I pulled my chair away. He glared. Daggers, crude like angry boys draw in notebook margins during class, shot from his eyes.

The stacking noises died and we sat in silence, turned at various angles to hear Gunn's announcements, rising finally to stand for the prayer, "Grace after Meals."

"Grace after Meals. Grace before Meals. That's how Prince Rainier likes it." The worst thing about Hank the Tank's level of humor was how funny he thought he was. "Monaco is a state of Grace."

"A pun is the lowest form of humor."

In the cattle crush of boys funneling to the narrow refectory exit, Mike Hager, seated at another table, had already heard about the fight.

"What's going on?" he whispered.

"Mutiny," I said.

"Why didn't you sign it, Ryan?"

"You're kidding," I said, not turning my head.

"You could have been one of the boys."

Hank the Tank stepped hard on the heel of my shoe, pulling off my loafer. It was an old trick, done every day to break someone's syncopation in the fast march-step of seminarians double-file down long hallways. I wheeled. The two of us stood, stock still, facing each other smack in the middle of the silent crowd of boys pushing out the door past us. My tongue licked across my two new teeth. In the free-for-all fury of the Mud Bowl, nobody but me knew exactly who had kicked me in the mouth. He knew. I knew. But I never told anyone. I wouldn't give him the satisfaction. He was afraid to claim the bragging rights.

His kicking out my teeth gave me the power to get him shipped any-time I wanted. So did his locked door.

The secret bonded us.

"Screw you," he whispered.

"You are more pathetic than boring," I said.

Around our little movie scene, the crowd of milling extras sniggered.

"Silence in the ranks!" Gunn yelled from half across the room. "Close up the file or I'll bring you all about-face."

In a high-pitched ventriloquist-whisper into the fist of my thumb over my forefinger, I said, "No! No! Not that! Not the 'about-face.' I might turn and see Hank."

All the boys near me laughed into their hands and into the crooks of their elbows.

I turned and walked out.

Hank the Tank was hard behind me as we filed two-by-two up the stairs, into the chapel where we all knelt together for our after-supper visit to the Blessed Sacrament.

March 17, 1957
Saint Patrick's Day

In the refectory, after supper, on the Feast of Saint Patrick, Rector Karg, in his *schnapps*, ordered me up the ten steps to the lectern, all the boys looking up, and made me sing "Danny Boy." Ha ha ha.

The Irish, Karg liked to say, missed twenty-five percent of Catholic history, because the Micks were pagans until 500 A.D. In the last election for U. S. president, when all the priests liked Ike Eisenhower, Karg had not liked me liking Ike's Democratic opponent, Adlai Stevenson, because he was governor of my home state. If Karg had a wrong side, I was always on it.

"Sing 'Danny Boy' again," Karg commanded. "This time, louder, in German." Ha ha ha.

Lock stood up and joined me, and saved me.

March 19, 1957
Feast of Saint Joseph

Two days later, in the middle of lunch, Father Gunn, the once-and-always Chaplain to the United States Marine Corps, strode like a Fury into the refectory. He rang the brass hotel-desk bell on his table—pounded it repeatedly, a touch of urgency—to silence the grand Peter Rimski who was reading from the *Martyrology* about the Patron Saint of Dentists, Saint Apollonia, the Egyptian martyr. After the anti-Christians broke out her teeth with pliers, she was given the choice of renouncing Christ or being burned alive, so she leapt onto the fire herself. Saint or not, she was no miracle worker, because when I had prayed to her, spitting mud and blood out of my mouth, she had not saved my two front teeth.

Gunn himself climbed up into the lectern. A shaft of noon sunlight blazed down on him from the high Gothic window. He and his strawberry toupee glowed in a dazzle of a thousand-watt divine wrath.

He held a plate.

"You'll never hear the end of this," Mike Hager whispered to me from the next table.

"Saint Apollonia," Lock whispered, "had it easy."

The priest elevated the gray plastic serving plate above his head as if he were elevating the Host saying Mass. "This," he said, "is the height of vulgar ingratitude. The good nuns are shocked. They were in displaced people's camps. And you shock them! The Father-Treasurer is beside himself with anger. We brought those nuns here, rescued them from those camps. And yet you, you, you insult them!" He read the inscription. "This seems to be the best that educated young Catholic gentlemen can do." He flourished the plate. "Who is 'Tank'?" he shouted.

He knew. Everyone knew. Everyone looked at Hank squirming next to me. He was a boy big in size trying to make himself very small. He raised his arm up, sheepish, not very far.

"Stand at attention, Mr. Rimski," Gunn ordered.

Hank's chair squawked back across the terrazzo floor and he stood.

"Who is 'Porky'? We know, don't we. Stand up, Mr. Puhl."

Three names later, five boys of our whole table of eight were standing in ignominy except for Lock and Dempsey and me. Every eye in the refectory turned toward us.

"Hey, Tank," I whispered. "You fub-duck."

He looked his famous daggers at me.

Gunn studied the plate, then looked down upon the room, the tables spread with the interrupted noon meal. "I need not say," he said, "how outraged Rector Karg has become at this terrible insult to the good sisters. It must be Providence that this note was found. Providence that the dishwashing machine did not scrub off the vulgarity, letting us discover at last the low ingratitude I always knew lurked among you. You come from nothing and we try to make you into something." His strawberry hair flashed in the sunlight as he rocked from one foot to the other.

"*Gott in Himmel, God in heaven!* The good sisters try," he said. "God knows they try with what time and money Rector Karg gives them. Anyone taking grievance about their valiant efforts certainly lacks the worldly detachment necessary for the priesthood. You should know the real hardship of soldiers at war, of nuns at war. Then you might appreciate what's given to you."

He began the Father-Treasurer's story of the blind German lady, but I hardly heard him, remembering Hank's bravado the night before. I started to laugh because Hank and his cronies stood shamed by the fable of the little old lady's quarter. I laughed harder and harder, Gunn up in the lectern waving the plate, unable to see me, because of the five disgraced boys standing all around me.

Lock poked me, worsening my laughing jag. "Nuns at war!"

When Gunn announced that the gang of five had to wash every window and every light fixture in the high-school building, even if it took all their free time till June, I dropped my head to the table. Tears rolled down my face. I was on the side of the angels. Maybe Gunn was right about Providence. This was almost a sign of something.

Lock poked me again as Gunn stormed down upon us. I regained some composure while he broke up the table, moving into exile, at a disciplinary side table, everybody but me and Lock and Dempsey, who the night before had, sly as a fox, rubbed out his signature during the "Grace after Meals" with the blot of mustard from my fork.

April 15, 1957

Even Hank the Tank looked a little broken after a month of climbing ladders to wash the high-hung electrical fixtures, especially when the first warm spring weather blew up the river valley to the hill. So long after the offense, the five disciplined boys began to gain a general sympathy. Misery had more than two thousand ornate light fixtures. Lock, as class president, had knocked on Father Gunn's door to get the stiff sentence commuted. The priest refused out of hand. He cautioned Lock not to abuse his position as president in matters that concerned higher discipline.

"Gunn is really down on the class." Lock felt dejected. "Karg backs him up."

"Hank caused it," I said.

"But it seems more than that," Lock said. "I thought we had Gunn to where he'd listen to us, or actually hear something about what's happening to us."

"That was earlier, much earlier, this year," I said. "It's probably the same hope every senior class begins with, to win the disciplinarian's heart."

"Institutions don't have hearts," Lock said. "None of the faculty wants our opinions. But I thought we could change Gunn's personal hard-line attitude and maybe achieve an actual 'first,' a high-school graduation this year. That's what I've been working towards. A graduation ceremony could symbolize our intellectual progress toward the priesthood. But no! Last night, Father Gunn told me in no uncertain terms there will be no high-school graduation this year, because there has never been a high-school graduation at Misericordia, and as long as there is an Ordination Day, there will never be a high-school graduation, because our focus at Misericordia is on the priesthood, and that, he said, closes the subject."

The next day the breach between students and faculty became even more strained. Gunn stripped Porky Puhl's last tatters of hierarchy. He shipped him out of Misery, on an hour's notice, for performing a scientific experiment on some sophomores.

Porky had put eight boys—each in a separate shower stall—and measured their privates. One kid got scared and told in Confession to a priest who refused him absolution until he told Gunn.

After that Gunn treated us like we all knew, I mean really knew, what Porky had done in the shower and all. Father Gunn rounded up the bunch of us senior boys and wondered, he said, about group guilt and one bad apple. It was one of his longest spiritual lectures, lasting over two hours.

Lock sniggered that Porky must have really been concerned about "the shortage of priests."

April 16, 1957

Late the following night, after lights out, I slipped out of the dormitory in my pajamas and robe. I carried my hard-heeled bedroom slippers in my hand until I stood barefoot outside Father Gunn's dimly lighted door, where I stuck my toes into them and stood on my sloppy crushed heels. I knocked and knelt down on both knees on his threshold.

He opened his door and looked down at me, kneeling, looking up at him. "Tell me," he said, "everything."

"Father, I think you ought to know...in view of what's been going on and all that Hank and Ski...Mr. Rimski and Mr. Kowalski, that is...have been caught locked in the storage room...Sometimes Porky Puhl was in there with them. They've been exercising, I guess, is all they've been doing, because here's this book I found on gymnastics that's from the library stacks. It's been taken out without being stamped...Also there were some, I think, secular periodicals, health magazines from Charles Atlas, stuck under the stored mattresses until yesterday, but today they're gone, except for this one called *Tomorrow's Man*."

To keep from smiling, I ran my tongue over my bridge of front teeth.

May 1, 1957

What I hadn't figured was how cleverly quick Hank could be appealing to German discipline. Gunn was so impressed with Hank's quick-flexing explanation of physical fitness that every boy in our class had to come up with seven dollars, so Hank the Tank could order us each a rubber strap with a handle on both ends to build up our chests and lung capacity. For the first week, our senior-class wash room, where twenty wash bowls stood side by side under a wall of mirrors, was dangerous with boys holding the red rubber strap straight out at arms' length and stretching—three, four, five, ten repetitions—till our faces exploded.

Hank the Tank, of course, had no trouble pumping the red rubber strap that looked like he was stretching a huge hot water bottle.

I waited my chance and when Hank the Tank was at full explosion, I snapped my red rubber strap like a locker-room towel at his backside and we both went chasing down the stairs, falling over hooting boys.

May 24, 1957

Lock called a senior class meeting and announced that we deserved to celebrate our high-school graduation with an actual ceremony. Dick Dempsey made forty-two diplomas out of typing paper, lettered them, and rolled them up. We all came together in our senior classroom the last Sunday afternoon in May. Actually, our intellectual independence was sad. Lock and Dempsey tried to make the occasion solemn and real. Father Gunn refused to come. The other priests said they were busy grading final exams or preparing for Ordination, except for one priest, who came and stood uneasy near the back door and left, embarrassed, as soon as all the rolled typing paper was distributed.

He was a young priest, new that year, quiet and unreachable. Maybe he ran out on us because it made him sad we were just a bunch of kids, just kids, trying to make something out of something that was forbidden. Lock, pleased that at least one faculty priest attended, ad-libbed into his valedictory speech that he was glad some older, more adult interest was being shown us.

But I felt more like a kid than ever, even if I was graduating, facing another summer in the world. I made up my mind. I was seventeen, about to be eighteen, feeling my innocence ridiculous. I had to know. One seminarian from Philadelphia was playing forbidden race records, Negro music, like Mickey and Sylvia singing "Love Is Strange." I was intellectual enough to know. I wondered how strange. I geared myself up and made up my mind and went without stopping to the priest in the Confessional and asked him point blank how it was done, how the two, like Charlie-Pop and Annie Laurie, got together for sex.

He told me all it was, and it was somehow terribly disappointing, because I had felt some tedious obligation to know one of life's big secrets.

Trying to be pure had been terribly difficult, because I had no idea of what the temptation was supposed to be. Sin had something to do with girls, but no one spoke clearly.

I had to know what it was besides interfering with myself that celibacy required I give up, so knowing that, I could leave it, not needing it, and be free to search in myself for the priestly self that needed finding.

My need to know was real enough. My mother wrote me a special letter. Charlie-Pop was so proud, she said. She was pregnant. I could hear the pitter-pat of little feet walking in to replace me.

They could have asked. Thommy was bad enough. I felt the way all first-borns feel, forever falling from being the only child.

"We're so happy with you and Thom," she wrote, "we thought we'd try again."

May 29, 1957

"I'll **never** forgive you, Ry-baby!" Hank the Tank jumped down from a ladder, his hands wringing a wet rag he threw at me. "I'll never forget."

He had me cornered on the third floor alone.

"Don't say anything, baby. You talked enough already. Ski and me came near to getting shipped out of here. Twice, because of you. And we would have, yeah, you would have succeeded, but my father's name saved us. Rector Karg didn't name you as choir boy, baby, but we all know, don't we, what you are and what you sang to Gunn. Don't flinch up. I'm not even going to threaten you, O'Hara baby. You'd only run and sing again. You're so effing pure. No man, I don't need to threaten you. You're so busy playing white knight to that pansy Dempsey, because I ride his tail. You wait till I ride yours. You like your new teeth? You ain't seen nothing yet. Fub your fub duck. I'm gonna fuck you up."

"Try it," I said. "You expect me to knuckle under? To you? I mean, how do you want me to play it? Get down on my hands and knees and worship you by burning incense in your big belly?" I threw the wet rag back at his face. "You found your vocation: washing light fixtures. Like father, like son. Your father washed out of Misery. What do you expect?"

"Not what I expect, O'Hara. But what you don't. This time you got me big."

"Confession," I said, "is good for the soul."

"You're supposed to confess your own sins."

"Oh," I said, "I always get that mixed up."

"You're gonna get it from me in the ass when you least expect it."

"I think my Confessions always are about my own sins."

"Remember that, baby—when and where you least expect it. And never mention my father again."

June 1, 1957

Baiting Hank the Tank was a thrilling contest. Hank and his crowd of glee club and choir boys and opera fans had those kind of ecclesiastical ambitions that made me wonder what was God's point in such a calling of such a lewd boy with such social-climber friends who all seemed like they were having forbidden special friendships, always together, the way Father Polistina—who could have caught mystical fire for all I cared— never went anywhere without Father Yovan, who taught theology, and had a giant body topped with a head even so much more giant he seemed deformed, even though he was overall very handsome. As if the priesthood itself weren't elevation enough, Hank's crowd wanted to be monsignors and bishops and cardinals, and Porky had wanted to be pope.

Actually, what is a vocation, but making the improbable probable?

God told me I had a vocation.

I told people God told me that and they all believed me.

As those years in Misery's high-school department changed into four years in Misery's college department, doors opened and closed. Many boys quit. Many more boys were shipped out. The priests were shaping the next generation of clergy. Some boys like Hank the Tank began to work the church-strings that would set them up for the four last years in Misery's theology department, and then in their diocese for life.

One older seminarian, everyone knew, had already played his cards right. He'd be a grand priest, they all said, a very young bishop, and an astounding American cardinal, called to Rome itself, and he'd be a boy from Misery. I understood his ambition, but I had studied his face and wondered under his impeccable grooming what was his secret heart.

We all knew how to reach Ordination to the priesthood, but I wondered about our personal identity and our individual integrity, and who that older seminarian really was behind the pose, the mask, the vestments, the incense, the music, the candles, the lighting, the architecture.

Hank's clerical ambition seemed to me to be a worldly vanity, because he was the kind of boy who, having survived public disgrace, could only rebuild himself up by tearing other boys down. In the end, I figured, even a priest had to confront his human heart.

June 6, 1957

As soon as I arrived home, as if she'd been waiting for me, Brownie died.

My poor little dog. Asleep forever. Sometimes when I was five or six or ten, I forgot you with a small boy's carelessness. Many's the time I buried my tears in your fur, laying my head on your warm and curly side. Sitting those last afternoons, reading, with you lying in the cool ground-cover of my parents' back yard. You lifted your head, looked at me, and rested your nose on your paws. Nearly fourteen years old. Ninety-eight in human years.

Finches and butterflies flew around the still pair of us. What a lovely afternoon was the last afternoon. I put my bare foot on your left forepaw. You looked at me and smiled, yawned, and put your nose down on my toes. I touched your head and said, "Such a good girl. You're such a good dog."

She was in no pain, but she would not eat. Last night I put my forehead to her forehead and said, "Whoever you are in there, I'll take care of you. I'll protect you. I'll keep you easy. You're still here, honey dog."

Starting on this somber little journey, where goes a little dog's soul? Moving inexorably to the inevitable. Soon no more cold wet nose resting forepaws on my mattress edge each night. *You love me. Only you love me.* No more being watched as we eat until the last fork is set down on the last plate, and you stand up for your turn. Your last night on earth.

My little dog died last night. I sat with her, breathing heavy and staring at me until 3 AM, finally falling asleep until at 4:30 she called out in four rising cries: mmm, Mmmmm, MMMmm, MMMM! I bolted up and held her, lay with her, comforted her, falling asleep together, knowing in the morning we'd have to decide something, falling deep asleep on the floor, holding her, waking at seven with my father, kneeling next to me holding her, rousing me.

Brownie? Brownie? She was dead. Still warm to my touch, kissing her, holding her, until my mother came with a red wool blanket and we all knelt around her, crying, stroking her familiar curves, our fingertips touching in her fur. "Our little girl is gone."

Her shoulders were still warm, her paws still so soft and tender. Her eye caught the light, but she was not looking at me.

I clipped some brown fur from her soft neck. My father brought his wheelbarrow. My mother cut bouquets of flowers from the yard and we lay the flowers, red and yellow and purple and pink, and fresh green leaves, all around her beautiful brown body, and wheeled her solemnly into the shade under her favorite tree where together my father and I shoveled silently in the brilliant light of a warm June morning.

4

July 4 Weekend, 1960

Three years later in a red Volkswagen Bug, I roared out of Peoria free, white, and twenty-one, north on a two-lane highway, singing along with the car radio, "There's a Summer Place." Destination: the home of Mike Hager. He lived in the resort town of Wisconsin Dells. We had planned at Misery how my family could meet his family the summer before by taking our vacation at the Dells. For some reason, maybe a funeral out of town, Doc and Mrs. Hager never showed. Mike came alone.

My father had shot home movies of us all on one of the small tour boats. On screen we cruised across mirror-smooth water, among beautiful rock formations with my mother pointing up at the delicate cover of green forest.

Thom stood in the background, smoking, hating the vacation, hating us singing along in the silent movie with the tour guide who was an Irish tenor happy to hear we were the O'Hara Family. Fluttering in 8mm Technicolor, we all took turns holding my little sister, Margaret Mary, *isn't she cute*, forever the new baby, who was three, and always imitating us, talking anachronisms about things the family did "before the baby was born," as if she had preceded herself, till I told her to cut it out.

When the boat reached "The Wonder Spot," a place in the forest where baseballs rolled up hill and we all looked like we were standing at gravity-defying forty-five degree angles to the ground, Mike and I had taken the movie camera from my father and we shot each other sideways and upside down, and when I ran the movie backwards through the projector, everyone laughed.

I even showed the movie once at Misery. I was the first boy in the whole history of Catholicism to return to the seminary with a movie camera and a projector, but I had to mail them both home because Rector Karg said, "Just when I think you've thought up everything, you think up something else."

At twenty-one, I was embarrassed because I looked no more than fifteen. My summer job was pumping gas at a filling station owned by my father's best friend who was the rich Mason. He had given me the weekend off. My red Volkswagen Bug, borrowed from my dad, hugged the unbanked curves, except when my speed swung my rear tires onto the shoulder, shooting small hailstorms of gravel into the birches and pines. I loved the radio competition between the bad boys and the good boys with Elvis wailing "Heartbreak Hotel" and Pat Boone crooning "Love Letters in the Sand." Nearly noon on the Fourth of July, and on the whole length of county road I had seen only two kids pushing a bicycle. Sunlight sifted down through the forest that arched high up and full over the road making a dappled green tunnel.

I slowed for a blind left curve, downshifting for the fun of it, still drifting a bit right, playing the small car's quick response. In the middle of the road, two human figures, jumping like startled targets ahead, separated fast a couple yards before my bumper. I passed narrowly between them at no more than thirty miles per hour. A thump hit the right side of my car. I held the center of the road, skidding to a stop on the shoulder. The little car rocked back on its brakes. The dust cloud caught up and settled like powder all over the red hood. I sat holding the wheel.

"Hey, kid, you trying to kill somebody?" One of the two men ran up to the car. He was shirtless and built bigger than Hank the Tank. He wore plaid swimming trunks, and he shoved his face with a red beatnik goatee into my window. He ran a hand through his red flat-top and shook his head at me.

"Say I didn't hit anybody," I said.

"You like almost killed my buddy."

The other guy appeared at my passenger window. "Hey, Rip, should this kid be driving?"

"I'm sorry," I said. "What was that thump?"

"Kenny kicked your fender," Rip said.

"See this fist?" Kenny leaned into the car, beer-breath first. "Rip's like the strongest guy in town."

"I said I'm sorry," I said. "Watch where you're walking."

"Don't get wise, kid," Rip said. He made a big left bicep and snapped it a kiss. "I can turn this Bug over like nothing in the ditch."

"He can. Like a turtle on its back," Kenny said. "With you in it."

I started the motor. "Back off," I said, "I'm tougher than I look." I raised my left fist and kissed it.

"Hey, kid," Rip said. "Don't kid a kidder." He reached his big arm through my window. "What are you? Fifteen with a learner's permit?" He clamped his hand on my shoulder. "Kid, you need like an adult in the car when you drive. I'm nineteen." He pulled open my passenger door. "You tried to kill us. You can give us a lift."

"Beat it," I said.

"Get in, Kenny," Rip ordered.

Kenny, playing Tonto, climbed into my passenger seat. Rip yanked open my driver's door, shoved my seat forward, and jackknifed himself into the backseat. My little Bug rocked under their weight. I sat stock still, kind of scared, kind of thrilled. Kenny sat next to me, with Rip behind me where I could keep an eye in the mirror on his face and his red flattop.

"So like drive on, James." Kenny leaned in and dropped the brake release. They both smelled beery.

"You owe us. You near killed us," Rip said. He rolled a cigarette paper like a farmer, licked it, stuck it in his red goatee, and lit it. "Hang a U-ey, Bug man, and drive us to the general store three miles back."

"I'm going the other way, toward the Dells," I said.

"Like tough nuts," Rip said.

The evergreen forest stretched for miles on both sides of the road. They were drunk boys and they were in the car and I didn't know them and the world seemed exciting because I didn't know them the way I knew everyone I knew way too much.

"You want a ride. I'll give you a ride."

"The kid sees it like our way." Kenny double-beat the dashboard like a riff on a bongo drum. He punched on the radio and twirled the dial through fast blips of sound to a station he liked. "Hey, man, you know 'Lullaby of Birdland, da da dee'?"

I whipped the car into a U-turn that threw Rip against the rear seat. They both started laughing. I started laughing.

"First you try to kill us, then you try to kill us," Kenny said. "Me and Rip were gonna hike the beer trip. Da da dee. You're like a lifesaver, Bug man."

"What kind of a name is Rip?" I said. "Is that—like—a Hollywood name like Tab and Rock and Troy?"

"His name is like Ripley," Kenny said. "Believe it or not. Ha ha ha. Da da dee." He turned the radio up louder.

At Misericordia, I had longing fantasies about disappearing into the real world like a real person instead of like a seminarian, so I could see what real life was like. "Lullaby of Birdland" filled the car. Doo wat da doo doo doo wah da. It was summer. The Fourth of July. I was free. Doo wah. Real.

Ahead, I saw a store called "Fred & Alice's" with a single red gas pump. I drove in kicking up our own cloud of dust. Rip and Kenny walked into the store as a really old Fred sitting on the porch looked toward me.

"Fill up?" he shouted.

I waved at him to keep sitting. I had learned how to pump gas filling up all those tanks at the Mason's filling station where hardly anyone who knew me even recognized me. A gas jockey is such an opposite of a seminarian. People don't notice the one and fall all over the other. Except for one time, a girl, when I was leaning over the hood washing her windshield, she spread her knees way apart and held her two dollars in her fingers between her thighs and neither one of us pretended to notice what she was doing.

"Hey, kid, like you want any?" Kenny yelled from the porch of the store.

All over the rustic wood front of the station, Fred had nailed metal signs for Coca-Cola and Lucky Strike. Kenny stood next to a three-foot thermometer shaped like a Drewry's beer bottle. The temperature was 94 degrees.

"Any what?" I yelled.

"Like beer, man."

"I'm driving." I walked closer to the porch.

"Don't be a dick," Kenny said. "I figured because you were underage, you were afraid to come in." He disappeared back into the general store. Fred thanked me for a buck-fifty for the seven gallons. I was happy. A guy I didn't even know called me names. I was passing. I was one of the boys.

"Yippee!"

"Put the beer in the back seat," Rip said. He and Kenny each carried two six-packs. "I wanna chug."

"Put it in the trunk," I said. "I don't want any trouble with the Wisconsin Highway Patrol."

"You boys be careful now, hear?" Alice came out to the front porch wiping her hands on her store apron.

"Hey, lady," I yelled. "You're a witness. I'm being kidnapped."

"To the Point, man!" Kenny yelled.

"I'll drive you, but I got to be going."

All the way back Kenny yelled "Lullaby of Birdland" and Rip would yell, "Da da dee" and they'd laugh like some Morse Code to a punch line of an in-joke. For the third time in twenty minutes I passed the two kids pushing the bicycle. This time they stared as the red Volkswagen roared by.

"Can you get like parts for this car?" Kenny asked. Then he turned to the back seat. "Let's get drunk."

"We are drunk," Rip said. "We are like so drunk we don't even know Bug man's name."

"O'Hara."

"So, 'O'! We're drunk and it's your goddam fault."

"My fault?" I said.

"No. I mean, his fault. Out there floating on the lake since six this morning. With the goddam car keys."

"Who?" I asked.

"Deacon," Kenny said.

"Deak's got the car keys like in his trunks," Rip said. "He never heard us yell at him once. We killed a whole case and he never heard us yell once."

"A third of the beer was Deacon's." Kenny looked crossed-eyed into the back seat.

The rhythms of the car seemed to be lulling them.

"A third was his," Rip said, "and we drank it. Therefore we are drunk. Therefore it's Deak's fault. Him out there with the car keys. Not coming when he's called. Making us walk all the way to good old Fred and Alice's."

"That's the turnoff road for the Point," Kenny said.

We swung off the blacktop to a one-lane dust path. Weeds scraped the bottom of the car. Finally, the trees ahead broke into a sunny clearing that fell down a gentle slope to the water and a long finger of sand bar. Strange for the Fourth of July, the place was deserted, like a resort lake closed for the season.

"Our car's off to the right in the shade," Kenny said.

I pulled up next to it. "Where is everybody?" I asked.

"Nobody here but us and Deak like out on the water." Kenny pointed to a rowboat drifting easy and silent, floating more on the lake glare than on the lake. "Nobody much comes out here anymore..."

"My dad owns the property," Rip said.

"...except at nights, they come."

"But only," Rip sniggered, "by like...my invitation."

"I'm supposed to find Mike Hager out here. His folks told me in town."

"You mean Deak? The Deacon's your friend?" Rip asked.

"You're from that weirdo place in Ohio?" Kenny asked. "Crap, man, sorry."

"That explains why you're so weird," Rip said.

Kenny laughed. "Hey, like we said, he's out there in that boat."

"Open the trunk." Rip pulled at the front bumper of my car with both his big arms. They carried the packs through the clearing. Kenny sat down, rattling the morning bottles ranged like dead soldiers across the heavy wood table. Two rolled to the ground. Rip didn't bother to catch them. He straightened up and rubbed the slight balloon of his stomach. "Damn," he said. "I'm getting a gut." He was hungry for compliments.

"How long's he plan to stay out in that boat?" I asked.

"It's not the beer," Rip said. He pointed at me. "It's your fault, O'Hara."

"Mine?" I said.

"Yours. Deak's and yours." Rip belched and became very precise. "Like you're one of his seminary friends, man. You tell me. His way's no way for a guy in college to spend his summer. You guys ain't castrated."

"Shut up, Rip," Kenny said.

"Remember that like fruitcake who came here last summer?" Rip was not to be stopped. He was one of those frank men whose respect Rector Karg said priests needed to court. "That pansy-ass seminarian what's-his-name we got so drunk he kept doing those goddam imitations of the friggin' Latin teacher, chanting 'Polly Polistina, Polly Polistina.'"

"The one that kept flipping the finger and screaming like fub duck, fub duck, fub duck!" Kenny said. "How could I forget?"

"Fruits," Rip said. "Fairies." He turned to me. "You a fub duck, O'Hara?"

"Is Mike?" I said. All I knew about fruits I learned from Rector Karg who always told us before we left on every vacation that if a fruit comes up to you in a bus station, kick him in the crotch and run. I turned toward the boat and yelled for Mike.

"It's okay, man. My folks raised me like Catholic." Rip belched again.

"Feel better?" I asked.

He sat down. "Yeah."

"We'll all friggin' call him," Kenny said.

The table shook as they rose and supported each other to the sandy bank. They lurched together for a moment, stopping to watch across the sparkling surface of lake the tiny figures in far-off animation at the municipal beach where Mike had worked as a lifeguard.

"Damn," Rip said, "I can like sniff it from here. Let's row on over where the girls are."

"You can't drink there," Kenny said. "Which is why we stay here."

"We're drunk anyway," Rip said. "Blame Deak." He put his hands to his mouth and bawled toward the boat, "Hey, Mikey-Mike!"

Kenny joined him. "Hey, Deak, come on in."

No head popped up in the boat.

"Screw it," Rip said. "He drowned."

"Bull. He's laying in the bottom asleep…"

"…passed out…"

"…on the life jackets." Kenny kicked at the sand.

I sat down on the beach and took a mental picture.

"He's been a screw-up all summer," Rip said. He led Kenny back up to the table and rolled up one of his cigarettes.

For a long time I watched the water lip-lap up on the sand. The glare darting off the waves was bright as Rip's squared-off opinions. Suddenly, way out from shore, Mike was sitting up in the boat the way you do sometimes when you've been drifting for hours and have forgotten about people and motors and then all of a sudden you smell the exhaust of someone's outboard.

I raced up the bank and beeped my car horn. Mike turned toward the shore. He saw me honking and flashing the headlights of my red Bug parked next to his car in the deep pine shade. He waved and started rowing toward us. "Ryan!" Mike called. He handled the old wooden boat perfectly, nosing it on to the narrow strip of sand. "Ryan. Welcome." He ran up the bank. We shook hands. "I didn't expect you till tomorrow."

"Surprised?" I said. "I phoned your folks this morning and they said come on today. I can't stay the whole holiday anyway. My pastor wants me back Sunday night for closing of Forty Hours Devotions. He crapped when I left this morning. What a tan you have!"

"You know I was lifeguarding at the city beach." He lit a cigarette. "What you don't know is my pastor said hanging around a pool wasn't a fit job for a seminarian."

"It's not," I said.

"Saving people?" He blew smoke rings that floated up in the still air.

"Never stretch a metaphor," I said.

"Ry, Ry. You'll never change."

Mike brought me to Kenny and Rip. "Two old buddies," he said.

"Like…I poured them into the car."

"We all got peculiarities," Mike said. "They think they're beatniks."

"One of you Deacons got a church key?" Rip yelled.

Was he maybe slamming me with some inside joke?

"That's a bottle opener, Ry," Mike said.

"Oh."

"We lost ours." Kenny cupped his hand to his ear. "Like I'm waiting."

"In my glove compartment, Kenny." Mike fished his keys from his swimming trunks.

"Finally we got the friggin' keys," Rip said. "You want like some of this smoke?"

"I don't smoke your kind of cigarettes." Mike punched a slow-motion punch onto Rip's big shoulder, turning him away. We stood alone. "You heard the news, Ryan?" He faced me square. "Dick Dempsey quit. He's not going back to Misery come September."

"He would have told me."

"Swear to God," Mike said.

"He would have written me."

"Lock called me long distance last week."

"Lock telephoned you?"

"I meant to drop you a postcard."

Dempsey couldn't have decided to quit without telling me. "He tells me everything."

"Nobody tells everything," Mike said. "Lock knew a month ago."

"Lock knew? You knew? Dempsey knew?"

Mike shoved me. "Ryan, you're famous for not knowing everything."

"Get out!" I pushed him back.

"You can't be told everything." He pushed me again. "You're a confessor." Smoke from his cigarette streamed from his nose.

"You're kidding me!" I pushed him harder.

"Don't kid yourself." He caught my head in a hammer lock and blew a halo of smoke around us.

"Misery loves secrets," I said, breaking free of his hold. "Maybe he's taking a medical leave. He had inner-ear trouble all last year."

Mike shook his head. Our horseplay evaporated. "Stop," he said. "Dempsey quit. Absolutely quit." He stamped out his cigarette in the sand.

Quit was an even more threatening word than *shipped. Quit* was something a boy did to himself.

"You can't quit a vocation."

"Why? Will God chase us down like the 'Hound of Heaven'?"

I felt jealous. In a world where special friendships were forbidden, Dempsey had seemed like a best friend to me. "He would have written."

"He didn't though, did he," Mike said flatly.

Loss in the movies has violins. I had the hiccup duet from Rip and Kenny playing bongo rhythms on the picnic table. My Uncle Les counseled me that in his own seminary he had watched good friends drop out who had more vocation than he did. Dempsey dropping out was a shock. Every time a close friend quit, I made an examination of conscience to see if my vocation remained sound. Any boy's quitting called into question my intellectual reasons for staying in the same way that priests feared other priests quitting the priesthood for good reasons other than alcohol or purity.

"Get changed, Ry," Mike said. "Let's swim."

Later, wet and cool in the shade, helping Rip and Kenny with the beer, I weighed the difference Dempsey's leaving might make on my life at Misery. Dempsey and Mike and Lock were best friends. Whenever Dempsey repeated that he was president of the Friends of the Friendless Friends, we always responded, "Who are the Friends of the Friendless Friends?" And he'd say, "I'll never tell." Our good times smoothed the rough spots. Any other boy in our senior-college class could have left without rocking my boat, but with Dempsey gone I'd know the difference. I was sure word from him would come, a letter from him, to my home probably today, telling me he was leaving the seminary and why. I hoped the letter would come, even though my hope was both a tiny sin of vanity and a venial sin of disobedience, because Dempsey had crossed over and we were forbidden to communicate with boys who left Misery. Not-knowing was proof I was left out of inner circles of fraternity.

"Later I want to talk to you," Mike said as we came up dripping to the table.

"Is this irony? You big deal want to tell something to somebody...like... famous for not knowing everything?" I waved my hand around my ears. "Damn the mosquitoes," I said.

"You'll get used to them." Kenny handed me a beer.

"Not in the daytime," I said. "Never."

"You guys like reject everything, don't you?" Rip was up around Cloud 9. "You never want to accept life the way it is." He groped himself.

"Hey! I only said I don't like mosquitoes." I turned to Mike for help.

Rip shrugged. "Sooner or later every conversation turns like to sex, so..."

"Rip, don't," Mike said. "You're boring."

"Sometimes Rip's the town philosopher," Kenny said.

"Big hairy deal," Rip said.

"The village idiot," Kenny said.

"Don't start the bit," Mike said. "You never understand. I'm not sure anymore I understand."

"You understand it?" Rip asked me.

"I can't follow pronouns." I played stupid to stay innocent.

"About how you're going to live without it," Kenny said.

"Deacon sure can't say how he's going to live without it, can you, stud?" Rip poked Mike.

"Uh," I said.

"Pick it up, fella," Rip said to me. "You ain't slow. Tell me how you're like gonna live without it."

"I don't know, well, really, if I can tell you so you'll understand exactly the theological position we're in."

Mike moaned and threw his head down on the table. He made me mad, knocking his forehead on the wood while I tried to unravel my real relation to the Church and all the souls in the Church who would call me their spiritual Father. Rip chugged the last of a beer during the most intricate part of my explanation. He tossed the bottle over my head into the pines. Wet drops sprayed down my bare back. I stopped. Rip and Kenny and Mike were all shaking their heads.

"See," Rip said. "You rejected my question. I asked you about women, man. You need, like, such a big bush ha ha ha to beat around?"

"Have you ever wanted to get married?" Kenny asked.

Mike rolled his eyes.

"No," I said. "I'm not old enough." I hated these conversations because I could never explain this part of a vocation to anyone.

"Have you ever thought about it?" Rip asked.

"I'll be the first one to admit," I said, "behind every man's a great woman. Priests have the Mother of God behind them."

"So you'll marry the Mother of God," Rip said.

"Not literally. Symbolically. Men and women in the religious life are married to the Church."

"You're nuts," Rip said. He was one of those people in the Gospel who scoffed at Christ. Why was he baiting me? Would men bait me after I was ordained? Or would they automatically like me because I was ordained? Or would I have to talk sports and drink bourbon and tell jokes about the priest, the minister, and the rabbi? Or would I be like Karl Malden, the rugged priest in *On the Waterfront*, who tries to save hard men like Marlon Brando?

"So these nuns," Kenny said, "who wear wedding rings. They're like married to the Church?"

"The rings symbolize," I teetered on the words, "their mystical marriage to Christ."

"You mean, they're married to Christ?" Kenny said.

"Yeah," Rip said. "Christ's in Argentina with like Hitler and Checkers and James Dean."

"Then what about these priests that wear wedding rings," Kenny pursued. "Who are they married to?"

"To the Mother," Rip said, "and to the Church, and, well, you know about Hitler and James Dean and Checkers."

"Who's Checkers?" Mike pretended to regain consciousness.

"Nixon's dead cocker," I said.

They all laughed.

"Ignore them," Mike said. "Rip's got a one-track mind."

"Damn right," Rip said, "and I think about it all the time. You read the Bible. You study it. The Bible says woman is man's helpmate. That's why I like them, plain and simple. I need lots of help."

"If you understand, it's all different," I said.

"Different? You're weirdos. You know it. We know it. We all pretend not to know you're wasting yourself." Rip turned to Mike. "Man, moping in a boat ain't curing the problem in your pants."

"Hey, Rip, is it really so important to you?" I asked.

"Sex?"

"Pussy." I stared him down with the word. I had played my manly ace-in-the-hole: bad language. I was one of the boys.

"I don't believe it," Rip hesitated. "Like I really don't believe it."

"Let's get out of here," Mike said. "Head over to the beach. Rip could use some food."

"Yes, let's," I said.

"Yes, let's," Rip mimicked.

"Give me the keys, Rip." Mike was angry. "We'll drive both cars back to my house and go to the beach from there."

"Like take the damn keys." Rip threw the ring at Mike. "You had them all morning anyway."

Kenny went and sat in Mike's car. "Come on. I'm hungry."

Rip stalked off to the shore. He was relieving himself, writing circles in the water, reporting what a like big thrill it was.

"Come on, Mike," I said, "let's clear this up."

We threw all the bottles into a trash barrel near the cars. Kenny set the barrel on fire.

"Some party," Mike said.

"I'll go ahead to meet you at your house," I said, crawling down into my VW Bug. I pulled out before Rip came back from the trees. I wanted to drive back alone. The sex talk hadn't much disturbed me. I ran into that all the time. I wanted to be alone to figure out Dempsey.

I must have been driving slow because they passed me on the way back to town and called me the big hairy speed demon on the way to the beach in Mike's old Ford. It was Friday, so the beach was a lousy place to eat, because we couldn't eat meat even if it was a holiday weekend. Even Rip and Kenny ordered peanut butter from the hot dog stand that was playing John Philip Sousa march music, and we all kind of goofed off sort of singing, "And the monkey wrapped his tail around the flagpole."

"You don't eat meat?" I asked.

"I have like enough," Rip said, "to confess."

The sandwiches lay like a rock in my stomach.

Two cute blonde girls in shorts and tops walked by. "Hi, Ripley," they said, running off, giggling in undisguised appreciation of his build and his face. He had what a priest should have.

Rip and Kenny sloshed on into the water diving head first and splashing a group of pretty girls. I said I'd better wait. A radio commercial jingled in my head. "Don't go swimming alone, because you can't reach a phone. When you're in Davey Jones' locker, it's too late to call. So don't take chances. Learn all the answers. Learn swimming today at the YMCA."

I was always treading water, alone, waiting, perfecting my backstroke, biding time for something. I was jealous of boys with red goatees who chewed peanut butter and jumped splashdown into lakes churning up the water, racing past my sidestroke with a freestyle Australian crawl.

In the Ohio winter, I ached for summers in the sun, beaches, bongo drums, and a beatnik beard. But I was drowning in inhibition and obedience. I was going down for the third time with purity. I was a seminarian, a theological student, and certain things weren't mine to expect. Hell! Why couldn't I be the first beatnik priest? I rolled onto my back in the sand. I had more than all those other boys. I had something. Not everything, but something larger than life. I rose to my elbows. They were all wilder than me, the boys who bought girls Cokes in the park and lay with them on beaches. I had always adjusted to this social difference as my special lonely way of life. They could all change faces for each other to get what they wanted.

I was pledged to stay constant. I spent my vacations with maybe one or two theological students from around Peoria, or was left alone with one of them, like Mike and I were now. We wore modest boxer trunks and swam together like little fish for protection. Sometimes we seminarians talked, lying on white towels we had ink-marked MISERY, about theological problems and how the whole world danced around ignoring the true meaning of life.

Seminarians either gossiped or talked obvious shoptalk. They bored me. I announced, "If our vocation could actually be explained, no one could ignore it." The other seminarians accepted the mystery of the priesthood so nonchalantly that I felt myself drifting away from them. They were unquestioning. My nagging analysis isolated me from them.

On the opposite side, I felt myself defending my vocation from boys like Rip and Kenny who were worldly the usual way with alcohol, tobacco, cars, and girls. No wonder faith had to rule reason. Maybe these unanswerable questions Dick Dempsey and I had discussed so often had caused him to quit. At least he wasn't shipped off to the insane asylum where I was obviously headed.

It was all too much on the hot beach. I wanted to plunge into the cold water, swimming out over my head to the raft. I wanted to watch the girls up close touch their blonde hair, wet in strings, finger-combing it, their arms lifting and tightening their small breasts under the swimsuits. I wanted to hear them scream and dive off the float, piercing the water around me when wild boys in red and blue and yellow racing Speedos pulled their arms or slapped at their hard little rears. They were golden angels chased by young devils and their play drew me fascinated toward them. If I were to be their priest, I had to understand them.

"Mike, I'm going into the water."

He groaned a bit, lying all lifeguard-tan on his white towel, stretched half asleep in the sun. I walked across the beach of hot sand through the wonder of half-naked flesh. They think nothing of tomorrow, I thought, circling the prone baking bodies, splashing into the green water. They're lost, nearly all of them, unless saved.

I swam out into the water, almost as far as I could, until the rock 'n' roll pounding from the speaker on top of the bathhouse grew soft under the lap of the waves around my ears and was lost in the quivering heat and voices on the shore.

I was out too far and began to swim back nearer to the diving raft. I hung on it, turned from the float, in over my head, treading water, feeling, feeling it warmer around my shoulders, feeling it bubble dark and cold around my moving feet. A girl swam up from the bottom so close to me her hands brushed my legs on her ascent and her solid breasts, wired in her suit, graded up my back.

My God, I want no bad thoughts.

"Sorry," she said.

"I'm sorry." I avoided her direct eyes.

"You don't live around here."

I prayed, wondering if male seed in the water could get inside their bodies.

"Tourist?" she asked. She was Sandra Dee. I was Troy Donahue. The lake was a summer place. Life was a movie. With dialog.

"Like...," I said, "...another tourist." I swam off in a fast Australian crawl, never looking back, hearing echoes of Rip's biblical "helpmate." Being set aside from sexual desire truly was difficult, though in a way Rip and Kenny would never guess. Not because desire was physical, but because it was mysterious.

I wondered, I really wondered, treading water, warm on the surface, cool around my feet, what she looked like, the girl I could love and take for my wife. Perhaps my surrender to celibacy would make it easier to give her up if I could lessen the mystery, actually see her, if I could know what my flesh was losing, like Grace Kelly, blonde, not Marilyn Monroe, peroxide. This was harder, not knowing, because the mystery of her never appearing visible, incarnate, was so great. To see her swimming in the water, face and body and hair, and still be able to say, "No, my dear, we mustn't," must be easier than fighting off the fantasy of what might be.

I turned to look for her, but she was gone. A vocation has its price. The priests always said that. But what of the girls men who become priests did not marry? What happened to them?

I wanted to leave the beach. I was vexed with, not temptation exactly, but with unfocused sexual unrest, and Dempsey dropping out, and all those beer bottles. I swam back to shore. Rip and Kenny, towels around their necks, sat with Mike on a bench near the bathhouse, talking to the blonde girls who smiled, and sing-song said, "Bye-bye-eye, Ripley."

"God, Ryan. Where were you?" Mike said. "Get changed so we can lose these two characters. My parents expect us home for supper."

"I'll go like this if it's all the same. Let's leave."

In my VW, Rip and Kenny sat in back. I was in no humor to talk.

Mike pulled his old Ford out of the parking lot, still in the blue mood that had sent him to the middle of the lake alone.

I drove my VW three car-lengths behind Mike, following him to his house. In my back seat, Rip rolled up another cigarette, and he and Kenny kept laughing, smoking, and bragging, like two drunks, about catching a train to Florida.

"We could buy like a case of bourbon."

"That's expensive. Cost you like a quarter for a 7-Up."

"We could pack it in our luggage."

"You know what'd happen. We'd get like halfway there and run out."

"We'd get off the train and like buy some more."

"The train'd like pull off like without us."

"We could borrow a couple bucks from your dad."

"Hey, dad, like I wanna take a little vacation."

"We could hitchhike down to the Keys. Take a month or so. Send back for the skis and get towed like a hundred miles. If you fell off, it'd be like a cool munch for a barracuda."

"Lullaby of Birdland, do wah doh."

I punched the radio dial as hard as I could and turned Pat Boone up loud: "Oh, Rudy! Tutti Frutti! A Bop Bop A Loopa!"

Rip pushed my shoulder. "Turn it down, Tutti Frutti, hey," he yelled.

I kept the volume up.

Two blocks later, Mike's Ford pulled ahead of me into the cement driveway of Rip's house. I backed in up the drive, so my window was next to Mike's window, the cool way of talking car-to-car, like cops do.

Rip and Kenny climbed out.

"Bug man, you're like crazy," Rip shouted, starting across the trim lawn. He dropped his plaid trunks and mooned us.

The three friends laughed so hard no one noticed I choked.

"See you," Kenny said. He slapped his palm on the car.

Mike stared at me, car to car.

I turned off my radio. "They both...like...live there?"

"Kenny cuts through the alley."

"Like damn, they're crazy," I said. "Worldly and crazy. But I like them. They actually live in the world."

"They're fub duck," Mike said.

"Are they?"

"Follow me." Mike backed down the drive. I swung after him, three blocks, driving under huge elm trees. Through the dappled shade of the afternoon, kids were already running with blazing bright sparklers. He pulled into the drive of a foursquare two-story house painted white.

"Nine rooms and a bath," he said. Next door, the neighbors waved and lit off a string of exploding fire crackers.

Mike's parents had more money than my parents. That was probably why they hadn't come to the Dells to meet my parents. We weren't rich enough. Annie Laurie warned me as I drove off, "Always act like you come from money, like you have money, like you appreciate what money can buy."

I pulled a Madras shirt over my trunks.

"You look like you're not wearing pants," Mike said.

"I'll tuck the shirt in." I was very insecure.

"I was kidding. Come on. We're late."

In the dining room, flooded with light, Julia and Doc Hager sat eating salad in silence. Her faded gentility perched on the edge of her chair. A lovely bygone sparrow, Julia was, in organza green-yellow as an August lawn. Doc wore white: short-sleeved shirt, trousers, and shoes. All white but for a red strawberry stain clotted above his fold of paunch. He looked as if he were wounded.

"Michael, we've begun," Julia apologized.

"You're late, kid," Doc said.

"Ryan. I was so worried you wouldn't find Michael." Julia motioned us around the table. "Ryan, this is Doc, Michael's father."

"That was settled out of court," Doc joked. "Hello, kiddo."

He finished his salad on his perfect china plate. Julia picked at a lettuce leaf, revealing a chip and a dark flaw running to the center of her dish.

"You've lovely china." I had been prepared to say it. My parents told me to say it. I said it for practice so I could feel what compliments felt like gurgling up from my throat, inflating in my mouth, frothing through my teeth and lips, floating bubbles of praise toward a host and hostess. Priests who have no money spend many a night singing for their supper wherever they are invited.

"Thank you, Ryan. It was from my hope chest."

"This is the last of it too," Doc said. "Four place settings."

"I had only eight," Julia explained. "One was broken years ago when we moved to this house, almost on our Wedding Day."

"Julia broke the other one herself," Doc said.

"It's an English tradition," Mike told me.

"When a child gets married," Julia smiled like a curator, "one is supposed to break his plate, symbolizing he may not come back. When our Julie got married, I broke her setting."

"She's not coming back," Doc said. He took abrupt interest in me. "What do you do, son, besides go to the seminary in Ohio? You have to be more than a priest to get into this house."

"Ryan is sort of a free-lance writer," Mike said.

"He means I've broken all my lances ha ha for free." I tried to put them off.

"Actually, Ryan is fairly well known in the Catholic press."

Julia fluttered. "I read your religious poems. The ones the priests printed."

"Mimeographed," Doc said.

"They were lovely," Julia finished.

"Ryan has sold at least a dozen short stories, but he's really good at interviewing missionaries for feature articles about cannibalism in the African church, and there's his radio drama called *Mister and Missa Luba*." Mike enjoyed embarrassing me while he needled his parents.

"It's such a comfort," Julia said, "to know a close friend of Michael is such a good influence on him."

"God knows he could use it," Doc said, squeezing more lemon across his finnan haddie. He sucked his fingers.

"That's enough, Doc," Mike said.

Julia offered me the basket of rolls.

"Were you busy at the office today, Doctor?" I made conversation.

Julia's eyes widened in her stare at Mike.

"With all the tourists," I said, "you maybe do a lot of emergency dental work."

"Doc, that is, the Doctor, doesn't like to talk about business at home," Julia said. "I'm sorry, Ryan."

"On the contrary, I'm sorry," I said.

"Don't be." Doc pushed his plate away. "I don't like to talk about dentistry, because I don't practice dentistry."

"But you are a dentist, dear," Julia said. "He has his degree. He received it the week before we were married."

"He announced he was never going to practice dentistry the week after," Mike said.

"Tell him why, dear. Oh, Michael, why haven't you explained all this to Ryan years ago. You're such friends."

"I'll tell you why," Doc said. "I decided I couldn't stand to put my hands in other people's mouths."

"That's a laugh," I said. "At Communion, priests' fingers touch people's tongues and teeth and lips and lipstick..."

"Disgusting," Doc growled.

"He only wanted the title of 'Doctor,'" Mike said. "That was the real reason. So he could be 'Doctor Hager' and move into nine rooms and a bath."

"Now I'm afraid I, his own wife, don't even call him 'Doctor,'" Julia said. "Even I, who should understand him, call him 'Doc.'"

"Everyone at the drugstore calls me 'Doc,'" he said. "I like it."

"Then you're a pharmacist now," I said. I should have shut up.

"Oh, Michael, how could you wait till now?" Julia cried.

"I think it's very funny," Mike said. "I don't tell everything I know."

He grinned at me. "Do I, confessor?"

Doc stood up. "I am not a pharmacist." His voice was imperious. He pulled a folded white Nehru cap from his back pocket, placed it on his head. "I am not a practicing dentist. I never was a pharmacist. I am a jerk. I run a soda fountain and milk bar." He saluted, making fun of us all.

"But you are a dentist?" I asked.

"You're like all Americans, sir. You question everyone who doesn't fit some national stereotype. The national syndrome is to question every-thing along preconceived lines. Ryan, what holiday is this?"

"The Fourth of July."

"The first Independence Day of the 1960s."

"Yes, sir."

"Are you a questioning boy?"

"He's questionable," Mike said.

"Have you noticed," Doc said, "that our national anthem, 'The Star-Spangled Banner,' begins and ends with questions?" He began singing, "Oh, say, can you see?" He stopped. "But no one ever asks me the most dignified of all questions: What do I prefer? What is my choice? Has any-one recently asked you what you're all about? What might be your choice?"

Julia broke into such tears she had to excuse herself. "Not this again." She headed to the kitchen.

"Good-bye, Julia, my wife," Doc said. He turned to me. "Are you an independent boy or a dependent boy?"

"I don't know. Independent, I guess."

"That's good for a guess and better as a choice...if it's true." Doc threw his napkin on the table full of china and stood up. He was quite tall. "Mike's an independent boy." He looked at his son and we all waited the longest moment. "Well...Good-bye, my boys. I'm off to the bright-lighted chromium drugstore to serve up malts on the Fourth of July. Later on, come on down, and I'll treat you to an independent independence sundae." He exited singing, "Oh, say, does that star-spangled banana still wave...."

Mike and I sat alone.

"My mentor is my tormentor, " Mike said. "Nine rooms and a bath." He gestured across the shambles of the meal.

"There was no call for you to lead me into an ambush," I said.

"They deserved it."

"Deserved it!" I yelled. "Your father's ego and your mother's humiliation?"

"He's crazy like a fox and she loves it. They sort of have this act. Besides, they stood your family up on your vacation last year. They didn't have to go away to a funeral. They're insecure. Julia thinks my family isn't holy enough for your family. She thinks you're great, because your poems show you have a true vocation." He rose and started for the front porch. "You coming?"

We tried to shoot a little basketball in the driveway. I beat him at a lazy game of "Horse," and he put a half-nelson on me and we wrestled around and then pulled free of each other.

Off down the block, roman candles shot through the twilight.

"The season's all wrong and it's too hot to wrestle," I said.

"You want to go out to the park or the lake?"

"What's the use? Tag-teaming Kenny and Rip? Seminarians on parade. We don't fit."

He led me upstairs to the screened porch outside his bedroom. For a long while we sat in silence, with the one little ship's lamp burning, listening to the evening sounds of the town beginning to ignite the sky. I rocked in a glider. Rockets whistled and flares went up and fathers lit fountains on the sidewalk across the street. At the Point, he had said he wanted to talk. I wanted to listen to him, but I sensed a danger, a chance of reaching out to him and getting hurt in the process.

He reached the lamp from his chair and turned it out.

I tried drawing a line between safety and charity.

Aerial displays exploded all across the night sky.

I was still looking for myself.

From way down at the park, some band played sweet patriotic music.

In all charity, I wanted to help him, but without losing the little self I had found. Confessions, especially late night ones, made me nervous. Boys always wanted to confess to me. That made me feel priestly, but I never really knew what to say.

In the sudden dark of the extinguished lamp came a moment more of silence while the bugs that had been fighting the screens so fiercely stood back stunned that their bright goal had been snuffed. The moon made blue-white tracings on the floor.

"This is the time," he said, "for telling you."

Out in the night of the Fourth, bombs were bursting in air.

I immediately sensed the huge substance of his Confession and prayed nothing Mike said would drag me from my vocation.

"I think I better not be a priest, Ryan. I think I been...I didn't know how much till this summer...pressured all my life. It's time I stopped."

I pulled at my trunks that had long ago dried on me.

"Doc's always saying he thought I'd be the salvation of this family.

And Julia! She keeps reminding me she was pronounced barren forever after my older sister Julie was born. She prayed for a son, hoping, I guess, to change Doc. Anyway, to hear her tell it, Julie at the age of two was praying for a baby brother."

He slapped the arms of his chair.

"Then, of all things, some clairvoyant nuns told Julia she'd have a baby and he would be God's child. That," he said, "that is when you start to find out where the pressure is."

"That baby was you."

In the yard across the street, lines of shouting children ran circles across the lawn with burning sparklers.

"Doc really elaborated on all this crappy family history when I tried to discuss leaving Misery. That's why Julia was so glad when you said you'd come visit. She thinks you'll be on her side. Your poems really convinced her you've got the perfect vocation."

"Uuuh."

"Maybe you do. Maybe she knows."

He lit his last cigarette, crushed the pack, and sent the smoke swirling through the moon motes. "Anyway, I hitched down to Sauk City, right after my pastor made me quit lifeguarding at the beach, to see 'Man of the Cloth,' Arnie Roth, the only priest I trust. 'Be an adult,' he said. 'Tell them you're not going back, tell them you're going where you want to go, to Madison, the Twin Cities, Chicago, wherever. Transfer over to some Catholic university like Loyola. This is between you and God, not mommy and daddy. Get away from them and this dead tourist country.'"

"But your father wants everybody to do what they choose," I said.

"Doc?" he laughed, "he's the original big noise from Winnetka. With a bad case of moral amnesia. Anyway, after I left Arnie Roth, I went straight to the drugstore. After what you saw at supper tonight, you know my father is obviously an escapist. A man who was told by his own father and mother that he had made his own bed and could rot in it. Every Sunday without fail he closes the dairy bar and gets dead drunk. Julia flits around him, still wearing the dress she wore to church, trying to humor him. Normally he's cynical, but Sundays he's unapproachable."

The orange tip of his cigarette arced from his lap to his dark mouth, glowed brighter an instant, then descended.

Far off, crowds applauded fireworks we could hear but not see.

"Anyway, Doc told me we could talk. So I sat there an hour, real nervous, drinking Cokes and smoking. At one o'clock exactly, he hung a *Closed* sign on the fountain, and we had lunch out of a paper sack. A few customers came and went about their business with the pharmacist. Weird. Doc didn't say one goddam word. So I put my hand on his and told him, right at the table where there were a lot of people around and he couldn't make a scene. All he said was, 'Number one made a mistake. Now number two.' He pulled his hand from under mine and reached in his jacket and gave me a dollar. 'What's it for?' I said. 'It's all I've got.' He was almost crying. 'It's the last thing I'll ever give you.'"

"Jeez, Louise..."

Brilliant fireworks popped streaming across the town sky.

I held my chair, pained, that for so long Mike had been wrestling alone, like Jacob with the angel. Wrestling somehow seemed the classic Roman sport of seminarians: wrestling with angels, devils, and sexual temptations. I knew that hearing Confessions would be like this. So I struck a more sincere pose, which felt terrible, really, and quite so false, that I added to seminarians' wrestling card: *vanity.* How would I ever pull off actually acting like a real priest, actually being a real priest, when I felt like an imposter distanced from my own self?

"By the time I got home," Mike said, "Doc had called, and Julia, my own mother, was in tears. 'Your father didn't let you down,' she said. 'There's some things you're old enough to know.'"

From outside and across the pines came the shrill cry of loons dancing on the lake, calm as a perfect mirror for the man-made displays of color and light.

"You know my sister Julie I used to tell you about? You didn't see her picture anyplace, did you? It went out with the broken plate. She married when I was in eighth grade. Doc and Julia didn't like that choice much and liked it even less when she divorced her husband for desertion a year later. She was eighteen."

All the pieces, things Mike had told me at odd times in long talks, began to fall into place. At Misericordia Seminary, where time was measured exactly into the defined periods of the liturgical year, we lost all sense of real time and urgency.

How many boys were hiding family scandal at home?

Mike, free of being a priest, felt freer to confess to me, because he said I had a true vocation.

"Let me tell you something," he said. "The year after the divorce, you remember Julie went to Madison for a rest." He stubbed out the last of his smoke. "There was no nervous breakdown. Just some blond Scandinavian guy from one of the tourist lodges. Damn, I'm out of cigarettes. Why don't you smoke?" He patted all his pockets, then settled back into the creaking wicker chair. "I'm out. Anyway, one night that winter, while you and I were holy little high-school sophomores at Misery, Julie came home all beat up. She'd told this Scandinavian social director she was PG with his kid and he slapped her up all alone outside the cheery lodge, right in the street. Left her in the snow. A great melodrama, but no hero saved her and that spring, late, she had the nine-pound nervous breakdown, and it was adopted. Doc hauled the guy into court, quietly. He was fined or something. That pushed Doc and Julie even farther apart."

"Mike, come on. Enough's enough."

"You don't believe it. You think it's *Peyton Place*."

"You say it, Mike. I believe you."

"God's truth," he said.

"But it doesn't explain you, just them."

"They're the easiest part," he said. "What happened to me even Rip and Kenny...like...don't know. There's Barbara."

Barbara? Oh, no; but, of course. Why not? Somewhere in all this muck lurked a Barbara. My grade school had been driven crazy by the sudden bloom of sweet little Barbara with the pointy chest the mothers said was prematurely developed. The priests at Misery continually warned us there would always be a Barbara.

I felt sorry for girls blamed for boys' bad thoughts.

I felt sorry for boys driven crazy by girls.

I didn't like playing at being Father Confessor. The priests warned us that penitents always try to confess with too much detail. Don't let them. You'll only hear things you'll try not to think about later, or, worse, their sins will become your temptations.

Mike was frightening me. He was no longer a safe seminarian. He had a Barbara. He knew what his girl looked like.

"You know," he said, "with purity everybody's got trouble. Alone or with others. Like Barbara. At the beach. When I was a lifeguard."

"Your pastor spoke too late."

"Thanks like a bunch."

I wanted to ward him away from me. My vocation was too important.

"Barbara's a good person." He was focused on confessing. "I think the world of her, though I'll never quit because of a girl. She's only a small part of the picture. In July she told me, after we'd parked at the Point a few times, she thought she was pregnant."

"Fub!"

"I never went all the way with her. She admitted it was someone else's. Ryan, I prayed that night for her like I've never prayed for anyone before.

She went to the doctor and he said her tubes were clogged."

What had to be the last barrage of rockets and flares popped and exploded over the rooftops.

I was trying to be matter-of-fact. But I wanted to laugh. I had to control myself. After Ordination, I could not laugh in the Confessional at the comedy of it all, because sin could send sinners to burn forever in hell. No sense of humor could change that.

During Mike's Confession, I had been afraid he'd seduce me to sin by example, by teaching me a tempting thing or two. But "tubes"? I vowed that after Ordination, hearing Confession for real, I'd not allow so many details.

"The doctor gave her some treatment and that was that. I don't know if she was never pregnant or if it was my prayers. At any rate, this mess adds to my terrible certainty that I don't belong in the priesthood. Doc and Julia have got me nearly to the edge. They want me to go back to Misery and talk to Karg and Gunn and maybe Polistina. So I'll know my own mind—which I'm nearly out of."

"Mike, what can I say? In a million years, I wouldn't know anybody's mind. Even my own. I can't push you either way. Why not at least finish your last year of college at Misery?" I couldn't lose him and Dick Dempsey the same September. "At least try it."

"I've tried it for seven years, Ryan. For seven years, we've been best friends, and you know nothing about me."

"You don't know your own mind. Go back with me to Misery and look at your vocation in the context of the seminary, where vocation is real and has objective value, and is not a joke to guys like Rip and Kenny. That's all I ask. Come back in September."

"What time are you scheduling the miracle?" he asked.

"Mike, don't," I said. "You can always be an undecided plumber or an undecided salesman."

"But not an undecided priest."

"Not an undecided priest."

Huge blooms of raining color burst in the night air.

"Thanks," he said. "I mean it, Ry. Thanks."

"The evening ends?" I asked.

"You go to bed. I'll sit awhile longer on the porch."

All around me in his bedroom were his things, all the junk a kid collects over the years and never throws out till all on one day. I figured Mike, like every other kid, had a shoe box full of stuff, but this kind of stuff! I had never thought of Mike being in the back seat with anybody, but I began to wonder what I would do if I ever climbed into a back seat, which I'd never do. The thought made me giddy. I mean, I stopped even picturing such a scene, because I didn't want to sin with that girl, that blonde girl from the lake. With the wired breasts, *no, my God!* I had to drive home on the highway and couldn't afford to go to hell for an impure thought.

Suddenly, I hated summers in summer places that threw us protected boys out into a wild world that asked questions, worse than Rip's, we couldn't answer. Misery, I had expected, to tell me everything, but I heard nothing. At least, I knew I knew nothing. I was glad I was not like Mike, not like other men. I had that special priestly grace setting me apart. Summertime was hell and maybe the priests would be right to do what was rumored: send us off to a secluded villa for the summer, to be alone and safe together, away from the clutches of the devil and the questions of the world, and all the wiles of Barbara.

In five years, the bishop would send me forth, baptizing and preaching. I was a child compared to Mike. How could I ever handle the priestly situations that might arise in real life? I felt hot, all wrong lying in that strange room in someone else's house. I knew all my life would be spent in rooms that weren't mine, in houses that were strange, taking orders obediently from old men.

What is it like in a rectory at night?

I grasped at straws that might delay my Ordination. Tuberculosis or something from the movies like a war. Anything, because so much was to be done to me in such little relentless time. *Tick. Tick. Tick.* The sacrament of Ordination to the priesthood puts a permanent mark on a man's soul. Once a priest, always a priest. Forever.

Mike lounged nervously out on the porch. He had found some cigarettes, stale ones, he had shouted, in the drawer. I threw back the clinging sheet, and knelt by the bedside in my swim trunks. My senses glutted with everything I had seen driving up, at the lake, and all I had heard tonight.

Something very loud exploded over the house and a rectangle of light from fireworks outside the window fell across me.

Dear God, I prayed, when one looks at girls for the first time, he's delighted by what he sees. That's fine and normal, but I should have done that at fifteen, not twenty-one. I'm even behind the normal calendar of my life. I'm too afraid to actually sin mortally. I have no idea of what goes on in a back seat. My conscience is too blunted to perceive the refinements of many venialities. I'm neither hot nor cold, Lord. *Hardening.* Don't vomit me into the pit. Every noble intention I had for the summer, every thought of Mass, meditation, almost of You, Oh Lord, has been drowned in the rush of this beautiful world, the land of love and sweetness for which I long but give up for You. *I don't want this pleasure.* It's the hurt of the wonderful things missed, gone-by, time-passed, when I'm alone. *Take this pleasure away.* My prayer is never good. My prayers are emotional sedative at one time, emotional catharsis at another. That's why I flounder so easily, why the world can swamp me, and not let me give a clear answer to people like Kenny and that stupid Rip. I will try harder, Lord, so I don't lose out like Dick and Mike. I will be Your priest and life will be hard. *I will never interfere with myself.* Because I've started to be good so many times, I have the habit of beginning and not the habit of perseverance in anything. I've got to find me in reality, Lord. Help me define my vocation. I'm kneeling here, on this hard wood floor, asking. Even my problems aren't real. *Please don't let me feel this.* I don't have a real bit in my body. Mike proved that tonight. Nothing will ever happen to me, unless I make it happen. Amen.

I knelt stock still.

In the hall, Doc banged into the bathroom, making asthmatic sounds. Then around the cracks in his bedroom door his light went out. Mike came in from the porch, dropped off his clothes, and crawled into the other bed. I heard him rustling the covers, settling down on the old creaky roll-away. Finally the room was silent around me as I knelt there, hiding myself, but only for a minute. One last burst of fireworks lit the room.

"For God's sake, Ryan," Mike said. "Get in bed."

5

September 1960

Eight weeks later, the first day back at Misery, Mike Hager ran down the front-porch stairs. He had decided to come back for our senior year in college.

Wearing black street clothes, I approached him from my taxi.

Tentative, somewhat embarrassed, he brushed at his cassock still wrinkled from the crush of summer storage. "What the fub," he said. He took one of my two suitcases and walked me down the long corridors to my room.

I avoided saying I was glad he had come back to get unscrewed. In fact, for weeks we talked around the summer, knowing his late-night Confession happened, pretending he was a full-spirited seminarian in his black cassock, pretending we had never talked at all in the summer.

Misery taught us to work around certain facts of life. The priests warned us: "After a vacation, never come back to the seminary because you've a habit of returning, or because you like communal life, or because you're afraid of the world." For me, each willful return to Misery became a greater tryst with grace. I wanted the priesthood with every fiber of my soul, but I hungered for some priestly fraternity more than the adolescent regimen of seminary life itself.

Seven years a seminarian, I was twenty-one, and desperate as a puppy for the priests to begin to reveal the words of their sacred mystery, to let me know from the inside out what it felt like to be a priest. My own uncle, the Reverend Ryan Leslie O'Hara, seemed totally indifferent to me in my vocation. He had his own private life as a priest, continuing to minister to hundreds of soldiers from the War. He stayed away from Misery, which was a far more famous and endowed seminary than the Kenrick Seminary where he studied. Maybe he was jealous. Maybe I wasn't good enough for him. Maybe he wanted to be the only priest in our family.

I loved the rich medieval life of study, prayer, and work. But each September, I grew mournfully homesick. By November, my longing for the summer turned into eager expectation of Christmas. My vocation, after all, was not to live in a seminary boarding school, but to be a parish priest working in the world. The seminary was a test of worthiness. So I diverted my agonizing for the world into tightly scheduled classes, exams, prayer, play, and work. I could only become a model priest by learning how to be the ideal seminarian. I never pitched a softball game where I didn't mean every pitch as an ideal pitch. Every class of the twenty-six hours a semester I aimed for the highest grade.

The silent priests, hands tucked up their sleeves, treated us ever harder, ever tougher, running Misery as a spiritual boot camp to make us earn our vocations. We had dues to pay. We were soldiers of Christ. Our goal lay in a most desired Jesus. Time and self-discipline were keys to success. So I kept climbing, each bright new September, back into the gladiator arena to witness to Christ that I was strong enough to be buffeted by other boys, educated by distant priests, and clever enough to survive to my Ordination Day.

Mike set my suitcases at the door to my room. If ever a seminarian crossed so much as the toe of a shoe over the threshold of another boy's room, he was shipped. Mike stood the required six inches back from my door so his whole body could be seen down the length of the hall.

"I'm glad," I said, "that you came back."

He said, "Yeah," and left me in my room.

The desk and the bed smelled not yet of me, but of the institution closed in antiseptic quarantine upon itself for the summer months. I piled clothes into my drawers, vowing to keep the white underwear stacked neat, knowing the reality that I was not the kind of boy whose socks ever stayed tucked away in tidy rows. My vocation absolutely needed the priests' discipline. To be alone at Misery for four months, with theater and lectures and concerts suspended; to be lacerated like the old monks with discipline, and worse than they, with loneliness; to be whipped into shape if I could not love my way to the grace of a vocation.

My tiny room closed in about me. Very *Pit*. Very *Pendulum*. Breathless, I pushed my empty suitcase on the shelf over my bed and desk. To flee the sinking sense of abandonment, to flee the panic of isolation, I left the other suitcase half-packed. I pulled on my black wool cassock. My body disappeared into the perfectly tailored shoulders and chest that dropped straight down to my black shoe tops. Black trumped the colors of the world.

I ran downstairs toward the laughter in the recreation room. Ping-pong balls popped back and forth. I shook hands with seminarians selling and trading cassocks they had outgrown over the summer. Lock Roehm had not yet arrived.

Mike sat alone on a window sill with an outdated issue of *Commonweal* magazine, which was the epitome of the serious Catholic press. He was intense as a Jesuit.

One boy, showing off on a bet to ten boys, stuffed a full pack of twenty cigarettes in his mouth and lit them all at once, puffing and huffing and choking to rounds of cheers.

The chatter in the room buzzed around Dick Dempsey and other missing boys who had dropped out, or whose rumored quitting was not yet confirmed or denied by their signature, or lack of it, in the official book sitting on the Reverend Treasurer's desk at Misery's front entrance. Each seminarian competed to be the first to know of any other who had lost his vocation. The opening-day tension was electric. Shock wanted. Shock given. For the first day, the missing boy's name was gossiped about, wildly, as if some boys had privileged information, but in time, mention and memory of him evaporated.

Dick Dempsey was doomed to disappear. He had sent me no letter, only a picture card of Philadelphia postmarked on Labor Day and signed, *"Pax te cum, peace be with you. —Saint Dick."* Always he played back, as a joke, the boys thinking he was a special kind of holy saint. We had been best friends, but I'd never know how his vocation ended.

Rector Karg forbade us, under "consequences worse than the pains of hell," to have any communication with former students. "No letters. No visits. No contact. Nothing. Ever."

Dempsey's leaving Misericordia terminated our seven-year friendship as finally as death. Dropping out made a boy invisible. Any communication with such a dropout got a boy shipped out immediately. No questions asked. But my feeling for Dempsey lingered. He had been in my crowd.

"Ex-seminarians can pull you down," Hank the Tank said. "We've only twenty-one classmates left out of our original eighty-four..."

"Eighty-six," I said.

"...somebody's done," he insinuated, "a lot of pulling to reduce our class seventy-five per cent in seven years." He eyed me suspiciously. "Weren't you a special friend of Dempsey?"

"Me? A friend of the president of the Friends of the Friendless Friends?"

We actually smiled at each other. "Hank." I greeted him by his right name and he called me mine. "Ryan." It was good to see the friends. And the enemies. Good to be warm to them, sensing their resolutions to come back and be Christ-like to you. But I knew, inside my human heart where no one ever entered, the truce might last a day or so before hostilities resumed where rivalries had left off in May. The venom and crotch-kicking would revive, deep as ever, and cliques of skirmishing boys would shift territorially shoulder-to-shoulder during chapel sermons about the primacy of charity in loving one another. The loving fraternity of seminarians was defined by grades, looks, sports, and piety.

Lock said, "The biggest sin at Misericordia is uncharitable speech."

The three of us, Lock, Mike, and I watched good resolutions disintegrate into calumny, slander, short-sheeting, and pink bellies. No one ever terrorized me that way, never held me down, never slapped my belly red, because I announced to everyone, I'd kill anyone who touched me at all, except, of course, in the on-going wrestling match.

Scandal launched our senior year in college. What started as a double-dare joke at a pinochle table grew into the Great Bermuda Shorts Rebellion.

Ohio's Indian summer turned Misery each hot October into a rain-tree garden of dusty flaming color. Long cobwebs drifted lazily through the air, caught silver, and matted across the shoulders of black cassocks. Brushed off, the webs floated up again on the lazy heat, tangled in the apple trees bent for harvest, and sailed out toward the sun. Across the long flaxen field grass, the trees in the deep woods crackled yellow.

The first autumn leaves fell into the still pools alongside the forbidden river that rolled slow and beautiful on the western edge of Misery's acreage. Leaves sank halfway under the quiet, clear-green water, suspended, beautiful, as if no winter rain would ever come, *wild river*, muddying and brown, to freeze them brittle upon the slate gray banks where boys, in warm weather and cold, often smoked and waded and skated against all the rules, because the river was out of bounds, *forbidden river*, and we were never allowed to leave the property. The river was the Beyond Which Not of Misery's western front.

Rumors from Rome came with every letter about the approaching Vatican Council. Prayers in English began to replace Latin in the Mass in the scorching October when a pair of seminarians appeared on the tennis courts wearing Bermuda shorts. Their daring display rippled through Misery. In Rome, the Pope was planning to convene, *aggiornamento*, all the bishops of the world to open a window that would let a breath of fresh air blow through the Church.

The next day two things happened: a seminarian played a guitar during Mass while we all sang "Michael, Row Your Boat Ashore," and later in the morning, a doubles set of four more boys, tentative in their own Bermuda shorts, joined the first pair.

None of the faculty noticed the high jinks. The priests were busy arguing the canonical correctness of whether a priest should say Mass the traditional way with his back to the congregation, or the new way, facing the people. The most senior seminarians, about to be ordained, wondered would facing 'front' or 'back' affect the design of their new gold-and-white Mass vestments.

Father Gunn, traipsing around in his full Marine Corps uniform, was preoccupied with a Misericordia reunion of military chaplains who had served in World War II, minus my Uncle Les who sent his regrets. "Who," Father Gunn asked me, as if I knew, "does that uncle of yours think he is?" He focused on me. "And what does that make you?"

I ran from Father Gunn. I loved my Uncle Les.

The following Saturday afternoon a Roman holiday spirit swept the softball fields as one or two boys, then whole teams of seminarians, appeared in Bermudas cut with scissors from black khaki wash pants.

Rector Karg made no comment. He paced the faculty walking path chain-smoking cigarettes and knuckling his black rosary through his fingers. He was nervous, in a personal retreat, isolated away in his dark front quarters, waiting for the latest alarming gossip from the planners of the Vatican Council in Rome.

Sunday the temperature reached ninety-six. Monday was hotter. By Tuesday, our black wool cassocks, wet from three suffocating days in chapel and classrooms, began to break unnaturally in their drape, about knee-high. Wednesday, shortly before noon, the fad escalated to barely disguised sniggering when a seminarian crossing his legs in Father Polistina's philosophy class hitched up his cassock and revealed an expanse of bare leg.

Still the priests said nothing. Thursday and Friday the movement spread, a week old. Boys began to take sides. In the overheated chapel, audible gasps, pro and con, interrupted the Gregorian chant as here and there, entering in procession, boy after boy genuflected, one knee forward, up, revealing through the slit in the cassocks the bare white flesh of hairy naked knees.

Saturday morning Gunn canceled our last study hall before noon and scheduled an unexpected assembly in the auditorium. He stood at attention in his dress blues.

"The ship's hit the sand." Mike sat next to Lock.

"As Cleopatra said to Antony," Lock whispered, "I'm not prone to argue."

Gunn called for silence, and exploded. "Three weeks you've been back here at Misericordia," he said. "Three weeks and already you stand in open rebellion. Another mutiny! I can somewhat understand you breaking rules three months from now. But at the beginning of the year, at least then, we expect you men to come back with certain resolutions. If you degenerate this far in the first three weeks, where will you be in three months?"

The hundred-forty seminarians of Misery's college department sat squirming in absolute silence.

"I have been busy in town," Gunn said. "I trusted you collegians to be beyond caprice of the high-school boys. But no. Not you overgrown boys. You've less internal discipline than the greenest boots I ever chaplained in the military. I need not mention what you've done. Your consciences will remind you not only of your breaches"—someone snorted a laugh—"of classroom manners but also of chapel reverence for our Blessed Lord in the tabernacle. There were naked calves in the chapel."

"How 'C. B. de Biblical,'" Lock whispered.

More snorts disguised as coughing.

"There is a poison upon us," he said, "and the only changes around here, Vatican Council or no Vatican Council, are changes I make."

In the nearly eight years I had known Father Gunn as disciplinarian, I had never seen him so viciously controlled. He was not lashing out, flailing in every direction. He had the focus of a rifleman sniping from the Dome of Saint Peter's.

"I know it will be nearly impossible to find the ringleaders of this insidious movement. But I plan, indeed, I intend to start right here right now. You will all stand."

"God, no," Mike said under cover of the sounds of the auditorium seats rising up.

"I intend to weed this hot bed." The set of his face had never been more calculating. "You will all hoist your cassocks up over your shoulders and file one by one down the aisle past me. If your bare limbs are showing, you will sound off as you pass. I will record your name which Rector Karg will add to his personal shit list. Action, I can assure you, will be taken. Some of you boys will be shipping out."

Even nervous laughter ceased at the fatal shuffling of feet as a long line formed through the room.

"Storm troopers," Mike whispered. "Never trust a German institution." In our fourth year learning "Hoch Deutsch" with Father Kleinschmidt, we were reading *Der Tod in Venedig, Death in Venice,* trying to figure out what Thomas Mann was actually saying about entrances and exits and gowns and uniforms as we translated him line by line day after day.

"Lambs right, goat knees left." Lock turned to me. "Are you washed in the Blood of the Lamb?"

I showed him my bare knees in my blue Bermuda shorts. "Goat knees," I said.

Ahead, first in line in front of Gunn, Hank the Tank stood with his cassock gathered up around his thick waist. Lock could see his chunky immodest calves. "Goat knees," he said.

Mike shuffled past Gunn. "Hager," he mumbled and let his cassock fall down his Bermudas around his bare calves.

"O'Hara," I said.

Lock came next, perfectly dressed as always, home free.

"Two-out-of-three boys: naked goat-knees," Mike tallied.

"Safety in numbers," I said. "Bermuda shorts: the new vestments in the coming attractions for *Vatican II: The Sequel.*"

"The most swift punishment I can mete out," Gunn said, "is to deny tonight's movie to this entire college department. No one will be allowed to watch *The Song of Bernadette.* The names I have collected certainly deserve no entertainment and you others deserve the same punishment, being collaborators in silence."

"What's the good of being good, Lock?" Mike asked. "You miss the first movie of the year same as anyone else."

In the refectory, we ate lunch in double-enforced silence, because Gunn was so furious he forbade us to talk at a meal during which talking was never permitted in the first place. In my sweltering room, I regretted I had been caught wearing Bermuda shorts. How could something that began as such a lark turn so serious that vocations ended up on the line with boys being shipped? I hadn't long to ponder before Mike and Lock coaxed me out of my room. "More absurdity?" I asked.

"Come on," Mike said. "Hank's got a bench down by Ski's garden."

The spring before, Ski had asked his mother to send him vegetable seeds so he could plant a garden in the woods near the pond we called Lake Gunn. He thought the spot secluded enough that no one would find it. But everyone knew and raided Ski's patch for what food it was worth, which wasn't much. Misery fed us, but we were five hundred growing boys who were always hungry. The German nuns who cooked for us served mystery meat gravied up in deep plastic bowls of noodles.

"Their specialty," Peter Rimski said his father said, "was pup-gullion where they'd take a pregnant dog and hang it by its feet and beat its belly till its guts fell out."

That's why the older seminarians taught the younger how to raid the priests' refectory, stealing their food and cigarettes. That's why we smuggled in food from the outside. Bad food caused bad behavior that led to a venial kind of scofflaw rebellion. All this meant that most boys felt no guilt stealing from the priests or stealing from the crop behind the pond where Ski had tried to grow his own food with a stolen hoe.

"I'll come," I said.

Lock had a transistor radio built into the false bottom of his shaving kit. Transistors made Rector Karg insane. Never before had radios been small enough to hide. Sputnik was shrinking the world in the space race. I threw in some candy bars my mother had hidden in my suitcase. Mike had nothing. He was trying scrupulously to keep the rule exactly, not to muddle up whether he had a vocation. That was his business.

The beautiful afternoon was ours, a chance to get away together from the turmoil about Bermuda shorts. No doubt, Father Gunn and Rector Karg would inflate the perceived disobedience to seize upon some boys they had been trying to ship out anyway, because they didn't any longer want to feed their faces.

Down in the woods, the slanting acres between Misericordia and the forbidden western front of the deep river at the bottom of the valley seemed a million miles away from Gunn's regimentation. If we could never leave Misery's five hundred acres, then we could disappear into the woods, thick with trees, moss, and gouged with dusty shale ravines where we exchanged the hot marble corridors of Misericordia for the golden October.

Mike skipped stones across the pond. He couldn't pass the still pool without tossing something in it. I felt, at least since I had been reading Teilhard de Chardin—one of the new anthropologically-minded French Catholic philosophers—that it was something atavistic he was expressing.

"Atavistic, my ass," he shouted, pitching another stone into the small pond, rippling the mirror surface into multiple circles. "Why do you think everything has a hidden meaning?"

"I think the reason people like the ocean so much," I said, "or lakes and rivers, is because one day man kind of crawled up on the shore. *Ka-boom*."

"Washed up," Mike said.

"It was a beginning," I said, "and we never forgot where we came from."

"If I was going to evolve," Mike said, "I'd never crawl up out of this pond on this shore. Little Lake Gunn isn't even a real lake."

"Gunn dug it with a road-grader."

"I prefer the river," Mike said. "It's natural."

We cut down the embankment through the undergrowth toward Ski's clearing.

"I mean," Mike said, "you know the lake's piss-poor."

"Quite the contrary," Lock said. "Boys piss in it all the time. Even Ryan's peed in it."

Mike stripped off a low branch. He flailed away at the brush ahead. We stopped.

Suddenly.

We stared at each other, *uh,* in one of those moments when truth surfaces.

"I wanted to get along in the seminary," Mike said to Lock. "Not to get in trouble." It was the first time Mike mentioned our talk of the past summer. "Ry said to come back and talk to some priest. I wanted to talk to Gunn, I guess, but I take one look at him and know what he'll say and do." He whipped at a small buckeye tree. "The rest of the faculty's worse. Wind them up, they say Mass and disappear for the day."

"Unless they come to inspect your legs," I said.

"Or to teach," Mike said, "which is worse."

"Congenital idiocy," Lock said. "Misericordia's holy reputation hides a history of intellectual incest. Take one student. Train him for twelve years to Misery's way of thinking. Pack him off somewhere conservative for a bit of advanced theological study. Recall him before he's finished, so he can teach for free room and board. Promise him if he's tractable he might someday get his doctorate in something not too worldly. Finally mince around so long both he and you forget the promise. Result: perfect blandness."

"The intellectual bloodline gets tired," Mike said.

"It's Appalachian when it's not Machiavellian," I said, leading the way toward the clearing. "That's no bench," I said. "It's a couch. Hank hauled it down here..."

"...on his back...," Lock said.

"...from Monsignor Linotti's suite. I think old Linotti died on it."

"Father Dryden," Lock said.

"Father Dryden," Mike said.

"Father Dryden," I said, "threw that cruddy couch out last week when he started remodeling Old Linotti's place." When Monsignor Linotti had died suddenly, alone, in his ascetic rooms, full of Greek classics, all Gunn had said was, "When you grow up and can't pee like a horse, see a doctor."

Six weeks earlier, the Reverend Christopher Dryden had returned to Misericordia, his alma mater, to teach. He quickly picked up a following. Boys favoring the progressive side of the Church announced a major breakthrough in seminary education: a faculty member observed speaking to seminarians outside of class.

Like a Kennedy, Dryden played tennis and touch football, and on Saturday afternoons after a game jumped into the traveling wrestling matches that continued like relay matches, boy tagging boy, on the lawns, in the gym, the halls, the dorms, the playing fields, the woods, the river bank, day in and day out, month after month, year after year. The wrestling never stopped.

Word was Dryden was a great guy, well rounded by his post-Misery years of study at Innsbruck and Rome. Brilliant. He could speak with authority on almost anything. One of the highest IQ's in Misery's history. The perfect model of the modern new-breed priest.

After the first week, I hated the Reverend Christopher Dryden for better reasons than his always jumping over the tennis net between sets. He usurped me. He quoted Catholic writers I felt were my Irish preserve. He knew Coventry Patmore's line that the poet Gerard Manley Hopkins was "the only orthodox and saintly man in whom religion had absolutely no narrowing effect upon his general opinions and sympathies."

Dryden was too much the wholesome type of priest pictured in the seminary brochures. No one could be that absolutely perfect, unless that kind of perfection was the secret of the priesthood itself. His kind of athletic good looks, exuding the untouchable masculine appeal that blooms in celibate men, was the kind that sets some women off on a mission to seduce virginal priests.

He seemed hired from some modeling agency as the perfect prototype for aspiring boys who hoped to secure some golden image of themselves in a seminary cassock and surplice. I never believed those seminary recruiting ads in the Catholic press any more than the ads around them for the truth about arthritis or how to be sure with the rhythm method.

Mike hit the late Monsignor Linotti's couch with his stick, flailing dust and dye out of the rotting print upholstery.

"Dryden's redoing Old Linotti's whole suite. Throwing out all the traditional early-Misery junk. He's reforming his rooms, he said, modernizing medievalism to make the medieval thoroughly modern."

"I bet Gunn never heard of that," Mike said. "If they didn't have it in the Marines, no one ought to have it now. Newfangled effeminacy. We got trouble in River City. Right here." Mike marched around the garden waving his stick like Robert Preston. Our glee club was always adapting show tunes for our concerts, censoring any reference to girls. We sang a song from *South Pacific* with new lyrics: "There is nothing like a steak." Such a twist, of course, only added mystique to the subtracted original lyric.

"What next?" Lock said. "What next?"

That precisely, I guessed, was what the whole faculty was asking about the dashing advent of Christopher Dryden. Something inside Misericordia was shifting on its axis. Years before, the seminarians had been docile, obedient, reading only the literature and philosophers required for class, and mostly outwitting the priests by drinking altar wine in the attic while sitting on the boxes of silks used for the Virgin's May altar. I saw color-slide pictures of one of those parties with seminarians, all fresh young veterans from World War II, later ordained priests, slugging smuggled bourbon right out of the bottle.

Gunn, I think, really preferred that kind of rebellion. It was easy to deal with. He caught them, if he could, and shipped one or two of the leaders. Then he had discipline. For awhile. Drinking didn't scare him, because he knew the thought behind a drink or two.

But with Dryden's coming, the old shenanigans had mutated and Gunn, consulting with Rector Karg, could not understand the refined edge of the new expressiveness. Change was blowing through the Church. On the sly, we read about the worker-priests in France who supported themselves at jobs and did not live in a rich rectory supported by their flock. Dryden had returned from two years at the Biblical Institute in Rome with a third glamorous year with the Vatican diplomatic corps, changed, despite all the formation of his years at Misery.

He had come back from the world to Misery. He had lunched with Sophia Loren, and he had met Fellini during the filming of *La Dolce Vita*, which was condemned by the Legion of Decency, and he had worked with Roman charities for destitute boys. He had sped through Rome in his own red Frogeye 1959 Austin-Healey. He was shocking. He spent time talking with the seminarians outside of class. Mike, who began seeing him for counseling, reported he gave a glimpse of priestly professionalism: what it was for a man to be a good priest on the human level.

Perhaps this priest was the priest I had hoped would initiate me fully into the inner secrets of the priesthood. He had introduced a new intellectual honesty. Our Misery education in humanities and theology had always been excellent even though rigid. Scholastically, Misery was the Oxford of Catholic seminaries, and Dryden was the new champion, at least, for those ambitious boys who planned to get ahead in the priesthood.

A few moral theology books written by the new breed of theologians approved by the Pope circulated more openly despite cautions by Misery's old guard. Boyish conversation became at times serious shop talk. Rules were kept and broken under a new rationale of personal responsibility that made Father Gunn angry and Rector Karg enraged.

"The Communists are bad enough," Karg remarked, "without this creeping socialism in the Catholic Church."

I hated Christopher Dryden, probably as much as Gunn did, but for different reasons. I disliked him as a person. Something about him I recognized without knowing what it was. Gunn resented his undermining Misery's safely institutionalized uniformity. I resented the way he made the priesthood into a show-business cult of personality. Dryden had emboldened, almost immediately upon his arrival in the small-town world of Misery, a disturbing shift in values. He was like one of those drifters in the movies who blows into town during a long hot summer and changes everybody.

His influence moved things fast. Suddenly, the unchallenged Reverend Disciplinarian, Father Gunn, ran into some opposition shipping a seminarian for reading books or for knowing the latest in Protestant biblical exegesis, though Gunn did construct an expulsion case for one seminarian caught reading Martin Luther's autobiography in chapel.

Books became a battle ground, and, though we shared a common roof, the faculty priests never knew a tenth of what went on. If, so quickly, the reading of rebellious theology books was allowed *sub rosa*, I went farther *under the rose* to read every novel and poem mentioned in our English class, even *Leaves of Grass*, which was so beautiful, I cried, and wondered why it was on the Vatican's *Index of Forbidden Books*. Unless a boy grew really careless, even Gunn wasn't so crazy as to try to explain he was shipping a seminarian for reading.

Getting even for many of the boys' late-night raids on the faculty food lockers, Gunn took to raiding our rooms, searching for books, transistor radios, and heating coils used to brew a cup of hot water for bouillon or coffee. Rector Karg himself conducted his own searches for forbidden books, magazines, anything that could justify him shipping out any boy who was wiser, and suddenly more aware, than they had bargained for. To protect true vocations from worldly poison, they needed concrete reasons to ship out the intellectually curious and the abstractly rebellious. Gunn grew clever building his shipping cases around, quote, minor infractions of the holy rule that fell into a not so minor pattern, unquote.

Misery had no mercy, especially on boys the priests had fed and taught and counseled for nine, ten, eleven years. It was not a time in church history for a seminarian to get careless or expose any weakness. I hid my shoe box full of personal things away behind some pipes in the boiler room where Gunn would never look.

"Beautiful day." Lock flopped onto the couch of the dear departed Monsignor Linotti. He peeled his shirt, planted his feet on a crate, faced the west.

"You'll burn with the late sun," I said.

"Here's a burn for you." Mike tossed a match at Lock.

"Watch it," Lock said. "You'll start the couch on fire."

"The burning of Rome," I said.

"Vatican II is burning down, burning down." Mike lit a cigarette and tossed the match at me.

"Lock's in the hot seat," I said, "on Nero's couch."

"Hank Rimski, the zero, is no Nero and no hero," Lock said.

Our ongoing war with Hank, his brother, whom Lock had begun to call "PeterPeterPeter," and all those holy seminarians who thought they were destined to be bishops and cardinals continued. Their attitude made the couch in the woods symbolic. Ski's garden had become their choice retreat. Hank said PeterPeterPeter and his crowd called the garden "Little Rome."

Mike lit a match. "Look at this." He set the whole matchbook on fire.

"You're demented." Lock stretched out his full length on the couch. "I'm not getting up."

"Wanna play Joan of Arc?" Mike threw the burning matchbook at the cloth-covered couch. The wind snuffed it out.

"Jeez, if you're really going to burn it," Lock stood up, "dump it over on the garden. The weeds are too dry out here."

We tipped the couch upside down. Mike lit the upholstery and the wind whipped a spiral of black smoke up into the bright air. "Ha!" Suddenly, brilliantly, fire engulfed the whole couch. "Jeez!" The wind cracked the flames. "Christ!" We retreated back from the blazing heat.

"Fire is amazing," Mike said.

"The whole woods will burn," I yelled. "We need water!"

"The pond's too far," Mike said.

"Throw dirt on it." Lock beat at the burning grass with his shirt. "Get that side of the clearing."

"Break up that crate box, Ry. Hurry." Mike stamped around on the burning grass, flames licking at his shoes.

We beat at it, clawing handfuls of smothering dirt. "Piss on it," I kept yelling at the visions of the goddam woods burning down, flames licking up Misery's bricks, burning the wood floors and desks and papers and books and chapel pews, melting the gold chalices and the gold tabernacle, fireballs shooting up the bell tower, flames roaring out the top, setting the bells ringing madly, like the fall of Troy, fire itself the flaming Trojan Horse, burning down the school house, sacking the seminary, like all the war stories in our Latin and Greek lessons, and Gunn shipping us out.

The wind funneled the main fire hot up through the frame of the couch that was blazing alone in the center of the garden while wider and wider a ring of fire spread out through the dry grass.

"Piss on it, goddammit." I really had never said anything like that before except once or twice to show off. Now the words seemed commanding. My heart pounded in my chest. We were choking on the smoke. But finally we beat the fire out. At the edge of the burned circle, grass smoked and died. The couch collapsed and crumbled all over itself on top of the scorched garden patch.

Lock and I laid down inside the warm circle of ash-white black, exhausted.

"Oh God," was all I said. "Oh God, Gunn would have killed us."

Mike was laughing, dancing, mimicking how I had kept screaming, "Goddammit! Piss on it!"

"This sure ought to fix Hank's buns," Mike said.

Lock, for the first time in his straight-A life, looked happily ridiculous, sitting with part of his burnt shirt in his blackened hand. Dust stuck all over him stripped to the waist. He looked like a wild blond Indian. I pulled off my sweatshirt to my teeshirt and tossed it to him.

We threw more dirt on the couch, and on each other, in a sudden wild dirt fight of dust and ash, jumping, wrestling, tossing each other to the ground, constantly changing two against one, everyone for himself in a free-for-all, until Mike stopped, leaving Lock straddling my chest, all of us screaming like Indians with laughter, leaping up, heading back through the woods to the school, laughing, running, the three of us almost hysterical with excitement, singing, "Cheer, boys, cheer! Old Misery's burning down! Cheer, boys, cheer! It's burning to the ground. The faculty will be run out of town. There'll be a hot time in the old Mis tonight!"

Hank the Tank was in a small basement room lifting a set of barbells and dumbbells Dryden had donated. We stopped at the door, still laughing, to make fun of Tank, who was working at making himself even bigger. Lock joked about how seminarians weren't sure about their body image. Dryden had talked Gunn into designating a special exercise room. Gunn at first protested such a gym would be temptation to a worldly preoccupation with the body, but Dryden reminded him of the disciplined Marines and their stamina.

Gunn half-capitulated and assigned over part of a boiler room, though he was by no means convinced of this kind of a *mens sana in corpore sano, a healthy mind in a healthy body.* Ever so often in assembly he made uneasy mention that it was all right to care for the body, but not to get all preoccupied with it, and not to eat spices or a lot of pepper, and not to look at it more than you had to for hygiene, and always to be sure to sleep on your right side with your hands folded across your breast so you wouldn't feel your heart beating and start thinking about blood and what it could do to a boy's body.

"Hey, Tank," Mike announced from the door, "we're from the Friends of the Friendless Friends Society and, we regret, we reject you."

"Drop dead," Tank said. He chewed a wad of bubble gum like chaw tobacco.

"Hey, Tank," I said from the door, "how much do you weigh?"

"What's it to you?" he asked. "You're all covered with dirt."

"The Tank used to be a two-hundred-pound weakling," I said to Mike, "and they kicked sand in his face at the beach. But they don't any more."

"Why not?" Mike said.

"Why not?" I said. "They blacktopped the beach!" *Ka-boom.*

"Ain't you guys funny as a rubber crutch," Hank the Tank said. He turned his fat back to us, pulled at his seat where his hacked-off khakis had ridden up, cut the cheese at us, then rotated his shoulders, spreading them, arching his elbows slightly from the sides. He stepped and turned. Like a strong man in the circus, he faced us, squatted behind a weight, gripped it, and began a lift. Showing off, he inhaled.

"Sniff that cheese," I said. "Sou-ee!"

Hank the Tank stood up straight with the iron weight at his huge thighs, curled it to his chest. He face reddened with the exertion and a vein knotted down his forehead.

As he pressed the bar with all his force above his head, Mike said, "Down in Ski's garden we burned up your couch."

"You freaks!" He exploded. He dropped the weight to his knees, threw it rolling across the cement floor. "You damn freaks." He moved toward Mike. "Get out!" His voice careened up in pitch. "Get the hell out of here before I rip your balls off. Aaaaaaah!"

"You're screaming soprano," I said.

"I'll ruin you," Hank yelled. "I'll get you three shipped out."

"Tough toenails," I said.

We retreated to the hallway. Hank slammed the gym door. He was cursing and shoving chairs around.

"He was so mad his voice squeaked," Lock said.

We looked at each other, blackened by the smoke, and suddenly found the leg inspection and the fire and the weight-lifting tenor hilarious.

"What a day," I said.

"We sure snapped his jock." Mike was swept up into our horseplay, happy, as if he never had a problem with his vocation during the summer.

"Come on, Lock," I said. "Toss me back my sweat shirt."

The gym door opened. Light silhouetted Hank the Tank, who screamed in his enraged soprano: "The glee club! The choir! The chanters! You three will never sing in this seminary again. I'll see to it."

"You?" I said. "You and what army?"

September 26, 1960
The Kennedy-Nixon Debate

Within a month, Father Christopher Dryden's Sunday afternoon soirees collected all the best collegians into his newly decorated rooms. His open-door policy was shocking. An affront to the established order. Until his return to Misericordia, seminarians were never allowed into faculty suites. That policy changed after Dryden and Rector Karg were overheard in a noisy argument that emerged from Rector Karg's office in comic dialog balloons: *Never!* Yes! Change! *No!* Brave new world! *Heresy!* Papal decree! *Against my better judgment!* Thank you very much!

Dryden had arrived crisp with the fresh smell of Rome on him. He seemed backed by all the power of all the bishops of all the world who would be called to the Vatican by the Pope to remodel the Church. That power made him exciting to some boys, but Rector Karg thought such leanings dangerous. Allegiances changed daily. Pre-council anticipation fueled change. Pope John XXIII had set the Catholic clock ticking. A recording of the African *Missa Luba* experimentally replaced Gregorian chant. Out in the world, nuns free of full medieval habit were teaching Catholic congregations at Mass to sing "Kumbaya, My Lord, Kumbaya!" Inside Misery, I feared that vocations and virtues like purity itself were being cracked open, maybe even redefined to suit the institutional worldly side marketing Church politics.

I felt like a spy on an inside track, because a small Catholic publisher hired me through a friendly faculty priest to translate from German into English a three-volume moral theology text written by the Reverend Bernard Häring, who was consultant theologian to the theological commission preparing the agenda of the Second Ecumenical Council of the Vatican.

My translation of Father Häring's ground-breaking *Law of Christ: Moral Theology for Priests and Laity* was my first free-lance writing job, and I earned about the same as the French worker-priests: ten cents a page for fifteen hundred pages.

My classmates thought the job was glamorous, the book maybe dangerous, and the schedule probably impossible. I added the translation work to my full study schedule to consume myself, to lose myself, and to test the expansive reaches of my vocation. "Many are called," Christ said, "but few are chosen."

Mike attended Dryden's Sunday soirees weekly, out of gratitude, he said, for the excellent counseling help Dryden was giving him. He almost apologized, Mike did, with every report he gave me. He saw me react to Dryden's immense popularity by throwing myself into making Father Häring's long German episodic sentences translate into short colloquial English. As I translated sheet after typed sheet, the intent of the new theology became clearer to me. I saw my chance, secretly, to be Karg's worst nightmare. I dared loosen even more the tone of some of the author's opinions about sin. I became the old Roman maxim: *Translator, traditor, The translator is a traitor.*

During those Sunday afternoons, I played basketball with another, less complicated, crowd of boys who cared nothing for seminary suckups trying Dryden's Mass vestments on for size. My skin crawled, imagining them posing, sashaying, and gesturing like some Vatican fashion show. I myself never entered Christopher Dryden's suite—never, that is, until I found him more useful than provocative, because he had the first and only television set in all of Misericordia, and he used it like an apple in Eden.

"Jack Kennedy's debating Nixon tonight," Mike said. "Dryden got permission for a few guys to watch the special up at his place. Why don't you come, Ryan?"

"There's a movie tonight," I said. "*Moby Dick.*"

"Which the freshmen think is a disease."

"Bad sex puns. That's the level of humor in this German kindergarten."

"You're so uptight. Come on. Relax. Live a little."

"Kennedy I would like to see," I said.

"You can catch a gander at Chris' rooms." He knew curiosity had me. "Only six weeks to the election." We had all turned twenty-one, old enough to vote for the first time. "Right after rosary."

Father Christopher Dryden himself ushered me through his door.

"Welcome," he said, "to my drawing room."

I was not about to be strong-armed. I kind of laughed, "Uh!"

He was towheaded and lean, right for a tennis player. His priestly hand, gaunt with gristle and calloused, motioned me toward his couch which was eight feet long. Those boys sitting there shifted on the single long seat cushion, but the "settle" as he called it looked too straight-back to be comfortable, so I veered to a corner near his component stereo tuner. I gauged the room from my standing vantage. Almost all the boys were smoking. Three college seniors, smoking lavish meerschaum, *mirror sham*, tobacco pipes, lounged together off the seat and arms of one Morris chair, behind which hung a painting of John Henry Cardinal Newman, whose book *The Idea of a University* was hidden under my mattress.

His remodeling completely transformed the original Misery three-room suite. To emphasize the natural woodwork, he had painted the walls in schemes of greens, browns, and yellow, stenciled around the top at the ceiling. He had stripped the heavy curtains from the trademarked Misery windows and left them undraped to exhibit the light spilling in the clear glass at the bottom and the ornate stained glass at the top.

Six or seven top boys sat around the dark oak library table where a tall ceramic vase, decorated with irises, stood beautifully empty. Two other boys, each almost disappearing in two deep wooden chairs, lounged gesturing languidly with cigarettes whose smoke curled up under a stained-glass floor lamp.

On a green-and-yellow area rug, showing off the bare wood floors, three boys sat paging through an array of worldly magazines they found in the glass-fronted oak bookcase, on which sat a hand-hammered copper lamp with a mica shade like I'd only seen in old Marshall Field catalogs from Chicago.

Everything in the room, including a richly framed color print titled "A Converted British Family Sheltering a Christian Missionary from the Persecution of Druids," bragged that Dryden's family had money. This was not the cell of a worker-priest. Overhead, the indirect lighting from a suspended stained glass shade lit the room like a set in a play. I recognized the taste and tone from the mansion of the parish rectory where my Uncle Les was assistant pastor. More than one vocation to the priesthood was motivated by materialism.

Dryden had defined the wall opposite the door with ritual masks and spears and textiles brought from his Ordination trip to Indian reservations out west. Several black-and-white photographs, taken years before, featured real Indians standing stoically outside their teepees. On his dark and ornate desk sat a lushly baroque ceramic ink stand from Italy. A single lamp shown down upon it, spotting, I felt, his cocky Roman credentials.

Opposite, under a priceless Venetian triptych of Mary, Joseph, and the Child, stood a French spinet he had purchased in Florence. His one uncontrollable passion, he had told the Sunday group, was music. He invariably entertained them with his greatest classical hits each Sunday. He played the piano, his courtiers said, expertly. With music and readings of poetry, he charmed the suckups at his Sunday soirees.

This night, two seminarians sat on the piano bench and knocked out the usual four-handed duet of "Heart and Soul."

"Penny for your thoughts." Mike edged up beside me.

"This all reminds me," I said, "of a poem by Robert Browning."

"I like Browning," Mike said, "but I like Kipling better."

"I don't know," I said, "I've never kippled."

We specialized in refurbishing old jokes.

"A poem," I said, "by Browning. 'The Bishop Orders His Tomb at Saint Praxed's Church.'"

"Ryan, why do you always confuse literature class with life?"

"For the same reason you confuse Bible stories with life."

"Ape!"

"Monkey!"

"Beatnik!"

"When's the debate start?" I asked

"Half an hour."

I felt tricked. "You got me here early."

"To get a taste of Chris' style."

"It's bourgeois," I said. "Not worker-priest."

"Also, he wants us all to mingle first."

"So," I said shrugging, "that's the curse that goes with the diamond."

"TV or not TV," Mike said.

From Dryden's corner of the room, the conversation heated up.

"But our battles don't carry any universal overtones," someone protested.

"Ah," Dryden prolonged the syllable as a sign. The room quieted. "The causes," he said, bringing his topic to the fore, "for the defeat of the human condition lie often in the individual, but more often within the institution which subsumes him."

Lock stood up next to the spinet. "That's not really true," Lock said, uncaged in the free atmosphere Dryden generated. "People fight themselves and call it the institution..."

"The seminary," a voice interjected.

"All right, the seminary," Lock continued, "or the world or whatever frame it is they're involved in."

"You're on to something there." Dryden retrieved his upstage position. "Several years ago at Catholic University we heard some rather shocking gossip about Misericordia. You remember, that fellow who took the freshmen to the shower room."

"Porky Puhl," Hank the Tank said, "was in our class, but he was definitely not in our class."

Everyone laughed, ha ha.

"But he did 'measure up,'" Dryden said.

The courtiers roared.

Dryden poured something into a small glass. "It's good to ventilate some topics."

I grew wary hearing their lurid details about a shipped boy's impurity.

"What's he drinking?" I asked Mike in a whisper.

"Pernod," he said. "There's Coke for us iced in the bathtub."

Dryden sniffed his glass. "My theory on that poor fellow is that the seminary merely provided, by its very nature as an institution, the hothouse environment in which the individual's neurotic tendencies could bloom."

"Then there is something wrong with such an institution," Lock said.

"Maybe," Dryden sipped at his glass. "If one subscribes to the theory that people are good and institutions are evil."

"Do you believe that?" Lock said.

"This is 1960. A new decade. I believe that when people are evil or misguided or mentally ill, it is the institution to which they belong, be it country, corporation, or church, that is responsible for their dis-integration."

"Then you don't hold Porky Puhl responsible," Lock countered.

"For his curiosity, no. Was his question intellectual?"

"It was cock-eyed." Hank paraded his pun.

Ha ha ha.

"His guilt, I contend, is mitigated, and is inversely proportional to the guilt of the institution which fostered and fed the growth of his neurosis."

I pushed Mike aside. "Personal guilt is impossible? I have always taken personal responsibility for myself in the face of every impersonal institutionalization forced upon me."

"Bravo!" Dryden beamed as if I were a new devotee. "Proceed."

"I'm responsible for myself," I said.

Sporadic applause.

"I have a social consciousness."

Ha ha ha.

"Nevertheless I have a Roman Catholic conscience. So I wonder, what if I am wrong in my personal stand within the institutional seminary or the institutional Church? Then what?"

"Yes, then what?" Lock asked. "We stand up to Gunn and Rector Karg. We read books the Church itself has condemned."

"We risk getting shipped. We risk our very vocations," I said. "Trying to learn something about the world without becoming worldly."

"We now talk to you, a priest!" Lock said. "What a contradiction. For all these years, the priesthood is our ideal, but the priests—our teachers—are our worst enemies."

"How do we know," I said, "you're not a turncoat?"

"Or a double-agent?" Dryden said.

"Yeah," I intoned comically, ambiguously.

"You don't," he said.

"We need you," Lock said, "or priests like you, to teach us how to be effective personal agents for Christ. That's what a priest is. Yet as seminarians we're trapped in an impersonal tyranny Christ never dreamed of." Smattering of applause. "We're supposed to be the institutional Church, but we can't stand its present condition."

"As priests, as persons, we need some safe harbor," I said. "A priestly vocation shouldn't have to mean personal isolation. Now, with all this change from Rome, where do we stand? I have a vocation to priestly chastity, but what if...what if the Pope, during Vatican II, commands priests to marry..."

Ha ha ha. He he he. Ho ho ho.

"Ahhh, then!" Dryden was triumphant, "what would we all do? What would you do? Or you do?" He looked around the very anxious room. "Or you? If the Church suddenly commanded priests to marry!"

"What?"

"Shocking, isn't it? Look at your faces. What a thought. How our lives would change." He stared the whole room down. "Would you do it? Would you 'marry' on command the way you 'don't marry' on command?"

Dryden circled through his crowded smoky room, taking random ecstatic kicks at furniture and pillows and doctrine and dogma. "I am," he said, "a follower of T. S. Eliot. I subscribe to his theorem that the greatest treason is to do the right thing for the wrong reason. I also very much think that all institutions would be better organized along the lines of the religious communities of the Middle Ages. A modernized reorganization, of course. Perhaps into communes of peace and justice and love."

I stepped back to the shadow of the corner. "Mike," I said, "something's got to happen to me this winter or I'll die."

"Cool it," he whispered.

"You each do what you must for yourself," Dryden said. "People always do. Priests are people. As persons, you must withstand the impersonal institution for the right reason, the reason proper to your own existential soul. The impersonal must be resisted. Resist it for whatever reason is right for you, not solely for the fashionable sake of rebelling. This suite I have changed into a personal statement that nevertheless remains true to the worker-artists who built Misery with their own hands."

"Hmmph," I said.

Dryden stopped beneath a large black-and white photograph of himself sailing with Senator Jack Kennedy on vacation at Martha's Vineyard three months before in June. "Priests, you say, need safe harbor. So true. Priests ought to be more than prayer machines, vending masses to distract their libidos."

"Two-four-six-eight," a boy chanted. "How we gonna sublimate?" He was hissed quiet.

Dryden laughed and picked up the word. "Some physical sublimation must occur, but such purity must find intellectual or esthetic expression, or the person the priest is will crack up, go crazy, turn to the bottle. Christianity is, after all, the ultimate achievement of Greek culture. But always there has been, and is now, even in this sweeping time of change in the Church, too much sterility, loss, and defeat in the priesthood. There need be no sterility in intellectual life, or in spiritual life." He turned, sweeping in the whole room, "We are surrounded by beauty. We are ourselves beautiful creatures of God's grace."

I thought to myself, this guy has escaped from a cuckoo clock. "This year," I whispered to Mike, "something's got to happen to me."

"You won't be a seminarian all your life," he said under his breath.

"Thank God! In four years, I'll be a priest!"

"You've got two hands." Christopher Dryden stared straight at me. "Start wringing them."

Everyone laughed. I pulled at my Roman collar.

"Resist institutionalization to the degree you must," Dryden said. "You must resist, if you have," he glanced my way, "any conscience. Make a stand, passive if need be, but a stand, a commitment, someplace in your intellectual life. There's no difference between praying and thinking."

He took a long dramatic pause that pulled the focus of every boy to him.

"If pushed by any institution to give up your intellect, your will, or your personal conscience, you must consider rebellion, civil war, disobedience. Even the bishops eventually to be seated at the Vatican Council cannot legitimately sit and argue about granting the right to the individual conscience. Every person has that right, bishops' ruling or no bishops' ruling. There is no such thing as a correct theology. The Church speaks, yes, but the Church has spoken, and the Church will speak. The verb tenses evolve. What the Church has said is not necessarily what the Church will say. The individual conscience, in the present, can live by anticipated future morality."

I almost liked him for redefining vocation in terms of the person who was called, and responsible personally.

"You all in one way or another," Dryden said, "must resist adolescence, isolation, and the lack of counseling the best you can. Opt for the original, personal experience of life," he said. "Don't settle for the institutional ritualization of experience. That can change, and is changing in Rome at this very moment."

He looked at his wrist watch, and gestured to a boy eagerly waiting to turn on the TV.

"This is no commercial," he said, "but I'm available at any hour to any one of you."

He dimmed the overhead chandelier. His twelve-inch television sprang crackling snowy to a stark rectangle of black and white coming live from Chicago.

Senator Kennedy smiling.

Vice-President Nixon nervous.

Questions.

Answers.

Quemoy and *Matsu.*

Kennedy trouncing Nixon with the two names of those two disputed Asian islands.

The television picture clicking, podium to podium.

Kennedy puncturing the air with his driving forefinger.

Nixon leaning back, clinging with both hands to his lectern.

Barrages of the right words. Kennedy unloading, growing more handsome, articulate, self-assured, youthful.

Nixon disagreeing, his lack of a forefinger, the words not coming, the sweat running down his nose, streaking the pancake makeup he used to hide his five-o'clock shadow.

Dryden's close, crowded room, dark, boiling with smoke, silhouetting heads wreathed with rolling blue halos of burning tobacco.

I was amazed, transformed, transfigured.

Irish Jack Kennedy was the first politician I'd ever seen who didn't look as old as my grandfather.

Leaving Dryden's for night prayers, Lock said. "Some advisor should have informed Nixon, off, exactly, what continent those two islands are."

January 20, 1961

The evening of President John Fitzgerald Kennedy's Inauguration Day, the after-supper ritual of our small lounge room was more excited than usual. The talk in the dim parlor, made dimmer by the smoke of the cigarettes allowed only in this room, pursued the new reality of our lives in the televised events of the Inauguration. Jack Kennedy was a new dawn of a new day. The feeling was palpable. The Oath of Office in the freezing snow. Himself, Kennedy, redheaded with a top hat, usually so bareheaded.

Cardinal Cushing reading a prayer while white smoke, like a hopeful omen, wafted out of his lectern from a short circuit. The ancient laureate Robert Frost reading his new inaugural poem in the biting cold Washington breeze. The triumphant parade through streets plowed clear of the deep snow that had blanketed the city quiet the night before.

John Kennedy was the ideal Catholic man. In our priestly quest for manliness, I wanted to be like him. I fully understood in my priestly heart what he meant on all levels, even the religious: "Ask not what your country can do for you, but what you can do for your country." The way my uncle had served as a priest-chaplain, I would be a worker-priest.

The air in the crowded lounge was blue. Cigar smoke, because Catholic Jack Kennedy smoked cigars, hung like a rug vibrating with the upper reaches of Puccini spinning rpm's at the delicate fingers of the opera crowd who fantasized political connection between Washington and Rome.

Christmas vacation had ended less than three weeks prior to Jack's exciting inauguration, so I was depressed, gasping for breath, afraid the old stuffed furniture would fold around and smother me in its worn unhappening arms.

A boy who carried himself as if he would be bishop turned the stereo louder. I cursed him, afraid I would never surface for air, suffocating in the room jammed with determined young men all dressed in black.

I was making extra visits to the chapel during play time to stare up at the huge crucifix over the main altar where hung the Christ I was to become when, as a priest, I became an *alter Christus, another Christ.* I always lived alone among all the other boys, but in the chapel, I could be left alone. I had been studying hard. Twenty-eight semester hours in physics and philosophy and modern history. Trying to decipher whatever anyone said about the needs of priests. Not only the way priests studied, and not only the way they administered the sacraments, or said Mass. Wondering how priests actually lived, minute to minute, how they felt emotion, how they handled temptation. Translating the daring Father Bernard Häring's German moral theology trilogy. Writing on the side for the Catholic press. Determined feature articles about *brazeros*, Mexican migrant workers. Winking allegorical short stories about "The Untimely Death of Juan Cristobal." Driven poems about men and women too busy in the world to realize all the grace God poured on them.

I wrote one feature article about James Dean, who had been dead only four years. To get it published, I passed it off as a moral cautionary tale: "James Dean: Magnificent Failure." Rector Karg, who censored every word of writing any seminarian mailed out, okayed the sinner angle, but said no one would publish it because James Dean was the glorification of sickness. He was very angry when he opened my incoming mail and found that the first place I sent it, *The Catholic Preview of Entertainment*, bought the fifteen-hundred word piece for two cents a word.

"Don't let it go to your head," he said. "Of course, you'll be donating your royalty check to the fund for the poor students, *die arme Studenten*." He handed me a pen to endorse the check. "I always keep my eye on you, and your accounts."

"Thank you, Rector," I said. I knelt down. I handed him my first royalty check. "Would you please give me your blessing?"

I had a seminar paper, "How Asceticism Leads to Mysticism," to finish and I was dead tired, an absolutely perfect state for mysticism. All my activity was making me more and more introverted. So much time to think. Six chapel periods a day. Thinking was the same as prayer. Writing was thinking. *Ergo*, writing was prayer. The syllogism suited me.

The priests said to look in on ourselves and find our identity and shape ourselves to Christ's priesthood. I was finding identity, or at least ego, but only between moments of almost compulsive plotting of story lines and distracted delectations on morose fancies that might lead me to find a potentially popular song hit to be lifted out of the hymns we sang, the way "Love Me Tender" came out of "Aura Lee."

I read *The Roman Martyrology* looking to adapt story lines of love and death and faith. I tried to discipline our long periods of classroom lectures, study hours, and meditation, like Gunn said, all the while we were tutored in the manly ways a priest must conduct himself.

"A priest can never be too masculine. A priest must be a man's man." Gunn advised that when we sat in the privacy of the rows of toilet stalls, we should concentrate on dropping our voices down to where we wore our jockstraps to make our voices deeper so our sermons would impress the men and women in our parishes. Sometimes, in the jakes, when all the stalls were filled, the room echoed with boys intoning, each competing to be deeper than the others, the first four notes of "Old Man River." All advice in any boys' school spins into jokes, satire, resistance.

Nevertheless, I prayed for the revelation of some priestly mystery to come and shine itself on me my senior year in college. I knew I was not like other men, not even like most of the seminarians sitting in the lounge arguing over "Kumbaya." But each is God's image, I thought, and God has many facets. They're drips, the Drips of Dryden, the way other boys were the Sons of a Gunn, and all were the Friendless Friends.

I vowed to respect both sides and worry only about the impossibly huge job of perfecting, dissecting, correcting myself. No one had appointed me referee in the seminary civil war. I had no right to force other boys to my choices of natural discipline, working my own way to mysticism through asceticism, physical penance, extra fasting, inserting a pebble in my shoe to hurt my foot when I walked, tying a hemp cord around the skin of my waist.

My vocation roared inside me. A fever was upon me. Perhaps I was not meant to be a traditional parish priest, or a French worker-priest, or even the editor for some bishop's diocesan newspaper. What if I were a mystic, like Father Polistina, in the Mystical Body of Christ? What if Christ's Stigmata, His Five Precious Wounds, opened in me and I began to bleed from actual wounds in my hands, and feet, and side, and ate nothing but the Communion wafer, and lived to be really old like saintly Padre Pio in Italy, curing people with my touch?

I knelt alone in the chapel. The red sanctuary lamp, signifying Christ's real presence in the gold tabernacle, burned steady in the half-light. Gunn startled me. He came from behind and tapped me on the shoulder and said, "Why aren't you kneeling up in those front pews? It's Church Unity Octave Week, but why save the best seats for the Protestants?"

I had to say, really say, I preferred kneeling in the back. For perspective.

"We can be," Father Gunn said, "too ecumenical. Move up and kneel in the first pew. The real reason you're back here is you don't want to miss seeing everything that goes on. That's your main problem, O'Hara. As God is my witness, O'Hara! Oh ha-ha! You think you are God's witness. You've got a lot to learn," he said. "You're no judge of us. You think you're something. Just like your uncle. You're nothing."

Gunn rattled me more ways than one. He was so crazy. He was jealous I had an uncle who was a priest who had been a chaplain exactly like him. Gunn pressured me because Karg was pressuring him because the Pope was pressuring the Church.

"Gunn and Karg are the Iago Twins," Lock Roehm said. "No one understands their motives. Not really. Not even them. Not any of us."

I always took Gunn and Karg, like all priests, at face value, always interested in my own good even when I failed to perceive what I needed.

Later, Lock stood in the doorway of my room. He motioned me out to follow him.

"What is it?" I walked fast down the hall after him.

We passed the closed door of the lounge room where everybody's favorite hit album, the Ray Conniff Singers' *'S Wonderful*, was playing. Lock dragged me into the corner darkness under the stairwell. "It's serious," Lock said. "Something's up."

"Way up," Mike said. He was waiting for us under the stairs. "Something bad."

I sniffed the smell of sin, of possible impurity, but in charity I could not flee from my two best friends. Besides, backstairs gossip was the salivating heart and soul of Misery.

Mike gushed with suspicion. "I've been seeing Father Dryden for counseling since September, four months," he said. "Believe me, without Dryden I'd have left Misery long ago. He encourages my vocation, but today he said the strangest thing, for no reason at all. He just said it."

"What did he say?" Lock demanded.

Mike looked at both of us. "Praying to have a nocturnal emission."

"Uuh," I said. My heart sank to the pit of my stomach.

"Dryden said it's okay," Mike said, "to pray to have a wet dream."

Anything but that, I thought. This was the heart of vocational danger. Could the new Vatican II theology be that progressive? Dear God, don't throw me in that briar patch.

Mike laughed at me. "Ryan, don't look so horrified."

"What's the punch line?" Lock asked.

"God's truth, Lock," Mike said. "Dryden says he prays for release all the time. As long as you don't touch yourself or do anything to cause it but pray for it."

"Pray for the spray!" Lock folded his hands in mock piety.

"Uuh," I said. I had never touched myself. I had never, would never, interfere with myself. Self-pollution was a mortal sin. I was afraid of burning in hell, alone, *nobody loves me*, forever in an agony of pain. Protestants and Jews don't know the secret penalties on Catholic boys.

"What are we going to do?" Mike asked.

"Stop finding loopholes," I said, "in the Ten Commandments."

Lock, incisive as the canon lawyer he hoped to be after Ordination, said, "I live for loopholes. Let's play detective and find out what Dryden's told other boys."

"Where there's talk, there's action," Mike said.

"Don't be scandalous." I turned away from them. "Let it alone. Prudence dictates we keep our distance from sin."

"Ryan," Lock grabbed my arm, "this has to be handled right."

"Don't start a witch hunt," I said. I'd seen what witch hunts had done to Hollywood. My forbidden reading under plain brown wrapper had evolved from novels by Charles Dickens and poetry by Walt Whitman to dramas by Arthur Miller like *The Crucible*. "We've got trouble enough with our own vocations. Let Dryden alone. Pursue this line and we're lost."

The bell ending the brief evening recreation period rang. The door of the lounge room opened to the hallway.

"Up, everybody," Hank the Tank yelled, "the wee-bitching hour."

He walked past us shaking his cassock down around his legs. His brother, PeterPeterPeter, was only eighteen months from Ordination, and their father, Mister Gustav Rimski the Huge, had come to visit several times to sit on the Board of Directors. Tank's family was everywhere at Misericordia, and he was full of himself. He walked up the stairs past us, leaned over the rail, and looked down on us.

"My, my," he aimed at me, "you're so young to be going bald on top. Your Ordination photo will look like Yul Brynner."

"Yours will look like Liberace."

I hated him. He was the first person ever to mention my deepest secret: my hair, like everything else about me, was exactly like my Uncle Les.

Tank shook his head. "'S Wonderful!" he hissed at the three of us.

"'S fub duck," Mike said.

"Jeez!" Lock said. He asked me again. "Will you help us get Hank, Ryan, and guys like him?"

Were we starting to decide who had a vocation?

"Yeah," I said. "So much for philosophies of 'I and Thou.' I guess I need to learn to listen." Sooner or later, a seminarian must start training for the rigors of the Confessional, where people who do everything can say anything.

The lounge crowd milled past us, out the doors, talk dying, stubbing cigarettes, still exhaling on the stairs, smoke rising up the chimney of the stairwell toward the chapel. I was afraid among them, the marionettes, marching up in line, wondering who was praying for nocturnal emissions. More than ever I lived alone in that crowd of boys. Their talk, their gestures, all more advanced. I was twenty-one and not feeling adult. Possessing vocation, same as theirs, aching to identify my specific priestly vocation. The throes of my adolescence, I called it, the last throes.

I felt the child in me, the boy in me, the *hey, kid*, in me telling me he did not want to leave his innocence, his purity, his joy, just so I—as if *I* were not *he*—could grow up, turn into a man, an adult, and a priest, but only if I grew away from the boy.

None of the other seminarians seemed ever to have spiritual crises about the obligation of growing up. They all loved acting grown up. All their crises were the predictable pecking-order problems with grades and sports and who was sucking up to whom. I felt no connection to ambitious older boys, closer to their Ordination, whose talk ran to the money management of parishes and dioceses, like my Uncle Les who showed me how in his own church he placed loose change in the collection plate at the foot of the Virgin's statue, because "If you don't leave pigeon feed," he said, "people don't know what the plate is for, and you have to cover your expenses to keep your bishop off your back."

I hated my overwrought sense of the dramatic and entered the darkened chapel for rosary. Shuffling feet moved off into the assigned pews. I dipped two fingers deeply into the holy-water fountain. I felt suddenly close to them, all those boys, dipping my hands into the same bowl where they had all dipped, almost sacramentally.

"I have a social consciousness," I had foolishly said in Dryden's suite. They had applauded, and giggled, but their applause repelled me.

My closeness to them chilled to my usual distant freeze-out. *I don't love them.*

Their ordinariness repelled me. *They don't love me.*

Their obedient subservience injured my sense of free will. The well-trained goodness of all those boys, called to be shepherds of the flock, seemed taught by Saint Pavlov, the Patron of Salivating Dogs. They understood ceremonial piety. They were all so pious. So pietistic. So instantly able to hit a pose like a Holy Picture.

I wondered what was the nature of true spirituality. Certainly spirituality was more than liturgical pageantry. Even the truly good boys hurt me with their ordinary goodness, because they were ritualized beyond personality. *Hello in there!* They were walking clothespiles of black cassocks and Roman collars and white surplices. Whitened sepulchres, Christ had said.

I hated them, because if I was like them, no wonder Thommy had called me "Phoney, a fake," and I had to punch him. What if Thom, who lived like a man in the world, was right. What do real men really think of real priests?

Immediately, I prayed to be forgiven for my vain pride, to be given the grace to mature finally without going mad, so I could become like them, because I so envied their uncomplicated vocations, and was desperate to be exactly like them, *simplex, simple,* not *complex, complicated,* because under the watchful eyes of Gunn and Karg and all the other priests, they had grown so fub duck perfect.

The hypnotic counterpoint of the rosary recitation–Angel's words, *Hail, Mary,* followed by sinners' words, *Holy, Mary*–seemed form without function. I knelt unfeeling in the crowd of seminarians hailing Mary's like taxicabs. Before I could save parishioners, maybe I had to save these lost boys themselves. I wanted to reach out in the chapel to the five hundred dark figures kneeling around me and give them all I had. Would they applaud? I feared the crazy Russell Rainforth in myself, the modicum of self-inflicted insanity no one admits to, till it boils over and Saint Nicholas' helper socks you in the face and blood runs out from ears and nose and mouth and the priests tie you to a chair and cart you away to an insane asylum for lost seminarians.

I stared hard trying to find the dark tabernacle. What was it John Henry Cardinal Newman had written back during the Oxford Movement, sitting among the Pre-Raphaelites, when he had been silenced by his bishop? "Lead, Kindly Light, amid the encircling gloom."

When things were good, Oh Lord, we should have stopped all the clocks. *Tick. Tick. No Tick. Nothing destroys me but myself. Pitiable destruction. So small a chastisement for my words. Unfair I should find myself capable only of destroying myself. If You will to drive me mad, Oh Lord, do it from without. Make Hank or Gunn or Karg the villain. Them I can handle. Deliver me from within. Don't turn my very insides against me. Don't let me destroy myself. Let me understand. Make something full of grace happen to me. Make me start to live. Don't bring me to the steps of death. Don't ever let me die without being ordained a priest. You could...push me into the darkness... easily...so easily...as once before when from outside, during the War, banging the gurney into that blazing white surgical room, before I could talk, pulling at me, they gassed me, to push me back to where there was no word and no time. Oh God, why do I hold back? If my vanity can't have a perfect vocation, my modesty will settle for an imperfect one. Whatever is Your will. Why can't I admit for all time I have a vocation, exactly as required, so finally I can grow into it? Why do I resist my superiors? I am vain. I am prideful. I want to be a priest, Oh Lord. I'll bend my will. You know You called me; so help me answer Your call.*

6

Winter 1961

The pages ripped off the calendar like months passing in an old gangster movie. In February, to celebrate Saint Valentine's Day, we watched Glenn Ford in *Torpedo Run*. In March, the movie for Saint Patrick's Day was canceled because of Ash Wednesday.

"We have to keep it bent for Lent," Mike said.

He was no closer to his vocation, but I was. Mike's questioning of his vocation clouded his quest with even more doubts. My questioning my vocation drove me closer to my calling, my surety in the priesthood. It was Lock, not Mike, who first lost interest in prying into the case of Father Dryden. No boy in our college department admitted to anything even worth telling in Confession. Seminary life thrived on hot juicy gossip that was forgotten with the new scandal of the next day. But about Father Dryden the talk was all about the golden priest.

"I was rash," Mike said. "I got excited." He shuffled around. "I guess Gunn's military methods have gotten more to me in eight years than I like to suspect. Father Dryden's a good guy after all. Very intellectual, satirical, ironic. Maybe I took him too literally."

"You're as literal as a fundamentalist Protestant," I said. "Never accuse me of confusing literature class for life again."

"I never..."

"You always make fun of me when I tell you one thing can mean two things."

"Father Dryden is a strange man," Lock said, "but a good one. He's opening the intellectual window to blow some air through this place."

"Thank you, Sherlock Holmes," I said, satisfied, and went off, grateful everyone was being true to his vocation and obedient to the purity required. I knew unprovoked nocturnal emissions were not sin, but I never touched the deep sweet privacy of myself. I let God and nature surprise me with the natural nights in the throes of sleep. I woke with only vague images, saying, "Oh, my God, I take no pleasure in this!" Impure imaginings quickly disappeared under the icy shower spray. Quick towel. Buffing. Secrets ever silent. Temptation. Thoughts. Star. Starlet. Starlet's chest.

Our new Jesuit spiritual director, Father Sean O'Malley, S. J., suggested that impure thoughts could be driven out by thinking analytically of something else: how many boat trips to get four elephants across a river if the boat can only hold a thousand pounds and the two grown elephants each weigh a ton-and-a-half and the babies five hundred pounds apiece.

In Father Yovan's class in Moral Theology, five hours a week, two semesters, everything was either good or bad. A morality to everything. Nothing natural allowed for priests. *Uuh*. Nothing unnatural allowed for Catholics. *Uuh*. Amorality was worse than immorality because amorality was nothing, neither hot nor cold and worthy to be vomited from the mouth of Christ. A moral dimension for everything. No situation ethics. Nothing ever neutral or what personal subjectivity made of it. No private interpretation of the Bible: look at the Protestants' Bible-thumping problem with that.

No telling ordinary Catholics, because the laity doesn't understand specifics, that Rome discreetly permitted abortions in cases of rape or incest, because the fetus was an unjust intruder inside the woman's body, so she could use self-defense.

No allowance for imagination while discussing in Monsignor Undreiner's droning class in Dogmatic Theology, six hours a week, two semesters, how many angels can dance on the head of a pin. I shouldn't have asked Monsignor Undy what style of dance? Ballet? Modern jazz? I received good grades in the Introductory Sermon class, but Undy warned me away from too much creativity.

I looked up at him over the pages of the forbidden book I was reading in his class, under his nose, *Fifty Stories* by Ernest Hemingway, and said, "Yes, Monsignor."

May 1, 1961

By May first, May Day, the Feast of Saint Joseph the Worker, in the month dedicated to the Mother of God, we were very near final exams for our last semester in college. Because Saint Joseph, the husband of Mary, was a carpenter, Rome honored him on May Day as a retort to the Communists' celebration of May first as International Workers Day. French priests honored Saint Joseph as a patron saint of worker-priests.

Lock and I hardly bothered that our exams would determine which of us graduated at the top of the class. Our college graduation's real import meant we had eight years down and only four years till our day of Ordination to the priesthood. The last third of the way to the priesthood was all that was left. Making it to Ordination was our work. My goal was to become a worker-priest living in a bare room, praying, helping the poor and the sick and the dying reach peace in this world and heaven in the next.

I stood on the edge of Misery's pond, Lake Gunn, where my crowd hung out, listening to Lock and Mike, not watching them. The Ohio twilight lingered longer in the spring evening. On the smooth mirror of water, Misery's tower and its lights rocked upside down on the surface, disturbed only by night creatures. The full moon hung low enough to touch twice: once wet, once dry. It washed down the beautiful slate roofs of Misery far up on the hill. Bats, whipping through the air, swooped close to the water's surface, visible for an instant, then lost in the darkness rising from the pine woods around the small lake.

"Forgive me, Ryan, for telling what happened," Mike said. "Lock and you."

I laughed. "Something happened? Nothing ever happens." Oh, God! I suddenly realized this was one of those awful spontaneous Confessions. "What happened?"

His eyes glistened. "You and Lock," he said, "will understand. You said something's got to happen to you this year, Ry. Well, something happened to me."

"Dryden!" Lock said.

Mike nodded. "Today for my regular conference—every Thursday I see him—I told him: 'It's the end of the year almost. I want to really talk to you.' He said, 'We have been talking.' I told him, 'You've got to help me. No one else is here to help me.'"

Mike had the Catholic need to confess details I can recall more vividly than a movie, but then the story was told and retold so many times it became a famous scene, an inescapable, probably obligatory scene in the history of Misery.

"Michael," Father Dryden says, "we've worked all year, changing your doubts into, well, an examination of what actually is a vocation to the priesthood. The puzzle is solvable."

"Solvable?" Mike asks. He lights a cigarette.

"I think you're afraid of your feelings."

"You'd be afraid of them too."

"Michael. Michael. You're so much unlike everyone else. And so much like me."

Mike sits silent before the ornate desk and the Italian ceramic in the tasteful drawing room lit only by the small pools of light from the mica shades on the copper lamps.

"What do you think has been my mission here at Misericordia this year? I have caused this institution to vibrate. I have come back to bring it freedom." He leans intent over his desk. "Why do you think I work an eighteen-hour day, by my own choosing and authority as a priest, counseling enough of the student body to keep three full-time counselors busy?"

Mike sits silent, biting his lip.

"Are you going to sit not saying anything?" Father Dryden leans back and laughs. "You little fool. You poor little fool. You think you're going to come out of this with Ordination bells ringing. Well, Michael Joseph Hager, I am going to be honest with you. I am going to be so honest with you your head will reel." He leans forward over the ceramic. "But you've got to trust me." He pauses. "Will you trust me, Michael?"

Mike nods.

"You are afraid of your Self, Michael. Afraid of your body."

Mike shakes his head.

"Of course. You're thinking of all those things you told me. That business of the girl at the lake and so forth. But don't you see, you only did that because you were running scared." Dryden stands up and walks around the desk. "I know, Michael. I know how it is. I was once the same my Self. When I was a boy, my father locked me in a broom closet for fourteen hours because he caught the child next door examining my body." He sits on the desk and leans over Mike. "Which do you suppose was worse? The examination or the punishment?"

Mike blows out huge flumes of smoke. "What did you do?" Mike asks.

"I found my own true Self," the priest says. "In that tiny broom closet, I began to find my Self. After years of guilt and torture, I found my Self."

"You found yourself?"

"Yes. My Self. And the seminarians that come to me? I let each find his own Self. *Gnothi sauton, Know thy Self.* After that, the rest is easy." Dryden walks across the room to a closet door. "Stand up, Michael."

Mike rises.

"Jesus loves you, Michael. Body and mind. Jesus loves you." He opens his closet. "Take off your cassock, Michael."

"Why?" Mike asks.

"I want to hang it up. I want you to look at your Self. Here in this mirror on the door."

Mike hesitates. He begins to unbutton his cassock.

"Trust me," the priest says. "This is different than you think."

Mike hands him the cassock. He sees himself standing in the mirror, black khaki trousers and white teeshirt.

"Jesus loves you, Michael." Dryden stands next to the mirror. He and Mike's reflection stand together. "Your body is good, Michael. Good as your soul. Jesus loves both, because both are you. Jesus loves you. Do you believe that, Michael?"

"Yes," Mike says. "Yes, I believe it."

"Do you believe your body is good, Michael?"

"Yes, Father."

"Have you ever looked closely at your body, Michael?"

"Yes. Kind of, well, athletically, like, am I strong enough for football."

"Take off your shirt, Michael, and look at your body."

"I don't really think I should," Mike says.

"Relax, Michael. Your virtue..."

"Yes, Father."

"Virtue."

"Yes, Father."

"*Virtue* comes from the Latin word, *vir, a man, a male, the quality of a man, goodness.* Trust me." The priest advances a step. "Jesus cured many by virtue of His touch. Open your shirt. Let me touch you, Michael. Give me your shirt."

Mike retreats behind a chair.

"Don't be afraid," Dryden says. "Trust me."

"Look, Chris, I'm twenty one years old. I don't think you're right about this."

"You've got to believe." Dryden spills a stack of *Holiday* magazines across the floor. "The others believe."

"I'm not the others," Mike says. "I'm myself. I have that much identity."

"I'm a priest and I love you as I love the others." Father Dryden's bright eyes burn in his athletic face. "You've all been isolated here with no adult attention. Now you wonder what is the connection between a priest's natural body and the chastity of his soul. The other priests touch your intellect. You let them. The spiritual director guides your soul. You let him. But none of those priests really loves you. A priest needs to love the persons under his care. They need to know a priest loves them. Really loves them for what they are." He falls kneeling to the floor looking up at Mike. "Michael, I love you for what you are. A real priest loves you, loves you all." His hands palm-to-palm implore Mike. "Michael, you must experience true *ens-qua-ens, true being-as-being*, true beauty, true virtue, true manliness, true Self..."

———————————

In the May moonlight, Mike turned to Lock and me. "I knocked over his palmetto fans, dodged him to grab my cassock, and beat it out the door. That was two hours ago."

The smell of sin was fresh. My breath came short. I wanted to plunge my body like a hot poker into the cold pond.

"What a scandal!" Lock said.

"Why did you tell me, Mike?" I said.

"Finally," Lock said, "we see the tip of the iceberg."

"I hate stuff like this," I said. I walked away.

"God, Ryan," Lock said. "You're such a damn baby."

"Sure," I said, "and you're Lochinvar Roehm, Vatican Detective."

"Dryden admitted," Mike said to Lock, "there are others. A lot of boys try..."

"Don't say it!"

"...expressing themselves and if they feel guilty, he hears their Confession."

"Uuh," I said.

"*Absolutio complicis*," Lock said. "If a priest in Confession absolves his accomplice's sin, he violates Canon law."

"And commits a mortal sin," I said, "so they both require forgiveness from yet another priest. It's endless! I...don't...understand...this!"

"I can't tell Father Gunn or Rector Karg," Mike said. "I'm trapped. I can't lie. I actually dropped my pants."

"They have to be told," I said.

"But Mike can't do it," Lock said. "Don't you see? They'd suspect him, because he went so often to Dryden for private conferences...."

"You dropped your pants?" I said to Mike.

"I can't lie."

"...It would be Dryden's word against his..."

"You dropped your pants?" I said. "You can't tell the truth either."

"...It can't be Dryden's word against his." Lock turned to me.

"Why not?" I said.

"Because," Lock said, "this is Byzantine, Roman, and maybe very Vatican II."

"We need someone who was never alone with Dryden."

Both Lock and Mike turned to me.

"Oh, no," I said. "Not me."

"You qualify, don't you?" Lock asked.

"So do you," I said.

"You handle it, Lock." Mike begged him. "This has to be handled right. I might or might not have a vocation, but I don't want to get shipped. If I leave, I want to leave by my free choice."

"You handle it, Lock," I said. "You're the most respectable seminarian at Misery."

"You've got clout," Mike said to Lock.

"You're actually ship-proof," I said. "You're the golden boy."

"I bet you, Lock," Mike said, "those old priests would believe anything you said."

"This is a temptation," Lock said, "to vanity."

"That's better than impurity," I said.

"But harder," Lock said, "to resist."

Mike swore us both to secrecy, which we sealed by each throwing a rock into the mirror of the lake sending Misery's reflection out in loony rings of moonlight.

The next afternoon, after Hank the Tank and his bevy of choir boys and sacristans had erected a lavish white silk May altar, the annual May Crowning of the Virgin Mother wound in long procession through the main chapel. In crisp white surplices over black cassocks, wearing our black biretta hats foursquare on our heads, we carried a hundred vases of lilies and lilacs and peonies and roses in procession to the statue of the Virgin Mary, singing in unison to the Mother of all priests.

> "Bring flowers of the fairest!
> Bring flowers of the rarest
> from garden and hillside
> and woodland and dale!
> Our full hearts are swelling,
> our glad voices telling,
> the praise of the loveliest
> Rose of the vale!
> Oh, Mary, we crown Thee
> with blossoms today!
> Queen of the Angels!
> Queen of the May!"

The next morning, Lock entered Rector Karg's office. From down the corridor, Mike and I spied Rector Karg rise quickly and close his ever-open door. Within fifteen minutes, Lock came out for Mike. "You have to go. You have to tell."

"Why did we have to tell at all?" Mike said. He started running down the hall.

"Why does anyone confess?" I asked. Lock and I ran with him. Our cassocks whooshed around our legs.

"In a school," Lock said, "where five hundred boys each go to Confession twice a week, you better confess to cover yourself."

"Lock's right," I said. We ran around a corner. "That's how Porky Puhl was caught."

"Confession is perfect, isn't it," Mike said, "for controlling a bunch of boys."

"Tattletales," I said. We picked up speed running for a stairwell.

"Dryden was right about one thing, at least," Mike said. "Communists and Catholics both rely on informants."

"But why do we have to tell?" Mike said.

"Because," Lock said, "we're good Catholic boys."

"It'll be the Inquisition all over again," I said.

We stampeded up the stairs as if we were somehow going to escape.

Mike disappeared into Karg's office. Doors banged shut. Mice scurried into holes. Sanctuary candles flickered. Priests whisked down hallways and disappeared.

Lock and I sat through the day's classes fearful that parts of the precious world of Misery were about to blow. Around our ears. After eight years of being good. A month before college graduation.

"I wonder," Lock said, "how many seminarians took, uh, interpretive dance lessons from Dryden?"

By supper Mike had returned. He looked terrible at table, but he hadn't been shipped, at least before supper. Maybe he could make it to our graduation.

Hank the Tank nosed around Mike's disappearance. "Where were you all day? You missed your classes."

"None of your beeswax where he was," I said.

"Mike had an appointment with the doctor in town," Lock said.

"He has polio," I said.

"Simple as that?" Hank made his bubble gum smack.

"Simple enough for you," Lock said.

"Drop dead," Hank said. He fisted his closed thumb and forefinger up against his belly and belched.

Everyone laughed, ha ha.

After supper, Lock cornered me. "Tomorrow, Rector Karg is bringing in the Bishop himself. Mike and I both have to sign depositions to the Holy Office in Rome. Keep pretending you know nothing."

"I really don't know anything." I feared our very innocence might be used against us. Like *The Crucible*. Awful to be accused of something you did. Worse to be named something you weren't.

"We're under oath," Lock said.

"They're acting fast," Mike said.

"*Festina lente*," I quoted the Latin maxim. "*Make haste slowly*. That's what they will do."

"Chips will fall where they may." Lock looked worried. "Heads will roll."

The little sanctuary of our lives ignited with anxiety, tension, and excitement. The drum roll of changes coming from Rome was interrupted by the whispered scandal we could not name. Priests fighting over Vatican II suddenly closed ranks. Purity was stronger than politics. Purity was ancient, legendary, basic. We had no words to discuss what could not exist. I knew purity was somehow at the heart of the *Dolce Vita* matter with Father Dryden, but how he had tempted Mike in his room threw my imagination akimbo. All the priests and all the boys once again knew something I didn't know, and I was too afraid of losing my purity to ask.

Mike had dropped a rock onto the still, perfect, mirrored surface of the deep waters that were Misery. The rock splashed and sank hard. Concentric rings rolled out across Misery's identity. For three breathless days, I saw priests skulking through shadows in the halls, whispering, and disappearing into rooms where we boys were not allowed. From our watchful vantage point, I was actually happy that the usual dissension among the faculty decreased as the priests prepared a united front for the coming investigation into what Lock called "The Secret Life of Misericordia Seminary." Yet, in reality, the secrecy was so tightly managed that even Hank and his gang of vigilante altar boys failed to notice how Mike and Lock appeared and disappeared and appeared again.

"I can keep," I said, "the seal of the Confessional."

"We can't tell you," Mike said.

"If the Bishop knows you know," Lock said, "you'll get shipped."

"So you don't know anything, do you!" Mike laughed.

"I know nothing about what you're talking about."

"God made us," Lock said, "and He matched us."

They both laughed.

"What's that supposed to mean?" I said.

"We're worse off than Dempsey ever was," Lock said. "How did we become the Friends of the Friendless Friends?"

"Fub," I said. "The Fubs of the Fubless Fubs!"

Hank the Tank, yodeling Gregorian chant, ticked up from his hymnal, eyes alert. "I sniff the blood of long knives," he said.

"You sniff your own shorts," I said.

Hank noticed that the Reverend Father Christopher Dryden was sick and confined to his ornate rooms. The following Sunday afternoon Hank tried to sneak up to see him, but a do-not-disturb sign hung sideways from his door knob, and an old retired priest sat half-asleep on a chair by Dryden's door.

"What happens to priests when they get old?" I asked.

"They die," Lock said.

"I mean before that."

"Not much."

"That's cynical." Father Gunn preached that cynicism ruined vocations.

"As you live, so shall you die."

"I can live lonely, but I don't want to...."

Led by Father Polistina, Misery's priests showed up on the hour for each and every class, keeping to the Latin grammar and the Church history and the geometry theorems and the philosophy texts exactly. Discipline ruled work and work was ruled by prayer. Our school year ticked like the clock. *Tick. Tick.* The humming big hand crossed the little hand. *Tick. Tick.* Tension mounted, yet nothing extraordinary seemed to be happening. *Tick. Tick.* Classes dragged on toward final exams in Greek, physics, and the philosophy of German Idealism. I wanted to go home to Charley-Pop and Annie Laurie and Thom and my four-year-old sister, Margaret Mary.

In the halls at Misery, I posted flyers announcing "The Theology Students' Year-End Musical Concert" for the next Sunday night in May. Whatever performer had been scheduled was not canceled.

"Appearances are everything," Lock said.

In the auditorium, I pushed Mike and Lock into theater seats directly in front of Hank the Tank and Ski Kowalski, so we could sit real tall, rock back and forth, hold up our programs, and generally obscure their view of the stage, because Tank's brother PeterPeterPeter was singing. The last of the student audience was filing in.

We heard Ski ask Hank, "Where's Dryden? He's late."

"He's either feeling better or he's dead," Hank said deliberately. "Chris never misses any student function."

"Ain't that the truth!" Mike whispered. "Function! Function! Who's got my function?"

"Shut up," Lock said.

I turned around in my seat and waved my program in Hank's face. "Your favorite priest is scheduled right here to play piano in the second act." I pointed to Christopher Dryden's name on the program I had mimeographed only the day before. No priests had dared break their secrecy by telling me to remove his name. I had received the typed original before the unspoken scandal broke. No priest said not to print the bill, and I couldn't very well suggest editing out Dryden's appearance without indicating I knew he was being ostracized. Or disciplined. Or worse.

"Chris will play as promised," Hank said. "Plague wouldn't stop him. Peter said Chris knows the show must go on."

I looked at him: "Why must the show go on?" I repeated the sentence five times with five different inflections.

"Shut up," Hank said.

"Hank's suspicions are dangerous," Lock whispered to me. "He knows we know something."

"If Chris doesn't show," Hank said, "I'll bet ten to one he's finally in Dutch with the powers that be."

"The powers that be!" Mike repeated.

"Oh no!" Lock said, "Not the powers that be!"

The auditorium lights dimmed.

Hank hit me on the back of the head.

I slapped him across the face with my program.

He popped his gum and belched.

"Stop it," Lock said.

"Chris is forbidden to eat with the other priests," Hank said to Ski.

The Misery pit orchestra of six boys hit the overture with bass and drums and piano and a blat of trumpet. The stage lit up on PeterPeterPeter, dressed like the Music Man, pattering out "Trouble. Right here in River City." Oh yeah.

"What?" Ski could not hear.

"Forbidden to eat...aw, wait till intermission," Hank said. "Watch my brother."

PeterPeterPeter ran and danced across the stage. I was jealous of him, or any boy who could sing and dance, but I was glad I couldn't because I felt sorry for boys that men out in the world might think made strange priests. Bing Crosby playing a priest in a movie was different from a priest playing Bing Crosby in a parish. PeterPeterPeter tap-danced his way off the stage to the wild cheers of all the seminarians.

The Theology Choir walked out on stage and climbed the three steps of the choir risers singing a romantic German drinking song, "Du, Du Liegst Mir im Herzen," then burlesqued themselves with "Wunderbar." The auditorium burst into applause and the applause rose when Father Gunn announced to the audience that the Reverend Mister Peter Rimski, who was only two weeks away from final Ordination to the priesthood, was making his last stage appearance at Misery.

Amid the polite applause, Lock and Mike and I cheered. "Good-bye! Good luck! Good riddance!"

The Theology Choir, arranged in three rows on the risers, parted in the middle, as PeterPeterPeter appeared on the top stair. The Choir applauded him. The stage lights dimmed as one of the vigilante altar boys in the light booth hit PeterPeterPeter with a pinpoint blue-white spot causing PeterPeterPeter to shimmer *vibrato* like an angel singing on the head of a pin, "Ave Maria."

"Gounod," Lock whispered, "is not good enough."

Hank the Tank leaned forward, his tobacco breath between our two heads. "You're cruisin' for a bruisin'."

The whole choir joined together for a selection of difficult Palestrina, concluding with an upbeat medley from the Broadway musical *Camelot*. When PeterPeterPeter burst into a histrionic "If Ever I Would Leave You," waving good-bye to the Misericordians, Lock and Mike and I were practically busting a gut laughing. We had more fun, off with our secret little crowd, singing along with Tom Lehrer, *"Genuflect! Genuflect! Genuflect!,"* satirizing Vatican II to the tune of "The Vatican Rag."

At intermission, I stood alone near Hank, who was holding court in the lobby.

"Chris is in Dutch with them," Hank said. His eyes burned holes into me. "Peter told me the whole long scandal."

Ha! Hank the Tank didn't get it!

"They're all mad he's brought fresh air into the place. The structure can't abide his civil disobedience."

Lock came up to me and stood with his back to Hank, listening to him.

"The faculty won't even let Chris eat with them," Hank continued. "All because he's so intellectual and has done so much for us."

"I saw Chris back in the kitchen tonight," Ski said. "He didn't say anything. He kept eating out of a quart box of ice cream near the freezer."

"Peter says that's all he's eaten for days. He has to raid the kitchen." Hank pulled his fan club in closer. "Gunn and old Rector Karg and their clique never did dig his ideas and now they're rebelling against him."

"Because," Lock said, "they can't rebel against Rome."

"Because of Vatican II, Chris has to eat it raw?" Hank the Tank said.

"You eat it like they feed it," Ski said. "I know how this works."

"Maybe this time..." I paused to yank their attention. "Maybe this time...they're shipping a priest!"

Phlewww! Hank blew raspberries at my idea. "Ship a priest! Ryanus!" Tank of the Imperial Roman Empire was holding court. If any boy was going to tout gossip, it was going to be him. "Misery gives you the dirty end of the stick. You eat it or else."

Was that the definition of a vocation? Eat it or else?

"Chris was crazy to come back to teach," Hank said. "Really off his nut. He knew what Misery was like."

"Isn't that why he came back?" a sophomore boy asked. "If the alumni don't cause change, who will? He's sacrificing himself."

"He's a regular martyr-saint," Mike said. "He missed the triple crown: virgin-martyr-saint."

"Most of us will get ordained," the sophomore said. "We'll leave Misery behind and forget it."

Hank spun the sophomore's idea. "Our seminary years will be the best years of our lives."

"Because," Mike said, "we've such poor memories."

"After I'm ordained," Ski said, "I'm blowing the whistle."

Everybody laughed, ha ha.

"Like hell," Hank swore. "Your bishop will crap daily so you'll always know where your next meal's coming from. You'll never tell anybody anything about the inside dope of seminaries."

"What priest would?" Lock said. "Seminaries make us weak, dependent on the institutional Church for bed, board, and shelter. We obey, because where would we go? We're unemployable. How would we live?"

The foyer lights flashed.

"Worker-priests know," I said.

"Mark me." Hank the Tank's eyebrows that had begun to meet in the middle glowered ominously. "Something's going on," he said. "The old guard is afraid of Chris' intellectual revolution. They don't know how to handle this new, serious, Christianity. I know what this is."

"What is this?" Mike Hager said.

"This is all nerves about Vatican II."

Like Meredith's nerves during World War II.

Christopher Dryden was a no-show in the second act. At the grand piano, a high-school boy with four thumbs and nine fingers substituted for the missing priest.

The next morning, the old priest sitting guard outside Dryden's suite was gone. The chair was empty. Hank dared knock and push on the door. He came running back to our classroom. "It's locked," he said. "There's no sound. It's like no one's there."

"They've martyred him," Ski said. "Behind our backs, they've martyred him sure."

Lock looked at me dramatically, as if to say, Oh God. Rector Karg had privately informed him and Mike that, last evening during the concert, about the time the dearly departing PeterPeterPeter was transfiguring his way through the "Ave Maria," Father Dryden had been cornered in his apartment, buckled into a straightjacket, and driven off to an institution. They were to tell no one, but they told me about his complete nervous breakdown. They put him in the booby hatch tied up next to Russell Rainforth.

The next four days were final examinations. The tension caused by the mystery of the missing priest raised conjecture to a fever pitch. Ski made a candle-lit shrine out of a can of Dryden's tennis balls you'd have thought were third-class relics. In a closed community where everyone knew everyone else's business, for once no one had anything right.

"This is being handled very badly," Lock said.

"What exactly is a nervous breakdown?" I asked, genuinely, because I had long feared I might have one.

"A nervous breakdown is what people say you have," Lock said, "when you don't agree with them."

"And," Mike said, "when they can't get rid of you any other way."

Mike's mother and father, Julia and Doc, always said his sister had a nervous breakdown.

"Sometimes what you have," Lock said, "is a nervous breakthrough."

"A nervous anything," I said, "can cost a priest his vocation."

"Wrong," Lock said. "A vocation is a personal calling from God. Lots of men have vocations to the priesthood, but not everyone answers, or is allowed to answer."

"You think Christopher Dryden has a vocation?" I asked.

We stood looking at the bulletin board. Gunn had tacked up new specific mimeographed rules. He renewed the ban on fiction books, and, backed by the faculty, stipulated only textbooks and authorized collateral reading in our rooms. Protestant and Jewish theologians, who had crept in during the year, were collected by very senior boys and locked away in a cage in the library.

"Pogrom," I said. "Inquisition." Philosophers like Paul Tillich and Martin Buber returned underground with the transistor radios. "Do not ask the 'I' for whom the 'Thou' tolls."

"Karg and Gunn are missing the point." Lock was disgusted. "Never throw the baby out with the bath water." He was tearing up a copy of Sartre which in itself was Sartrean. "Rules of grammar and laws of theology they understand, but anything modern proves they're more medieval than this wonderful new Pope."

"But look at their logic," I said. "The worst sin has indicted the whole progress of theology."

"Vatican II and Father Dryden. Sheer coincidence."

"Were those priests spying on us all year?" I could imagine Gunn and Karg rooting through our underwear drawers, flipping through my notebooks, picking at my treasures in my shoe box. "Dryden maybe proves them right in their caution." Many boys' rooms in the last twenty-four hours had been ransacked. "Dryden ruined whatever he was trying to do."

"You never liked him," Lock said. "Ever."

"He scared me."

"You're amazing, Ryan. What is it about you? It's like you can smell a sin of impurity at a thousand paces. I'm not sure that's a virtue."

"I hated him, even though he breezed through in a fresh way."

"Dryden's ruined everything," Lock said. "At least because of him everything's ruined."

"He told us," I said, "about T. S. Eliot, and then he went and did the wrong thing for what reason I don't understand."

In the room, the boys come and go, posing for Michaelangelo.

"Rector Karg has acted even worse," Lock said, "handling this situation with all these gossiping boys. Old-guard priests don't like to see the new-guard church replacing them."

"Maybe," I said, "Father Dryden really did nothing wrong. No more wrong than me translating Häring. Maybe he's only a symbolic target."

"But Mike said..."

"Mike has a great imagination. Nobody has actually proven Father Dryden committed any sins. In my vocation, I want to be sensible about hysteria."

"Ryan," Lock said, "If you write stuff like that in our moral psychology exam tomorrow morning, I'll graduate top of the class."

"You want to fight for number one?" I said. "You can have 'Valedictorian, Misery, college class of 1961.' Help find me an extra packing box. Tomorrow I'm taking home anything they can object to. I'm purifying my life."

"Ryan, you're afraid too, aren't you?"

"It's ironic. The minute I started to understand the requirements of a vocation to the priesthood in the Catholic Church..."

"Deep down," Lock said, "you feel maybe Gunn and Karg and all the old fogies in this sterile hothouse are right to hold off change."

"A vocation happened to me this year," I said.

"Ha! You...don't...want...to...change!"

"I don't know whether I'm protecting my vocation running with them or from them."

"There's many kinds of priestly vocations," Lock said.

"So which kind's mine?"

"You'll be the first beatnik priest. That's the beauty of the new Church."

"As God is my witness," I said, "I will be a priest, and if you want valedictorian, you'll have to kill me."

Lock jumped me with a full nelson. We wrestled and laughed and ran down to the swimming pool and raced each other in furious laps through the slapping bright chlorine water.

Hank the Tank stuck his head out of the lifeguard's booth and flicked the overhead lights on and off. He was stealing a pair of flippers to go swimming himself down at the river, where he and his kind had started to hang out to separate themselves from our crowd, who had taken over the pathway circling around little Lake Gunn.

"I dare you to come race me down at the river!"

He turned the pool lights out.

"I'm the king of the river!"

He slammed his way out the door, and left us bobbing in the dark.

May 31, 1961

Three mornings after Mass, which I offered up so I'd score good grades, I carried my school books and suitcase to our rented car. Mike was to drive a Ford with three passengers to Chicago, drop us individually on Randolph at the Greyhound Terminal and for trains at Union Station and LaSalle Street Station. I hung around Mike's car under the mulberry trees, waiting for him to come unlock the trunk. He had packed everything he owned, finished with Misery and the priesthood, he said. Doc and Julia would have to eat it.

I brushed several fallen mulberries from the white car.

Hank the Tank stormed up. "Have you heard," he said, "what they're doing and what they've done?" He set his valise on the ground.

I tried to look shocked as he spouted old news that was new to him.

"They canned Dryden. Framed and trumped-up. God, they were always jealous. Half the seminary stopped confessing to the old priests. All the best seminarians went to Chris for counseling and Confession. Rector Karg knew that Chris found out more in two years what was going on around here than they knew in two generations."

"Confession is information," I said. "Even if you can't break the seal of the Confessional, you can't help acting on what you know, like if a priest's mother confessed adultery to him, he'd look at her differently, even though he could never mention he knew."

I tried not to picture the images Mike had conjured of Dryden kneeling before his Danish modern crucifix praying to a half-naked Jesus for dreams of release. Hey, Father, is that a serpent in your cassock or are you just glad to see me? Engorgement, Christopher Dryden had said, was a richness, an overflow like grace, to be attended with no less joy than running naked through goldenrod or drinking cream and feeling full and good and human and like men. Actually, I was incensed that Hank gave the distinct impression he knew more than the rest of us.

"Who told you?" I asked him.

"It's out," Hank the Tank said. "My brother, Peter, found it out."

"And what is it?" I asked him directly.

"What it always is," he said. "S-e-x. Rumors of s-e-x."

"You say Dryden was framed?"

"Some truth to tell. Certain activities were politically reinterpreted for Rector Karg's convenience in reporting to Rome."

"It can't all be true," I said to Hank's fat face, "because if it's true, it means you were involved. And who'd have sex with you? Isn't that why you came to Misericordia, because girls ran away."

Hank the Tank rumbled toward me. I shoved him. I pushed us apart. He let me push us apart. For the first time.

"I'm not involved in anything, Ryan."

"Deny me three times."

"Screw you, Virgin Mary." Hank the Tank tugged at his shirt. "It's true!" He wouldn't stop. "The old priests manufactured the story, twisting it the very way they wanted. They already smashed his piano and the

Broadway original cast albums."

"But that stuff's his!" I said.

"Not in their minds." Hank moved in closer. "Did you know they're saying Chris had an open affair with one of the most famously flaming *maître d*'s in Rome?"

"What's a 'flaming *maître d*'?'" I said.

"You are impossibly naive," Hank said, "and maybe even really as innocent as you act, you poor fub duck thing."

Mike returned and opened the trunk. He looked me full in the face. "I've heard," he said. "Everyone knows. *Roman Holiday* turned into *La Dolce Vita*, with a lot of *dolce*. Get in the car. I need out of here."

"And last night!" Hank oozed up against the white car, practically performing "The Snake Dance" from *The Garden of Eden Ballet*. "Last night, nineteen high-school boys were shipped out under cover of darkness."

I reeled with the news. Sunlight hurt my eyes. The cars of parents arriving to pick up their sons roared in my ears. "It's true," Mike said. "Nineteen. Gone so fast they couldn't even take their luggage. Some of these parents arriving today to drive little Johnny home will find little Johnny disappeared last night on a Greyhound bus."

"This is disgusting." Lock walked up to the car. "A real witch hunt."

Off to the side a mother of a shipped boy cried out. "Where's my son?" A father grasped his chest. "Shipped?" An old priest talking to them pointed to their son's suitcase. "Perhaps another seminary will take him." Three or four other sets of parents were leaning against their cars in shock and despair. "You sent him away last night knowing we'd be here today?" One father kept slamming his car door. "What kind of people are you?" A mother fainted. "You're supposed to care for my son." A shipped boy's little sister, no more than eight, started a wailing cry. "Where's Bobbieeeeee?"

A bird, crammed full of mulberries, dropped a load that splat across the shiny white car and dirtied Hank's fat fingers spread on the hood. So much for the wonderful hands of a priest.

"Stop laughing," Hank said. He wiped his hand in the green grass. "I'm not stupid. I don't know about you guys, but I suspected something. Those old priests were not paying attention. Gunn was checking our legs for Bermuda shorts while half the high-school department was being raped."

"You can't rape boys," I said.

Hank the Tank grinned. "Maybe for one or two it was rape. Chris is a very attractive role model."

"Oh, jeez," Mike said. "I'm beginning to get it."

"Every ring," Hank said, "has a ringleader. You're never sure who it is."

Mike walked around to the driver's side of the white car. "I'd say, 'Be seeing you,' Hank," Mike said, "except I won't 'be seeing you.'"

"Better you should know who's on first." Hank picked up his valise. I thought it was like his mind, a tight little box full of dirty linen and bound with straps. "I must find the new Reverend Peter Rimski. His Ordination means a lot to our father."

"Yeah, yeah," I said. PeterPeterPeter was a priest! I picked a handful of mulberries from the tree and bit into them, their little grits pricking my mouth. Mike's exit from Misericordia was final. He was driving home for good, but I had my vocation. If PeterPeterPeter could be a priest, what was the nature of Christ's call? My vocation would not be lost because of outside forces that suckered those nineteen shipped boys into whatever happened. Inside my soul I was growing more secure. Christ, with time, was drawing me close, fitting me with less pain into the molded vocation He desired.

Our two freshmen-college passengers climbed into the back seat, slammed the doors, lit up their cigarettes, impatient to leave Misery. Mike and I shook hands with Lock, who was flying out on a plane to New York and then on to a summer internship as a page boy at the Vatican in Rome.

"Don't let it get you down," Lock said to Mike. "You did right. Never think you didn't."

I got into the car. The two freshmen were combing their hair from the way they'd worn it all year to the way they wanted to wear it for the summer.

"Good-bye, Lock," I said. He was standing, framed by the perfect geometry of Misery's tall red bell tower. I wanted to tell Lock I loved him, the real way a priest loves a brother priest, the way my Uncle Les loved his priest friends from the War. I had the feeling he would go to Rome, be liked, study there, be ordained, join the Vatican diplomatic corps, turn into Tom Tryon in *The Cardinal*, meet Sophia Loren and President Kennedy, resist the *Dolce Vita*, and never come back, maybe never even approve of a worker-priest from miserable Misericordia.

Mike slid behind the wheel. He turned the key in the ignition, looking straight ahead. "So long, suckers!" he said.

The two freshmen laughed like he was the funniest guy on earth.

"We're dropping out too," they said.

I stared straight ahead. I was the last and only vocation left in the car. What difference did it all make? They had to do what was right for them. *God bless them.* Their exit didn't threaten my vocation. Mike slowly drove us, his last time, down old Misery's drive out onto the two-lane stretch of highway. On the car radio, Andy Williams was singing "Moon River" from *Breakfast at Tiffany's*. It was summer. We were free.

I quickly put my fear of Rector Karg out of my head, waving over my shoulder at him, at him, *der Herr Rector*, watching out his windows with the pontifical binoculars of God.

7

June 20, 1962

Tick. Tick. Going home summers was like rowing out in a boat chained to the shore. I paddled out only to be jerked back, tethered forever to the land. I was true to my school and for me girls could not exist. I could not run with the hot boys of the town. They always chased down the same one track, luring the girls who actually existed into cars into parks into bushes for short-breathed twitchings in the darkening twilight. I had to go everywhere alone or with a few other seminarians home for the summer from other seminaries that were not as top-notch as Misery. That was the same as being alone.

I sought sanctuary in the dark of movie theaters that disguised my estrangement from a world of couples who saved no place for me. The theater seats could be old and ripped, the floor could be so sticky I couldn't lift my feet when the mice ran by, the new wide screen could be winging precariously out of the old proscenium arch, but I loved the silver screen and the muted blue lights high in the arc of the movie palace dome.

I laid my head back on the seat and stared up at that hypnotic blue circle, losing all my bearings. The cone of projector light flickered and the stereophonic sound bounced around the walls.

People sat in two's and four's and people sat alone, sitting like me two or three times through the same double feature. The world I was giving up really didn't seem like much, but the world was all some people had. I pitied them. I pitied anybody who hid out at the movies from the world I was sent back to for three months every summer.

Some boys fell in love with the world and never returned to Misery again. I valued the world, but I was not cut out to be part of it. As a priest I would be in the world, but not of the world. I would save people from their worldliness.

October 11, 1962

Pope John XXIII finally opened the Second Vatican Council in Rome on

October 11, 1962, while at Misery, the 16-millimeter projector funneled its own ray of light through the darkened seminary auditorium, over our heads, down the middle to the screen. The movie actors' mouths had to work around a hole where some wild boy had shoved a chair through the grainy canvas. The movies were old, scratched, and wholesome.

The Mudlark, a movie about Queen Victoria, broke off flapping repeatedly during its three reels that had to be switched by hand. The lights came up and the boys moaned and I couldn't be inside the movie any more.

The sound went out of synchronization. The frames stuck and burned and the black-and-white image on screen turned orange and melted from the center out as we'd all boo. The movies were rated by the Legion of Decency, but the decency of seminarians required even stricter watch.

Whenever anything slightly suggestive came on the screen, one of the priests held a filing card across the projector lens. I always wondered if he watched the scene on the card like his own private peep show. We snickered our first years at every carded scene, when the screen went dark, or almost dark, and the top of actors' heads bobbed around, and the dialog continued, strident through our one-string-and-tin-can-loudspeaker tethered on a long cord and set under the screen.

In our later years, we laughed up our cassock sleeves because the priests always told us that we were adults who should be acting like adults and then they whipped out the filing cards. At least I was able to retrieve a strip of twelve frames that broke off one reel and save them in my shoe box. The movie was *The Left Hand of God* with Humphrey Bogart posing as a priest in China. The thought of someone posing as a priest intrigued me and I studied those twelve frames of Bogart's face over and over, holding them up to the light.

Movies at Misery were far from glamorous: no marquee to stand under, no coming attractions, no popcorn. Most boys filed into the auditorium in bleary-eyed compulsory attendance at movies I called "vitamin-enriched" because they were supposed to be good for us. I had hopes for each movie, but the priests succeeded in making every viewing a season in purgatory.

When we once saw a movie about convicts watching a movie in prison, the movie prisoners acted the same way toward the screen we did. I laughed out loud. I knew the screen was a mirror. I realized that whatever was on screen was really about life, the way novels and plays and art were really about life.

Sometimes the movie provoked discussion afterwards, with all the boys standing in hallways, the older boys smoking one last cigarette in the last few minutes before night prayers and the Grand Silence.

After every movie, Father Gunn stood outside the auditorium, cross-armed, ill at ease, trapped like a watchdog in the hall, forced to make small talk.

"You really picked a doozie this time, Father." Keith Fahnhorst, the best wrestler in the history of Misericordia, had liked the month's only feature, *The Long Gray Line*, a drama about an Irish coach's life at West Point Military Academy. Parts of the movie mirrored Misery perfectly. "But a couple scenes might have been a little too much for the high-school boys," Keith Fahnhorst said, "where Tyrone Power and Maureen O'Hara were kissing and then sat in bed and talked."

Gunn frowned, recrossed his arms, half-smiled. Uncomfortable. He'd seen the film a few summers before on the ship when he sailed to Europe to visit the Vatican and he certainly hadn't recalled the marital scenes, which had not seemed suggestive to him on the high seas. He was, he said, embarrassed to have exposed tender minds to such emotions. "But the scene where Maureen O'Hara died," he said, "with the rosary in her hand, right there on the West Point grounds was excuse enough for the emotional exposure."

My God, I thought, my God. That movie was approved for family viewing by the National Legion of Decency and these priests carry on like these kids don't see and do far more when they go home for the summer. "Here comes the double standard again," I whispered to Lock. He laughed.

"What was that, O'Hara?" Gunn asked. "You aren't related to Maureen O'Hara, are you?"

Hank the Tank sailed by. "He is Maureen O'Hara."

"No, Father," I said.

"I once met a movie star," he said, "during the war. Ann Sheridan. She rode in my jeep."

"My uncle," I said, "also met Ann Sheridan. Their picture was in *Life*. 'The priest and the movie star.'"

"Your uncle is," Father Gunn said, "a true marvel."

"About tonight's film," I said. "Could we send away for some quality films? Some European films. You know, Bergman, Antonioni, Fellini. For the older seminarians. Real movies might be helpful in our study of philosophy and moral theology. We could show them through the winter on Sunday afternoons when there's too much snow to play or work outside."

Gunn looked at me in astonishment. "They're not even in English."

"Exactly. A chance to use all our Latin, German, French, and Greek."

"Don't try to intellectualize simple entertainment."

Some of the seminarians around me, including several of Tank's vigilante altar boys, nodded me on with guarded approval, fearful we'd sound like the disappeared Dryden.

"We might raise the standard of viewing," I said. "There's immense psychology, real religious psychology at that, behind a director like Bergman. He won the Academy Award. Did you see *The Virgin Spring*?"

"How high did she go?" Hank the Tank asked.

The room exploded in laughter. Humor, St. Thomas Aquinas wrote, is the unexpected juxtaposition of opposites.

"No more suggestive talk," Gunn said.

"Films examine interpersonal relationships." I was coming on strong, surrounded by classmates who were quite happy for me to climb out on a limb that allowed them to watch more movies.

"Interpersonal relationships?" Gunn recoiled visibly.

My long-contemplated chance, my opening, my plan to catch him in public, where he was on the spot, had found its natural moment. "Priests are supposed to be educated. The most educated of all. This seems a perfect chance for broadening vicarious experience."

"I can guarantee you, O'Hara, you don't want experience."

"But I do."

"Experience comes slowly," he said, "if it comes at all."

"We clergy must see there's more to films than we've seen tonight."

"We don't have to," he said, "see anything!"

I fell back a step.

He crossed and uncrossed and recrossed his arms.

I took a step back toward him.

"Priests need movies like a hole in the head." He uncrossed his arms, extended his wrist, tapped his watch, held it above his head. "Night prayers," he announced. "Time for night prayers. Let's have absolute silence!"

"Told you so," Hank the Tank said.

As I stood by Father Gunn, I let the other seminarians walk away.

Father Gunn was perturbed. "What do you want now, O'Hara?"

"I just wanted to say," I whispered, "that I really like your new toupee."

Communication is a brief encounter, I thought. That was my sole meditation before bedtime and it wasn't a good one: too many negative un-Christlike thoughts about too many negative people. Why try to change the seminary at all? We had agreed to bring light after, not before, Ordination.

I was angry at Father Gunn for his mean sense of discipline. Every move was a battle of wills. I had been thwarted all evening because I hadn't wanted to attend the picture. The mailman had lost the film for a week, delaying the screening to the very last night before first-quarter exams. Where was the faculty's logic? First they cut our films from ten to six a year so the movies wouldn't interfere with our studies, and then they pulled a trick like this, forcing us to watch sentimental drivel when we should have been studying moral theology, physics, and German.

I hadn't wanted to go to the movie because of studies and because the last time, some puling high-school boy had sat on the floor between the chairs with his back to the screen, holding his ears to protect his purity from Elizabeth Taylor in *Ivanhoe.* I mean I try to be pure, but some of these boys are ridiculous!

I had to stop myself. I was thinking again. Or reacting. I had to stop reacting; that was childish. I would become a sane viable adult only when I began acting. Well, dammit, I had tried after the movie and received for my grown-up stand a paid religious announcement that it was time for night prayers. I hadn't wanted to see *The Long Gray Line* because of its sentimental reviews. I wasn't some stupid Danny Boy interested in a corny take on being Irish.

Actually, I was twenty-two and in my ninth year at Misery, almost a year past college and well into the graduate courses in Misery's Theology Department, studying old-style Dogmatic Theology and Moral Theology and Canon Law. In Pastoral Theology, I was learning how to hear Confessions and how to say Mass. I was on to the last leg of preparation for the priesthood with less than thirty-two months until my Ordination Day.

So much to do, I cried out to the Lord, so much to do before I was turned loose to minister to the world. Urgency and responsibility and insecurity drove me to study what they offered, to read what they didn't, to write continually the papers they didn't really care about.

"Misery's grading system is so strict," Rector Karg said, "that if you were studying anywhere else your grade would be ten points higher. Even at Ohio State."

I tried to polish myself by writing stories and feature articles with which I could effectively extend my ministry to spread Christ's word and love on earth. So what, I said to myself, if priestly writing puts art at the service of religion. So do stained glass and Gregorian Chant. Writing's purpose is goodness. Someday after some remarkable visitation of Christ, I'll actually have something to say. Something great and inspired and revelatory to help the world. Something just short of an epiphany or, maybe, an apocalypse. People always brag they have something to say, but when it comes time to say it, they take a pencil and go blank and drive people crazy on trains and busses with their life stories. I knew God called me to invent a special vocation for myself inside my vocation to the priesthood.

All of America had watched Bishop Sheen sweeping across the black-and-white TV screen talking to millions in prime time. I was driven, sanctioned even, by grace to make the tools of journalism sharp against the day when the great message would come to me and I, the best editor in the Catholic press, could spread it in headlines from the worker-priest garret, where I lived, to the very ends of the diocese. Writing sermons was almost the same as writing articles and stories.

Certainty of this special calling, of this vocation within a vocation, had come already. Almost. I had seen its faint glimmerings on my knees before the tabernacle where the Word Made Flesh, Love ineffable, Jesus Himself, the Prisoner of the Tabernacle, reigned in terrible confinement. Love would be everything. If only I could find love certainly and translate divine love into human terms to all men, Christ could come to them through me. But to be a vessel, I had to grow into a rich relationship with Jesus so He could fill me to the brim, even then to overflowing, so that the thirsting thousands I would touch could drink and wash and be refreshed in the abundance and overflow. My excess of spilling grace could change deserts into green pastures.

In the chapel I begged I might become fully human, fully a man, that in such perfection an abundance of grace might be founded.

Grace builds on nature, Saint Thomas Aquinas wrote in his *Summa Theologica.*

That was the key. That was one secret revealed. If it was so, because it was so, I prayed, then make my nature the more perfect that my grace might be increased and I might be a better, self-effacing instrument moved by the hands of Christ. The hypostatic union of His Person had been so perfect that Godhead could be joined straight to manhood.

His body had to be perfect to match His perfect divinity. From foot to sacred head, He had to become, and be, the most perfectly formed body to have such a perfect informing soul as deity itself. On the cross over the altar, the athletic Christ hung crucified but all-powerful, the almighty God in the perfect body of a man.

"Misericordia's main crucifix," PeterPeterPeter told guests on tour, "was carved in Northern Germany from 1929-1932. The Cross is fifty feet tall, carved from black oak, and the Corpus is forty feet tall, carved in blond oak. The sculptor, actually the sculptors, several monks, chose an Olympic diver as the model for the idealized Body of Christ. Hung originally in the Cathedral in Berlin, the crucifix, so decreed by Pope Pius XII, was shipped to Misericordia for safekeeping in the spring of 1939. The Pope formally pronounced the crucifix a permanent gift to Misericordia, to honor the seminary's unspotted German heritage, during the Holy Year, 1950."

The world waited, not for me as a person, but for all boys called to the priesthood. It is a terrible vocation, frightening, majestic, more self-defying than self-defining.

I knew that most people cannot be reached by most priests. I knew that certain people can be reached by certain priests. I knew that if I struck a tuning fork in the key of G and put it near to another tuning fork in the key of G, it would start the second tuning fork humming.

But if I put the humming tuning fork in the key of G next to a tuning fork in the key of C, nothing would happen. No energy would be transferred.

So, all people can only be saved by some priest who is in their key. That's why the world needs so many different kinds of priests, because there are so many different kinds of people. That's why there are so many different kinds of vocations.

I shuddered to think where the people Hank the Tank might be in tune with would hang out, because I wanted to stay away from that place. A priest needs to go out in the world and find the kind of special people he is called to save, whoever they are. Only that priest, and only those special people, in some kind of divine destiny, would fill certain spots of place and time in the world, in history, in the tumble-down mad affairs of humans.

Only the right priest could bump into them on special street-corners, *hello*, and special Confessionals, *Bless me, Father, for I have sinned*, at three o'clock on Saturday afternoons and hear the hot muttered admissions of guilt and sorrow, *alone and with others*, and repentance. Only a special priest could raise them from the stifling despair, *my husband*, and sweaty loss of, *my wife*, eternal hell. One thing I know: hell is not fire and flames. Hell is isolation, loss, despair, and depression when nobody loves you.

Responsibility for creating my specific priestly vocation rolled down upon me. Already I prayed for souls I would meet at some future date. That our coincidence, our mad falling together in the human chaos of a divinely planned world would be grace-ful. I always hyphenated that word. The punctuation made clear to me its real metaphysical meaning. I tore down the walls of myself day by day to grasp my true metaphysics, to bring my true self to the fore. I had so much to prepare to bring Christ to the world.

I talked to Him on a level of personal relation that soothed me with sweet rushes of grace. I cut dialogue short with the unfeeling, unthinking seminarians about me. To only a few could I express these thoughts. Someday I'd tell everyone about divine love in wonderful sermons. I was so full of raw thought and soaring feeling that I was frightening myself with a divine panic.

As if talking directly to me, Gunn preached a sermon in chapel, and eyes turned my way. I looked down at my hands. Gunn thundered that seminarians had no business writing or reading extraneous materials, especially the works of rogue theologians.

"You will only hurt your grades and your spiritual life."

But my grades were excellent. I wanted to stand up in chapel, to cry out, to protest. I was stopped only by a tremendous interior discipline that made me quietly strong against him and his kind. A splendid sense of mystic isolation thrilled through me. I liked not being him.

I kept to myself at free periods after supper and before rosary. I was effortlessly able to sit tight at my desk, writing in my room, resisting outside in the early October twilight a guitar and a couple of ukuleles pounding out "Sweet Georgia Brown" and "Who's Sorry Now?" while those who didn't know, who hadn't found the secret, sang and yelled around the drinking-water fountain outside the back stairs, screaming occasionally as a water balloon tossed from an upper window exploded among them, wetting the ankle-length flaps of their black cassocks.

The Great Either-Or reared its head. The clock was ticking toward Ordination Day. Time was short. Choices had to be forced. Would I serve God or the world? I could take vows of chastity, but what of obedience? I could dedicate my body, but my mind kept on thinking. Either total dedication or nothing.

Why couldn't I be like the other boys who had become men certain of their path toward the priesthood? Why should I sweat making real analysis of the priestly vocation they were moving toward in obedient ritual? Hank's only dilemma, perfect for an adolescent gorilla, was asking either-or questions at table in the refectory like, "Hey, Ry, would you rather slide naked down a fifty-foot razor blade into a pool of iodine, or suck snot from a dead Protestant's nose until his head caved in?"

December 5, 1962

The night St. Nicholas appeared annually with Ruprecht, Hank the

Tank, in the merriment of the Free Period before Night Prayer, walked up to me, smiled, said, "Merry Christmas," and pushed my chest, shoving me backwards over a boy kneeling on all fours behind my knees, to make sure I was flung back, out, and over, falling on the concrete floor.

I felt the lift-off from his hands raise me in slow-motion in wonder, in surprise, until I cracked down on the floor, trying to catch myself, the laughter around me already screaming funny, and broke my finger, felt the middle finger of my left hand snap back, crack through my hand, the beautiful hands of a priest, with the middle finger bent back over the ring finger and the little finger, swelling up fast.

Lock, the wonderful, lifted me up, took me to Father Gunn, who explained he'd try to find a priest to drive me to a doctor in the morning.

"It was only a prank," Hank said.

"Boys will be boys," Gunn said.

"But what about my broken finger?"

At Christmas Midnight Mass in Peoria, I walked out on the altar, the less-than-perfect altar boy, to serve with Father Gerber, hands folded, with my middle finger, the dirty finger that had made all the seminarians laugh, sticking up stiff in a metal finger-splint cast. Nothing was ever more embarrassing. In the front row of St. Philomena's was a small mercy.

Danny Boyle was too busy to laugh at my hand. He was holding a wiggling infant on his shoulder, trying to hand it off to his wife, Barbara, with her hands folded on top of another pregnancy under her cloth coat. A third child, a toddler, clung to Danny Boyle's leg.

Charlie-Pop asked Father Gerber if my injured hand might disqualify me from Ordination. Father Gerber told him to have my Uncle Les telephone Rector Karg. Uncle Les told us all to relax. He was, he said, spending the holidays on vacation in Key West. My broken finger concerned him less than that for the second New Year's in a row he had not been able to go to Cuba since Castro turned Communist. What a shame, he said, because at first he had so approved of Castro's revolution against the Batista government he felt was irretrievably corrupt.

"But what about my finger?"

"What," he said, "about Cuba?"

March 17, 1963
Saint Patrick's Day

The Jesuit priest, our new spiritual director, sat wild and wiry and full of life behind his desk. He was what Jesuits are supposed to be: the Marines of the Catholic Church. The huge desk and windows dwarfed him. He was Irish, of the redheaded and strong kind, a drinker and a smoker, sitting in a rolling blue cloud of smoke. A large ashtray, half-full of butts, lay under his tapping fingers. The toasted smell of his cigarettes saturated the room. He had lived in this suite at Misery only four months, and his bright, freckled, fearless personality lit up the room.

"Ryan Steven O'Hara. What's a Mick like you doing in a seminary full of Krauts?"

"Father, we pay no attention to that. We're all American boys, Catholic boys."

"Do you smoke?" he asked.

"No, Father."

"Good. It's an indulgence and indulgences aren't good for the young. I smoke."

I wanted to say, "You're not young. You're forty." But I didn't. I thought he might laugh, think it humorous, and be yet another priest who every time I tried to talk with him held me off with a joke. I didn't need another punster who saw two meanings to words but only one meaning to life. I hoped as mysteriously as this Irish priest, whose name was Sean O'Malley, S. J., Society of Jesus, had come to Misery, just as mysteriously he could help us all.

His predecessor, a pink ancient German priest predilected to saying *hence*, till all we could do when he preached was count the *hences*, had explained spiritual counseling to me definitively. When the German Jesuit was more than eighty, and I was only fourteen, he told me that I'd see him for spiritual guidance once a year and when I had twelve marks for twelve visits, I would be ordained a priest, and he'd be nearly a hundred years old. Then he talked about Maumee in Ohio and how he used to swim there, centuries ago, before the turnpike ruined everything.

I didn't want to talk about Maumee then with that old German Jesuit and I didn't want to talk about superficialities with the new Irish one.

"What do you want to talk about?" he asked.

"People and me. And God. I'm almost twenty-four and I'm in love."

"With a girl?"

"No."

"With someone here."

"Oh no." I looked at him. "Of course not."

"Thank God and Saint Patrick. Go on."

"All last fall semester I thought of coming to see you, but I was busy. Studies, and editing the Misery newspaper, and sports. After Christmas vacation I thought I'd procrastinated long enough to have committed at least a venial sin of omission."

"Don't be scrupulous, boy, finding sin where there is none."

For an older man he had a fresh tone for a priest.

"This is March." He lit a cigarette. "March first. March fourth. March forth. A month whose dates are a command to go forward." He exhaled clouds of blue smoke. "And March 17, the day for driving snakes out of Ireland."

"I have made progress. I've meditated and thought and prayed a thousand hours to get where I've gotten. I care about people and about God and I'm hurt because so many other people here don't care at all. About anything. I've written editorials about apathy in seminary life. That went over big. Rector Karg screamed at me that I might be the editor, but he was the rector."

"Priests and seminarians don't like criticism."

"I wasn't being critical. I care. That's all. I see this tremendous sense of social responsibility. Don't I have a responsibility now to awaken seminarians the way later I must awaken my parish? We all need to care. I don't think most people realize their potential for caring. They never stretch their lives."

"You know your potential?"

"Not yet. I'm discovering it. Pushing the sides out farther and farther. It's..." I stopped because the Reverend Sean O'Malley, S. J., didn't act as if he understood.

"What?"

"Oh, convoluted, involuted, upside down. Nothing's either black or white to me any more. I see an awful lot of gray. I see meanings to life, and double meanings to everything, and the meanings have been so hard to come by that I want to explain them to everyone else."

"Through Christ."

"Of course. He was a worker. I want to create and run before the wind. I want children. Not my own. Not just the selfish satisfaction of one child. But hoards of everybody's children. And everybody."

He chain-lit another cigarette. He said nothing.

"I'm sorry," I said, "that I talk to you like this. Without any preface. But I talk this way to my closest friends. We had to learn to counsel each other."

He looked hard at me. "I'll not be saying anything bad about my predecessor."

"You must know, it's been so long, it's been never, actually, since we've had adequate spiritual counseling."

"You boys are vain and demanding boys."

"Forgive me, Father. Don't get mad at me. I'll be ordained in two years and haven't the time to waste in preliminaries, in getting to know you. I welcome your objectivity. I open to it. I need direction. I've gotten this far. To this plateau. Where from here?"

"You hide behind too many metaphors, too many images. Where is this plateau? What is it?"

"It's love. I work out of love. That's the meaning of everything. To feel deeply and strongly enough about the world so that Christ can work through me. I know who I am. I've solved all that. About identity, I mean. I'm a child of God. Plain and simple. I arrived at that nearly two years ago and it still satisfies me. But that's a state of being. Where's all the action of life itself to be filled in? I want to give myself. I must give myself. There's no choice any more. My vocation has passed the chance of choice. Only how do I give myself? How do I know myself? Maybe I've never felt anything deeply. I've worked hard studying, reading, writing, praying, to prepare myself for my priestly life in the world. But that's not enough. I don't want to be a standard-issue priest growing fat living isolated in a rectory."

"Watch your mouth."

"I'm sorry. Why do I want to reinvent the priesthood? What can you tell me? What is the secret knowledge and the secret power of priests? Somewhere there's a short circuit. Am I dumb or numb, or do I feel too much?"

"You are having a spiritual crisis."

"Yes, Father."

He talked for a few minutes and said we could both read, think, pray, and make a novena to Our Lady of Knock."

"Knock? Knock?"

"Don't mock me, boy. You Americans!" He handed me a holy card with a drawing of the Blessed Virgin appearing in the village of Knock in Ireland. He would be able to see me again in two weeks and I should continue to work at God's will, discovering it and expressing it.

Two weeks! Damn nondirective counselor! Exiting his door, I asked for his blessing and knelt before him outside his threshold. He made the Sign of the Cross and put his hands on my head and gently closed his door. Clouds of his blue smoke, *incense*, rose off my cassock. I actually felt better. I believed in the craft of Jesuits over ordinary priests. I had dared express myself to a complete stranger. I was a twenty-three-year-old boy and he was a grown-up. Adult help was at hand, even if he was in the FBI of the Foreign-Born Irish priests working in the States.

I went straight to my room and impulsively wrote a short letter to the long-departed Dick Dempsey. Word had come back through the grapevine that he was sick. The implication was he had a...*drum-roll*...nervous breakdown. I thought Dempsey and I had been so alike, I had a vague fear that if Misery made something go wrong with him, the same thing might go wrong with me. I wanted to get in touch, to be of some help; but even Vatican II had not quite loosened the ban against writing, under pain of expulsion, to any former students. So I took the letter, reluctant to let go of my concern for my former friend, signed it whimsically, "Yours truly, Untouched by Human Hands, Raised by Monkeys," and folded the note paper in a kind of silly ritual, and obediently filed it away in my shoe box of historical treasures, knowing I'd never see him again.

Work clears the head. I resolved to stretch my capacity. Once again, the sympathetic older priest, who was himself a writer, hired me at ten cents a page to translate a second volume of Bernard Häring's German moral theology book. The practice at being a working-priest distracted me from the abstract thing I could not grasp.

The first day after the nine-day novena to Our Lady of Knock, actually four days before the two weeks to the next appointment with the Jesuit, I pounded on his door. I didn't cry. I didn't scream. I simply sat down in his chair and tore page after page out of my copy of St. Thomas Aquinas' *Summa Theologica* while I sang the blues and he stared at me.

"You've got the Irish flu," Sean O'Malley, S. J., said.

"What?"

"Most fellas think the Irish flu is drink. Truth be told: it's depression."

"I'm not depressed. This place is depressing."

He gave me a bottle of pills.

I was turning into Russell Rainforth.

I could see stern priests coming to take me away tied to a chair, carried on their shoulders, bleeding from a punch in the face. Soon enough they'd be stashing me in the loony bin between Rainforth and Dryden and Dempsey, in one of those special loony bins for wayward priests we heard whispers about.

It was weird how the core of me dried up, midway through March, into the spring when life is supposed to bloom. Somehow the buoyant balloon of my life deflated and clung to my face like the gas mask of the doctor who had circumcised me as a child. Somehow I went dead emotionally. I was paralyzed. Totally unable to feel. Only fit to curl up and ask why. I stood outside my body and myself and my soul and my mind. I was a question mark left over after everything had been said and nothing had been explained by mystics writing about the dark night of the soul. I committed my entire being to my vocation, but God in His immense silence said nothing. Would I never be able to sink the whole of myself into whatever this mysterious vocation was? I became a spectator of the movie of my life, watching the daily rushes unreel. I could only compare this to Christ's agony in the garden when He sweat blood and begged His Father to reveal the secret reason for such despair and isolation and fear.

I crashed flat on the bed in my own room, trying to breathe, too panicked for tears.

I lay on the bed.

I stood across the room watching this happening to me.

I cursed because I wasn't insane. This is what I got for pushing God for fast answers. A goddam cut-rate breakdown. *Step right up, folks.* I could feel the Librium. Father Sean O'Malley, redhead from the Society of Jesus, fresh out of Dublin, had liberated me with Librium. Lovely Librium, caught *knock-knock,* in my chest. Damn capsules. Lovely capsules. Damn freckled, flat-top Jesuit! Lovely Jesuit.

All I could think of was Annie Laurie saying that the first day she held me, newborn in the hospital, the vegetable man's horse crashed into my father's car parked out front and ruined it and made a great noise and made me cry. On that day of my birth, for little reason I cried. My poor parents would never understand this. Suddenly, I was stone.

I will. I will. Through clenched hands and teeth, I will my way through this. If this is the way from the plateau, then I will that this dark night clarifies my vocation. I will that it shall pass. And pass. And pass. And pass. Mir Mir untha whull, hustha ferst uthum ul? I felt light. Outside myself. Silly. Giddy. Dizzy. Spinning. Happy. Sad. Tangled in life. Threaded. Nobody loves me. Me, not nailed big and strong to a cross, but threaded. A child's beads strung tightly on taut string. March. The river melts and floods. Life is young, poised, free. Threaded. Young goats rolling in long wet grass. Tearing up the mountainside, tumbling down. Unthreaded. Laughing wind in trees, water and spray bubbling near moss beds and skimming over shallow cool sand. Claustrophobic shepherd trapped. Poised, balanced rock, ready to fall. Either way. Either. Or. Confiscated. Not really poised at all. Unthreaded. Marbles caught up in a leather pouch. Discontinuous bits of movie film. Fish in a bowl. Time snowballs. To another time. I will. Life and time and what? Responsibility. What the hell are you talking about? Fancy ramrods. Through a small splintered crack streams a coveted wisp of promise. Bits of songs. Typing ribbon eternally winding and rewinding itself. Paint oozing from tube to palette. Delicious are tastes and smells of dream. Picasso on the sidewalk. Existentialism on a picket fence. Not everyone wears a melted watch. Haunchers along a stone wall. Whispers under the droning harangue. Self-appointed Gantry. Yoo-hoo, Elmer! Fighting in others what afraid to fight in himself. I'm not like other men. Everybody sing. Vienna psychologist down for count of ten. Faith means I don't have to understand. Take it from the top! God said to Moses, Beat me, daddy, eight to the bar.

Ohmarywecrowntheewithblossomstoday.

Sixteen millimeter. Queen of the Angels. The wreck of my happiness. Queen of the May.

Every night, I pulled on my flannel pajamas.

Every morning, I woke up naked.

May 1, 1963
May Day, May Day

An evening rainstorm was approaching in a curtain across the Ohio valley, sweeping across the winding river, the wild, deep, flooded river, over the blowing trees, and up the windy hill. I could dare the spring rain and wait till the very last minute, the very last second, to pull my window closed. The edge of the storm hit, pounded pellets on the glass, washed down the beautiful May twilight. The sky grew orange when the front passed. Behind the clouds, the sun had set, leaving us all bathed in the trailing after light.

Outdoors, arm in arm, two quartets of boys stood in lamp light, sheltered under the stone vault of an entrance stairs, catching the echo, harmonizing German *lieder* and the sweet, sweet air from *Fiorello*, "Twilight descends, everything ends, till tomorrow." Out on the wet walkways, other seminarians strolled back and forth, and forth and back, cassocks snapping like windsocks about their ankles, talking shop, they called it, smoking, and waiting for the call to rosary. I did not follow them to chapel. Out of self-defense.

By the Irish Jesuit's orders, I took a vanishing powder. Now you see me. Now you don't. I disappeared for nearly five weeks into an underground of my own making. In theology lectures, I perfected a look of attention while I read novels under the priestly noses of ancient professors droning on about the Council of Trent and the horrors of Albigensian heresy. I filed with the boys into chapel often enough to keep up appearances. This too on Jesuit orders.

The crowd of five hundred seminarians and priests praying in unison, alternating the responses of the rosary in the dark, the beautiful hum of religious male voices chanting code, or spinning at Mass in rich vestments swirling in pirouettes of liturgy and clouds of incense, stole not my breath away, but my credulity. Ritual was surface. What was the secret behind it? What were they really up to?

Among so many seminarians, all dressed in black, hair cut in flat-tops, my withdrawal from their subjectivity to my objectivity, as a spy on them and on myself, went unnoticed. In the huge conformity, even Rector Karg had trouble keeping track of who was absent from morning prayers and mass; from chapel visits after breakfast, before lunch, after lunch, and after supper; from rosary; and finally from night prayers.

Rosary ended. I sat in the dark in my nine-by-twelve- foot room. I listened to the thudding lockstep of hundreds of boys marching silently from chapel, reluctantly turning into their rooms for the last study period, slamming doors. A tap sounded lightly on my door. I didn't answer. Always some trickster, in a tiptoe sprint down the hallway, knocked once on fifty doors causing fifty boys to break from their studies, open their doors, and all have a good ape laugh. The tap came again. The door edged open a crack. A figure was backlit by a sliver of hallway light.

"Friend or foe?" I asked.

"Ryan, you awake?" It was Lock.

I grunted.

"Where are you?"

"Over here by the window."

"Why so dark in there?" Lock reached only his hand into my room and flipped the switch to the overhead light. My windowful of wonderful twilight dissolved into a mirror reflecting me sitting in my room, desk and bed and wash sink, cassocks and black corduroys and white teeshirts neatly folded, a piece of driftwood Dick Dempsey had given me carved so subtly Rector Karg could never accuse me of collecting art, books all over, spilled, purposely spilled, with theology and philosophy books prominently strewn, hiding almost in plain sight the forbidden novels and plays from the secret library of Sean O'Malley, S. J., who claimed his own father had met James Joyce, in fact, had bought James Joyce himself a drink in a pub.

"Another sinus headache?"

"Yeah." Nobody's sinuses could act up so much, but Lock was kind.

"I thought so." Lock counseled me more than once that I had been communicating less and disappearing more. Lock knew how to play what game there was. Our classmates had begun to miss—not me so much—as my class lecture notes that I shared with them. They figured, because I could write and type, they didn't have to take notes. A true community, they informed me at a class meeting, should share everything beginning at Mass in the morning right on through to study notes and meals in the refectory. One thing was meaning two things. They were literal boys; I was a walking metaphor. I didn't want to be their secretary, but I wanted to be really well-liked by them, so I could levitate and wake them. I even made up subliminal messages hidden in my class notes to motivate them from apathy and fundamentalism. But a chasm gaped between us. Words didn't focus.

I had taken my vocation into my hands to make something of it in the seminary itself. I tried to warn them away from the institutionalization of priests. They were the sons of farmers and factory workers who had survived the Great Depression and many of them wanted to raise their station in life. They talked about not wanting to worry where the next meal came from. They competed about the real estate of their future dream parishes where they'd live in the biggest house in the neighborhood waited on by a housekeeper, a cook, and a gardener. They were not amused by the Christian Family Movement in Chicago. They shook their heads over Canon Cardijn's beginning of the Christian Workers Movement.

Many, choosing designs from Romanesque and Byzantine styles in sample catalogs, had already paid one or the other of the traveling salesmen from the competing liturgical supply companies for their own personal gold chalices. They examined the competing salemen's chalice displays the way customers shop jewelry.

They compared designs of Mass vestments, especially vestments for their own First Mass after their Ordination, at modest little vestment fashion shows, staring at themselves, parading out in the invited salesmen's finest traditional vestments and newest Vatican II styles.

They staked out bragging rights on the monsignors they knew, and predicted how they themselves would climb up the ranks of the clergy. They talked of the apostolate, about working with people, as if they were going to be sociologists or psychologists, not priests. Their vocations were defined by the world. The most ambitious boys loved the study of Canon Law and were set on becoming powerful ecclesiastical attorneys serving bishops and cardinals and the Pope. God told them so.

My very panic was caused by believing that God should be speaking to me, whispering reassurances about my vocation in my ear. Why was God apparently using semaphore flags to tell them to be canon lawyers, dragging their rich vestments down the halls of bishop's mansions, when He wasn't even speaking to me? The panic grew worse when I recalled that only saints heard voices, well, saints and crazy people. So, knowing I wasn't a saint, and estimating that I wasn't yet crazy, I should have been happy I wasn't hearing God's voice.

I wanted to hear what the other boys heard, but I didn't really want to hear the voices of the boys themselves, because, as they grew more mature, many of those German farmers' sons became hard silent dour athletic sergeants on the Misery construction crew, or worse, porky gossiping biddies singing along with opera on stereo recordings in the community room, where they auditioned boys with perfect enough pitch and graceful enough hands to be picked as cantors leading Gregorian chant in chapel.

The seminary was an institution, but I could not surrender to institutionalization. I thought a priestly vocation was a personal calling. I had found, vague as it was, a tempest of self that needed protecting. I'd be content, as Sean O'Malley, S. J., had asked me, to be a wee assistant priest in a wee parish in a wee town, living the wee hidden life of the Carpenter Himself.

"You missed the comedy after supper," Lock said. "Down by the kitchen, Alfred Doney was sitting naked in his room, painting by numbers, and everybody stopped in the stairwell. You could see right in. The jackals in our class thought it was hilarious." Lock leaned casually against my door.

The Doneys, mother and son, worked in the kitchen. She really had mother love to come to a place like Misery to be able to keep him with her. Alfred was retarded and looked like Mickey Rooney. He could have been any age, short, with vacant pink rabbit eyes and a high-pitched voice. His hair was cut under a bowl like a medieval monk. Mrs. Doney was as small as he, far older, with a shock of steel gray hair also chopped like a monk. She was sharp and but for Alfred would have taken the first bus out, migrating to some trailer park down among some sheltering palms in Sarasota or Phoenix. We were not allowed to speak to the lay help, especially this one female, but Mrs. Doney repeated within all earshot, loud enough and often enough for the dead to hear, that for us boys she had given up on ever having her sunglasses, her beautician's rinse, and her Mai Tai. I thought she blamed us for what she could not blame Alfred, whose room was filled with paint-by-numbers.

"Tomorrow night," I said, "you'll see Mrs. Doney standing on a table, posing for Alfred, with a rose between her teeth."

"She'll have numbers on her body...."

"So Alfred can paint her!"

"We could move the numbers around."

"That's what they did to Picasso's mother!"

"Move one eye here."

"Move the other eye there."

"Here an ear."

"There a nose."

"We're so uncharitable," Lock laughed.

Suddenly, Lock was shoved aside. "That'll be all, Mr. Roehm." The Full Gunn thrust my door open the rest of the way. He held Lock by the nape of his blond neck. "Your foot's over the threshold, Mr. Roehm. A mortal offense. Not even the toe of a shoe enters another seminarian's room. When I come down a corridor and see you visiting anyone, I want to see your full body in the hall." He shoved Lock away, and turned full on me. "You should have told him, Mr. O'Hara, to stand back."

He pulled my door closed with a slam and made a great noise bitching Lock out in the hall. All the other boys could hear, but everyone knew Lock Roehm was too golden to ever be shipped. He was temporarily stuck at Misery while the Vatican old guard and the Vatican new guard fought over him.

A guy couldn't win for losing. Screw them all. I picked up one of the many novels the Jesuit had bundled over to me from his private collection, still stowed in his unpacked trunk. He warned me if Father Gunn or Rector Karg caught me with his books, he would have to deny he ever had such worldly goods.

"But this is," Sean O'Malley, S. J., confided, "best for you."

Priests know best, and Jesuits trump ordinary priests. Wasn't that why the Pope himself had ordered the Jesuits to be spiritual counselors to make Misery's seminarians into parish-ready priests who belonged to no religious order? My nerves, my underground books, my blue pills, my big recovery were all top secret; privileged, entrusted, professional secrets for Sean O'Malley and necessity for me. Misery and Gunn and Rector Karg looked with disfavor on any personal crisis. We were supposed to come to Misery in a state of perfection and remain so. Latitude for crisis and growth frightened them. Somehow they had missed or forgotten the physical and spiritual crises of their youth. No potential priest was supposed to destabilize into damaged goods; that was why the priests kept the contents under pressure for twelve years.

But how, I wondered, can even the Pope expect seminarians, who come to the seminary at fourteen, not to suffer not only the normal crises of adolescence, but also the additional ones caused by struggles in the religious life? Realism says seminarians have to develop as much as anyone else. Karg can't expect us to have any interpersonal relationship with Jesus if we can't have one with our friends. Would Jesus want an interpersonal relationship with some boy who had only a stunted, inhibited persona to bring to the relation?

I wrote journal notes to myself on stationery I stuck into my translation papers for the book on moral theology whose German author, *that renegade priest, Häring*, speculated a forward thrust to the evolution of Christianity. Maybe the electricity of the wild May storm shocked me up like Frankenstein's monster. Maybe Gunn had gone too far. I felt wonderful. Screw them all! I tore open Hemingway's novel, *The Old Man and the Sea*. Someday I'll remember all this and it won't be any of that Mr. Chips crap.

May 14, 1963

Two weeks into May I told my Jesuit, *my* Jesuit, that I felt restored enough to begin a gentle preparation for final exams. All-important grades I couldn't fake. The clock was ticking. The calendar was turning. My third-to-last year, drawing to a close, promised a summer dedicated to apostolic work, maybe in some Negro parish on the South Side of Chicago. Ordinations to the priesthood for the twelfth-year deacons approached, propitiously, I announced to everyone, on President John Kennedy's birthday. That was a good omen.

They stared.

My Jesuit gave me copies of two recent Broadway plays, *A Streetcar Named Desire* and *Suddenly Last Summer*. He said that the author understood human nature, Christianity, and God. "Literature," he said, "precedes psychology and theology. Freud turned to Greek drama to find names for his conditions. In these plays you may rather quickly find the face of God."

Actually, rather quickly I felt bound to study for finals, so I skipped the plays, but after four days of deep study, I fell suddenly depressed. The Fathers of the Church in the "Patrology of Ancient Christian Literature" were dry texts we studied in Latin and were tested on in Latin. The Fathers lived in caves and sat fasting on top of stone pillars and cut themselves with sharp stones and whipped the cuts. I threw them aside and read *Suddenly Last Summer* which frightened me because, if literature was life, suddenly those Latin histories of martyrs and saints, and especially mystics mutilating themselves and starving themselves and living in solitary confinement of their own choosing, seemed insane, like psychosis transubstantiated into something believed to be bigger than our human experience, when they were just nuts.

I needed my upcoming summer vacation. The thought of twenty-four semester hours in "Church History," "Exegesis of the Old Testament," and "Ascetical Theology" sucked the breath right out of me.

Suddenly that spring, I started thinking with a southern accent.

I had a vision of heaven and a vision of hell, and the Virgin Herself appeared to me, or then I ate a leftover Easter egg that poisoned me so that I voided myself top and bottom in the white porcelain hand-sink in my little seminary room, wishing Saint Dick Dempsey was around to clean up the mess of pretend-Jesus.

I was dizzy, mystical even, beyond making any excuse to Gunn or Karg or the Jesuit. I lay exhausted on my bed, without my black cassock, in only my shorts and my teeshirt, holding the Jesuit's *Suddenly Last Summer*.

This attack was finally the tuberculosis I once hoped for, to delay my studies, to stretch time to think about being, and becoming, and love, and death. Months of rest someplace. Someplace existential with a veranda. Months defining me in terms of calling and ability. My vocation was absolute surety. A fact. But toward that fact I had so much to do.

I trembled, head to foot. God was speaking to me. This was a sign. I would be a priest.

The ceiling revolved, going round and round, spinning faster and faster around the light fixture. The transcendence was wonderful.

Like the last time, the first mystical time, I ate a stale Easter egg and threw up all over the shower room. Only this time I didn't throw up.

I remembered I had only one mystifying Easter egg left in my shoe box.

I passed out, halfway, or fell asleep.

Perhaps only minutes, seconds, later, an hour maybe, the door opened. Rector Karg stood there. I saw him, felt him, two hundred pounds of him, staring down. I could not move. His enormous chin protruded out of all proportion. The rest of his face, his eyes, peered down from behind his chin, like peepers over a huge cliff. The light burned in his eyes the way it had when he preached his sermon about self-denial, telling us how one day, years before, a house where he lived burned to the ground destroying all his books and papers and dead parents' pictures. He had offered his loss up to the will of God. But standing, watching everything burn, he had clenched his features into an expression of hard resignation and when the fire was out he could never remember how to unlock his face.

Looking down at me, he seemed to be seeing the fire engines of hell arriving again and again too late.

He looked immensely funny. I could not care to move. I was inside the transcendence of egg.

"Why aren't you in class?"

He put his huge hands on my shoulders and sat me up on the bed.

"I didn't feel like going."

"You didn't feel like going? Is that a reason or an excuse?"

"I have a headache."

He yanked me up from the bed.

"Get up. Get your cassock on."

"Get your hands off me."

"What kind of strange little boy are you?"

He slapped me hard across my chest.

The flat of his big Iowa farmer's hand stunned me. Nobody had ever hit me before.

"Get downstairs with the other boys."

My eyes burned with tears, but I held back, so tight, the tears stung like steam evaporating.

"Why don't you fit in here?"

"I fit in here fine."

"Don't contradict me."

"I fit in here fine."

"You're not one of us."

"What the fuck do you want?"

He slapped me across the face. He screamed: "Are you the Boy Anti-Christ?"

Water, not tears, ran down my cheeks.

He hissed: "You're the reason Jesus wept."

He watched me silently vest, take my theology books, and leave him standing alone in my room.

When I returned after class, the novels and plays were gone. The driftwood sculpture was splintered. The bed lay ripped to shreds. My shoe box was tossed spilled-out across the floor. I slammed the door on the mess he'd made.

The Jesuit clucked and shook his red head. "When Rector Karg calls you to his rooms tomorrow," he said, "be honest."

"You like contests, don't you?" I said.

"Are you one of the fighting Irish?"

Rector Karg had focused my resolve. God had spoken to me, but a man had slapped me. I meditated all night: Ryan, old boy, you had enough emotional strength to survive ten years in Misery. Hold together and win. He's a stupid ass. Be careful: that stupid ass has the power, stupid ass or not, to ship you out and ruin your vocation for good. In the long run, Ryan old boy, that's what counts. It's not God who decides you have a vocation, it's Rector Karg. Dear God, o-boy, help me now. You've got to, because if You don't, no one will. God helps him who helps himself, I repeated over and again. I vowed to forgive him.

Finally Karg called me to his suite.

He was prepared to torture me, and I was prepared to play martyr to ensure my vocation, like centuries of seminarians and priests before me.

"I don't like you," he said. He sat behind a carved mahogany desk. On it lay a prayer book, a letter opener, and a manila folder. Long ago when he first was made rector, he had inherited the room as his quarters. Nothing in it matched his personality. If anything, the room defied him completely. Misery's antique German wooden pieces, the brocade draperies, the ornamental carvings spoke of lush medieval days that had enjoyed the meadhall but had not yet learned of Port Royal and its doctrine of Jansenism that stripped art and images from the churches. The hot blast of his personal asceticism was too obedient, too institutionalized, too *'umble* to assert itself to a point of exterior expression in his rooms, so he turned his insane discipline hard in on his own soul. He could not bring himself to empty his sumptuous suite that Rome had years before assigned him. He tolerated its luxury as another cross to bear. Deep back the small human part of him was strictly Inquisition.

He opened the folder, obviously mine, and paged through it. He had spent the night scrupulously examining the little he knew of me officially: my Baptismal Certificate; my parents' marriage license, because no bastard could be ordained a priest; my grade sheets, all more than satisfactory, even if ten points less than at Ohio State; a few letters of official correspondence with my bishop concerning Ordination of each of my four minor orders as Lector, Porter, Acolyte, and Exorcist. I felt strength that before him I stood, an exorcist, ordained by the Church to cast out demons.

It wasn't working.

He reached for another sheet of paper.

"I don't like you," he repeated.

"I love you," I said. "In Christ's name."

"I also hold you...in charity."

"Thank you, Rector."

"You've been taking Librium."

"No more than I was given by my spiritual director, Rector. It's like an aspirin for nerves."

"You have a nervous condition?"

Not till now, I thought. I was still my own best observer. "I was working very hard. Studying. Writing. I had begun translating a German moral theology book, but stopped already early in the spring. My studies come first."

"Yes. That book by that heretic Häring."

"I was told, Rector, that he is one of the new theologians."

He glared at me. "Häring is a radical rogue priest." He pulled a sheaf of loose pages from his desk drawer. "These pages came from your room. There's words in here. Words that...one word...mentioned twice. You have dared to write it."

"I only translated it, Rector."

"No seminarian should even know that word exists."

"I looked in the dictionary, Rector."

"That word does not exist."

"When I become a priest, hearing Confessions, that word..."

"Do not listen to everything you hear in the Confessional. Do you understand me?"

"Yes, Rector."

"I shall take these pages and burn them myself."

"Yes, Rector."

He was an assassin. I sat across from him, intent on playing his game, intent on outmaneuvering him. This was about survival. I was certain I had a vocation, and if God were trying to tell me I didn't have a vocation, God would certainly find a better messenger than the pietistic Rector Karg.

If I was not to be a priest, which negation I sincerely doubted, then I would leave Misery by my own will. I would not let this assassin twist ten years of my pure motives of study, prayer, work, and virtue into some weird pattern that would justify his shipping me.

If I were to be removed, I would remove myself. All my life I lived to protect my vocation. Could I be faulted for grooming my specific vocation as a worker-priest, writing for my supper, in the general calling to the priesthood? I would not relinquish my lifetime of focus now. Not to an assassin who knew me only as a name in roll call, another mouth to feed, and a brain that was so *cogito: ergo sum, I think: therefore I am, that he feared, what? My powers of analysis?*

"You're the most analytical little boy I've ever seen," he had said, "and that's not good in the spiritual life!"

He knew nothing of my heart and my soul. He shuffled the sheets of my ten years of excellent grades and solid reports on my behavior. He mumbled over the early chapters of the discontinued translation. I felt secure because my purity was unassailable. Sex alone, or with others, was a mortal sin of impurity against the sixth commandment, and against the priestly vow of celibacy. I was a pure boy. I had never ever even touched myself, never ever interfered with myself, so even if I didn't have a vocation, no one could question my purity which the Church declared the barometer of a vocation.

"More seriously, however, I find this other matter." He paused expectantly.

"May I ask, please, Rector, what that is?"

"You don't know?"

"No. No, Rector, I don't."

He reached again into his drawer and pulled out a folded piece of stationery that had never been placed in an envelope.

I found this letter in your room." He handed it to me. "This is your handwriting?"

I looked at the letter I had never mailed to Dick Dempsey. It was an invitation for him to come some visiting Sunday. I had thought his talking to an old friend might help. I thought I might play a bit of the worker-priest, and be very Vatican II, and maybe help him. "I wrote this," I said. "Actually, I should say that I composed it. I never mailed it. I think I never thought to mail it."

"Why did you write to this boy? He is a former student. The rule forbids you to correspond with former students."

"Yes, Rector. But I wrote that note hoping the Vatican Council might allow..."

"You dare contradict me?"

"No, Rector."

"You still know this student?"

"I knew him, Rector. We were friends while he was here."

"Friends?"

"We were classmates, Rector. For seven years, Rector. We knew each other quite well."

"Then you know this man has been afflicted?"

"I heard he was not well."

"You knew it was not physical?"

"He was physically sick quite a lot when he was here. I thought perhaps he was a little emotional."

"You know what is wrong with him?"

"No, Rector. What is it?"

"You don't know?"

"No, Rector."

"I won't say."

"Say what, Rector?"

"If you are innocent, your innocence will protect you."

Suddenly, something unspoken leapt up in the room.

Rector Karg pulled himself up to his giant size. "Are you like him, boy? Are you like him?"

Dick Dempsey was nothing but innocence when he was at Misery and so nervous he wet the bed and was often in the infirmary, absent from class. I knew nothing unspoken about him. But everyone else knew. All of them, I bet, Lock included. Their goddam community. It was some strange Christian charity, all right, that kept them from telling me. Just because we had been friends. They told me only enough to make me feel a priestly responsibility to reach out to a friend in distress. How could I tell that to this assassin? How could I tell him an unmailed letter dated two months previously, written in hopes of the openness of Vatican II, had not been mailed because in the tension between the call of charity and the call to obedience to the holy rule, the rule had won out.

"Are you like him, boy? Are you?"

"No, Rector."

I did not lie. I was not like Dick Dempsey. I was not like that at all. Sean O'Malley, S. J., told me I was "maybe a wee bit soft from seminary living," but he thought I was "not like that at all, not at all, at all." O'Malley had asked me, "When you draw pictures of boys, are they erect or not?"

I was shocked. "I don't draw pictures of boys."

Suddenly Rector Karg slapped my records closed and terminated the interview. "We'll meet again tomorrow. You have placed me in a delicate situation of conscience. I must pray over this." He stood up to his full height in the big room of big furniture and big walls. "Tell me. How many other rules have you broken? I have confiscated your so-called literature books. I suppose you have a transistor radio."

I didn't say, "Every single seminarian has one." I didn't say, "Couldn't you find it?" I simply promised to surrender my only connection to music and the news within the hour.

"Give the radio to Father Gunn," he said. "We shall have to confer much about you. Your status is extremely precarious. We may have to ship you, boy. I suspect you may have lost your vocation. "

"Thank you, Rector," I said, "for your kindness." And screw you. I was in mortal danger. My soul and heart and intellect left my body and I watched myself walk out of his suite. Oh dear God, protect me. I went directly to my Jesuit, who to that moment had been only my spiritual director and not my confessor.

"Let me hear your Confession," Sean O'Malley, the clever priest from the clever Society of Jesus, said, and sealed his lips with the seal of the Confessional forever.

I confessed misdemeanors of the radio, and venial sins of unkind thoughts about Rector Karg, and how one time I had stood for three hours inside the tiny cupboard where the priests locked up their television so I could watch the Academy Awards. I confessed the same venial sins I confessed twice a week very Wednesday and Saturday afternoons waiting in the long lines of boys standing in the chapel at the curtains of a dozen Confessionals. I really and in truth had never committed a mortal sin in thought or word or deed. That was my ironic, intellectual problem: without knowledge of sin, how would I ever grow up emotionally and know anything about life in the world?

I was not like any boy at all.

I became even more fierce in my self-defense.

For a week Rector Karg, Father Gunn, and Sean O'Malley, S. J., rummaged about in my life. I pictured us all sitting at a round poker table covered with green felt, each one fitted with an eyeshade. I held my cards close. I was playing for my spiritual life, my soul, and my vocation. The Jesuit played by proxy; because of his privileged knowledge as my spiritual confessor, he could not talk directly to Rector Karg, who had to believe what I told him the Jesuit told me. Rector Karg was bound in conscience to believe me. His fundamentalism made him dangerous. He was a literalist trying to keep his balance in a trickster world of spirit.

"You," Sean O'Malley said to me, "are facing the world you said you wanted to embrace."

"I thought Librium was like aspirin. We have no newspapers, no radio, and you didn't tell me about it."

"I knew what you needed."

They all seemed to know what I needed.

"How did Karg find out?"

"I have to report any medicine I dispense."

"You didn't tell me that either."

"I'm a Jesuit," he said.

I actually short-circuited into laughs, big ones and small ones. Ryan Stephen O'Hara, I thought, you do get yourself in fub duck situations. In mortal danger of losing my vocation, I laughed, standing outside myself. Even fighting for elemental survival, I could not walk into a believable grown-up version of myself, because some grown-up was always standing in my way. My only strength lay in my creative resistance to Rector Karg. Again I felt like a moviegoer, watching myself act out the opening reels of my life done with smoke and mirrors. What he saw was not me. It was what I let him see. What I knew he wanted to see. What I knew he needed to see if I were to save my vocation.

Finally, Rector Karg called me to his suite. "Your grades are good," he said. "Your faculty recommendations are high. You tell me the Jesuit spiritual director says your interior life is progressing. There may have been some circumstantial misunderstanding. Your uncle, who is a priest not without influence, spoke up for you, both as a priest and a relation. However, we have uncovered enough that we can only encourage you to work to full capacity, that is, to full responsibility of Christlike perfection." He folded his hands. "If you are concerned about your status, let me ask you, do you feel the grace of God?"

"I do, Rector. I really believe I do. That I have all along. Even in the depths of this trial." I sensed he approved such dialogue.

"Do you feel you truly have a calling from God?"

"I've never felt my vocation more strongly than I have this past year. This last week has increased my sense of its value immensely. I had to make a concrete fight for it."

"Then you should rejoice, my son. Let me counsel you to take your examinations with a full heart and join in next week with all your soul when the Holy Spirit shall be called down on the candidates for the priesthood who are only two classes ahead of you. Ordination Day is a time of great hope and grace for all."

"Yes, Rector," I said and I knelt on the floor before him. I directed the movie perfectly. "Will you please give me your blessing?"

Rector Karg moved toward me. His shoe tips touched my knees. I could smell the hot metal of coins in his pockets. I imagined nickels and dimes and pennies tangled in with his rosary beads and some lint. My eyes crossed, focusing directly on his Knights of Columbus belt buckle. He put the palm of his left hand against his chest and with his raised right hand made the Sign of the Cross in the air over my head and then rested both his thick cold priestly hands on my hair. "No one of us," he said, "can stand the close scrutiny of God."

"None of us," I intoned.

"There is one condition more."

Still kneeling, I looked up at him with his hands open in the gesture of priestly blessing.

"Yes, Rector?"

"I forbid you to write one more word."

I wanted to punch him in his consecrated groin.

8

May 31, 1963

Things grew worse. Suddenly someone in Rome, some Machiavellian cleric slinking around behind the open-hearted Pope, probably some Borgia cardinal at the Sacred Congregation of Universities and Seminaries desperate to preserve traditional Catholicism against the progressive theology of Vatican II, promoted simple Rector Ralph Thompson Karg up to the exaggerated rank of Papal Chamberlain with the title Very Reverend Monsignor.

As a young man, Karg had first been a freshly ordained priest saying Mass in a parish in an cornfield in Iowa before the War Department had commissioned him a chaplain in the Air Force with the rank of lieutenant colonel. He had come out of combat in the War into combat in the Church as the longest reigning rector of Misericordia. He had become a soldier-priest championing the discipline of a muscular Catholicism.

He accepted his elevation to Papal Chamberlain like a blister on his 'umility. He wore his new black and purple robes like a penitential hair shirt. He preached to us that the title and robes were vainglorious. He tugged at his cassock and shoulder cape. His rank embarrassed him. He knew he was a lightning rod for both warring sides in the civil war of Vatican II. I hoped the lightning would strike him and kill him.

I had watched him for ten years and I could only wonder if his promotion was the old Roman rule of thumb: *Promoveatur ut amoveatur, Let him be promoted so he may be removed.* Maybe someone in Rome wanted to get rid of him and remodel Misery. Karg had lectured us with his story of his 'umble beginnings so often, my mind's eye had long before fantasized the fub duck movie version of his life to which I added adjectives.

He had been born the only son of an Iowa farmer whose lean-boned German face was permanently sunburned up to the cap line across his forehead. His father rarely took off his cap, and when he did, sitting with the other German farmers at Sunday Mass with their blond-braided wives and towheaded stairstep children, all the men's big-moustached faces were uniformly sunburned red up to the same cap line, above which their bald round heads were stark white, and their blond-white hair was cut short.

"Those Catholic laymen," he told us, "those farmers and fathers, are manly measure against our soft lives at Misericordia. A priest in his every action must always consider what other men will think. You must be manly men."

He regretted his own face was no longer sunburned. Something secret in him made him resent that someone in Rome who had elevated him out of any return ever to his farm parish in Iowa and vested him in robes that left Iowa behind. Such honor from the world of the Vatican affronted his conserving sense of personal asceticism. Obediently, he submitted to honor his superiors, the bishop, and the Pope. His obedience made him meaner.

Invested by the Church in Rome, a city he had never seen, he interpreted his new commanding rank as Misery's rector to mean Rome delegated him to use his tight-lipped Iowa ways to rein in liberal tendencies creeping into the seminary. He had swept the pride of the world from his soul. He shaved his face so close his hard jaw looked permanently scraped raw. For himself, to be saved, he had only to obey. Even as commander, he commanded only under a higher obedience which he commanded in all us boys. His one great pride was in his simple priesthood, for without his vocation, he was nothing more than an Iowa farmer's German son with the rank of lieutenant colonel from a War that was over except for its lessons.

As the new Papal Chamberlain, Karg set out to preserve the old ways of Catholicism, without distinguishing between traditional Catholicism and institutionalized Catholicism, even as the progressive Pope John's Council of bishops convened in Rome *aggiornamento*, to throw open the windows of the Church to admit the fresh winds of ecumenical change. Rector Karg preached that the glory of simple, blind obedience kept priests free from every sin.

He went on a rampage, disciplining or shipping boys not because they had no vocation, but because they were willful boys, bright boys, boys crying, begging not to be thrown out after six, seven, ten years in the seminary studying for the priesthood, foregoing all worldly pursuits and education. His reign of terror raided our study halls in wild scenes that made real the hilarious Christmas visit of St. Nicholas and his wild fiend Ruprecht. Parents who thought they were one day soon to be the mother and father of a newly ordained priest called Rector Karg begging him to reinstate their sons. Whole families fell instantly from honor to shame.

Rector Karg told them all the same thing: "Only ten percent of Misericordia's boys reach the priesthood. I'm going to make it five percent. The cream of the cream. Many are called, but few are chosen."

He sent letters to our parents and cut the number of Visiting Sundays from eight Sundays in nine months of the school year to three Sundays, between 1:15 and 3:45. He began opening all our incoming mail. He called me to his room for discipline because my mom and dad wrote me apologizing that they could not drive five hundred miles to see me for two hours and thirty minutes. He told me, singled out in front of all the other boys, that my parents were worldly. He shipped a studious older boy who dared tell him publicly, "You see the priesthood more as a reward than a sacred calling." He said to us, "A boy's only pride can be his priesthood in Christ." The priesthood was his horizon and his sun never rose on a day better than the morning of final Ordination to the holy priesthood.

"Ordination Day," he preached, "is the day that the Lord has made." He turned thumbs down. "No high-school graduation. No college graduation. No days to distract from Ordination Day which comes once every May for boys who have prayed and studied for twelve years." *Ka-thud.*

On the first Ordination Day after Karg's political elevation, on a particularly beautiful Saturday morning in May, Misericordia's chapel, bursting with flowers, was crowded with the fathers and mothers and families of the twelfth-year seminarians who had completed their studies in the Latin and Greek classics, philosophy, and theology. I looked down from the choir loft at Rector Karg far below in the sanctuary. He stood to the side of the main altar. His head and huge jaw sat on top of his purple monsignor's robes. He looked satisfied as the assassin who had whittled down the last of what had been a class of ninety-six boys to sixteen.

I knew that only the night before, he had called one of the brightest young men in the Ordination class aside and told him that he should, even with his family waiting for the glorious morning, withdraw from Ordination. Rector Karg did not think the young deacon was worthy of the tradition of the priesthood, but the young man told Karg he would report him to the Apostolic Delegate, because no one but God at the eleventh hour could stop his Ordination. Karg had raised his hand against the twenty-five-year-old who had said, "I wouldn't if I were you. I'm younger. I'm stronger. I'll sue you in a court of Canon Law."

The ordaining bishop knelt at the main altar and intoned the 142 invocations of the "Litany of the Saints." On the marble floor of the sanctuary, behind the bishop, the sixteen seminarians in white robes lay prostrate in four rows of four. "*Sancta Maria, ora pro nobis. Sancte Joseph, ora pro nobis. Holy Mary! Saint Joseph, pray for us.*" The prayers and the Ordination Mass called God's grace down on the sixteen young men about to receive an indelible mark on their souls from the sacrament of Holy Orders.

Only the Communion rail separated those special ones from pew upon pew of lay people kneeling at their seats and overflowing to stand in the aisles. An invitation to an Ordination was a social and spiritual coup far beyond any wedding. Watching the women and men and children all directly beneath my perch in the choir loft, I could close my eyes and hear how different the chapel sounded than when filled with five hundred silent, obedient boys. I loved the visitors' attentive reverence, their awe, their whispers, their voices responding to the bishop, their palpable happiness that their son or brother was about to be ordained a priest forever. I loved the powdered scented sweet smell of their bodies.

I drifted, *Sancta Lucia,* with the hypnotic sing-song, *Sancte Johannes,* of the Litany. I wondered if anyone famous, *Sancta Agnes,* sat in the chapel crowded, *Sancte Philippe,* with a thousand outsiders. Once, years before, Pat O'Brien, the movie star, had come to a second cousin's Ordination and the priests had told Pat O'Brien they hoped sometime to have his movie where he played Father Duffy to show the seminarians. They were sorry they could never remember that picture's name. I could not see the visitors' faces, but I knew they were the army of parents and relatives and nuns who followed the Pope's admonition of "nurturing vocations." I wondered if I invited President Kennedy or Princess Grace if I'd even get an acknowledgment.

Actual Ordination occurs when the bishop anoints the young man's hands, which are tied together with white cord. The bishop lays his hands on the young man's head and says, "Thou art a priest forever according to the Order of Melchisedec."

At that moment, God brands an indelible mark on the soul of the new priest—a mark so indelible that no one, not Rector Karg nor the Pope himself, can ever take it away.

So great is the sacrament of Holy Orders that all the clergy in the sanctuary rise up and join in a long line. While the bishop and Rector Karg and two dozen monsignors and the hundred visiting priests imposed their hands one after the other on each of the sixteen heads, in the choir we sang the surging hymn, "Holy God, We Praise Thy Name."

> "Holy God, we praise Thy Name.
> Lord of All, we bow before Thee.
> All on earth Thy Scepter claim.
> All in heaven above adore Thee.
> Infinite Thy vast Domain,

> everlasting is Thy Reign.
> Infinite Thy vast Domain,
> everlasting is Thy Name."

Chills ran through me. Boys were changing into priests, their souls marked for all eternity.

Their mothers and fathers pressed and craned toward the sanctuary where the drama of the ancient ritual unfolded in incense, robes, and music. I could see perfectly down into the sanctuary, but somehow my vision veered off-kilter. I wanted to witness the miracle of Ordination without fearing that a jaundiced old priest like Rector Karg might steal my Ordination away. I wanted to anticipate the very instant the sacrament of the priesthood would mark my own soul indelibly.

Once a priest, always a priest! A priest forever! Nothing more could Rector Karg do about it.

But my joy slipped. Even perfect ritual cannot deliver perfect moments. I suddenly felt sorry for the people down below, for the mother or father who was shoved off to the side or behind a pillar while I could see so well. Rector Karg threatened my path to this day. Always in awe of my vocation itself, I was suddenly overpowered by him.

Our whole seminary year was built up to this supremely metaphysical moment when boys became priests who could conjure Christ's body and blood and soul and divinity under the appearance of bread and wine. My blood flushed with anger. I felt simply, with all my clothes on, high in the choir loft above all those people, naked. I felt stripped, even under my wool cassock, naked, nude as a sculptor's model who, locked and tensed into position, remains totally, separately, existentially himself despite the artist's devouring eye, despite the brush-brush of charcoal sketches, despite the soft slap of hands laid on clay to give it shape.

My very desire for the crystalline purity of the priesthood caused an unaccustomed hardness in me. Perfume rose on the warm air. No, my God, I said calmly, I want no pleasure from this natural feeling that will go away if I distract myself. I concentrated on singing our rendition of the hymn, *"Veni, Creator Spiritus, Come, Creator Spirit."* My body was betraying my soul, so I stepped outside my body. Everything, I realized is not either-or. Some things are plain neutral. I wanted nothing: not pleasure, not indistinct desire. Nothing in the world could matter. Not even the world. No one could get in my way. Not even Rector Karg. I stepped fully into my vocation. I could will my way over anything, even the hard physical joy in the very idea of the priesthood.

In the faraway movie down in the sanctuary, the sixteen new priests in their new robes moved about con-celebrating the mass with the bishop. A thrill passed through my soul, but I would not be seduced by spiritual emotion any more than by physical pleasure. I was not stupid. I wanted every kind of purity possible: physical, intellectual, emotional, spiritual. I was a syllogism.

I possessed my vocation with a surety transcending emotion.

The only good Rector Karg had done was warn me off emotion.

The Jesuit O'Malley himself had said that my emotion had too much driven the intellectual and moral responsibility I had taken toward my studies, until I could work so intensely no longer.

Only by abandoning all feeling had I been able to defeat Rector Karg.

I vowed to express my vocation only through clean, clear, crystalline intellect.

This was the safe path to the distance of holiness.

I vowed to be analytical, chaste, and obedient.

No one could assail such Jesuitical heroism.

A priest could not leave himself open to any emotional compromise.

Circumstances of feeling cannot be logically explicated upon questioning.

The rationale of intellect can always be examined, clearly, objectively, without suspicion.

Rector Karg had taught me that. I learned it from him.

I learned about the triumph of reason.

My vocation was no longer based on a swell of boyish feeling.

God had used Rector Karg to redefine my vocation with reason.

I could think.

Therefore, I existed, cool, distant, high above them, and I hated Karg.

"Never become cynical," Father Gunn had warned us. "God knows there's nothing worse than a cynical priest except an ironic priest. Irony versus sanctity. Like chastity, the choice is not a choice."

I watched my classmates and the younger and older seminarians all swept up in Misery's chapel and choir loft into the hot May emotion. Ordinations came every year and each class of boys took one giant step toward the altar. I had written a progressive article about "The Objectives of the Second Vatican Council" for *The Misericordia Review*, and gotten in trouble. The other seminarians spoke in slogans.

They said, "The priesthood is a sacramental change of your soul." They said, "Ordination is a metaphysical change of your person." They said, "We've got to pray for our vocations to feel the totality of grace."

They said, "You lose yourself to become an *alter Christus, another Christ.*" They said, "Every priest has to pay for his vocation. Far better to pay for it in the discipline of the seminary than later on in the practice of the priesthood."

They defined my goal and my cross.

Disappear, vanish into Christ.

Every boy seemed hypnotized. Every boy except Lock and me. Even during this Ordination Mass, I didn't want to feel my vocation. I wanted to think it. I'd felt too much in the last months. My best feelings had been misunderstood by the priests who should have respected them most. But Rector Karg's raging at the top of his lungs that I could be dismissed for feeling, his way of talking to me as no one had ever talked before, delivered me. Having reached two awakenings after ten years of flat seminary life, I was delivered by reason. I stood outside the pale of traditional Catholic feeling. I vowed not to be swept up by pious claptrap. I would never again tell any priest, any teacher, anyone anything that could not be explained to lions in sheep's clothing like the sanctimonious Rector Karg.

I liked seminary life, but I wouldn't be taken in by its sentimentality of pious little boys with rays of light haloing their heads, because my call was not to be forever a seminarian, but to leave the seminary by becoming a priest. I stood away from the other boys. The gap between us became wider. They posed and pranced. Two years before, in all sincerity, I had requested, according to our custom of praying nightly as a group for sick relatives and friends, that three Hail Mary's be said in chapel for a sick woman. The next day when Father Gunn asked me in front of Hank the Tank and his brother, PeterPeterPeter, and another older seminarian if my mother were sick, I said, "Oh, no, my mother is fine."

When they pressed to know the name of the woman, I told them that they had prayed for Elizabeth Taylor because she was nearly dead in London and needed a tracheotomy so she could finish filming *Cleopatra.* They were shocked. "You brought a scandalous woman into our prayers." They said the Vatican newspaper, *L' Osservatore Romano,* had called her morally bankrupt. They accused me of condoning adultery. They said the world condones sin.

Actually, I told them, the world never has condoned sin like they thought. The world is always fundamentally righteous. Christ, I said, had to save thieves and harlots and sick people from the stones of the righteous world. Besides, I said—because I wanted them to talk meaningfully to me—after the War and Auschwitz and Nagasaki, you can't stone people any more. They shook their heads and told me I was worldly, and I told them they were righteous, and the distance between us widened into sniffy suspicions and whispers. Hank the Tank said in German, *"Der empfind-same Mensch, cheap sentiment.* What else can you expect of a Danny Boy?"

The Ordination ceremony ended with all us fifty boys in the choir singing "Handel's Anvil Chorus" out over the heads of the crowds flooding the aisles. Parents ran to white-robed sons giving their First Blessing, dropping tears and Kleenex. People hugging, giving kisses. The voices of the world crashing into our retreat. Pretty girls in summer dresses kneeling for the special indulgences that come with a priest's First Blessing, and boys, shooting their cuffs and tugging at shirt collars, intending to use what they had, awkward before ordained brothers they did not understand. Fathers in suits, and mothers in summer fur and perfume, and aunts and uncles all eddying around their beloved fresh new priests who were all completely handsome on their Ordination Day the way grooms are on their Wedding Day.

Above it, above it all, Rector Karg stood between huge bouquets of roses and peonies, above the love and effusion of the world of families. Off to one side, bearing it, alone, as if to say pay me no attention, because I'm the long-suffering servant of Jesus the High Priest, he tugged at his robes, and behind his ashen face, I could hear his voice, the rhythms of his voice, the way he lectured us, wishing to God that the celebrating crowd would move out the doors, away from the silent center of the gold tabernacle where Christ resided behind a locked door under the appearance of bread, attended only by the candle burning inside the red glass of the sanctuary lamp. I prayed that God would forgive my nasty, uncharitable thoughts.

I stood alone in the choir loft, behind the organ scattered with sheet music. Forty-nine singing boys, minus me, had run down to congratulate the new priests or to roam curiously among the guests. Rector Karg, seeing the crowd receding, walked purposefully behind the altar to the sacristy. I could hear him sputtering, roaring at finding the seminarian sacristans drinking unconsecrated altar wine, on this special day, right from the jug. Even some of the visitors noticed. I was happy he screamed at everyone and not only me. I figured the Pope knew Karg was crazy, and that made him infallibly crazy, and made me suspicious of Papal Infallibility.

I pushed open an old door behind the organ pipes in the choir loft. It led through a neglected attic stacked, *creepy*, with boxes of dead priests' effects, to another door that opened outside to a high parapet on the upper church. A hot rectangle of sun spilled into the dark cool of the attic. Pigeons cooed, flapped, flew up, and circled. Swallows swooped to farther battlements or perched far below at gabletop on the limestone crosses of Misery. The world fell down and away from this upper porch, down the falling lines of stone, across the slate-roof dormers, down the ancient red-brick walls to the green firs and red cannas and cement walks dotted with visitors.

Men in suits stood near willowy girls in dresses that lifted and floated in the spring breeze. Little groups crowded together, lined up smiling in front of cameras, and surged in circles around newly ordained sons. Junior seminarians, high-school boys in ironed black slacks and starched white shirts, and college seminarians in black cassocks with red sashes, moved through the throngs of visitors. All the boys were on their best behavior. Rector Karg told us to act like hosts to the visitors to Misery, because you never knew when one of them might die and leave a bequest large enough to fund one boy's entire twelve years of education.

"Every boy must replace his scholarship," Rector Karg said. "If you can't secure a bequest, you'll have to repay Misericordia yourself."

The threat was considerable because most priests earned no more than a hundred dollars a month.

I stood on Misery's rooftop looking down on the world below. God Himself must have such a view, and from God's perspective I watched all those people down on the lawn. Unlike God, I could not will them to move or not move, to wave or not wave, to open car doors or not. So much for priestly providence. They had a life of their own. For minutes, hours, years the world was down there before me. I could not hold back the joy of the day. O my God! I turned, ran back into the choir loft around the organ, down all the marble stairs, throwing open the doors, wanting to run across the porch to be down with them on the lawn, walking among them, almost touching the women in wild hats that floated over everything. I ran for the main foyer, my heart hurting, pumping beneath my cassock, trying nonchalance, weaving upstream among the guests working their way from the church to the front garden.

They walked, stood, milled about, talking, congratulating, hugging, eager to spy out the halls of Misery where their sons and brothers had spent twelve secret years of youth. Their laughter rang liquid down the marble corridors, banked against the stone walls, and echoed back like ripples on water over stones. I pushed through them easily. *Excuse-me, excuse-me, hello, congratulations, excuse-me.* An Italian family caught me up, *bellissimo* and *ciao,* and we all spun out onto the porch blinking like babies strollered suddenly into the sun. Other families, mostly German, some Irish—all Americans—mixed in and we were all swept down the steps, to the lawn, in the May. Together. Italian and German and as my parents both said,

"Irish and Catholic, thank God!"

Life poured into my very being. Senses glutting, digesting. Soul expanding like a sponge in sweet deep water. I, among them, moving, smiling, seeing, hardly being seen, listening, nodding, smiling, feeling, leaping nearly, wanting to reach out, touch, grasp all to me to protect them, to save them, to lock them all forever into their happiness.

My own mother was thrilled at the prospect of being known as the mother of a priest. My own father counted the days until he was the father of a priest.

Sun soaked deep into the black wool of my cassock. I felt like David Niven in *Around the World in Eighty Days,* floating in a balloon high above the world, watching out for it, landing on a white bench among the shade trees where three little girls in Sunday dresses played hide-and-seek.

"Ryan," Lock called. "Come here."

I turned, seeing him all in black break from the colorful crowd.

"Come quick," he said. "Live ones."

I walked toward him. He took my arm and I went cold. On no day but this would one seminarian dare touch another without wrestling for a hold. On Ordination Day, Lock thought nothing of it, forgot the rule completely. He wanted me to meet, I had to, really had to, he said, meet this wonderful group of lay people come for the Ordination. He'd run into them, quite by accident, them asking for directions on the lawn. I really had to meet them. Particularly this one couple who were writers. I really had to, he said, and he pulled me toward them, a rare cast to his always precise eye.

Five guests stood in an eager, curious circle that opened expectantly to receive us. A gaunt thin girl with a high forehead stood between an acne-faced boy and a tall smiling man with yellowish skin. The girl gestured frantically across the circle to a shorter man. He reached into his green suit and produced a package of cigarettes. The big woman next to him frowned, started to speak, but seeing us, instead showed her teeth and placed a small white-gloved hand lightly across her enormous breast.

"I could cry." She was being wonderful. "I could just cry meeting all you dear sweet dedicated boys at once."

"This is Ryan O'Hara," Lock said.

"How do you do?" I looked directly at the thin girl with the unlit cigarette. She looked petulant. I spoke directly to her. "How do you do?" She seemed as if speech were an effort beneath her.

The big woman intervened. "How do we do? Not so well as you, Mr. O'Hara," she said. "Not nearly so well as you. Or should I call you 'Father

O'Hara'?"

"Call me 'Ryan.' I won't be ordained for another two years."

"You've a great future, Ryan O'Hara," the man in the green suit said. He toted his publican's stomach toward me to bestow the confidence. "The wife and I are writers too."

"That's very nice." I looked at Lock.

"This is Mr. and Mrs. Thuringer," Lock said.

"Berrengar," the man said. "Not Thuringer. Berrengar. Thuringer is a sausage."

"I told them," Lock said, "you do a bit of writing."

"A bit!" Mrs. Berrengar exploded. "Why, my dear Ryan, we have read several of your stories and I said immediately to Mr. Berrengar that here certainly was a writer of great Catholic promise." Mr. Berrengar's green suit rocked back and forth in affirmation, smiling. "Walter, that's Mr. Berrengar. You can call us 'Walt' and 'Mauve.' Walter and I do a bit of writing ourselves. Free-lance, of course."

I smiled. The thin girl, tired of the useless waiting, lit her own cigarette. I knew the tip would be pulled wet from her mouth. I knew that any hotel room she would ever be in would have a flashing neon sign outside the window. She looked to be their daughter-in-law, the wife of the tall yellowish man, perhaps his college acquisition.

"The money in writing isn't important," Walter assured us. "We can make enough at our jobs to get by on. More than get by, I guess." He coughed modestly. "It's the good...son...Ryan...may I call you...'son'?...the good you can do."

"It's such a thrill to know you're doing something for somebody to see your name in print," Mauve said. "Maybe you could read some of our stories," she said directly to me. "You helping edit on *The Misericordia Review* and all. Of course, we haven't hit the big Catholic magazines yet."

"But the little ones love us," Walter said.

He only needed to slap his thigh and stick a red ping-pong ball on his nose. Oh God, I thought, help me to be kind. These are nightmare people from some nightmare parish in some nightmare town. They're not at all like the other guests. Lock searched hard to hunt these clowns out for sport. It was a cruel game we often played with unsuspecting visitors, especially ones more Catholic than the Catholic Church.

"For instance, take Skippy's best friend there." Walter motioned to the boy with acne. "Why, we got a feature article out of him that might save hundreds of teenagers' lives. Why that little boy, Skippy's friend—Jim, Jimmy, his name was—went off and shot himself right in the head in a field not two blocks from our house. Had felt down in the dumps, his folks said. Good people, his folks, but not too cognizant," he lingered over the word, "...cognizant...of what goes on in modern kids' modern-day heads. We wrote it up and called it 'Teenage Doldrums.' Of course, we never said in the article that Jimmy shot himself for sure; said it could have been an accident, like the coroner told his folks. It could have been an accident."

"You always leave room for hope," Mauve said. "I certainly wouldn't want it on my mind if one of my boys, or Edith there, went off and shot their heads off on my account. Edith won't have to shoot her head off. Edith smokes cigarettes. Edith is my daughter-in-law, Chuckie's wife."

"That poor man and woman have never been the same," Walter said.

"That's sad," I said. "There certainly is a great opportunity to express social responsibility in the Catholic press."

"Yes," Lock said. "Our *Misericordia Review* has a circulation of 20,000 souls."

"Think of that," Mauve said.

"Jimmy's parents never will be the same either," Walt said. "Always thinking they might have caused him to do it. Skippy here don't know why he did it."

"He certainly doesn't." Edith said her first words.

They looked at her. A kind of fear flushed suddenly in their faces. Chuckie, the man with the yellow skin, shifted slightly, touched her arm, and said, "Now, Edie, honey."

"Christamighty," Edith said, "the Catholic press stinks."

They stood in silence before her. Lock and I said nothing.

"Edith, please," Mauve said, her white hands fluttering to her powdered head. "I'll have an attack."

"Jesus will cure you and make you well." She mocked the older woman.

The two men, father and son, moved, each to his own wife.

"We'd best be going," Lock said. "We've some things to do for Rector Karg."

"He's such a lovely man," Mauve said.

"Ordination Day is a busy day today." I moved back, smiling. "Nice to have met you." *Liar.*

The five of them stood there, Walter and Mauve and Skippy and Chuckie and Edith, caricatures of themselves, glaring. Skippy, the boy with acne, turned rosy red. Only he nodded good-bye.

"Damn you," I said to Lock, "they were finally getting like interesting. Whose guests are they?"

"Somebody's aunt and uncle, I think. How about that Edith."

"Some witch."

"Some bitch. Damn intellectual girls," Lock said. "That's the kind of college graduates they keep warning us about we'll have to preach to."

"I doubt if she even goes to Mass on Sundays."

"Girls like her with a chip and real hostility," Lock said, "I always want to go up and ask, how old were you when you were screwed, my dear. Ha ha ha. Screwed by the existential."

We laughed, wandering curiously through the crowd, smiling back at people, seeking some new adventure, feeling guilty at our pleasure in examining them, and them us. Up on the front porch, back among the arches, the faculty stood huddled together, priests playing at Roman nobles, aloof on Nero's palace steps.

"It's a beautiful day," Lock said, turning about, gathering in the crowd.

Over his shoulder I saw a prominent guest, a priest, his cassock cuffing about his legs, walking quickly toward us.

"Batten the hatches." Lock sounded a warning. "Here comes the Reverend Cyril Prosper." Lock turned toward the porch.

Cyril Prosper, like his once-upon-a-time classmate, Christopher Dryden, thought of himself as one of the leaders of the younger clergy, the hope of the new Church. A Misery alumnus, coming back every year, a buddy example for the Big Day. He was four years a priest, but still had the look of his seminarian days: a big, blond man, heavy in shoulder and chest. His eyebrows had bleached to near white over the dark frames of his glasses. He looked like an athlete gone esthete. As if one day he'd hung his jersey up and seen a book, really seen a book, for the first time and felt bound to like what he saw, because it was good for the priesthood.

"There you are," Cyril Prosper said, extending his hand, the blond hairs on the back catching red from the sun. I could tell he was very conscious of keeping the beautiful hands of a priest. "There you are, the two of you, same as last year. Not changed a bit."

"You either, Father. How are you?"

"Cut the 'Father' bit, man. I thought I broke you of that last year." He was in very good humor, come neat from the faculty lounge. His mouth was slick with a little good bourbon.

"Putting on a little, aren't you...Chick?" I said, recalling his old nickname, barely.

"A mite." He patted his cassock over his belly. "I got me a little pooch. About twenty pounds here that was never ordained. Mean to work it off this summer. Get back in the old shape, you know."

"Still the good confessor you were last year?" Lock asked.

"Better, much better. There's no sin I haven't forgiven."

"I'll bet."

"How's Dryden?" Lock trusted Cyril Prosper. "Seen him recently?"

"Cut it, man," Cyril Prosper said drawing closer. "Don't mention Dryden around here. You know that." He moved in confidentially. "Actually, I stopped to see him at the sanitarium, but they wouldn't let me in. Misery left orders. Misery doesn't love company. You know?"

He enjoyed feeling conspiratorial gossiping about the "retreat facilities" where bishops send disobedient priests off to secret little Catholic jails, little cells in little monasteries administered by great big monks with great big keys to the little tiny doors.

"Nobody can get in," Cyril Prosper said. "Nobody can get out. But I did pick up a few things."

"Like what?" Lock said. "Like what?"

"Like Dryden wasn't all as knowledgeable as everybody thought. So offhand. He'd drive to the library in town and check out lecture tapes and listen to them in his room. Obscure tapes, you know, by real authorities on a subject and then he'd come down and introduce the topic to you guys in the lounge and pass it all off as his own thought. Neat, huh?"

I wanted to say, I knew it. I guessed it all along. There was something phoney about him. Dishonest. But now, after the act, it seemed too pat to say.

"That means trouble," Lock said. "Plenty of trouble for us. And it explains a lot."

"How do you mean," I asked.

"Listen to me," Cyril Prosper said. "What drives Karg so crazy that all the priests on the faculty are getting so afraid of now? Reading. Books. Being intellectual, radical, prideful, undocile. It's all the same serpent to them. Dryden undermined a good thing." He looked very stern, and I wondered whose side he was on. "Anybody," he said, "caught thinking now is suspect because somebody once who was thought to be thinking was that forbidden word that doesn't exist. Cribbing ideas wasn't even thinking. It was memorizing."

"Doesn't that last part sort of cancel out their major premise?" I asked.

"How?"

"I mean if he wasn't thinking in the first place, then what does being that word..."

"You can say that word, Ryan."

"...that word have to do with thinking in the second place. He wasn't thinking at all."

"But he was clever," Cyril Prosper said. "The Reverend Christopher Dryden was the epitome of everything clever. That really scares them. You've got to give him credit for that. He sure as hell was clever. 'The *ssserpent* in Eden,'" he said, imitating Rector Karg, "'hath many ways even unto the days of our own.'"

A thin stiletto voice cut into our laughter. "I'm surprised. I didn't think Catholics could quote Scripture." Edith Berrengar, that girl, had followed us, smoking, her black dress flecked gray with tiny ash. She was alone. Chuckie and the rest were lost in the crowd.

How ugly she is, I thought, how very horsy, how kind of...attractive, sexy even.

"Your persuasions, your persuasions," she continued. She gestured toward Misery's huge red-brick buildings. "I'm glad, really so glad to see the priest-factory. Where they take men and wrap them in the sweet bosom of God."

"Your terms sound mighty religious," Cyril Prosper kidded. He thought she was joking.

"Religious!" Her laughter cracked dry, crumbling down. "Christa-mighty. I got tired waiting for the new revelation by the time I got to be twelve. These two here," she waved a gesture of bracelets at Lock and me, "haven't reached twelve yet. I can tell. Oh, brother, can I tell. They're all kind of wrapped up in the old religious womb. Singing some prosy, rosy prayer of semiconsciousness. Look at them!" She chain-lit another ciga-rette. Smoke enveloped her face. She didn't smell as if she'd been drinking. "And you, priest, dear, you're the same. Just older, not wiser."

Cyril Prosper looked at her, amazed, his cool, priestly suavity almost swept from him. "Miss? Miss? I'm sorry I..."

"Mrs. Berrengar." She waved her ring in his face. "Mrs. Berrengar, the younger. As opposed to Mrs. Berrengar, the older and uglier, the mother of my husband, Big Chuckie, who probably only loves me, Big Edie, because he's afraid not to. Tell me, priest. Priests. Priests and priestlings. How to cope with that. You're supposed to know all about love and marriage. Your guns all unshot under all those skirts. Your bodies may be virgins, but your minds are fucked."

Violent, smoking, ugly standing there, she made me feel hot and mov-ing, wanting to mate with her, throwing her to the damp filthy straw of some medieval lodging. The summer before I'd split the back of my head water-skiing and told the barber to be careful, *be careful of it*, and he, not knowing me a seminarian, presumed, "She slugged you, huh?" She could have, Edith could have, standing smoking, could have been the one if ever one was to be the first one to knock me senseless, and it would have been more pure than impure.

"I went to Confession two months ago," she said, "and I asked the priest a question and told him my opinions about marriage and sex. He asked me what I'd been reading. I told him de Chardin."

"You read Teilhard de Chardin?" I was amazed.

"Shut up, Ryan," Lock said.

"Anything you can read I can read," she said. "Anyway, do you know what this Father Abortionado said to me? 'My daughter,' he called me—imagine!—'we should be wary of the pride that makes us attempt intellectual pursuits beyond our capacity. De Chardin,' he was telling me off, 'tries impossibly to marry biblical doctrine to theories of evolution. We must leave theological speculation to the experts and be content with the simple definitions of Holy Mother Church.' I gagged, really gagged. I wanted to say, oh, you stupid, stupid old fool, wasn't Holy Mother Church ever a girl? I haven't been to Confession since. I'll go again. But I haven't been since."

"He was probably one of the older clergy," Cyril Prosper said. "Some of them don't understand the new Church too well."

"They better," Big Edie said. "They bloody well better. Christamighty. I won't, I won't be part of their scapular-kissing, medal-jangling crowd. And you! Kid! What's the matter with you? You're young. What's going on? How do they do it? How do they do it to you? How do you do it? Is it some course they teach you here? How do you learn to go around reducing ordinary good people to gibbering idiots? Why do you do it?"

I was quiet before her because she sounded somehow right and I knew she was more right than kooky, though vocationally I was unable to agree with her. But she was right, crazy right. Next to us, all around on every side, on this very Alice-in-Wonderland lawn, the power play was happening. The Bishop had shooed the black-cassocked faculty out among the colorful crowd to play their roles as priests. Visitors, grown and successful men, disintegrated into the masks of what they were in high school when confronted by clergy in authority. The visitors shuffled, looking at their shoes, laughing at anything or ready to, because good Catholics always laughed at priests' jokes. I wondered what they really thought.

"And sex!" She raised her voice. Several faces panned politely shocked and amused toward us. "If the clergy knew anything about sex. There's such a gap between you and we marrieds..."

"...*us* marrieds." I found myself editing her.

"Ryan!" Cyril Prosper called my name.

"Why is it," Big Edie said, "that any Catholic boy who fears he's not very masculine thinks it a sign of a vocation? Christamighty, who knows where vocations come from? How they get here?"

"You certainly think a lot," Cyril Prosper said.

Lock and I laughed.

"You're charmed, aren't you," Big Edie said to Cyril Prosper. "I'm so charming. I'm everything you gave up. Ain't you lucky!"

She was nothing like the nuns and aunts I'd spied earlier in the day from the choir loft. I hated this ugly jaundiced girl. I hated her because she had brought to flower in herself cynical seeds I had recently been finding in my own soul. Narrow, oh narrow, I thought, is the gate of heaven to the cynic, oh Lord. She was a warning to me of what not to become, and I wanted her, or wanted the idea of her.

She looked at Lock and me. "That boy in the story. Jim. Jimmy. The boy that shot himself. That was Walter and Mauve's boy. They'll never admit it. Their pastor has been helping them 'bow to the will of god,' encouraging them to go out to others. He prints their pathetic little paragraphs of hope and despair on the back of the Sunday bulletin. That's where they write. That's their big-deal idea of the Catholic press."

She could not stop blurting out everything she ever knew or wanted to confess.

"That boy with them. Skippy. He's not their son. He's a foster child. The pastor arranged a whole bunch of Skippiness for a distraction. They don't need a distraction. They need a doctor. A psychiatrist. But they won't go because the pastor has talked them into being happy in accepting their *cross*. He calls it that. The Church needed a new saint in heaven, he said. Saint Jimmy. God! Can Saint Skippy be far behind?"

Strands of black hair had fallen sticking damp across her forehead. "You're such dummies at this miserable school of ventriloquism." She shook her head as if she might be sick. "Christamighty. What's wrong with me? I don't want you to go out and do the same stupid things most stupid priests do, mouthing pat answers to questions no one can answer." She backed a bit away. "I'm not sorry," she said. "I...I thought you ought to know...about their son."

Then she ran away. She was gone.

"Oh," Cyril Prosper said. "Oh!"

"Some girl," Lock said to him.

I felt sorry for her, married into those people. Maybe two dirty coffee cups left in her sink, waiting for her, deadly, when she returned from the wide world with Chuckie, the yellowish smiling man. Coffee stains in her sink. She'd work for days to soak them out. In frustration. Ring around the sink, around her whole life. Because, poor thing, she felt too much, could accept too little the given limits of life and grace itself. "Ventriloquists," she had said. "Dummies. Parrots. Magicians. Hocus Pocus." She had blasphemed the very words of the consecration of bread and wine: *Hoc est enim Corpus Meum. This is My Body. Hocus Pocus.* She asked too much, expected, what? Something.

I felt she had a right to expect me to answer her dilemma as much as I expected the priests to reveal to me the secrets of the answers I needed for my sake as much as hers, but she was an occasion of sin, her voice, her body, her snotty arrogant way intimating she came from some place better, and deserved to be, needed to be, was really asking to be fubbed, because her vocation was seducing innocent priests like Charles Prosper who had been turning chivalrous and dandy toward her, following after her with his eyes.

"Mr. O'Hara," Rector Karg stood suddenly next to me and squared off his place opposite Cyril Prosper and Lock Roehm. "May I see you a moment? Excuse us, please, gentlemen."

I followed Rector Karg into a cove of evergreen that sheltered a small outdoor shrine to the Virgin Mary. He looked straight ahead and made a big business with his Army Zippo of lighting a large candle among the many small candles already burning. We were alone. He had, he said, by chance happened to see me. How fortunate, he said. He had, he said, wanted to remind me of my situation. Finally, he turned and faced me.

"You came so perilously close, son. Your honesty, that's what saved you. Had you lied once, about the transistor radio or anything, the smaller lie would have exposed larger lies, larger faults. Small things fall into large patterns. Are you innocent? Have you innocence?"

"Yes, Rector."

"Forgetting nothing, I will forget everything so we can begin anew next September. But one caution." His face folded deeper behind his jaw. "You must be prudent. Prudent enough not to tell anyone what happened. Not your uncle. Not your parents. Lay people can never understand what occurs in seminaries. *Silencio.* Do I have your word?"

"Yes, Rector."

"Promise me."

"I promise you."

"You will tell no one."

"I promise."

"Your uncle has promised."

"I promise."

But more, I promised God, for I was not like other men. I would be the perfect young seminarian. I would go back to my German translation on summer nights at home. I would apply myself to apostolic work in my parents' home parish. I would keep a cool reserve of myself, but I would fire up all the warmth of Christ in my personality. I would work with the poor and help keep the parish records. I would work at the teenagers' center and teach catechism classes. Everyone would see the emerging young priest in me. They would all know the difference once I was there. They would find me warm and loving. Empathetic. Emptied of feeling. Solid in my vocation. They would look at me and see actually the essence of the priesthood. They would see an *alter Christus, another Christ.* I would disappear into Christ and Christ would appear and no one would even see me. It was perfect. I would live on Communion wafers and I would say Mass and people would ask me to pray for them and I would be handsome and gaunt from living on wafers and I would baptize and confirm and marry and bury them and I would be personal with Christ who would Himself protect me always.

I promised, really vowed, to tell no one the intimacies of our seminary life.

Rector Karg pulled from his sleeve a sheaf of typed pages. He held them up in front of my face. "You recognize these papers?"

"Yes, Rector."

"What are they?"

"The title pages of my new German translation."

"You know what I want you to do with them."

"You gave me permission."

"I'm taking it away," he said, "for the good of your soul."

"I never know what you want."

"Maybe you should go home and never come back."

My face blushed red enough almost to betray me.

"I prefer you speechless," he said. He looked deep into my eyes. "Your renegade Häring's work is under the most severe examination by the Congregation for the Doctrine of the Faith." He stretched out his arm until his hand, full of the pages of my translation, was near the Virgin's bank of candle flames. "Promise me," he said.

I promised hoping my promise would save my work.

"Promise me again." He moved the papers slowly into the candles. A flame licked up to a page. "Promise me again." The pages browned and curled and flamed. He held fire in his hand. The pages burned and burst and dropped off to ash. "Promise me you will be good." He dropped the burning ends of the pages to the floor. "Promise me again."

"I promise. Oh, I do promise."

I was twenty-three years old.

In the escalating mystery of change, seventy-two hours later, on June 3, the open-hearted Pope John XXIII suddenly died.

On the Vatican chess board, everyone moved.

August 29, 1963

Threats work. Karg scared me to death. My well-intentioned summer collapsed in a June panic. My secret reading of the *Index of Forbidden Books*, the Church's feckless guide to good reading, had led me to Richard Wright's autobiographical novels, *Native Son* and *Black Boy*. My dad's collection of James T. Farrell's *Studs Lonigan* trilogy led me to Chicago. Farrell was a Chicago writer, Irish and Catholic. Jack Nicholson was starring in the movie of *Studs Lonigan*. The Christian Family Movement in Chicago was promoting the idea of worker-priests. *"Observe! Judge! Act!"* Chicago was the logical escape, north 150 miles, from the provinciality of Peoria. I needed a place to hide out, regroup, and plan my strategy to survive Karg.

By July, the humid heat of the South Side of Chicago spiked my moral urgency to a crisis. I gasped for breath inside the once-grand mansion of the parish house where I had told my parents I was under Church orders to go to live for three months. I lied to them. Of course. As usual. To protect myself. I ran away from them, my own mom and dad, and my five-year-old sister, Margaret Mary, even though I loved them so much that my love for them verged on worldly attachment. Karg told me so. "You must leave father and mother for Christ's sake."

I was under more fear than orders.

My family did not see me that summer, because I had to experience what a priest's daily life was like in a parish of two thousand souls. I knew nothing of any folks, especially black folks, but figured they were like white folks, except somehow more full of secrets they might reveal. I sat beneath a ceiling fan at Holy Cross Rectory trying to decipher sense in the parish records of the pastor I had begged to take me in. His parish had changed from all white to black in less than twenty-four months.

Father O'Farrell welcomed me, and any help he could get, with open arms. With a couple other seminarians and young priests, he put us to work days, and he set us up evenings in the rectory library with parish paperwork and some books of essays, Jimmy Baldwin's new *The Fire Next Time* and *Nobody Knows My Name*. We read Ralph Ellison's novel, *The Invisible Man*, and Chinua Achebe's *Things Fall Apart*. The themes of estrangement thrilled me. Father O'Farrell was a working-priest creating a new kind of parish.

"Want to deal with change?" he said. "Change."

Through him, I disappeared under the crush of new parishioners moving from the Deep South of George Wallace's Alabama and Orval Faubus' Arkansas to the formerly white parish at the El station of 63rd and Cottage Grove.

Daytimes, in the parish office, I mouthed words of encouragement to people in trouble and in sorrow. In the school gymnasium, I could hear myself, *shut up*, make pious admonitions, *yes, almost a priest, really,* to hold off, at arm's length, Negro teenagers almost as old as I was, being friendly with boys talking about Chicago soul and the guitar of Buddy Guy, and nice to girls singing sweet but raunchy along with Etta James, "Somethin's Gotta Hold on Me," so they would not ask me questions, "Baby, What You Want Me to Do?" or tell me Confessions about their experiments in the Sixth Commandment.

I typed up sheets with lists of doctors and clinics and libraries and turned out purple mimeographs of school services and went door to door, *go 'way, boy,* knocking, knocking, talking through doors that would not open, *you got a doctor name?,* on all sixteen floors of the new high-rise monoliths of the Robert Taylor Homes.

Hank the Tank sent me a postcard: "Keeping tabs thru the grapevine. What movie are you now? Peter says, Angie Dickinson in *The Sins of Rachel Cade*." One of the other seminarians or young priests was a spy.

In the churchyard, old women and old men pulled on my sleeves. They wanted exactly what white folks wanted, but they wanted it revivalistic, singing where the Church met the Top 10, "For Your Precious Love," biblifying with Curtis Mayfield, "People Get Ready," pushing before them any fresh young priest who could save them before he became like the old priests silenced by the world and woe and women and whiskey.

Christ was bread and wine. Christ was flesh. Christ was a man. How could I ever be another Christ?

With another seminarian, I escaped uptown one night to a theatre in the Loop to watch James Earl Jones performing live in *The Blacks*. I wanted to hear his voice, learn some secret, see some scene. I tried to add up the equation: literature plus metaphor equals real life. Do actors understand literal Transubstantiation? Does anyone? The other seminarian was happy the theater manager invited us two white boys to sit front row center, until we figured it out. The play could not be performed unless at least two white people were present, and if no white people were available, then two dummies dressed as white people were to be placed in the front row. The casting was perfect. Ha ha ha. All the white couples in from the suburbs laughed, relieved they'd got off scot-free.

I gave the people at Holy Cross Parish, kneeling at the Communion rail, Christ's body to eat and Christ's blood to drink.

Actual body.

Actual blood.

No metaphor.

Real.

But it was my body and my blood. They demanded the be-all of something, life perhaps, and maybe with good reason because they had been promised life everlasting, and what they got was me, very *Suddenly,* very *Last Summer.* They judged my vocation a sign that life to me was no riddle. They said, *Help me!* They cried, *Answer me!* They said, *If priests don't know, who does?* I envied them. I suspected their particular answers lay in themselves particularly.

Irony, the sin of irony, if irony is a sin, was rusting the edges of my soul. The other seminarian, probably Hank's spy, the pipeline to Peter-PeterPeter, told me so. God! What must Vatican politics be like at Saint PeterPeterPeter's Basilica in Rome!

The people pulled at my black cassock in the poor parish church, tugged at my Roman collar on the street, shredded my soul to bits seeking the Jesus-comfort in me. They took Communion on me, and the other priests, and left satisfied, for awhile, until some next great hunger called them back.

"A priest," Father O'Farrell said, "needs a spiritual life. Anyone dedi-cated to public service needs a spiritual life to survive." Very *Jack.* Very *Kennedy. Ask not!*

The work was hard. Very hard. Self-effacing. A priest's work is not about the priest. A priest must be all things to all men. A priest, who is truly another Christ, must remember eventually he will be crucified. A priest must give the people everything, including the hammer and nails. Black or white made no difference when life squeezes a person down to scary questions about what happens when we die, or worse, fearful terrible questions about what happens when we do what we have to do to survive in dirt and poverty and crime.

I got what I wanted. An element of blank. I became some black-dressed

Jesus-blur, *a two-hundred-pound old lady, nice old lady,* regarded maybe more kindly than the older priests in residence, because I was a young seminarian, *help me, she begged,* a terribly serious white boy, *my son done gone,* a jokey transient peckerwood novelty, *cleaning her up from excrement,* of the long hot summer that peaked in the heat of August, *changing the sheets.* The priests in the house, *remembering Dempsey pretending he was cleaning up Jesus,* were kind that I was not up to their speed in civil rights experience, *a future time exists, she said, when you are already dead,* even though I had marched with them and The Woodland Organization, learning on foot in the streets the words and rhythms and meaning of "We Shall Overcome," and sat in at Mayor Daley's office, where the marble floor was cool, cooler than the humid air, *she was the old religion of conjure voodoo,* until the police dragged us out, women and children and men, back to the street and dropped us on the curb and called us *niggers* and *nigger lovers,* and we bussed back to 63rd and Cottage Grove, laughing and clapping and dancing, discussing the kind of folks who sat on the front porch, and why black women never much cared for the foundation garments that girdled into shape the figures of white women, and all of us tuned listening to WVON, the Voice of the Negro, spinning the records and screaming and scratching and knocking out the blues on the radio in the night.

The group of young priests invited the labor organizer Saul Alinsky to a supper at the rectory, and when we asked him a question about President Kennedy, whose newborn son had died the week before, and about Martin Luther King, who the day before had marched on Washington, *I have a dream,* Saul Alinsky for some reason looked straight at me, as if I had asked him a question, and he told me, "Kid, here's what you got to do and how you got to do it."

Why he looked at me, like I was there, really there, present, when no one else could even see invisible me seated like a dummy in the front row, shocked me with stage fright that I might somehow have to perform, or actually do something, because he was somebody important and famous in the world, and I was the new kid in town, new in the world, and ready to be used. I knew what the young are for. He made me gasp. I ran from the dining room.

Escaping up the rectory stairs, climbing up, shoes thumping up wooden steps, I heard from outside an El train's metal wheels pitch a long, whining squeal against the hard tracks. Suddenly, deep in that hot August night, in that rectory, in that attic, I really fully knew no one had looked at me, at the real me, in years. My parents looked and saw a priest, but I had never looked at me. I had never ever even seen myself. In my small room, high up under the eaves, I threw myself down on the bed covers and fumbled to turn off the lamp. The window shade, drawn up, revealed the black city night bright with light and with the moon. Sirens shrieked down streets, avenues, boulevards. Sirens shrieked down me. Years of prayer and examinations of conscience and soul and intellect had plowed me back into myself. I at least stood on hope's margin. I might have a self worth finding.

Heat lightning flashed across the sky.

I bolted up and stood in front of the one luxury in the room that had, in the better days of the parish, been the second housekeeper's quarters, a three-quarter-length mirror. I took off my shoes and socks and shirt and slacks and underwear. I dared stand naked. White and naked and more naked than white. Blind parents raise invisible child. Another invisible boy turning into another invisible man. In the summer suddenly, I could die like Schwerner, Chaney, and Goodman, virgin-martyr-saints of civil rights. The shell of my outside was new, forbidden. I looked at every part of it.

Except for the unseen soul inside, *corpus meum, my body* could have been any young white man's body, naked, downed downy with Irish down, passably athletic. Inside me is me. Outside is me too. Ridiculously obvious. But meaning much more. My body a metaphor of the veil between me and all the world. Pushing tongue against the permanent gold bridge backing my perfect white teeth. For years when I was a child, men spoke to me as a child. Paralleling Saint Paul, I put away the childish things and men spoke to me as a seminarian. The second state little different from the first. Child and seminarian. Seminarian and child. *Childseminarian.* The darkling umbra penumbra of labels. I had always handled myself well without ever touching myself. Without interfering with myself. I stared into the mirror.

For years, no one had seen me. I only that night stopped to look at the white dummy from the front row. "Child of God," I said. "I am that they see, but they've never seen me." Never seen me: Ryan O'Hara, Person. A young person. Trust in Jesus. Trussed in Jesus and Rector Karg and Father Gunn, because they went *lickety-lickety,* the way James Earl Jones could in his "Old Man River" *basso profundo* intone *lickety-lickety,* wagging their pious fingers, saying I could have no crisis, no growth, nothing but the innocence of my childhood from which I was to come to them perfect, remain untroubled, and survive without blemish.

Blue sheet lightning crashed off in the night. Hopefully a bit to the west, over the Iowa plains, striking the birthplace of Rector Karg, and burning it down.

Misericordia didn't give an inch for any bent to the normal adolescent crises of the very adolescence it protracted. I was shocked at my physical boldness. I had never seen myself naked. Even as a metaphor. Oh Jesus! I was no Dryden! I waited for lightning to split the hot humid night air, lighting my body, finally hearing thunder roll in from the flat Illinois plains and prairies toward the third-floor attic of the parish house at 63rd and Cottage Grove *and the spoom tilly* in the darkest meanest part of Chicago *doggley bedeep* where the main difference between me *gaspoom toggley* and the black folks was that I could leave the ghetto any time I wanted. "Lullaby of Birdland. Doo wah doo."

September 5, 1963

A few days later, I dared myself to return, despite Karg, to spite Karg, to Misericordia to begin my eleventh year.

"You came back," Karg said. *Check.*

"God told me to," I said. *Checkmate.*

"The clock is ticking," he said.

"Do not ask for whom the clock ticks," I said.

My summer masquerading as a worker-priest in Chicago fascinated Lock. "How can I now regard myself?" I asked.

"What possessed you to come back?" Lock asked.

"How do you regard yourself?"

"You might have disappeared bongo-bongo into some neat, beat Chicago writer's garret."

"I disappeared years ago. I'm trying to reappear. That's the point. I haven't been seen in years."

"Then why come back here?"

"Karg was betting I wouldn't. Nobody can use my vocation against me."

"Karg can."

"No one can use my purity of vocation or purity of intention against me."

"He does treat you strangely."

"I came back for perspective."

"The only perspective here is Ordination, and getting picked up by a progressive bishop in a liberal diocese."

Lock, for all his Vatican diplomatic corps promise, was not much help. The intensity of Chicago had diverted me even farther from my classmates writing little blab-blab sermons to have on file once they were priests. They sat in circles in discussion groups gibbering endless spirals about "the social implications of religion." Jesus H. Christ. They ought to spend one hot, humid, muggy hour, sixteen flights of stairs up, on top of a public housing high-rise and listen to the roar, screams, and sirens of the world below.

My German translation was out of the question, so I started reading again. On my own. Secret stuff. Little Modern Library books that felt good and handsome in the hand. Thomas Wolfe. John Dos Passos. James Joyce. John Steinbeck. Ah, the rhythms of the writing in *The Grapes of Wrath*. The stories of Ernest Hemingway. I might have to go across the river and into the trees. Like a convict, I watched the calendar: September to May, I had nowhere to go. The Church feasts pointed up the days, weeks, months, hours, minutes, seconds of the semester.

My physical boldness I spent among the other seminarians on the playing fields. Softball in September and football in October and basketball all winter. A writer's garret in Chicago sounded as sweet as a mystic's cave, but I would never have anything as personal and romantic as that. My life was dedicated to the service of God through service to others. Around me, some boys achieved good grades and other boys were shipped. No matter what happened, I kept focus on studies, prayer, and my spiritual life.

Objects on my desk in my private room moved about mysteriously when I was in class. Rector Karg was everywhere around me, like a monster you have to kill in a movie to save yourself. I prayed that God would give me the strength to embrace my vocation which is, oh my God, I know, so much more than fantasies of You whispering in my ear. I pray for some wonderful mentor of a priest to come along and take my hand and lead me through some spiritual boot camp of the soul that will strengthen me, that will make me grow up, that will deliver me from perpetual adolescence where all I have to do is be a good boy, a good seminarian, and a good priest. What, oh my God, does *good* really mean?

Alfie Doney, the retarded man, was good, and I knew I was no better than him, trying to read Saul Alinsky's book on the sly.

September 22, 1963

"Alberto, a brave boy, is dead, *muerto*."

Movies can change on a dime. Characters die suddenly. The audience gasps. Rector Karg stood in the pulpit and announced, "Hank Rimski is dead, drowned."

For three days, we five hundred boys had prayed for Hank's safe return. The weather that autumn, blowing up from the South, brought a strange flood of rain. Lake Gunn filled to overflowing across the rim, across the path where we walked, barely wetting our shoes at first, spilling in an inviting waterfall down to the river beyond which was the Out of Bounds where we could never go.

The river rose out of its lazy banks, flowing grandly, gently it seemed, carrying ducks quacking happily downstream. Boys stood on the hillocks in the woods watching the silky muddy water swirl around the high necks of trees ten feet from the small river's usual banks. Nature was our only entertainment. We waved at a couple of boats, one wood and one alumi-num, that floated past, shouting to the men, *Hey Mister!*, who used their oars only to guide their boats propelled along by the current. A couple of boys splashed into the water, calling to the men, asking for a ride. Everyone laughed.

Hank grabbed someone's hat and skipped it like a stone across the eddies. The river was splendid, flooding its banks after the dry summer. The hat spun and swirled and caught in tree branches and freed itself and floated left and right, and once, even floated back upstream for a moment, riding across the deep pools of water that made the tiny, silly, negligible river suddenly magical, flowing up, flowing down, flowing across, as boys, stripping to their underwear, one after the other jumped from overhang-ing trees into the water, floating easily, borne almost sensuously on the slow rolling current. I waded in up to my knees, and I heard my mother's father's Irish warning, "Stay away from water. Drowning runs in our fam-ily," even though no relation had ever drowned coming from Ireland or since.

"Come on in," Hank the Tank called to me, "You're a duck. You can float like a duck, a fub duck."

His crowd laughed. My crowd booed, but only one or two boys dared to leave the bank or the shallows to join him out as far as he was in the sky-blue water reflecting the last gold on the autumn trees.

Hank the Tank rose up in the water, shirtless, strong, lit suddenly brilliant by a shaft of sun cutting through the clouds. He swam against the current, making some headway, then stopped and floated laughing downstream, catching a tree branch with his hands, proud of his strength, pulling himself up into the tree, where he stood in his wet underwear like an acrobat on a branch, about to swing out on a trapeze, bowing to the shouts and applause of the boys who were some meter, I guessed, of the kind of applause Hank would win as a priest. Men would like him. Women would confess to him. His feet gripped the branch and he turned backwards to the crowd of boys and pulled his undershorts, white-cotton briefs bagging with muddy water, tight against his buttocks, standing in the tree like a photo-plate of a gladiator statue in our Latin books. He turned his face over his shoulder, looked at us all, laughed, and pulled his shorts down, dripping mud, mooning us with his bare butt, which was the most shocking thing I had ever seen at Misery.

That was the last time I saw him. That evening at supper, when all the boys who had been at the river returned, Hank's chair at table was empty. Every boy thought another boy had stayed behind for one last water frolic with Hank in the muddy river. It was biblical, exactly the way Mary and Joseph lost the Boy Jesus in the temple when He was twelve. Mary thought Jesus was with Joseph on the walk back to Nazareth, and Joseph thought He was with Mary. I could imagine their hysteria, losing their Child, by the wildness that broke out in the dining hall of Misericordia. Boys disappeared, but no boy had ever gone missing.

Outside the high red-brick walls, new sheets of rain lashed through the night against the windows of Misery lit bright by the light fixtures Tank had been sentenced to wash. Death never came to Misericordia except for old priests. Young boys never died. One time all five hundred of us had been sick with the flu, but no one had ever died. Boys don't die. But Hank the Tank died, swept away downstream, missing three days in a flood that lasted a week. My mind went blank.

At the funeral for Hank, in Misericordia's main chapel, PeterPeter-Peter returned to say the Mass for the Dead over the coffin of his brother. Their father, who had once been a boy at Misery, sobbed on the arm of their sobbing mother. The choir and the sinecure of Gregorian chanters made the hymn *"Dies Irae, The Day of Wrath,"* into pure opera.

Rector Karg preached that death was God's will. "You should all be happy that Hank is in heaven, having died in the state of grace, a good seminarian. He will never be a priest, but he is God's new saint."

All the boys were whimpering, but I cried out in real despair.

He'd fub duck, but somehow he'd won. Saint Hank.

Ka-boom.

Even so, tonguing my new teeth, I loved the mud flowing through his death.

Now *that* was irony!

———————————————

The next morning, two boys, smoking cigarettes in the attic where Karg stored dead priests' stuff, found Father Polistina, Misery's mystic, hanging, dead, naked, from a rafter, swinging above an overturned chair. The rope around his neck was the rope he had worn for years wrapped tight three-times around his waist, knotted every six inches, to rub his skin raw and calloused for penance, to remind him always under his clothes of the suffering of Christ. Karg buried the overworked Polistina, *his kind*, without ceremony, *always*, under cover of night, *kill themselves*, and he was never mentioned again.

October 22, 1963

At table in the refectory, eight of us sat at supper laughing and talking over a pupgullion of noodles and boiled meat.

"Can you guess," I said, "what happened a year ago today?"

Ski stared straight ahead. Minus Hank.

"It was a year ago today," I said, "that Gunn first let us listen to the radio while we ate lunch and supper."

"It was a month ago today," Ski said, "that Tank disappeared."

The whole table of boys kind of grinned, watching Ski dog-paddle in the debris of his special friendship.

"Tank was a pain," Lock said.

"Where a doctor couldn't reach and a nurse wouldn't dare," Ski said, "but that Tank, he was quite a guy. Makes you wonder."

"Wonder what?" I said.

"Why the young die."

Lock and I both rolled our eyes.

"Why does anyone die?" Lock asked.

Ski slurped up a fork of pupgullion. Gravy splashed, landed on his black cassock, and disappeared into the wool. He was crying. I felt sorry for him in a way. Hank the Tank had never recovered his reputation from the plate caper. Ski was alone now. Like me. But I had chosen my aloneness. Not he his loneliness.

"How can anyone," I said, "explain Tank's lapse in the river–uh, I mean, laps in the river. I thought only the good die young."

Ski looked daggers, the kind he scribbled on paper during class, arrows shooting out of the eyes of one stick figure at another.

"If only he were quick," Lock said, as if Ski were not sitting broken, crying into his pupgullion. Time had bored us with each other and whittled us down from eighty-nine boys to eighteen.

"Hey, numbnuts," Ski said. "I'm sitting right here."

"But do you remember Gunn's radio a year ago?" I said.

"I remember the first day I saw you eleven years ago, you stupid mick, you and Lochinvar there, and you haven't changed."

"The Cuban crisis, stupid. When JFK made us finally take a stand against Khrushchev and Castro," Lock said. "Gunn brought in the radio and put it on the corner of his table. Were you out to lunch?"

"If Kennedy had sent in the Marines, I would have gone," I said.

Ski spit pupgullion all over the table. "Oh, Mary! And Joseph!"

Lock put his hand to his mouth.

"My brother Thom is in the Marines," I said. "Gunn was trying to inspire us to be patriotic priests, maybe turn out to be military chaplains like he had been."

"War is immoral," Lock said.

Ski blew raspberries.

"Hey, you, Ski," Lock said. "Stop spitting out your food!"

"My uncle was a chaplain," I said. "He was in the Battle of the Bulge. He had his picture in *Life* magazine saying Mass in front of a Jeep in Belgium."

Ski scowled. "Kennedy stopped the Russians, didn't he?"

Keith Fahnhorst said, "If he hadn't, and if there'd been a war, the government would have made us stay here inside Misery all year round to keep our clergy exemption. Like in the last war."

"If Kennedy and Khruschev had gone to war," Ski said, "there wouldn't be any Misery. There'd be fallout all over the place. My pastor says so."

"Phooey."

Everyone had a two-bit opinion. We argued on till Gunn rang the bell for silence and we stacked the dishes. I loved Irish Jack Kennedy. His call to arms was stronger than the call to the priesthood. I was committed to Jack Kennedy. If he had taken us to war, I would have knocked on the redheaded Jesuit's door and said, "O'Malley, I cannot sit still at Misery while the world blows up." I would have joined my brother Thommy in the Marines. Kennedy had drawn a line with the blockade of Cuba. Washington peaked at war intensity. Any Soviet arms-running ship refusing inspection and immediate return to Russia, he ordered sunk.

Gunn and Karg and all the old priests who had served in World War II grew more excited than I'd ever seen them. They brought radios into the refectory, and we ate quietly listening to Kennedy's Roman-orator's voice crackling direct to us between reports from on-the-spot announcers. In a day, the first letters from home, stuffed by boys' parents with newspaper clippings, showed us how frightened the world had been with civilization and mothers and fathers and children teetering on the brink, the real brink, of real nuclear annihilation.

Himself I blessed: John Fitzgerald Kennedy. He committed himself. He took a stand. He dared face the bravado of the Communist dialectic. He remained calm. He resisted dropping nuclear bombs. Finally, after four tense days, when I did not know if I would live to be a priest or die fighting in a nuclear war, the blockade lifted and U Thant went from the United Nations to Cuba. We were wary: when on a Friday Khrushchev can deny Russia has bases in Cuba, when on a Saturday he admits them, saying he will swap his Cuban bases for our Turkish missile sites, when on a Sunday he suddenly capitulates as he's never capitulated before, anything could be a ruse, except for an encounter with the committed greatness of John Fitzgerald Kennedy. Weeks later I told the Jesuit, I would have followed Jack Kennedy to Cuba, to the ends of the world. From Jack Kennedy I tried to learn calm in standing up to the Very Reverend Monsignor Ralph Richardson Karg, Papal Chamberlain and Rector of Misericordia Seminary. I hadn't been dragged out of Mayor Daley's office without learning something.

"Your idealism," Lock had sniffed, "is crap. The religious vocation is what's important to save the world."

"What came first," I had said. "The soldier or the priest?"

"The fried chicken or the scrambled egg?"

I had handed Lock a letter from my brother, Staff Sergeant Thomas a'Becket O'Hara, USMC, stationed at Guantanamo Navy Base, Cuba.

"So life's a Rimski Brothers vaudeville routine," Lock had said. "For the Christmas skit, you can dress up like Mrs. Doney. I'll make you a poster that says 'Kennedy, *Si!* Cuba, *No!*' You can sing a chorus of 'I Didn't Raise My Boy to Be a Soldier.'"

November 1963

Late on Halloween night, after lights out, Rector Karg stood with a flashlight at the door to my room. He tilted the beam up, lit his face from below, and then aimed the beam at me. He ran the light up and down my body like a gunsight.

I looked at him and he looked at me. Neither said a word.

As quickly as he appeared, he swept off in silhouette down the dark hall. I stepped to my threshold. His flashlight preceded him left and right, and then he turned around once and shined his light down the length of the hall and again right at me. I felt the force of the light as a kind of cold heat penetrating the dark night of my soul. *E! E!* The shrieking violins of the *Psycho* score!

I closed my door and ran to my bed, hoping he wouldn't come back. Always I had set impossible tasks for myself, because the thrill of defeating the threat of failing caused in me a rush that always caused me to succeed at the very last moment. When I was a little boy, I often laid on my stomach lengthwise on the edge of my bed, whispering *nobody loves me*, inching over bit by bit, till half my body was on the edge, then half was over the edge, *nobody loves me*, then more than half, and still more, as my pajamas clung to the sheets, until in a slow tense avalanche of bedclothes, *nobody loves me*, I slid ever so quietly, ever so thrilled, chest, stomach, thighs, knees, and ankles, to the floor. I had fallen in love with anxiety. Oh God, life would be perfect if I weren't mentally ill.

The clock was ticking.

I had known, felt, for four days, at least, that, as sure as Tank sank, I must leave Misery. Hank the Tank had got out easy. Come our Ordination Day in fifteen months: subtract me, one less boy. I would not be white-robed in the chapel. My impossible task was to escape Misery even if I had to delay or deny my vocation to the priesthood. I had been sliding out of this miserable bed for three years. My breathing stopped. The difference between my vocation and my seventeen classmates was a simple matter of talking out timing with the Jesuit. For a month or two. Until Christmas. To be certain. Wait until Christmas. Eleven years. My parents. My uncle. My brother. My little sister. Me. Knowing nothing of the world.

What I will do, oh Lord, I prayed deep in the night of my room, the secret my own—no one else's—I do not know. Why, my God, are You doing this?

I have a vocation, but this is the wrong time in the world and in the Church to become a priest.

Vatican II is an earthquake.

The dome of St. Peter's Basilica in Rome shakes over the epicenter.

Misery is trembling under my feet.

Priests, once simply Catholic, good Catholic priests, are shaken by Vatican politics, scurrying right to tradition and marching left to change.

Maybe I lack real faith, my Lord, but how dare I promise a permanent vow of celibacy in the sacrament of the priesthood that puts an indelible mark on my soul during a civil war of politics and purity?

The faces of Gunn and Karg tell me who will win this time around.

Oh, I recognize this.

Once again the Germans are coming to get me, like a patient etherized upon a table, a rubber mask tied over my face, pushing me back down where words cannot exist.

I will become a simple, honorable man. My profession or career I do not know. My wife, if any, I do not know, and my children, if any, I do not know. My home and country I do not know. My friends I do not know. My happiness I do not know. My sadness. My life. This litany is late in beginning, oh my God, but I must be free, my Lord. I am smothering in the security, the safety, the conformity. I regret it is late. Eleven years of my life on the bittersweet block. How long, oh Lord, have You hidden Your face from me? Why play coy with me who have loved You so long?

At chapel I wanted to shout with fear and excitement and warning. *Enormitas conformitatis, the enormity of conformity!* I was so depressed I thought my heart would break. In the mirror, I saw the saddest boy in the world, betrayed by the only world I had known. I prayed for clarity as much as purity. Make me clear. Question myself. Question them. Question everything. This is sin. Sin. This is Adam's sin: wanting knowledge of good and evil. All my classmates were careening toward the priesthood, toward an indelible mark on their souls, toward something you can't get out of in this life or the next.

Run. I wanted to shout, *Run. Churchquake. Run.*

I could not breathe looking at them sitting in row after row in chapel, wearing the same black cassocks, singing the same antiphons of Gregorian chant, itself fading away under the strumming strumpeting approach of folk music. "Kyrie" versus "Kumbaya." Our seminary life had once been all so beautiful, so medieval, something in a book, something in a movie, but it was horrible, awful, the denial of self and independence. I collapsed before the paradox. Can one have the talent, morals, health, have all a vocation needs, but not be able to accept because his personality wants to run naked down the main aisle to the altar for absolutely no reason but freedom?

Why not climb the cross and rescue Christ? Salvation dictates you can't stop a crucifixion. It's like being possessed, twice. I slid from the safe schoolish life I'd known, and from the safe rich life that lay ahead of me, only this time I wasn't slipping off a bed to a floor, *nobody loves me,* where my father would come in and ask me, *are you okay, son* and pick me up, rescued in his arms, *I love you, honey, your daddy loves you,* and put me back in bed. I was slipping down a rope, rope-burned, my hands were rope-burned so raw no anointing could ever balm away the blood in my palms.

Oh God, help me. My creative unbridled attitude is immature. I'll have to tone myself down no matter what my vocation. Or perhaps the priesthood will give me greater freedom than any other life. The point of my independence, after all, is freedom to express myself by creating something, anything, new, adding part of me to the sum total of humanity. But what am I trying to express except some weird metaphysics of life?

Oh God, I'm going to explode. I'm dying. I need salvation. I need a play, a concert, a foreign film. A movie. A radio station. I'm so worldly I can taste it. I'm too young for this. Uncle Les said so. Maybe I should wait till I'm older. If you're older, at least you don't have to live with your decisions so long. Saint Augustine waited till his death bed to be baptized. I mean, how much of me can I abdicate hoping God will fill the void? Is this the devil calling me like Bali Hai? Is this that first night, all over again in a different way, when the Polynesian girl sat on my bed, arms gesturing in a slow hula, trying to lead me out of the dormitory. Why not? The Jesuit, the crazy mad redheaded Irishman, says the Holy Spirit is talking to me.

I realize the insane temptation.

All I have to do is say *God told me* and they all believe whatever I say.

So basically I'm alone on my own.

I could make all of this very easy for myself.

The Jesuit sees my coming back perseveringly every year to Misery, despite my awful agony of adjustment to captivity, as a sign of my selfless wanting to serve. But why do I have this love-hate attraction to the people in the priesthood? These actual seminarians and actual priests. I could fubbing murder them where they fub-duk kneel inside their fubbing little cliques. What's one more *Murder in the Cathedral*?

What don't I get?

When will I get it?

Perhaps I should spend all the rest of all the Sundays of all my life saying two Masses in the morning and in the afternoon sitting in the rectory basement slitting open the envelopes of dollar bills and checks from the parish collection basket. If I take that road, if I accept the cross of loneliness, of a long-distance runner, with all my priestly heart, I shall still, with all my human heart, my frail human heart, my unseeing, my fanatic heart, miss what could have been on the road not taken. No other vocation is forever, and no other vocation makes you be alone forever.

Can God—and I shook my head not wanting the question—ever mean as much to me as does my possible life or my possible wife and my possible children and my possible creative work? But if it turns out I decide to follow Christ in the priesthood, then it will prove only that although Christ might not mean so much to me as my life, I love Him more, the Word made Flesh, the Man-God, divine and human, noble, naked, nailed, huge up on a fifty-foot cross, seventy feet high over the chapel sanctuary, agonizing, dying to save me. He hangs, transcendent, glorious in this salvific, romantic moment, this epic moment chosen by theologians and artists, this crowning single frame of western culture, crucified, high over the small red flame of the sanctuary lamp.

My ambivalence seesawed across the November days. Misery's code of silence meant I could not discuss any of these doubts with my friends. Just me, Jesus, and the Jesuit. It sounded like a song in a Misery skit: "Me and My Shadow." The roundelay repeated again and again till on a cold November morning I meditated. *The Lord is my Shadow.* In the cold chapel in the long dark before dawn, with the radiators knocking with the first stingy heat of the day, I said, *there is nothing I shall want. He leads me to lie down in green pastures.* My prayer book fell open, full of trust, to the pages worn thin through eleven years of prayer. But the pastures, the pastures. During the autumn, the fall, the long fall from the bed, I volunteered for the Misery farm crew to harvest the corn on our land and bale the hay. I craved the physical resolution of work, the need to feel close to the earth, like Levin in my secret copy of *Anna Karenina* to help me think. Or to keep me from thinking.

But signs and omens were everywhere.

At the farm, the lay tenant's son, a little nine-year-old boy asked to ride the tractor with me. He wore an outgrown crewcut and faded jeans and an old denim jacket and he was like some long-ago far-off ghost of me come back. I had not wanted to grow old the way of Misery. But between me and the boy on the tractor, between me and the boy I was, lay an infinity. Me seated, driving; him standing, holding on to me. I felt ponderous, grown older, certain that life required more than mere physical survival. I wanted to hold him close as myself, and one afternoon I took his picture, him sitting in a barn window, as if I was photographing the last instant of my own boyhood, that last afternoon that I ever saw him.

My own private Jesuit thinks beneath all this German *Sturm und Drang, Storm and Thunder,* is the right stuff that defines a really true vocation. My Jesuit leads me to waters where I may rest. He refreshes my soul.

He says I have a true vocation to the priesthood.

He plans to work the final wrinkles out before my yes-response to God's calling me. God guides me along straight paths for His name's sake. *Even if I shall walk in the valley of darkness, I shall fear no evil, for Thou art with me. Thy rod and Thy staff, these comfort me.* I will willingly give up myself to serve you.

Later, after lunch, I dropped my copy of Sigrid Undset's novel *Kristin Lavransdatter*. Just dropped it. Dropped it right to the floor. Lock told me, dumbfounded, stood in front of me, crying, weeping, and told me.

He was dead.

Jack Kennedy, my Jack, was dead.

The day had dawned so gray and sweet, so muted in dry November. April's fool, a joke, had come to November. Till that noon hour, till today, April was the cruelest month. This feeling. Fragmented. What makes a man so alive one minute? What lays him low, snuffs him out the next? He was the only person I really knew in all the outpost of the world. With any other death, the past could have died. But with him, all the bright future, somehow linked with my passion of giving, vanished. As long as he was being president, I could see myself being priest. *Alter Christus. Alter Jack.* Oh, God. Civilization slipped from us. Violent. Bloody. Jack's brains were all over Jackie's yellow roses. *Big D, little A, double L, A, S.* All the boys were in tears. The priests were in tears. For the first time in history, television sets were carried into the recreation halls and left on and on and on. I could talk to no one. Alone in my room, hours later, the night of the longest day, I pulled my tiny journal from inside my torn shoe box and wrote before the onrushing terror of darkness, psalmish, sighing, keening, kaddish, half-dead myself.

22 November 1963
Tonight, oh Lord, the dun land mourns
disbelieving believing,
dessicated leaves of this week
before Thanksgiving (feast from his New England)
rattle and skitter across brown grass.
This Fall's been a drought on the land,
ended now,
well-watered by weeping.
John Kennedy has passed.
Safe-comfort they had hawked,
sixty-nine cents a pound.
He could have bought it and did not,
chose not to recline in wealth.
Sought rather service.
Sacrificed until sacrificed.
By a young man in the Texas Theater.
Tonight the networks say nothing so well as it is true.

And outside, where there is no moon,
the dessicated leaves rattle across November.
It was gray and wet,
unseasonably warm today.
But in the unloved wind tonight,
unnumbing, beginning to believe,
I taste the coming bleak
of the world's most lonely winter.

My heart broke that day the earth stood still. The world quaked, fell to its knees, stopped, not knowing what to do, where to go, feeling time itself divide into *before that day* and *after that day*. Oh Jack!

December 5, 1963

Days of mourning later, after the Widow, after the tiny daughter, after the young son saluting, after the saddled black stallion, riderless, with the boots turned backwards in the stirrups, after the days of drums, Lock kind of slapped me around. He said my sentiments were hopeless, *God rest ye,* so hopeless they weren't even Christian.

It was again the Eve of the Feast of Saint Nicholas, *merry gentlemen,* and while Ruprecht ran wild through the study halls exciting all the boys, *let nothing you dismay,* with thoughts of Christmas vacation, I told Lock, my best friend, nothing of my decision to abandon my vocation. He would have judged cause and effect in what was only sad coincidence.

John Kennedy was dead and I was done a-grailing.

I had saved enough money in my shoe box for a one-way train trip home to Peoria.

Later, in the dead of the night, at 4:30, before dawn, fourteen days after the martyrdom of Jack Kennedy, the martyrdom of my vocation, I left Misericordia Seminary.

I walked quietly down four flights of marble stairs, alone, and with one suitcase, into which I packed eleven years of my life, I pushed open the heavy wooden door and stepped out into the snow still lit by moonlight. Misericordia stood dark and separate behind me.

I was a twenty-four-year-old boy, and I had never ever in eleven years of keeping the Grand Silence from dusk till dawn been outside the seminary buildings after night prayer.

All the other boys and all the priests lay asleep. Only the sacristy light, high in a chapel window, showed out in the cold air. The sacristan was already up preparing the vestments and chalices for early Mass in honor of Saint Nicholas.

An incredible sadness took my breath. I stood on the steps staring up at the moon over the silent white snow.

Oh my God, I offer the rest of my life to You. I offer You all my prayers, works, joys, and sufferings of this day, of this life, in union with the Sacred Heart of Jesus and the intentions for which He pleads, and offers Himself in the Holy Sacrifice of the Mass throughout the world in reparation for my sins and the sins of the whole world. Oh my God, I am so scared.

I trudged through the snow, feeling the true knee-deep meaning of trudging, out the stately drive winding like a postcard out to the highway. To leave the property was a mortal sin. The moonlit night was freezing cold. I stepped off the drive and put my foot down. A semi-truck roared passed. I walked along the shoulder of the forbidden road toward the town. Kennedy was assassinated and so was I. Misery was growing distant in the dark. Cars and trucks swept by me, wheels swirling snow, flakes caking my face.

Several times I turned and looked back, and, as Lot's wife turned to salt, I turned to ice. My heart turned to stone. My breath turned to steam.

I stood on the shoulder of the highway and watched a few early lights at Misery come slowly on. A horn swooped wailing beside me. The headlights and the gusts of traffic overpowered Misery itself. The swirling snow turned Misery into one of those toy miniatures in a glass dome of water that kids shake to watch the snow fall. I picked up my suitcase and left Misery behind me swirling like a tiny fortress in a snowy medieval keep.

Down the highway, I walked into a drive-in coffee shop decorated for Christmas. On the jukebox, Bobby Helms was singing, "Jingle Bell Rock." The waitress took a look at me and nodded to a couple of truck drivers sitting at the counter. I was one of them now. I was no longer set aside from life.

"You're from that place, aren't you," the waitress said. "They always come here like you with their suitcases. You all have the same hangdog look. Maybe I should call the SPCA."

They laughed, but they didn't laugh at me, so I smiled. Maybe they thought Misery was a joke.

Eleven years...and I choke.

"The pay phone's over there," the waitress said. "Here's a dime. Call yourself a cab."

"Hey, kid," one of the truckers said. "Have a cup of coffee. On me.

Merry Christmas."
I tried to feel their cheer.
I had told none of my friends of eleven years goodbye.
None of them, I knew, would ever contact me.

9

December 25, 1963

Silent Night. I faced the music. Christmas at home was a showdown game of chicken. Like Kennedy daring Khrushchev, I risked announce into the oncoming headlights of all my parent's friends: "I quit." *Oh, Come, All Ye Faithful.* On Christmas Eve, before Midnight Mass, people still reeling from Jack Kennedy's death stammered in the snow outside my parent's parish church and looked at my face, looked at their feet, and started to say, "Oh, I'm sorry," then stopped.

"I quit," I said. *Dashing through the snow.* "The world is changing. Faster than you know." They buried their heads in their fur collars and scarves. "Even in Peoria." I could never have preached to them. I could never have warned them. Christmas was lights and presents and "Yoo hoo, Santa."

"You would have made such a handsome priest." They looked at me, really looked, perhaps for the first time, at the amazing invisible boy, then said the same lines, all of them, the same lines: "Better to find out now, courage of your convictions." *Chestnuts roasting.* They stared at me like some shape-shifter. *Come and behold him.* "Girls?" they asked. "Who's the girl?" They drew their daughters in closer to them. *Round yon virgin.* They kidded me. "Now I don't have to watch my language around you." *Barump a bum bump.*

My father's best friend, the rich Mason, pulled me aside and said, "Congratulations. You were always too good for that." *Everybody knows.* People took my hand and pulled me to them. "Now you have to make up for lost time." *Jingle all the way.* I was shocked they were so relieved. *Oh, what fun.* Grown-ups who loved me had kept their opinions quiet out of respect for my vocation. *All is bright.* They breathed a sigh of relief, as if abducted, I had rescued myself.

They welcomed me back. Quitting made me one of them again. For the first time in almost eleven years, I had no identity. I was not the best little boy in the world, up on the altar serving the priest at Midnight Mass and ringing the altar bells and swinging the incense in the faces of two thousand parishioners. Oh, Lord, I prayed, I can't trust anyone. They all hide their true feelings. They never really cared what I did: go or stay. It's Your birthday, but I'm the babe in the manger. I withdrew. They all lied to me. *We fell into a drifted bank.*

My father, in tears, said, "If you had left Misericordia, ten years ago, five years ago, but now, so close to Ordination." My mother said to my father, "Honey, Ryan didn't know for sure till now." *Mother and child.* "Whatever," my father said, "you want, son." Kids my age, Danny and Barbara Boyle, stared at me. I had run from them after grade school. *They never let poor Rudolph.* I had not penetrated to the deepest fraternities of Misery. *Play in any reindeer games.* I was isolated, alone. *Star of wonder.* I had run from the seminarians at Misery. *Star of might.* The huge gap I felt separating the clergy from the laity was the same huge gap separating me from those pietistic twits at Misericordia. They would never change from how I left them. They lived to fight their tattling way up through the ambitious pecking order of opera clubs, the cliques of the Gregorian choir, and who was holy enough, with enough martinet snap, to be the showy Master of Ceremonies at Ordination services. *Guide us with your perfect light.* I was not Misericordia. I was not Peoria. I was on my own.

Except for the draft board. The day after Christmas, I walked into the Selective Service office and asked to change my exemption from "1Y" for "theology student" to a regular student deferment.

"A deferment for a big, healthy, strong boy like you? With Krushchev running around? And Castro? Ha ha ha." The lady who ran the draft board had steel-gray hair combed back into a D.A. "I have 15,000 boys," she said, "in Southeast Asia. Ha ha ha." She typed up a new draft card that said "1A."

Some group was always wanting me to join up body and blood.

The huge snowdrifts across the flat land of the Midwestern winter cracked. My life was a silent movie. I faced an ice floe of dangerous bergs: Misery behind, Peoria present, the draft board tomorrow, girls forever. At Misery, my vocation was on the line. Ten days outside of Misery, my life was on the line. My draft card ticked in my wallet. Forces were at work. In silent movies the actors jumped across the river from one bobbing ice chunk to another. Life lay across the ice floe on the other bank.

"A penny for your thoughts?" The blonde daughter of my father's rich Mason friend smiled. "Do you like Paul better than John?"

"The Popes?"

"The Beatles."

Her brother, home from college, came over to us with a bottle of wine. He reminded me of Lock. My brother, on leave from the Marines, folded himself in. "The more the merrier," Thom said. He felt he had won the unspoken competition between us. His military career was no longer trumped by my vocation. He had married a girl named Sandy Gully. He had felt sorry for her standing outside the Marine Base at Camp Pendleton, choking on the Southern California smog. She was sixteen, old enough to marry Thom, *The Gully-O'Hara Nuptials*, but not old enough, her father said, to travel, especially her mother said, being pregnant and all.

No one spoke of my past. I was different. They acted normal, trying to fold me back into their world. I was the alien from another planet. *Karma barana nick toe.* They had always talked to the seminarian. Suddenly I was real to them. I was back among them: Lazarus come back from the dead; a childhood friend hit by a car lying in a coma for ten years, the Sleeping Beauty of boys; *The Creature from the Black Lagoon.*

They covered their puzzlement with laughing, back-slapping, and contests of singing parodies of carols: "I wouldn't trade brass monkeys for a one-horse open sleigh."

Not one of them believed an "I quit" rubbed out ten years and four months. *Tick, tick, tick.* The rich Mason faced me toward the facts of life: the ten years and four months, the nearly four thousand days and nights, the ninety-six thousand hours, the six million minutes, the three-hundred-and-fifty-million seconds, at five dollars an hour was $480,000 I could have earned.

Divorce of any kind interested them. They sniffed at my reasons. They all had heard of "spoiled priests" ruined by alcohol and women, but the spoiling of the best little altar boy in their world created a mystery. Where was my cocktail glass? Where was my girlfriend? Eyes watched from church pews. Faces glanced over plates at holiday supper tables. They stared on the sledding hill in the park where I took my six-year-old sister, Margaret Mary, rocketing down the toboggan run.

I was no great mystery.

I had no scandal.

I had no vocation.

My father explained to my mother, "He's a cover without a book."

"What?"

"His life is beginning."

I could never write or phone or visit Misery again. *Ninety-six thousand hours.* I could never change my mind. *At five bucks an hour.* I could not go back. *$480,000.* I forced myself forward into the future. No longer was a bed and a supper waiting somewhere in some rectory. Life had no net. I sensed danger and adventure. I had a draft card. In six weeks, I could be in Vietnam, with no Jack Kennedy to lead me. In seventeen months, my classmates would be ordained to the priesthood. I panicked. I missed Lock. I fantasized saying good-bye to him at Misery. No real good-bye. So no experience of a personal good-bye. An imagined good-bye no more real than a grade-B late show starring Lock and me.

Lock: "Did Karg give you his farewell sermon?"

Ryan: "I stopped him. I said the Jebbie Jesuit took care of anything that needed to be said." *Close-up. Ryan. His face shows he remembers how he had lied to his father when his father had tried to explain the facts of life.*

Lock: "Good. I heard it's terrible."

They look at each other as the swirling decked holiday halls of Misery empty around them. Carolers, far-off, sing, "Fa la la la."

Lock: "Priests are like gypsies. We're always saying good-bye."

Ryan: "Life is an endless succession of good-byes."

They begin to make dialog...

Lock: "Everything goes too fast, I guess."

...to cover the end...

Ryan: "It seems all my life I've been standing in bus stations saying good-bye, leaving people."

...of their friendship...

Lock: "On cold platforms."

...each never to see the other again...

Ryan: "In clouds of blue exhaust."

...like the movies...

Ryan: "Be a good priest, Lock."

The two young men shake hands like comrades parting in the trenches.

Lock: "A good person. That's what you'll be. A good man."

Close up. Ryan. He wants, for all the warmth of ten years, to hug Lock shoulder-to-shoulder. But he cannot. There can never be special friendships, because special friendship never existed. Even at Christmas. Camera: medium shot. The walls of Misery press too close. The face of Rector Karg appears. Lock himself begins to fade to black.

Ryan: "Remember the spiritual autobiography Raissa Maritain wrote about her life with Jacques?"

Lock: "*We Have Been Friends Together.*"

Ryan: "Good-bye, Lochinvar."

I dissolved out to my real self, on a walk into the cold December, taunting the world to receive me newly arrived in the world, but not yet of it. No longer unlike other men. Other Christmases the bus out of Misery had roared past filling stations where grease-smudged young men stood intent around the raised hood of a truck, absorbed in tangled wires and steaming radiators and universal joints. They were in the world, unbeaten, unbowed, heroic, anointed in crankcase oil, unafraid. They were workers, not priests. They knew how to make motors work. They were serious about their women and children. They had focus, fraternity, codes, secrets I wanted to learn. This time I would penetrate the tightest circles. I promised to know their essence and match it. I would no longer be Saint Analogus, the Patron of Those Who Always Stand on the Outside Looking In. *Ryanalogus, the Latin word for fool.* I would be the real thing if it took alcohol, tobacco, firearms, and Masonic women. I knew how to make ready the way of the Lord, to make straight His paths.

I must have looked fierce at our supper table.

My father put his hand on my shoulder, looked at Annie Laurie, and announced, "He's a solid man." He said what Lock had said. That compliment was the supreme compliment to an Irish boy. "You can do anything," he said. "Solid you are. Solid enough to calm down."

"You are," Annie Laurie said, "the spitting image of Charlie-Pop. He decided to quit smoking. Period. Cold turkey. He stopped."

"So indeed I did," Charlie-Pop said.

"He can do anything," my mother said. "So can you."

Somehow Christmas made me feel as turned away as Saint Joseph searching for a room at an inn. Jack Kennedy was dead. All connection to Misery was dead. I was dead like a stillborn child needing aid to breathe and kick and scream. Freedom's slap was shocking glorious. I flew up in free-flight. I hung on the edge of the bed, *nobody loves me,* sliding out of the bed, *nobody loves me,* hitting the floor. Accidentally, I touched myself during the night and the accident repeated every night two or three times. I felt no guilt. How strange. After all I'd been told. I would never confess it. *Nobody loves me. Who cares!* I felt the wild way the whole world had felt, flown up in joy, when the war had ended. I was capable of choosing anything. I had free will. Potency veined sensuously about me in my bed. I would never go to Confession again.

Pine and mistletoe twisted into sweet peas and myrtle. How could such a grasp of self be a sin? Had I won some race? In the mirror, vine leaves twined time-lapse through my hair. Hell did not open up and swallow me. I loved the world and the world loved me back. Had those priests lied about grasping yourself? The world vamped me. I had always gone starved to bed. What else had they lied about as well? On the streets, billboards, small at a distance, loomed up large showing how much I needed all the world could offer. I understood the last temptation of Christ: Satan took

Him up to the parapet and showed Him the whole world and said, "All this can be Yours if You will fall down and worship me."

I began to nibble at the world. Tiny bites. Baby steps toward everything forbidden to a pious seminarian. I had changed movies like a double-feature. *Good-bye, Misery* with co-hit, *Hello, Life.* I remembered how the panicked priests had turned off the projector and ripped off the reel of *Auntie Mame* while all the boys were laughing at her yelling, "Life is a feast and most poor suckers are starving to death."

To try life on for size, I read each billboard and movie marquee along the way. I sopped up the way of the world, the way it walked down the street, or shifted lanes with one arm and no backward glance. Clark Gable had died, like Marilyn Monroe and Montgomery Clift, after the three of them filming *The Misfits.* Jack was gone. James Dean was gone. Hemingway was gone. Marilyn, Monty, and Gable were gone. Gable was the man's man women loved and men wanted to be like. Same as Jack Kennedy. Suddenly, all the grown-up people were dead. My little world shifted crazily on top of the great shifting shelves of the big world. Something was happening. Outside Misery, the world was picking up speed. The world needed new people. No more misfits. I bought the long-play album, *Meet the Beatles,* because it was new and an antidote against the universal sadness after Jack's assassination. John and Paul and George and Ringo made me happy. "I Want to Hold Your Hand!" Rector Karg would ban them.

I asked our parish pastor, Father Gerber, could I go to the Varsity Theatre on the Bradley University campus. "It's an art theatre."

"They show condemned movies." he said. "But with your education, you can go if you go in the side door, so as not to give scandal to people who might not know what you understand. People will never forget," he said, "that you were nearly a priest. You must conduct your life with that caution."

In one week, I saw *The Longest Day, Long Day's Journey into Night,* and *The Loneliness of the Long-Distance Runner.*

"I can't," Annie-Laurie said, "keep it straight where you're going."

"They're wonderful black-and-white movies about life."

"Be careful of movies about life."

I grew hungry for humans. *I want to hold your hand.* I wanted to see people wearing tweeds and corduroy and the foreign black sheen of faille and the weightless blue of nylon tricot. I smelled the world up close in the warm fragrant female smell entwined in long loose hair, bare scented arms pulled warm from greatcoats. I dreamed of the world applauding exhibits and lectures and theatres, till all its clapping became concerted applause, heady as Chanel and cigars, sumptuous cheeses carved on old wood with a silver knife, warm breads washed down with fine wine. What had happened to that world with Jack dead and Jackie in mourning? Hard work could move me through the world. Whetted appetite grew to craving necessity. For all the sports at Misery, I felt weak, enervated by Misery itself. I had been a priestling. I joined the most forbidden Protestant gym in town, the Peoria YMCA. I did sit-ups and pull-ups and push-ups and watched the other men lift weights until I could lift them myself. I read the pamphlet in the lobby that explained that masturbation was recommended for students and workers to help them keep studying and working. I was shocked to see in print in a public lobby, another word, one of the very words I had been punished for writing from translation. In the beginning was the Word and the Word was made flesh. I never even had to think how fast I must move.

I had been kidnapped.

I screamed.

I had been in real danger.

I'd been circling the drain.

Time so lost had passed with no trace of me in the world. Streets and movies and people rushed into my senses. Who needs salvation when you need rescue? Jack had his brains shot out in a car. I panted for life's embrace. I sat crying in the movies. Where was my wife? Where were my children? Had they gone speeding by in a car? I had been robbed of any head start in life. What now? Is now enough? And Jack dead. Dear Jack. Gone, taken lost from us. Seeing double: his death, my death. Death should end the past, not the future. I escaped one world to find another. Adrift, untied. Without him. Where? Barbarians reared up in the uncivilized street. His brain blown away. *Zap. Zap! Zapruder!* The wind, the blowing wind, Dylan, blowing in the wind. Jackie climbed across the car. Dropped the yellow roses of Texas on the blood spattered black upholstery. She didn't remember crawling across the trunk of the car. *I love you, Jack*: she placed her ring on his finger. Parkland. Bethesda. Oh Love Field. Women in leopard-skin coats like to make love. Arlington and crepe. Jack and Jackie. The curtain descends. Everything ends. Too soon. A simple matter of a bullet through the head. *Ich bin Berliner. Auch Ich.* A fear more than grief folds its black wings hovering over everyone crying from Thanksgiving through Christmas and into the new year. *Happy Birthday, Mr. President.* I should have held things closer when I had them. *Shalom, shalom!* Oh not like other men. *Kaddish.* I am worn from weeping, the psalmist cries. Night after night my pillow is drenched with tears. I weep till the tears flood my bed. More compassionate and understanding and loving and human than before that Friday. Valleys are filled, mountains brought low. *Oh Adonai.* In Advent, I advented out of Misery. The helplessness of carrying on like this. He was the best of the world I did not know. Gone, with him, that world. I open doors to Advent deserts. Crooked ways promised straightness. So golden, lord Jack, so golden. You promised never to leave me. Then you left me. I escaped on my own through the snow. I don't disintegrate, don't die till the end of days. Feel nothing. Felt so much can feel no more. They made me what I am. The one question at the dusty bottom of the academic box of philosophy and theology: How many angels can dance on the head of a pin? How many times can you die in a single 8mm Technicolor frame? I, human, shriven, over-shriven, shriveled. Nearly died. Escaped into the snow. To run time backwards, like film, to warn you not to fly to Texas. Running Zapruder in 8mm reverse: 26 seconds, a fragile six feet of film, final harrowing moments, soundtrack, Gregorian chant, Irish lament. Each instant of the 485 frames another frame of past, broken in two places, with sprockets torn out and burn marks, another frame of experience *née* innocence running round and round looped through the projector, every way but upside down.

The mother, my mother, a mother awoke before dawn, got up. Beat the alarm. No jangle. Floor cold. She turned. Some former rich fullness of the morning was missing. The room was right, a bit mussed. Her house quiet, husband gone early. She remembered the smoke. No cigarette smoke languishing in the morning air. He kept his resolution, eating mints from the grocery. Today she remembered a letter would come. *That day she opened the letter.* Her son would write again. *I would write again.* Her boy's voice on paper in that strange faraway style he'd fallen into during all those sheltered isolated years. His gift of a silver letter opener. His mail made her happy. Not this time. *I'm coming home.* She cried, she cried. For the lost vocation. For the lost May chapel, for the lovely scene of Ordination in lovely summer clothes, bishop humming above window-fan, snapshots, First Blessing of a newly ordained priest, her son. The greatest thing a woman can be: the mother of a priest. Oh *him.* What about him? All her hopes become luggage shoved back into a closet because of a splendid trip that would never begin.

Oh gone! *Oh Adonai.* Gone from me, I took the dream from them. No chance of home movies. No 8mm Technicolor Ordination Day. I was steady as a beam of light through a pinhole in an eclipse. An apocalypse. To sail beyond the sunset, and the baths of all the western stars, until I die. I sit tonight without my lord, *uh*, without my bucko, without my Jack, in eternal November's eternal Friday. Oh, everyone. Take me as me. Veils stripped away. Be thou my vision, so unlike other men. Flags go up the mast, up from half-mast, to forget, to forget. The first weeks of all the weeks of the world that must pass without him.

I want to go to the sea he loved. To see the clouds scud along the sky of Martha's Vineyard, wind whipping gulls to flight, to watch one impossibly white bird rocket up like a jet, becoming smaller and smaller till eyes ache to see the white spot in the pale flat sky.

Press the liquor from the loss into a cider's cup of meaning. Guinevere mourns. "Roe O'Neill. Sheep without a shepherd, when the snow shuts out the sky. Oh why did you leave us? Why did you die?"

Oh world. Oh litany of lost people, bleached girls with tight-lipped smiles hiding braces feather-dusting cosmetics in drugstores. Acne-boys under sudden mop-top hair and jeans and boots trying to be strong, smoking. Bald-headed men with lunch spots on their ties and old women who dress too young. Poor world. Life. Lost so long in the bowels of the Church. Ancient priests slipping down the drains of ancient corridors. How come to world, me, him gone. One world abandoned. I excess.

Sitting with Annie Laurie and Charlie-Pop watching the new nineteen-inch black-and-white screen after New Year's. Jack Kennedy lived and died on black-and-white TV. On television, everybody faking Christmas joy that this year cannot trump grief. My parents, me, the whole country, like the 1930's Broadway Baby belting it out, proving she's still got It, then life goes on. Ethel Merman brought to you by Ford Automobiles. *Gee, but it's good to be here!* She waves in that vaudeville way she learned. Old tendons in her underarms shadow obscenity under the bright lights. Her brave old sag propped by sequin-cinched waist. She finished getting *a kick, a fabulous kick out of you.* Annie Laurie likes Merman.

Charlie-Pop nods off, waiting for *Gunsmoke.* Television is all new to me. Amazing. I sit, a weird hybrid of Aquinas and Dos Passos, watching black-and-white TV variety shows like *The Judy Garland Show* strain desperately to entertain a grieving country. Annie Laurie dislikes Judy Garland. *She tried to kill herself. She doesn't know what to do with her hands. She makes me nervous. She's a wreck of a woman.* My mother doesn't know she's a Platonist, and married to a Platonist, and the mother of a Platonist. She leaves the room.

Judy Garland, alone on an empty stage, sings "The Battle Hymn of the Republic" and makes it about Jack Kennedy. Sing it! My God, she's so scary you can't turn away. She makes you root for her. Makes the anthem a hymn. Lifts us up and carries us onwards. *Glory, glory Hallelujah.* Close-up: painted face of Garland in torture. Her hands framing her face like white gloves around black face in a minstrel show. She carries us on, JudyJudyJudy, always a favorite of PeterPeterPeter. Picks the nation up. Television's prerecorded chilling crescendo of background voices. Mechanically reproduced audience. Sent to *glory hallelujah.* She tried to kill herself, but couldn't do that. *Glory, glory, Misericordia.* Back a tremble, a hit on TV. Lady of the World. Shredding emotion with all the feeling she can pull out of a top hat and tails. *Katharsis, catharsis.*

Don't make me cry. Don't let me feel. *Stop her, stop her.* Let me be sick first. I have to think. Stop. The world begins to glut me. The world. The word. What is the word? What is the word made flesh? What is the world made flesh? *Stop the World! I Want to Get Off!* I seek to pull my life from the wreckage of eleven lost years. The clock is ticking. The chase is on. Move it or lose it. Make up for lost time. No more circling the drain. Is it always high noon when your shadow stands around your feet in a puddle?

February 1964

In February I came from the family limbo of Peoria, north, to a new life in a new school in a new city. I met Joe and Louisa Bunchek in the *Chicago Sun-Times* classifieds. They provided board and an attic room for twenty dollars a week near the Loyola University Lakeshore Campus. They were real and suited my mood. They let me alone at first, only expressing wonder at all the books I had moved in for my first semester in graduate school.

"Those Jesuits at Loyola," they said, "sure make you crack the books."

They introduced me to visiting company, even on my way through their kitchen to the bathroom, as a seminarian.

"The last two boarders were in the seminary too," Louisa reminded her guests who were all relatives. "God must sure think we need watching over."

Everyone smiled as I disappeared into the toilet. Someone was always coming and going at the Buncheks. They lay in wait outside the bathroom to stare at me, glowing like a holy picture, when I came out.

Alone in the kitchen, sitting with Louisa Bunchek, I felt she was racier than any woman I'd ever known. Night fell fast in deep winter in Chicago's Rogers Park. I liked her.

Outside the back door, across Sheridan Avenue, closed by the loveliest blizzard in the world, I watched a lone woman sit reading in the ornamented glass ticket booth, frosted like an igloo, under the bright marquee of the Sheridan movie theater. Sometimes I'd call her, watch her look up, bored, as her phone rang, and, invisible, across the drifting distance of the frozen night, I'd ask her what time the next feature began.

The forbidden *Cleopatra* was playing out our back door, across the snowy street. Inside the huge movie palace, one ticket made winter into Egypt with Liz Taylor repeating, two showings a day, "Now will I begin a dream of my own." Twice a day, Richard Burton's Antony announced, "The ultimate desertion. Me from myself."

Signs and omens were everywhere.

Loyola Campus lay frozen, covered with snow, on the icy banks of Lake Michigan. The muffled city shimmered in streetlight and moonlight and starlight.

Who needed Egypt?

"A beer sounds right," Louisa said. "Stop calling that girl in the ticket booth. Her job is bad enough without you." Her housecoat opened as she pulled the metal can cold from the refrigerator, stabbed it with a green-handled opener. The beer bubbled up over the can. She threw the opener into the drawer, picked up the beer, and savoring her foamy fingers, bumped the drawer closed with her hip.

"Want one?" she asked. She sidled over to the kitchen table. "What you reading?"

"Big test tomorrow. Chaucer."

"Aw, you'll do good in it." She nudged my shoulder. "More's the pity."

"What?"

"More's the pity. All your brains and nothing to show for it. No money. No fun. No girls. All for a big fat report card."

"For now."

"You're not like my three boys."

She was a famous conversationalist in her family. Often I chose not to study in the attic so she could trap me in the kitchen where I listened to her, all the while moving my pencil across my yellow legal pads of notes. She always sat up, late and alone, the nights of that winter and spring. She wanted to talk. She was interested in the scar of vocation not yet closed on my skin. She wanted to rub her finger across it. She knew I was an open wound pretending I was a brave boy.

Joe Bunchek peered into the kitchen. His bare feet padded across the scrubbed linoleum. Like a little boy himself he wore jersey pajamas, maroon, that in walking made prominent the loose sway of his equipment which was the constant center of Louisa's comedy patter.

"Get those big old things away from me," she said to him. "Haven't you caused enough trouble?"

"Listen here, Queenie, lay off the beer. That's the sixth one since supper." They often quarreled openly for sport. Joe could only beat Louisa by silence. Too often he forgot to use his best weapon.

"Joe Blow, do you have to watch everything I do?"

They both acted like I was an invisible audience invited into their house. The twenty bucks for my room was the price of admission to their floorshow.

"Who earns the money that buys your beer?"

"Do me a big favor, Joey. Take the money. Run off to Florida."

"Don't tempt me twice."

"Take the money and run off." She taunted him beyond belief. Her body had given out before his, earning him her undying resentment.

"Money I don't need," Joe said. "I can go out and earn it."

"Take it anyway. Go ahead." Louisa became grand. "I'll get a room by myself."

"Kid, are you looking for women?" Joe said to me. "Forget it. Queenie's worse than when she was sixteen. She was frustrated then."

"I should have gone out and had some drinks by myself tonight."

"Oh *mother*, you talk like a lady with a paper nose."

"Oh you, you're so funny." Louisa turned, her face flushed under the thick permanent swirls of her very fixed black hair. From her depths she shot tremendous strength to her middle finger, thrusting it manfully in Joe's face. "Take that," she said and turned to her beer.

Joe reeled. "Women don't give men the finger."

"What planet are you on?" Louisa said.

Joe fell into a kitchen chair and put his head in his big arms on the table. I sat quietly across from them, sorry for him at the mercy of her change-of-life. She had taken away his part. She had gestured like a man. He was a handsome middle-aged man with big-nosed Balkan features and a drayman's pride in his body. It had given him three sons and he knew how to strut. His hard high chest had not softened over his strong belly, and Louisa maybe shunned him, but he had heat, he jibed at her, at the house where the girls knew all the tricks. He was a proud man. He worked. They owned a brick house. They had cars. He was not falling apart. She was enjoying falling apart. She had gestured like a man, not graciously like the nice old lady, refinished with a doll-face of her choice, that his old age had envisioned for itself.

Joe raised his head from his arms. He grimaced at her. "Nyaaa," he bleated.

Louisa threw her can in the sink. "Men!" she said and left the kitchen.

Joe sat uncaring. As quickly as Louisa disappeared, he could not remember why. Her gesture was already a joke to him. Even I had heard to the fourth power, in my three months in their attic, Louisa's endless stories. *Yellow legal pad, number 4, page 16.* She should have been a show-girl, she always said. Her mother had been in an act with Marie Dressler and Polly Moran, but pulled out right before they hit the big time in Hollywood. She could still turn an ankle with the best she said, even though—without much connection—her father deserted them leaving her with, *cue the miniseries,* no money or music lessons and at the mercy of her handy curious brothers. She had let Joseph Bunchek penetrate her secrets at the wake of one of her uncles. I had visions of them doing it on the casket, they were so open about everything. He knew she wanted what they all wanted, seed and cash, but she was easy and Catholic, so he married her a week later in Indiana. She followed him doggedly through the Navy camps on the East Coast during the war, dropping three babies in quick succession. She never forgave him for what it did to her hips and rear.

"Kid," Joe said, "you still looking for a job?"

"I got a test tomorrow." I looked at the clock. "Really, I got to study."

He did not hear. "I heard of one through Lou Lou's brother. You can make good wages. Union, like that. 'Course, you'll have to be able to work. Get your hands dirty. You ain't built like I was when I was your age."

He read my scar and rubbed it raw. He carried himself with authority.

"When I was your age, I was married, with two kids and knew what-for. I didn't sit around schools all day. I took my back and my pack and hired out for what I could get. Not for what I was worth. I was worth a hell of a lot more than I got. Ask your daddy about the Depression."

"I have. Lard sandwiches. Snow. Six miles to school." I looked at my watch. "God, it's late."

"Go to bed, kid. We're in the same boat, don't you know." He stood up.

"What?"

"Man-to-man. Some day I'll tell you."

"Tell me now."

Joe Bunchek hinted at the secrets.

This time I was not going to lie as I always had and say, "You don't have to tell me. I already know."

I needed the Buncheks.

"Say 'good-night,' kid," he said.

April 14,1964

Whan that Aprille with his shoures sote, the droghte of March hath perced to the rote, when April showers have pierced to the roots the drought of March, many mornings I woke wet, tented like the human tripod. *Don't touch it.* To head to the bathroom and kitchen, I sidestepped into the old Misery dormitory trick and pulled on my Jockey shorts under the covers, flipped the blankets, and stepped into my pants.

Even in April, 120 days out of the slavery of Misery, I could not believe I had bought my way upriver. Gunn and Karg warned us regularly about ex-seminarians. "They go off the deep end, lose their faith, stop going to the sacraments. The ruin of the best is the worst." *Touch it.* I woke each day hoping to be swept away, but life was as ordinary as Louisa's cupboards stocked with bread and canned goods.

Misery was a past I had to live with, like a girl who got pregnant and gave the kid up for adoption. I remained a jerk. *Touch it. Don't touch it. Which is sweeter?* You can take the boy out of Misery, but you can't take Misery out of the boy. Jacob wrestled with a goddam angel. I fought the good fight. I wrestled with priests to beat those priests and priestlings at their own game. What had I done? I denied my past and destroyed my future.

My Uncle Les said, "God ordered Adam and Eve out of the Garden. You walked out on your own."

I had moved from Gregorian chant into the polkas of Rogers Park and the hootenannies of Old Town and the jazz clubs of Rush Street on the Near North Side. I stared at the lights shining from the windows of the *Playboy* mansion on the Gold Coast and watched the crowds coming and going at the Whiskey-a-Go-Go, not yet prepared to walk through any doors.

'This is my philosophy: If you aren't adjusted where you are," I told the Buncheks, "then go where the adjustment is."

"So you studied philosophy," Louisa said, "in a fortune cookie factory."

"I want to go where I want to go and do what I want to do."

"Suit yourself," Louisa said. "I'm staying put."

"You need to get around a little more," Joe said.

April descended on Chicago. My first spring. I was free and ready to defrost. Blankets lay in the streets along the curbs where drivers stuck in the blizzard had thrown them under their spinning tires to escape. Little yellow crocuses bloomed around the edges of dirty frozen snow drifts. Vine leaves grew in my pants. I walked through people in the Loop. I sat with steaming coffee along the cement walks and walls of the Chicago River the city dyed green for Saint Patrick's Day. I had never watched skyscrapers light up by night. Never had I felt such wind. Evenings, coming back to Louisa's, I ran down the streets from the El train, jumping from pool to pool of lamplight in the spring rain.

My one attic window, large and round, looked down on Magnolia Street, where cars maneuvered silently between two parked lanes as furtive as great dark beasts hunting a curbside lair for the night. I owned no car. I owned no house. I was free beyond belief. I felt wickedly suspect: I was alone, rattlingly poor in someone else's attic. A dream come true. I had finally ended one world of my life. Everything seemed possible. I wandered into coffee shops and bookstores, watching people. I wrote notes in my yellow legal pads. A Journal. Twice a week the double-feature changed at the Bryn Mawr Theater. On the marquee at the Devon, *A Thousand Clowns* was in its second year. Louisa rattled out the wonders of money and a good job. Her middle son—my age—was a junior accountant in the Loop.

"I'm not sure yet how important money is to me," I said. "Roof, bread, tuition."

"Make sure you have twenty bucks a week." She kept the rent money powerful between us. She grinned when I found a job. "Doing what?" She hooted with laughter. "Demonstrating Hoover vacuum cleaners?"

"Shut up!"

She was a comedian.

"In department stores?"

"Really, shut up."

She was a lounge act at the local bar...

"In Marshall Field?"

...appearing nightly in the Plywood Room.

"So?" I said.

"Throwing baking powder on the carpet?"

"It's a job."

"Vacuuming it up?"

She had us both doubled up with laughter.

"Yes."

"Blowing the beach ball in the air..."

"I make $3.25 an hour."

"...on a wand?"

"Yes."

We were screaming with laughter. She was the funniest woman in the world. I fell into her arms.

"Hey!" she said. "Hey! Hey! Hey! I ain't your girlfriend."

"Sorry. You kill me."

By the next afternoon, opening a beer, she said, "Joey found you a better job."

"Part-time?"

"Yeah. You can't spend all your time studying and working blowing beach balls." She toasted herself. "You've got to date too." She trailed off into the living room. "You've wasted too much time."

"Thank you," I said. "Thanks so much."

"Think nothing of it."

"What's the job?"

"I don't know. Joey will tell you."

Any revelation Joe had I trusted.

Louisa plopped down on the couch. Her thighs scooting back on the plastic sounded like a martyr's flesh tearing. She loved plastic. On the lampshades. On the footstool. "If I didn't rent out a room, I could uncover this furniture, but I wouldn't."

"Save me from studying Victorian lit," I said. "You want to watch the late show tonight?"

"What's on?" she asked. "Not another one of those gladiator movies."

"*Never on Sunday*," I said.

"Already on the late show? I should have gotten more beer. *Never on Sunday* is not very old." She was feeling fully Queenie enthroned on the couch, a mystery woman, a woman of mystery, revealing everything, revealing nothing, an object lesson in something. Her feet rested up on the coffee table. "Sit down," she said. She made busy, buttoning her housecoat to her throat, but over her breast the cloth hung loose and apart, a dark tunnel lit by the alternating light and shadow from the TV screen. One pendulous sag was visible and moving, blanched white by Channel Five. She reached for her beer and the movement of her arm lifted, then closed, the view. We sat watching the news. *Never on Sunday* never showed up.

"Maybe the soundtrack was going to be on the radio," I said.

"I thought it was too new for TV." She tilted the beer can all the way back. "Guess I won't stay up. Too good a night for sleeping anyway."

"Every night's a good night for sleeping."

"Even that gets hard on the back," she said.

"I never have any trouble," I lied.

"Six-thirty comes early," she said. She shuffled towards her room, then turned. "So you got a regular job like a regular guy," she grinned.

"I'm a worker."

"Well, well."

April 28, 1964

The brewery sprawled huge across three industrial blocks. It was red brick, like Misery, but taller, and workers were free to come and go. At the entrance gate to the yard, the amber smell of cooking grains sifted down through the ring of cyclone fence. Men in blue twill stood smoking near the time clock, jowls grizzled from the third shift, but scrubbed fresh in the workers' shower.

I waited near them, glad to be in from the morning cold, listening to their words, trying to find what was to be expected in another new segment of my life. I would make a go of this, the same as my new school. I had to know what I was. I had to push myself in every direction. I had functioned well in the sweet security of the Church, claiming I had a vocation only God could underwrite.

I had to know if I had self-reliance, on my own, nothing mystical to fall back on. No terrible sweet ecclesiastical security to remove the ordinary tensions of existence. I willed to worry about food and a roof. Every new meeting made me further incarnate in the world.

I watched the men each push his timecard into the clock. Chunk-*ping!* They were faces marked by their lives, same as everyone else. On Ordination days when the new priests' brothers came, I always wondered at the telling differences life, not heredity, wreaked. Two brothers with the same bland faces as babies grow up marked with a difference, because the one sells used cars and the other says Holy Mass. The lay brother's skin is different, creased in premature lines, like my brother Thom's, about mouths and eyes that have tasted and seen and coped with the stress of real life. If it weren't for their vocation, I knew seminarians who'd stand in this same line, chunk-pinging their days like their fathers and brothers, not getting plumper in rectories claiming to be gourmet chefs. They flashed the ID of their priestly vocation like a passport exempting them from the slow-ticking clock on the factory wall. No one, not even Rector Karg, Papal Chamberlain, not even the Pope, the new one, Paul VI, could tell if they were palming off a forgery of a vocation. Where spirituality leaves off and social climbing begins is a thin red passive-aggressive line.

I was led deep into the innards of the plant, a movie set right out of *Metropolis* that I'd seen at the Chicago Film Society. In the section producing malt syrup only the center of the rooms was lighted. The walls receded into murky darkness. Half the malt building was storied, floor above open floor, with the steel skeletal anatomy of the cannery. Empty tin cans rattled down forever, cause and effect, from the third floor to the carousel spigots on the second where they were flushed full of syrup, lidded and cooled, whipped through a labeling chute and stacked automatically twelve on their sides, still warm, ready to be pushed by a button into a cardboard carton held by a man who started the boxes through the sealer, its brush tongue and harrowing lips gluing and folding the flaps down hard, pressing the boxes against the rollers moving toward the final chute to the busy shipping dock.

The rest of the building was open-storied like a Spanish mission built around an internal plaza, jammed with furnaces and boilers and copper tubing. Vats from the basement, explosive with pressure, flowed up to the second floor, their small openings steaming in the close hot air. Piping raveled through them like catheters rinsing steel patients. Everything was connected, explicit, unlike the Byzantine tunnels and pipes under Misery. Brown sacks of flaked green-yellow hops stacked in acrid bunkers stood ready for brewing. Periodically, tugging men emptied them into the small mouths of the vast pressure cookers that exploded in heat and steam and froth churning a full story high. They flushed the crude syrup up through the swollen tubing to a black steel hop-jack for rinsing and cooling, then drained it down, dropping it a floor to twin one-story vats separated by a catwalk, there to lay for final straining and cooling before canning.

That first day was like all first days for the new guy, isolated, abandoned, *nobody loves me*, consigned to the shit-work high on the catwalk. At least I was new. At least I was a guy. Fifty feet above the floor, vertiginous, alone on a small platform, learning to be one of the boys, I had to turn three-foot water valves from flow to ebb and back again on tanks as big as a school bus. *Angel of God, my Guardian dear.* I was standing on top of a kettle in hell, making thick tea by sloshing a thousand gallons of water back and forth through two tons of soggy tea leaves. Turning water into beer. The screen baskets of the final seining filled with a brown wet sawdust steaming like hot dung. The boiling brew, falling through the seine, bubbled down from the hop-jack hissing in wet clouds from the small door opening into the huge tank which I had to climb into with a shovel to scrape out the last waste. *If not a worker-priest, a worker.* Many men feared climbing into the small hole of the big tank. *I was big. I was tough. Liar.* That's why I got the job. I feared nothing, because nothing was more claustrophobic than Misery.

As the last syrup trickled into the tanks, I climbed a twenty-foot ladder, like Tony Curtis in *Trapeze,* leading straight above to the hop-jack where most of the waste had settled. A man stood beside it waiting for me, the first time. His cap was pulled down to his eyes and he seemed to have no face. He had an immense potbelly. A worker could drink as much as he could hold. He wore a see-through white nylon sport shirt that buttoned tight across his chest. My chest had strengthened at the YMCA. He motioned me to watch. He turned on the cold water to flush the heat from the hop-jack waste. He said nothing and I felt awkward, the two of us standing like acrobats on a platform, waiting, high above the rest of the plant. Finally he motioned for me to climb higher up the next ladder. I had to do it. Below me was all the world. I had to prove I could function where Rector Karg's Holy Mother Church was no net to catch me. I peered down at him.

He smiled beneath his cap. He placed his hand sideways in his crotch, drove his fingers in flat, index finger up, and pulled his hand out loosely and snapped it from the wrist as if flinging sweat from his fingers. He shook his head side to side, laughing, *boy-o-boy.* He was making like my buddy signaling me we were both hot and tired. He was telling me I was doing okay. Then he motioned me on, to enter the jack.

I peered in through the small porthole door, down at the ladder, into the steel submarine of the copper tank. From theological study to graduate school to this noisy, dangerous factory, and maybe to the war far off in Southeast Asia, I had to meet the world on its terms. That was always my point. Lots of workers become priests. I never heard of a priest becoming a worker. I looked inside the tank, pulled my work gloves on my hands, over the once-broken finger, and vowed I would make it back to Louisa's, because the stranger, my new buddy, had given me more encouragement in one gesture than any priest.

I climbed feet first through the porthole and ten feet down the rungs of the ladder into the isolation tank of the vat. Six inches of hops waste mattressed under my new work shoes. My buddy threw a stoker's shovel in after me. It cut through the wet heat and landed on the cushion of waste.

"Take off your shirt," he said. He peered down on me through the small porthole at the top of the ladder. The tank was ominous with sprinkler cooling jets. *In the showers of the concentration camps, a million Catholic martyrs.* "Every fuck ever worked in here says it's too goddam hot."

His face disappeared and I was standing alone on the spent hops. I gouged an opening in the carpet of wet waste nearest the sewer trap and slugged a couple shovels down. In two minutes I was soaked through, sweating like other men. I threw my shirt over the ladder rungs, to grab it in scrambling escape should the machine begin flooding with me in it. I was not going to drown like Hank the Tank. I was in the tank and one with the tank. I worked, shoulders, arms, back, legs, to clear the serrated floor, stopping to gasp under the draft of the tiny incoming flue that smelled like the cooler brewery air of the far outside.

I leaned panting against the black walls of the tank, larger than my room at Misery where Karg had slugged me across the chest. I paced myself, laughing, knowing I was strong enough to do the job. The shiny copper floor of the tank finally gleamed spotless, flecked with a few brown flakes, like cereal dried on the rim of an unwashed bowl. My jeans were soaked. I was elated, touched sensuously by a strange fatigue of pleasure. I could make it to Louisa's, I told myself. Dead tired, I would make it to Louisa's. I climbed out of the tank, shirtless, laughing, popping the can of beer handed by my buddy. In the sweat running salt into my mouth, I tasted the promise of the world.

May 14, 1964

My cherry depressed Louisa all through the spring into the first of my summers among grown-ups. Lilacs in the dooryards bloomed all down our street the way I always dreamed spring would be in the world. I no longer knelt, kneecaps on wooden kneelers, in the impossible indulgent stretches of introspection. I traded mystic meditation for rational thought on buses between graduate school and the brewery and Louisa's. I could have cared less that, back at Misery, Ordination Day was coming.

In the city, I pulled myself together, hungry for adventure. I walked the night streets of the Loop, eating up the downtown lights of the huge marquees of the brilliant movie palaces, wanting life as perfect and big and sweeping as a wide-screen movie, hoping history would happen to me, doubting it would, buying front-row seats to see Albert Finney in *Tom Jones* downtown and in *Saturday Night and Sunday Morning* uptown, double-billed with Richard Harris in *This Sporting Life* at the Bryn Mawr. The British invasion was everywhere. The Beatles were coming to the Amphitheater.

"You're begging for it," Louisa said. She was making me a cottage-cheese salad.

"My father once told me," I said, "that anticipation is greater than the actual thing."

"Then your mother must be a lousy lay."

"Hey, Lou Lou!" I said.

"Don't call me 'Lou Lou.' I was kidding."

"Don't insult my mother."

"We're all virgin saints, us mothers," Louisa said over the refrigerator door. "I'm going away for two weeks."

"By yourself?" She wouldn't travel with Joe.

"I'm not telling where I'm going."

"Don't put lettuce under my pineapple."

"Don't get smart," she said.

"Who's getting smart?"

"Men. Males, whatever ages."

Good. I warmed at her thinking me like all other men. I was changing.

"They ought to do with men like they do with girls in China."

"What?"

"Take 'em out and drown 'em."

"What a waste."

"Don't get smart or I'll give you your rent back."

"Louisa." I said her name strong as Joe. "What's the matter? What do you really want?" I tested only her honesty.

She licked her thumb, glancing my question away from her privacy. "A millionaire who'll give me two hundred a month and be gone all the time. No sex allowed. That's the perfect husband."

"'Can't Buy Me Love' ain't your song. Put my pineapple on top of my cottage cheese."

"Don't be funny. I'm miserable enough."

"You know, if I'd met you another time another place, we could have had a good laugh."

"Not me, dolly. I'm nothing but a miserable b-i...do you want me to spell it?"

"No."

"Then quit trying to hear my Confession. You *left* the seminary. God! There's hot dogs for supper and Jewish rye I bought. Why don't you get a girl—the poor thing—but get a girl for godsake. Call Miss Ticket Booth." She stared at me. "Get yourself loved..."

"Yeah, yeah, yeah. She loves me, yeah, yeah, yeah."

"...and get loved in return."

"Like you and Joe? That's the secret?"

"That's the ticket."

"Is that theology?"

"Ain't it the movies?"

She wiped her hands clean on her apron.

"Do you have any sauerkraut, Louisa?"

"In this house? This ain't Germany."

"You can get it at the A&P." I wanted to say *for Chrissakes.* I sounded like Joe. She had sucked me into her movie.

"I told you anything you want, pick it up. But you're probably not too hot at picking anything up." She slung the salad into the refrigerator. "You might as well never left the seminary. You live exactly the same. Study and work. You never go anyplace. Not like my boys." She untied her apron. "I'm going to lie down. You can put your own hot dog on. I understand boys," she said. "I understood mine and all their friends." She took a can of beer from the refrigerator. "But you!"

"Do you have another saucepan?" I said. "So what's the matter with me?"

"I don't want to insult your mother again."

"What's that mean?"

"Maybe she doesn't love you enough."

"Shut up, Lou Lou. You are a b-i-t-c-h."

"Yeah, well, here." She handed me her beer can. "These new pull-tab cans never work." She made a face. "Here, you try, Mister Big Brewery Worker. Watch you don't cut."

I pulled the tab open for her and tossed the ring into the waste can.

"Boys always have understood me." She winked. "Do you understand me?"

"I understand you."

"Joe says you could do with a good roller-coaster ride with Miss Slammo, the girl contortionist of TV wrestling."

"That's dumb and clear as mud."

"Mud covers the ground."

May 15, 1964

I hated Louisa. She stripped my need down like a bed for washing. Something no Jesuit had ever done. Every day of the spring I thought, now today, I'll meet the sweet girl, the one I'll love the first. I saved so long, everything I had to give was ripe, blooming, poppable. All unknowing they competed, girls seated in classrooms, animated in halls, talking over coffee in the Union. Perfumed, wrapped in folds of cotton and silk, cupped, teased, combed, heavy with languor, small hands in white gloves, studious beneath a professor's drone, each girl scanned, computed, sought eligible. I cruised among them, outside their sweet dimension.

A tremendous disconnected sense of being unloved, *nobody loves me,* crossed over me, who had words for everyone and everything at Misery, *your mother doesn't love you enough,* with nothing to say to the men at work, not speaking the language of girls, with inchoate desire sounding like a prayer, *Dear God, she turns me on,* dreaming of them all, of a face, faceless, beautiful, pure, small white breasts, coming to me, me bending to them teaching me, heavy with desire, with vine leaves in my hair, white godlike linen wrapped crisscross, *Christ's Cross,* around my loins, heavy with pure virgin love.

I thought of a boxing match at Catholic Boys Camp one summer, and Hank the Tank kicking out my teeth in football and breaking my finger, and returning more than twenty times after summers and after Christmases on busses and trains to six million *tick tick* minutes at Misery. I always went back for more: it took me almost five rounds to lose the boxing match, because I was rough and tough and ready to beat them all up. Louisa intuited some things about me, but she didn't know everything. She didn't know about the vast experiments in the South State Street dives, parlors of tattoo and pool, or about Jocelyn. When I experimented with giving up Confession, I stopped telling everybody everything.

Besides, Louisa never would have believed the gang of younger brewers, five or six, who let me tag along to Rush Street and Wells, drinking, and then four of us, *come on, kid,* to South State Street, stepping over winos, where we yelled, "Go-go, baby, go, go," at the white-booted strippers bumping it out over the ancient plush seats of the burlesque theater. "Take it off, take it off!"

Very jokey, very drunk, two or three of the brewers played at playing pocket-pool in their pants and moaning and laughing and mooing like bulls, and we all palsy-walsy went running drunken out into the spring night, stopping in later at the tavern where the older whores came to play tennis, and the guys, *come on, kid,* enrolling me in higher education, kidded them, *the old whoors,* all night, buying plenty of drinks, jeweling them down from twenty to five bucks a throw, until all their other prospects had stumbled out, and then laughing in the old cosmetic faces and hooting at them, *Oh, sister, how much will you pay us to gangbang you?*

The bartender laughed. He thought it so funny them, *the old whoors,* cheated out of their tricks, because the cops could arrest him for prostitution, because the gag kept everybody drinking longer and later, everybody so drunk even the old whores were laughing, because the bartender paid them to keep us all spending like drunken sailors.

At four in the morning, when the bars closed, that world, *Oh, Jesus,* was a cold place, *Oh, Jesus*, where street lights shined, *Oh, Jesus*, hard down on hard men hardening me.

May 20, 1964

So Louisa didn't know about Jocelyn Jennings. She was a professional graduate student. Her course work completed, she was in the sixth year of the seven maximum allowed to write a dissertation. Hers happened to be on Virginia Woolf, who had drowned herself twenty years before. Jocelyn had bussed her torso into college from Jamestown, New York. She specialized in taking new graduate students down to a cellar jukebox bar on Rush Street to twist to Chubby Checker, and frug to Ramsey Lewis' "I'm 'In' with the In Crowd," and slow-dance to Ray Charles records, "I Can't Stop Loving You" and "Ruby (You're Like a Song)."

One night, in the group of us, she took a pen from her bag, wrote something, leaned into me, and said, "Phone me."

I did, because hers was the first phone number I received, and she was editor of the graduate school literary magazine.

"You could get me published," I said, "for the first time outside the Catholic press."

"Did you notice you're in a Jesuit university?" she said. "Everything here is the Catholic press." She was something extraordinary among all the other well-bred girls and their blond beehive hairdos. She was tall, thin, and mysterious. Her long curlicue black hair flew loose, wild, around her face. In an instant, she could change, pulling her hair back and piling it on top her head like the women in ancient Greece, and behind her head, like Virginia Woolf herself in the photographs she had clipped from British magazines.

She was perfect for Rush Street and Old Town, where she lived at 60 East Chicago, Apartment 403, a block from the Water Tower, and a block from the Lawson Y. Many students hived together in tiny apartments. Artists and musicians and underground filmmakers hung out at the bars and coffee shops and the Russian tea room and the Cinematheque which, she told everyone, was always getting busted by the police, because the Chicago Film Review Board were all the widows of cops and politicians. She was a presence in the Student Union cafeteria, something like Urania, the earth mother, with her special chair at a special table. Everyone in graduate school seemed to know her, nod to her, suck up to her. I kept my distance at first.

We were like one of those old big-band songs of the 1940's where the whole tune, like "Sentimental Journey," is played through as an instrumental and finally some featured singer like Doris Day tags in at the end with the lyrics. Jocelyn and I only became vocal like that after a long period of, not flirting, but watching, studying, eye-balling each other. I missed the barracks of the seminary. I missed the Misery gossip. Jocelyn was the eye and center of everything. I missed knowing someone like that. She was the Ruler of the Union, the editor of the paper, and a favorite of the faculty.

I gave her a manuscript on J. D. Salinger. "It's okay," she said. We were dancing together on Rush Street to a jukebox full of 45's, Ray Charles singing, "Georgia, Georgia." She led me. "We have to discuss your writing. *J'accuse!* You were in the seminary." We stopped dancing. "Don't lie."

I was a seven-year-old caught with my underwear dripping. "It shows?"

"*Shows?*" She shot the word back from the side of her mouth. "The 'theology of this' and 'the theology of that.' *Crap.* Must you see a 'theology' in everything? There must be a thousand ex-seminarians on this campus. You're new, but you're not fresh."

"I can get fresh."

"I mean you're not original."

"You want me to get fresh?"

She slapped my face. Not hard. Everybody stared. I felt like one of those chickens they crucify in Mexico and watch die, taking bets, while the stage fills up with its blood. "Georgia, Georgia." She took my hands, lifted my arms, and pulled me into her. "Dance," she said. I hated her. I loved her. I pushed into her. She pushed back. We danced until Ray Charles stopped singing. "What do you think of Negroes?" she said.

"They need their rights."

"What's your 'theology-of' that?"

I told her about living as a worker-priest for three months at Holy Cross parish and marching on Mayor Daley's office with The Woodlawn Organization.

"From 63rd and Cottage Grove?"

"With Saul Alinsky."

That was when she said, "Phone me." That was the night she gave me her number. "Saul Alinsky, huh? Still waters run deep. We'll discuss it."

"*It?*"

"All of it."

"Have you read Alinsky's manifesto, *Rules for Radicals?*"

"I proofed the galleys."

"Liar."

An hour later, too eager, I called her from the elevated station near Louisa's.

"Can I see you?"

"Tuesday at eight."

"Shall I bring my manuscript?"

"Down, boy," she said.

"Go get her," Joe said.

Louisa laughed. "You're so sophisticated. Certainly, I did not see the fifth of Southern Comfort stashed under your bed, and your handwriting is terrible."

The thought of Louisa trying to decipher my yellow legal pads was a comedy compared to Rector Karg sniffing through my shoe box of papers word by word. Something had been stolen from me. Some secrets had not been revealed. I had escaped from Misery, a missing boy, gone in the middle of the night, and no one, no priest, no rector ever even called my parents to report me missing, or to see if I arrived home in one piece.

"Aaawgh," Joe said, "we all waste our youth some way."

"So us three got something in common," Louisa said.

"Aaawgh, Queenie," Joe said.

In the Buncheks' attic, I stood naked, couldn't keep my clothes on, transfixed in the mirror by who's that? Naked, I rose, untouched. Spring blew in the window. I threw myself into my bed, tossing, planning my first literary engagement with Jocelyn, whom I thought of as my editor, Jocelyn.

"I want to introduce you," she had offered, "to LeRoi Jones. I want to listen to you reading out loud, 'An Agony. As Now.'"

In my *Journal,* I wrote the declarative sentence Jocelyn had told me was the declarative truth of the declarative Virginia Woolf: "What secrets men know are revealed through women."

I was determined to be like other men, and learn the secrets I had always missed in all the other inner circles of boys.

Tuesday I stood, early outside her address, her salon, her apartment, her two rooms, for fifteen minutes, in the dark, under the lamplight, actually lit by the bright light of the Communist bookstore on the first floor of her building, looking up through the curtains of her window, four floors up, watching her arranging flowers she had bought herself. "I always buy my flowers myself," she had said. She saw me, shook her head, and waved me up.

"You're laughing at me," I said.

"Never." She ushered me through her door. "My roommate is out," she said. "Does that make any difference to you?"

"Should it?"

"Cary Grant," she mocked me, "come in." She received me in one of those *Breakfast at Tiffany's* black hostess outfits with long pants and a long skirt open in front, where you'd notice, pocket to pocket.

I squeezed past her in the narrow hall. She handed me one of the two glasses of wine in her hands. She smiled, closed the door, and leaned against it. "You've never seen anybody do this before," she said.

"What?"

"Lean back against the door."

"Nobody in real life."

"Darling," she said, flagging a hand from her chest out to arm's length where a finger wriggled at me, "you've never seen real life."

"Yes, I have," I said to contradict her. "But I've never seen a movie where a woman closed a door without leaning on it."

She looked annoyed, *baubles, bangles, bright shining beads*, then recouped. "You need a...big glass of wine. Drink up." She swung easily by me. She wore one earring, gold and pendulous, that told true gravity even as she rushed to fall posturing on the couch. "Sit down, oh, please, sit down, do," she said. "Welcome to my movie."

I wanted to ask who she thought she was, and who she thought I was.

"What movie am I?" she asked.

"What movie are you?"

"Darling, I'm Maya Deren in *Meshes of the Afternoon*."

"Never heard of her."

"I'm *Pussy on a Hot Tin Roof*."

"Very funny. That's not Tennessee Williams."

"That's the Kuchar brothers."

"What are you talking about?"

"Darling, underground film. Experimental cinema. Don't you know anything about the *avant garde*?"

"At Misery, I was the *avant garde*."

"Darling, I must take you to the Cinematheque."

"Don't make me feel ignorant."

"This is how the world opens up. New words. *Discotheque*. Dancing to records, discs. *Cinematheque*. Cinema, movies. Like *Bibliotheque*. Library, books. You told me you loved words. You told me you love movies." She handed me a sheet of screening dates and times, with photos, and titles like *Little Stabs at Happiness* and *Fireworks* and *Scorpio Rising*. "Wonderful films by artists, not studios. *Flaming Creatures* and *The Sin of Jesus*..."

"You can't scandalize me."

"I'm practically on the selection committee at the Cinematheque. You've seen Second City? Yes? No? Oh. In fact, I'm polishing up shooting notes, as an appendix to my dissertation, for an improvisational film of *Orlando*, a novel by Virginia Woolf..."

"*Who's Afraid of Virginia Woolf?*"

"...that's something else again, that play, but my film, I mean, will this graduate faculty ever catch up? I want to direct, but a film, even an underground film, takes money. Do you have any money?"

"Me?"

"You look rich."

"I just spent $480,000."

"Don't kid a kidder."

"Why are you at this school?" I asked.

She sipped her wine. "Virgins."

"Virgins?"

"Catholic boy virgins. Like you."

"I'm not a virgin. Stop trying to scandalize me."

"I have a fetish for Catholic boys."

"I'm not a virgin."

"How does it feel to be a fetish?"

"What's a fetish?

She went ha ha ha. Her mouth went ha ha ha. Her hair went ha ha ha. "You reveal yourself in your writing," she said. "You must be careful ha ha ha."

"Why? Writers are, like, strippers, revealing themselves ha ha ha." I said it, but her mouth and hair made me say it, revealed me saying, Hemingway was, and was not, *The Old Man and the Sea*.

"True." She pretended to weigh her words, trebling wine on her tongue. "Unless a writer comes out and says, I mean, really makes the personal explicit, 'this is me' or 'what happened to me,' well, the reader can hardly know what is an autobiographical act, or what is manufactured."

"Fiction."

"Your essay exposed you ha ha ha as an ex-seminarian."

"A former seminarian. I'm a former seminarian."

"What's the diff?"

"An ex-seminarian is one who didn't get over it."

"Humph! Jesuit! I hope you didn't mind my grilling you in the Student Union."

"No."

"How did you find it? I'm curious."

"The grilling?"

"The seminary. I think you were there a very long time. How over it are you?"

Her apartment was one of those semi-furnished flats fitted out with odds and ends. The orange couch, where she enthroned herself, sitting with her feet up, her knees folded under her, all in black, was the center of the room. Piles of cushions scattered in small archipelagoes across the floor. She said furniture was bourgeois, and marriage, and religion, and how did I like sitting cross-legged as a beatnik in a beanbag chair?

Behind her, in blue, greens and yellows, a print on textured cardboard, of a painting, "by Carrington," she said, a portrait, head and shoulders, of a florid young man, "you notice, but, of course, you think you look like that, romantic, a lover, painted by a woman," a prize, British, imported, from the bins of textured cardboard paintings sold at Barbara's Book Store in Old Town.

"Actually," I said, "I'm, uh, trying to be honest."

"As an artist," she said, "I'm interested in faces, portraits, films cast from life, faces, not actors, real people, and real writing, personal, reflexive."

At Misery, I could have projected her, Jocelyn Jennings herself, face and body, from real dreams. I had known her apartment, if not her, already far back, distracted by Plato in Misery's chapel, dreaming about a Greenwich Village garret. I was not disappointed she was so literary, so bohemian, so free, so pretentiously beyond the pretenders preening in the Misery opera and chant society.

"I was in the seminary longer than most murderers are in prison, but don't get me wrong, as fub duck..."

"Fub duck?"

"...fucked up as it was, it was one of the most positive experiences of my life."

"What did they do to you?"

"They never did anything to me."

"They never touched you?"

"They never touched me."

"Maybe not your body."

"I tried, really, to be creative, find myself, get the most out of it."

"Hasn't every boy in a seminary, everyone thinks, presumes they, you..."

"No."

"Perhaps, not you."

"Not me. Definitely."

"And you're jealous ha ha ha that they didn't do...you, choose...you."

"Ha ha ha. One day I discovered I'd milked the experience dry. I'd learned, taken, everything they had to give, and shined it back at them. The priests had no more to offer me. I had to leave, and fast, or watch my creativity," I wanted to say, my very self, my soul, my life, "curl up and die. As simple as that."

"But what did they do to you?"

"They gave me drugs."

"Priests are not doctors."

"They said I made myself nervous."

"Darling," she said deliberately, sitting up, "you didn't leave the seminary. You left the Dark Ages."

I could touch this worldchild. Grace could still work through me. She could introduce me to the world, and I her to heaven. Oh, God, shut me fub duck up. Spinning, falling, rising, lying, hoping, begging, pretending, faking, wanting to fall into all the troubles of the flesh, the glories, sitting cross-legged, containing myself, wanting not knowing what, everything, from her.

"You're positively Gothic," she said. "At least you're making yourself up." She rose. "We had an ex-seminarian up here to dinner last week. He acted like we were going to rape him. He sat there, on the couch, right on the edge, his knees together." She lit a cigarette. "I guess he thought he ought to go out with the girls. Priests are such boys, such...virgins." She smiled at me, really smiled, looking for all the world like everything I'd never seen. "Care for another drink?" she asked. I heard every apple in Eden fall.

I pushed my package of Southern Comfort towards her. "It's a house gift."

"Thanks," she said, "wine's my limit. Yours too. Stand up." She poured the wine into our glasses. "Can you manage the stereo? I've stacked six or seven LPs. You know how to manage the stereo, don't you? You lift the arm, set it on the lip of record, and make sure the needle rides on into the groove."

"Lauren Bacall. *To Have and Have Not.*"

She kissed her finger and put her finger to my lips.

I dropped the record already set on her phonograph, and turned up the low, surging Mikis Theodorakis' soundtrack to the movie, *Phaedra,* so popular at the Bryn Mawr theater, crashing violins, deliberate picking guitars, soothing, the huge crisp black-and-white faces of Melina Mercouri and Anthony Perkins and Raf Vallone playing Aristotle Onassis erasing the faces of Karg and Gunn and all the priests and all the sweet, sweet nuns.

Melina Mercouri's deep voice, silken as cigarette smoke curling around grape leaves, saying over the music track to Tony Perkins, "Falcon of the cold north. Eagle of solitude. I give you milk and honey. You give me poison." Oh, if the priestlings could see this occasion, this Jocelyn Jennings, this living occasion of sin, ah, not sin, they'd scream perdition and mortal sin, yes, mortal, not venial, mortal sin, and ruin, lovely ruin. I stood ready, waiting my cue, waiting the director to call "action," but there was no director, and no action, and I stood embarrassed by the phonograph, breathing with the recorded actors' voices speaking now and again over the music, watching Jocelyn Jennings watch me, silken cigarette smoke rising through her hair, listening to the music.

"Lovely," she said, meaning the music, watching me. All the stuff of seduction surrounded us, but something was amiss. I smiled ha because we felt ha ha nothing for each other ha ha ha. I mean I. Not her. Who knew about her? What the virgin-slayer really felt? The whole charade made me suddenly sad. My spirits nose-dived. How could I make the first time, so long saved, be perfectly right? My breath came short. Get it over with. Maybe it didn't need to be right; maybe it only needed to happen: no plot, no props, one take.

The room was hot, "too hot for May, don't you think, maybe it's not the heat, but the humidity."

Sometimes people panic.

Sometimes a glass or two of wine turns out to be cheap wine, sangria, even, in a jelly glass, with a record playing, scratched, even, and the apartment, a far cry from Misery's luxury, fifty bucks a month, and all the stuff, phoney stuff, a reproach, going down the old evolutionary ladder, and the record turning, the clock ticking, and actors saying lines, written lines, scripted lines, about wasted lives and time lost, and the other person keeps on being glamorous, not noticing that sex, lurid, bumping sex has reared up in the room, wrestled itself around, hardened itself, denying, desiring, delaying, coming undone, scared, spent, thankful, happy to get out alive.

"So you liked *Phaedra*?" she asked over her glass.

"Yes."

We listened for a while not speaking, she smoking, until the record finished Side Two. I said I had to go, and left her my manuscript. At her door, searching for ignition, I asked, "Maybe, that is, if you're not busy or anything, we could go out Saturday night. To a movie or something."

"I'm afraid not," she said.
"Not even a virgin to the Cinematheque?"
"Another time."
"Oh, sorry..."
"Ryan, that's not a 'no.'"

June 20, 1964

Summer struck with new classes and thunderstorms. Lake Michigan rose and fell with a week of seiche that ripped the beach raw, crashing waves against the huge boulders protecting Loyola's Lakeshore Campus. Huge walls of water rolled in every ten hours, big as tidal waves. Between *bossa nova* cuts from the new Getz/Gilberto Verve album, the radio warned everyone away from the beaches of Lake Michigan, "The Girl from Ipanema," where lifeguards stood watch. Even the constant Chicago wind could not relieve the humidity, and the suck and pull of barometric pressure, rising and falling, teetered always on the edge of cyclone and tornado.

I retreated to Louisa's attic, studying late, feeling unloved and lost, listening to Stan Getz' saxophone mix "Desafinado" with the piano of Antonio Jobim and the guitar of João Gilberto. I hated the House of Lou Lou. She thought me like other men the way the priests had thought all vocations were the same. I hated me in her house. She was too personal. I wanted to escape from my past to my future. I stopped going to Mass. I thought of Ted in that grade-school nun's story, how he committed a sin with his girl and died in a car crash. The fires of hell got him, but at least he got the girl. The priests taught that girls were the main occasion of sin, but girls treated me almost formally, as if they and the world had not exactly been waiting for me to show up.

Could the world feel what I could not feel? At Misery, I had felt compassion for the world, but in the world, I lost empathy toward everyone, victims in burning buildings and children with cancer and people in ghettos, slipping and sliding since Jack died in Dallas, six months out of Misery, having gained the world and lost my soul. I wrote in my yellow legal pads those old lines of Wordsworth that "the world is too much with us, late and soon, getting and spending, we lay waste our powers; little we see in Nature that is ours."

On the lonely sands of Edgewater Beach, where Lake Michigan rolled up to the neighborhood of apartments where I looked for rooms to rent, no girl dappled with sun rose from the waves. I was doomed to innocence.

No sweet girl would ever appear. I'd stayed too long at Misery, and she had become lost, or impatient, or whatever happens to women whom priests' celibacy declines. At least Lock, one New Year's when he was in Cuba, had a real choice when a woman had said to him, "Give me an hour with you in a room and I'll change your mind about being a priest." After eleven years, I had nothing.

I had been *Seduced and Abandoned*, the title of the Italian movie at the Bryn Mawr. That's what movie Hank would have said I was. Maybe I was lucky. In California, in some Marine Corps hospital, Sandy Gully handed my brother, Thom, a baby, a second baby, a third baby, triplets, the curse of the Irish triplets that ran in our family. Thommy named the babies Abraham, Beatrice, and Siena. *Abe, Bea, and Sie.* Our six-year-old sister, Margaret Mary, *star of wonder*, was furious enough to want to run away. Thommy was twenty-two, way ahead in life, way ahead of lucky me.

I avoided Louisa, suspecting her wise eyes could see I wanted to move out. I saw more of Jocelyn. We borrowed Joe's car, his Lincoln, *take it, kid*, to drive to Ravinia's evening concerts on the grass. We walked to the movies the way I thought it would be. Summer evenings after the brewery, after classes, after the library, I came more and more to her apartment, taking blankets over to the beach.

"Sidney Poitier gave me goose bumps in *Lilies of the Field*," Jocelyn said. "That body. No shirt. His smile. Negroes are so sexy."

"I can't compete with Poitier," I said, "but there's no nuns like the ones he helped. They prayed and hung medals all over the desert, and pretended they were experiencing a miracle, but they all knew it was him that built their chapel for them, not the archangel Gabriel."

"Always so analytical," she said. "I'm cold."

I put my arm around her. The rising moon hung low out over the still Lake. Somewhere far behind us an elevated train rattled late up the rails toward Evanston. The night was quiet. She lay back on the blanket. I folded next to her, over her, like Burt Lancaster up on elbow over Deborah Kerr in *From Here to Eternity*.

"I'm cold," she said.

My arm covered her gently swelling chest. Her ear lay cuplike near my mouth, tasting the sweetness of her hair. "I'm cold too."

"Your legs are quivering."

"We're crazy. But you're sweet." I nuzzled her ear, wondering was she really too cold and maybe wanting to go, or was she the kind of too cold that was an invitation to hold her.

"How long have you been out?" she said.

"You're cute, you know."

"How long since you left the seminary?" She pushed me away.

"Six months."

"Have you dated much?"

"Of course, selectively."

"Anyone besides me?"

"One or two others. An army."

"Anyone besides me? Come on."

"Fffub!" I hesitated. She'd think me a punk. "Of course."

"I don't believe it." She laughed and lay back.

"You don't?"

"No."

I thought the unsayable thing, judged it, reached out my hand, placing it over her breast. "Believe it," I said.

She did not push me away. I was uncertain. Was one thing two things again? One to her, another to me? We lay together a long while, not moving, not talking. From somewhere a dog trailing its leash rooted by, circled us, some kind of hunting dog because it stood, looked at us, and pointed.

"Bang-bang," she said.

I rose part way up, not moving my hand, joking in my best German accent, "*Meine liebe fraulein*, do not tell me you are part of the resistance."

She pulled me to her. "*Cherie*, I have never resisted anything."

I felt those vine leaves growing through my hair.

My legs quivered. Would she notice?

"I'm a passionate French woman."

Oh my God! I felt the lump of myself growing towards her.

Her mouth fit agreeably to mine, different from the soft kisses at her door. She frightened me with her teeth against my lips.

"No one understands all of me," she said. "But you're a man. An innocent man. Perhaps you can."

In gratitude I kissed her, to try it, to quiet her, to hear the truth to be found in her.

"No," she said, "like this."

I'm sensitive, my God.

"Don't pucker up."

Hypersensitive.

"Relax your lips."

Oh.

"I always pick flowers myself."

No one can save everything so long...

"We're too intellectual."

...and not be easily disturbed.

"We need to feel."

I pulled her to me.

"Like this."

I pulled her in close.

"Like this."

I tightened my arms around her.

Her arms tightened around me.

I hurt with undecided tension. I wanted and did not want. Song lyrics rushed through me. "Quiet nights. Quiet stars." Astrud Gilberto, "Corcovado, Oh, How Lovely." The lake and moon and sand and stars, the city, the world fell back from us lying in the late darkness. Under the thin lisle stretches of her swimsuit, I felt her warm white body like a night-blooming orchid. My nature quivered through me. Other men would take her, would have taken her long before. I was like other men. I wanted to slip deep down into her, into the idea of her, to be lost forever.

She knew my nature. "Ryan, oh, Ryan. We're more than intellect." She touched me. "Let me make you feel."

I was in a new world...

"Let me love you."

...on a beautiful beach...

"Let me breathe your breath..."

...faced with the mortal sin...

"...and breathe back into you."

...that could make me fully human.

Swept away, I rose to my knees, vine leaves curling down from my hair, around my chest and arms, lifting her effortlessly, she gasped, half-laughing, half-loving the gesture, like a lake dance on the sand, like King Kong carrying Fay Wray, like Hercules lifting a beautiful girl, feeling some old miraculous Jesus out walking on the water, all white and glowing with starlight, smiling, winking, like Rhett Butler carrying Scarlett, I lifted her, carrying her clinging into the lake, the warm water rising on my thighs, she murmuring, *oh love, oh love*, invoking love, the water rising around us, her legs locking in the vine leaves around my waist, in so deep the surface of the flat water spread out a dark saucer around us, night and moon and city lights, swirling, she sat on my thighs, her arms given over, around, cooing *love, love, love, fuck, fuck me do*, her hands fluttering like little fish, touching, holding, squeezing me, shorting out, trying not to think of Hank the Tank drowning, how it must have been like this, wet, and so I saw him, Tank, panicked, breathless, going down once, floating, spouting, going down twice, spurting, lost, pumping the cold water, drowning, her, breathless, floating, laughing, her arms and legs twined around, veined around me, the sense of being not myself, of turning inside out, forgetting her, forgiving her. *Oh, love, love,* she cried, slowing, tendering care. I did not, could not, was not like other men. Something held me blank, blanked out, blanketed. I could give myself to nothing, not even this, this, this ultimate act of creativity, this drumming tribal demand, this pleasure, this beautifully mortal sin. I could give myself to nothing all the way. *Oh,* she said, *love me,* and, *oh, please,* she said, *hold me,* and *let me,* she said, *hold you,* and she was perfect, and I was emptied of lust but not desire, starting to tickle her, to bring her up out of any misconception, beginning a laugh, slowly, coaxing her, shivering in the water, the cold up to our necks, cooing her head to quiet on my shoulder, loving her for what she was, no matter what, steadying her head, palming her hair close to me. *Hold on,* I said holding her tightly, *hold on, hold your breath,* and I sank us both inches below the surface. The dark water was cold, but she did not fight to come back up. My thumb signed her forehead with a Cross and I thought the words of Baptism, *In the name of the Father and of the Son and of the Holy Ghost.* I stayed under, held us both under, as long as I thought we could both hold our breath.

"Jesus!" She gasped for air, came up clawing at me, slapped me hard across the face.

We swam and waded toward the beach through the warm night air, dressed silently, quickly, and one went one way, and the other, the other.

At Louisa's, standing alone on the dark porch, I banged on the door. She came in her wrapper. "What in the world," she said through her sleep.

"I lost my key," I said.

"Men," she said. "You've been up to something."

"Nothing."

"You all lie." She yawned. "I don't believe a word men say."

"I don't lie."

"You! I don't believe a word you say." She rocked with sleepiness, talking in her sleep. "You!" One of her eyes opened wide, wider, widest, *malocchio,* evil eye.

"What?"

"You lie like a rug."

"I never lie."

"I've read in your shoe box."

"Bitch."

"B-i-t-c-h, I may be. But, kiddo, I know what they did to y-o-u."

"Nothing."

"Liar." Her wrapper parted between her breasts, opening down her torso. "Liar! Liar!"

I backed away from her up the stairs. "What am I supposed to do?" I asked, waiting for no answer, treading on up to her attic, packing my suitcase, lying alone on the bed, grasping hold of myself, hanging on, interfering for dear life.

www.ingramcontent.com/pod-product-compliance
Lightning Source LLC
Chambersburg PA
CBHW051259210726

48287CB00002B/575